T0372982

# That'll Teach Her

Also by Maz Evans

*Over My Dead Body*

# MAZ EVANS

# *That'll Teach Her*

HEADLINE

First published in Great Britain in 2025 by
Headline Publishing Group Limited

1

Cataloguing in Publication Data is available from the British Library.

Hardback ISBN 978 1 0354 1326 3
Trade paperback ISBN 978 1 0354 1327 0

Designed and typeset by EM&EN
Printed and bound in Great Britain by Clays Ltd, Elcograf S.p.A.

Headline's policy is to use papers that are natural, renewable and recyclable
products and made from wood grown in well-managed forests and other
controlled sources. The logging and manufacturing processes are expected
to conform to the environmental regulations of the country of origin.

Headline Publishing Group Limited
An Hachette UK Company
Carmelite House
50 Victoria Embankment
London EC4Y 0DZ

The authorised representative in the EEA is Hachette Ireland,
8 Castlecourt Centre, Dublin 15, D15 XTP3, Ireland (email: info@hbgi.ie)

www.headline.co.uk
www.hachette.co.uk

*For my Robocoppers*

*Karen Jeffery*

*&*

*Sarah van den Brink*

Couldn't have cracked primary school without you,
you brilliant babes.


*And in loving memory of*

**Sophie Pemberton**

*The fiercest of Tiger mums.*
*Until we dance again, my love.*

# The Flatford Gazette

Monday 24 October

## High Times For St Nonnatus Caretaker

A local school caretaker was arrested last night on suspicion of cultivating a 'substantial' cannabis farm on school grounds.

Douglas 'Dougie' French stands accused of using a disused potting shed on the St Nonnatus Primary School allotment to grow multiple plants of the Class B drug. Officers were called to the scene around 7.30pm when the shed caught fire due to an electrical fault.

'It was chaos,' an eye-witness reported. 'The whole lot literally went puff. Thank God the kids weren't here – you could smell it everywhere. Firefighters were wandering around the playground calculating the square root of a ladybird. The pensioners' ukulele club in the hall went from "Living La Vida Loca" to "Comfortably Numb". And when Ahmed's Curbab Van pulled up outside, you had more chance of getting the last lifeboat off the Titanic than a chicken shawarma.'

'Mr French's employment has been terminated with immediate effect,' confirmed long-serving headteacher Claudia Stitchwell, 63, on the last night of the half-term holidays. 'I will not tolerate vice of any kind at St Nonnatus. School will open as normal tomorrow and I will be broadening my exclusion policy on harmful substances.

'From Monday, the following will be strictly banned from the grounds: chocolate, crisps, ice cream, football, skipping ropes, stickers, post-colonial children's novels, merchandise from Smiggle, the *Guardian*, the oeuvre of Taylor Swift, discussion of Netflix sitcoms and Liberal Democrats.'

But many were quick to defend Mr French, a much-loved member of the school community who has been tending the grounds for over thirty years.

1

'Dougie's totally harmless – he just can't tell his grass from his elbow,' one parent insisted. 'He thought he was growing oregano, bless him. Which, now I think about it, might explain the immense popularity of his spag bol at the church's last potluck supper. And why five of us then signed up for a timeshare in Giggleswick.'

## Unexploded WW2 Mine Removed From Play Park

'It felt like the right time,' says council health-and-safety inspector.

## Local Artist Sets New World Record

'It was worth it to see all the pieces come together,' says the architect of the million-matchstick model of the Burj Khalifa. 'Although, with hindsight, I wouldn't have stored it so near my sandpaper collage of Dusty Springfield.'

# St Nonnatus Primary School Class List (Confidential)
## Tiger Class – Year 6
## Teacher: Mr Ben Andrews
## TA (shared with Owls): Mrs Kiera Fisher

### Autumn Term

| Child | Parents/Carers | Siblings |
|---|---|---|
| BOLTON, Emily | Eric Bolton (Mr) | Katie (Owls – Yr 4) |
| BOURNE, Maisie | Alistair Bourne (Mr) & Naomi Klein (Dr) | Leo (Owls – Yr 4) Millie (Bumblebees – Yr 1) |
| BRIGHTMAN, Phoebe | Jane (Mrs) and Nigel (Mr) Brightman | Kitty (Dolphins – Yr 3) |
| BROCK, Simeon | Dustin (Mr) and Barney (Mr) Brock | n/a |
| BROWN, Damian | Laura Sullivan (Ms) | n/a |
| DARWISH, Omar | Mariam Darwish (Mrs)*** | Suleiman (Badgers – Yr 2) |
| DAVIES, Oliver | Florence Bryant (Ms)* Karl Davies (Mr)* | *Matilda (FHS)* |
| DOOLEY, Matthew | Sharon (Mrs) and Stanley (Mr) Dooley | Hope (Tigers – Yr 6) |
| DOOLEY, Hope | Sharon (Mrs) and Stanley (Mr) Dooley | Matthew (Tigers – Yr 6) |
| FISHER, Grace | Kiera (Mrs) & Matt (Mr) | *Taylor (FHS)* |
| FORMAN, Beth | Karen (Mrs) & David (Dr) | n/a |
| GHANI, Adel | Local Authority (Key Worker = Tom Munro) | n/a |

| | | |
|---|---|---|
| JAMESON, Amelia | Felicity (Mrs) and Brian (Mr) | Daisy-May (Dolphins – Yr 3) |
| JONES, Verity | Tanya (Mrs) & Susan (Mrs) | Hope (Koalas – Yr 5) |
| KACZMAREK, Aleksander | Zofia (Mrs) & Marcin (Mr) | Albin (Dolphins – Yr 3) |
| KHAN, Khadija | Fatima (Mrs) & Rayan (Mr) Khan | Bushra (Dolphins – Yr 3) |
| KOVALENKO, Ivanna | Maria (Mrs) & Borys (Mr) Kovalenko*** | Yana (Owls – Yr 4) |
| LEONARD, Archie | Petra Forrest (Ms) & Anthony Leonard (Mr) ** | n/a |
| McCALL, Sasha | Annie (Mrs) & Ian (Mr) McCall | Amy (Owls – Yr 4) |
| McENZIE-ROBERTS, William | Stella (Mrs) & Richard (Mr) McEnzie-Roberts | Henry (Dolphins – Yr 3) |
| MISTRY, Anya | Priya Mistry (Ms) | n/a |
| MONTGOMERY, Elijah | Sarah (Mrs) & Ian (Mr) Montgomery | Bess (Badgers – Yr 2) |
| PHILLIPS, Zac | Leanne Potter (Miss) | *Julia – FHS* |
| RICHARDSON, Jacob | Jenna Richardson (Ms) & Mike Cone (Mr) | *Beatrice – FHS* |
| ROSE, Finley | Donna Sargent (Ms) | n/a |
| THOMPSON, Theo | Rosemary (Mrs) & Nigel (Mr) Thompson | n/a |
| WHITE, Riley | Jennifer (Mrs) & Felix (Mr) White | Lily (Rainbow – Nursery) |

\* = Contact Separately
\*\* = Contact details missing/form not returned
\*\*\* = Language support required
*FHS* – Flatford High School

Every Friday, the Star of the Week will take
Tickly Tiger home for the weekend!

Use this diary to tell us all about
his adventures with you!

### Tickly Tiger's Diary!

Date: Monday 24 October
................................................................

This weekend I went home with: Theo
................................................................

On Saturday, my mum made Tickly Tiger
homemade quinoa pancakes with an organic
strawberry compote. Then we did some yoga and
mindful meditation before Tickly helped me with
my homework as we both believe that a good
education is important for my development. In
the afternoon we went for a long walk in the
woods to get some fresh air and then we gave
money to a homeless person outside Waitrose.

On Sunday we did a jigsaw puzzle together as a
family while listening to Mahler before making
musical instruments out of our recycling and
pretending to be our own orchestra with Tickly
as the conductor! Mummy said we should do
something for charity, so we cleared out our
cupboards and took lots of tins of chickpeas to
the food bank. Then we went to the Flatford
Museum to learn more about our town's heritage.
It had some old farm equipment and paintings
of girls getting drowned for witchcraft.

Normally I just play on my X-box and mummy
and daddy drink wine out of a box, so it was a
good weekend.

# PARENTCHAT

Clearer Community Communication

## ST NONNATUS CE PRIMARY

*Ora et labora*

### Year 6 Tiger Class

click here for group info

**Mon 24 Oct**
18.17

**Tanya**
Hi everyone!
Hope you all had a great half term?
Anyone else coming to school tonight?
I made cake...
Kids can play in the library (my pair are there).
Miss Stitchwell has a special announcement.

**Priya**
Ah Bitchwell.
Please let it be true she's retiring 🙏
And nah – I'm stuck here.
I have to nit-comb my bloody daughter before
Brownies.

**Al**
*Please let it be true she's retiring.*
Amen.
Claudia Stitchwell
Worst head ever.
(And that includes your Anya – nits again, Pri?)
My sitter Casey's got Covid, sorry Tan.

**Priya**

*Worst head ever.*

She is a shocker.

Who bans stickers?!

(@Al – didn't Casey have Covid three weeks ago?
Although not so badly she couldn't snog Dean Blunt
outside the chippie instead of letting you go to
SuperSpin?)

**Sharon**

*She is a shocker.*

My Matthew got a playtime detention for laughing!

**Zofia**

I heard that she charges her own staff for tea and coffee!
And has banned birthday cakes as 'sinful'.

**Priya**

Have you seen her go at the bake sales?
She nearly took Fiona Churchill out over a
marshmallow slice!

*Donna has joined the group 'Year 6 Tiger Class'*

**Donna**

Er – Hi everyone!
I'm Donna, Finley's mum – new to the school
👋 👋 👋

Just moved in today, we start tomorrow!
Tanya gave me this group's login...
Hope I'm in the right place!

**Tanya**

Oh Donna!
So sorry – meant to introduce you.
It's been a bit mad here this afternoon...
One disaster after another!
Welcome to Tiger Class!
I've got Verity in Tigers and Hope in Koalas (Year 5).
I'm also class rep and PTA chair so if you need
anything, just sing out.

**Petra**

*I'm Donna, Finley's mum – new to the school*
🖐 🖐 🖐

Hi Donna – I'm Archie's mum.
Has anyone seen his PE top?

**Priya**

*I made cake...*
Why waste one on Stitchwell?!
Your cakes are the best! Save me a slice!
And hey Donna! I belong to Anya.
(We only just joined last year, so we're noobs too!)

**Felicity**

I'm on my way Tanya!
But I'm not staying long – I'm off tomorrow!
And if I'm not eating for a month, I'm doing it with your
cake in my guts!

**Priya**

Oh – your wellness retreat!
It would take more than four weeks in Turkey to detox
me...
Have fun Flick, you've earned it.

**Felicity**

Thanks lovely!
See you all when I'm back xxx

**Al**

Have the best time, Flick.
Hello Donna!
I'm the proud(ish) owner of Maisie (Tigers), Leo (Owls)
and Millie (Bumblebees).

**Sharon**

I won't be there, Tanya – it's Hattie's cookery class tonight.
Coq au vin, right up my street 😂😂😂 !
And hi Donna! Matthew and Hope's nan here.
You can't miss us!
(See ya Flick! Hope they don't stick too much up your bum.)
(Unless you paid extra 😳 )

**Tanya**

*Worst head ever.*
Miss Stitchwell's not that bad...
Can't believe it if she's really going.
St Nonnatus won't be the same without her.
And the cake has nearly gone already!
Serves you right for not coming...

**Petra**

*Has anyone seen his PE top?*
He definitely had it when he left home this morning, so
if you could please check your child's sports bag...

**Sharon**

*Miss Stitchwell's not that bad . . .*
Tanya. You're a sweetheart.
But Stitchwell's an arse. Always has been.
The Reverend was no better, may he rot in peace.
Like father like daughter.
I hope to Christ she is leaving, not a moment too soon.

**Donna**

*I'm the proud(ish) owner of Maisie (Tigers), Leo (Owls)
and Millie (Bumblebees).*
Wow – you've got your hands full!
I only just about cope with one!

**Tanya**

So Donna:
Miss Stitchwell has asked everyone to come to
the hall tonight.
To commemorate her late father.
And because she has an announcement.
(Oh – and put the Xmas Fayre in your
diary for 17 Dec.
We'll need all hands to the plough.)

**Al**

*I only just about cope with one!*
Ha! I stopped coping circa 2015.

**Zofia**

I heard that Kiera was asked to make the Rev's
sympathy card!
Apparently there wasn't enough in the whip round to
buy one.
I put in 10p just to make the point.

**Sharon**

I'd love to have been a fly on the wall when Kiera told
them where to shove their sympathy and their card!
I gave 5p in protest.

**Priya**

I donated £25 to Stonewall, just to piss Stitchwell off.

**Donna**

Kiera?

**Al**

*Kiera?*
Her Grace is in Tigers, but Kiera's not on here.
She's staff, so separates church from state.
She's a TA for two classes, plus lunch shifts.
I've known her since school, she's a powerhouse –
we're all in awe.

**Priya**

You might be...

**Al**

All we *nice, normal* people are in awe...

**Stella**

*But Stitchwell's an arse. Always has been.*
*The Reverend was no better, may he rot in peace.*
Sharon – might I remind you again about our
community guidelines?
I'm sure our newest member doesn't want to hear your
potty mouth.
Hello Donna. I'm William's mother in Tigers and
Henry's in Dolphins (Year 3).

**Mike**

Does anyone know if it's swimming tomorrow?
(Welcome Donna – I'm Jacob's stepdad xxx)

**Jenna**

Mike – it's on our fridge, you doughnut!
I'll be home late, but I'll put the dates in the calendar xxx

**Mike**

Thanks babe.
Thank God for this group or you and I would never
speak!

**Sharon**

*I'm sure our newest member doesn't want to hear your*
*potty mouth.*
Sorry, Mother Superior...
And to you Donna.
Forgive me, I'm common as muck.
(And Mike and Jenna – keep your marriage in the
bedroom where it belongs 😊 )

**Donna**

*And to you Donna.*
*Forgive me, I'm common as muck.*
Haha! None taken. And me too!
You're a lot livelier than my last class!
They just asked for the spellings!
You all sound fun!

**Sharon**
Yeah we are, darlin... 😈

**Tanya**
Right – Miss Stitchwell's asked us all to put our
phones away!
(Well, told us really!)
Speak later xxx

**Priya**
Nooooo!!!
No! Send us live updates!
It's you or *Love Island*!
Let us know it's happened!
#singlesaddo!

**Zofia**
*Does anyone know if it's swimming tomorrow?*
No – there's been an outbreak of threadworm at the
council pool, I heard about it from Rachel S's mum.

**Tanya**
No! Send us live updates!
OK.
Txetng in my handbig.
Soz 4 mistaaakers.
STIChewll spking on stag
Tlaking about the late Rev.

**Sharon**
Arsehole.

**Stella**
Sharon!
The dear Reverend is still warm in his grave.
Show some respect.

**Sharon**
Oh please.
He was a nasty, nasty bastard.
Good riddance.
What do you think she'll do?

**Al**
Rachel S?
Have a bum like a Mr Whippy machine, poor kid.
We used to dread worms on the ward...

**Priya**
Stitchwell, you fool...
That school is her whole life.
What will she do now?

**Sharon**
That woman has terrorised generations of my family.
So long as she's gone – who gives a crap?

**Al**
Still Rachel S...

**Petra**
*Has anyone seen his PE top?*
It has a small tear in the collar and a bit of discolouration
from where I tried to bleach out a nose bleed.

**Tanya**
OMFSTG!!
Shs nit gnggg!!@!!!

**Priya**
What?

**Al**
Speak English, girl?

**Jennie**
Does anyone know how to get Tippex out of a jumper?

**Tanya**
OH MY DAYS!!
Stitchwell isn't going!!
I repeat, she's not retiring!

**Priya**
WHAT?! No?!

**Al**
You're fucking kidding?
(Sorry Stella – needs must.)
That's it.
Screw being a stay-at-home dad.
I'm going back to nursing.
We're going private.

**Sharon**
What gives?

**Tanya**
V quick – Stitchwell's gone to switch the
dishwasher off.
(I'm sure Hattie did that on purpose!)
But she's just announced she's staying.
For another FIVE YEARS!
Ben Andrews looks like he's going to
have an embolism.

**Zofia**
Not surprised.
I heard he turned down the deputy headship at
Shottsford House.
Apparently Stitchwell told him he was a shoo-in for
the Head job when she retired.
I can't believe it, he would have been SO good, I love
Ben...

**Sharon**
Oh yeah – Mr A's the best.
Cute too...
If I were 20 years younger...

**Al**
You'd still be 10 years too old for him... 😶

**Eric**
Hi Everyone!
Just to say that the girls and I will be at Flatford FC's
cup game on Saturday!
We're home to Easthampton – local derby!

**Donna**
Ben Andrews?

**Priya**
Sorry Donna... Ben is the deputy head.
And Tiger class teacher this year (yay!)
He's the best, Finley will love him.
All the kids do.

**Sharon**
And the grannies...

**Tanya**
Bick again.
Ben lks like hes chewed s wasp.
Clive is grnning.

**Sharon**
Clive's such a creep.
Gives me the willies.
And not the good kind.
(Calm down, Stella)

**Donna**
Sorry. Again.
But... Clive?

**Priya**
Mr Baxendale.
He's to school bursars what Ebenezer Scrooge was to
Just Giving.

**Eric**
*We're home to Easthampton – local derby!*
So this Saturday.
Pies and pints (or pop) at the Crown and Anchor after.
This is our year!
I can feel it!
Anyone in?

**Sharon**

*He's to school bursars what Ebenezer Scrooge was to*
*Just Giving.*
And not at all cute.
I just can't believe Stitchwell.
She's worse than Rasputin.
Or a cockroach.
She's Cocksputin.

**Stella**
Sharon!

**Sharon**
Oh, keep yer wimple on...

**Laura**
Yup – can you get the chunky knit, it's better for socks...

**Laura**
Sorry – wrong group!

**Al**
It's the kids I feel sorry for. They hate her.

**Priya**
We all hate her.
At least we're leaving this year.

**Al**
Speak for yourself!
Millie's only in Year 1. We're lifers...

**Petra**
*It has a small tear in the collar and a bit of discolouration*
*from where I tried to bleach out a nose bleed.*
Archie thinks he got changed near Simeon and Oliver,
so if their parents are on here, could you just check?

**Tanya**
OMG!!
999
999
999

**Priya**
Don't tell me...
Stitchwell's starting an after-school club for oppressing
minorities?

**Al**
She's representing the UK at Eurovision?

**Sharon**
She's surgically removing the stick up her arse?

**Dustin**
*Archie thinks he got changed near Simeon and Oliver,*
*so if their parents are on here, could you just check?*
Hi – one of Simeon's Dads here – we don't have
Archie's top.
But I just checked his bag and we do have Zac's shorts,
Khadijah's sun hat, Phoebe's sock and Oliver's pants...

**Priya**
Tanya? Tan?
Everything okay over there?

**Karen**
Hey – Anyone got this week's spellings?
Sorry – 'Wow Words'?
Beth's are already in my tumble dryer filter.

**Al**
You okay Tan?

**Eric**
*Anyone in?*
Perhaps I'll start a separate chat group!
Things get a bit lost on here, don't they!

**Rosie**

*Hey – Anyone got this week's spellings?*
Yes. They are:
Incredible
Beautiful
Terrifying
Vicious
Intelligent
Exuberant
Colossal
Skilful
Adventurous
Abrasive
Or at least, those are Theo's.
He's in the Purple group.
The top one.
I think it's his strong spellings that earned him Star of the Week.

**Sharon**

Tanya?
You okay, love?

**Flo**

*But I just checked his bag and we do have Zac's shorts, Khadijah's sun hat, Phoebe's sock and Oliver's pants . . .*
I'm so sorry!
I have no idea how my son managed to come home without his pants...
(Must take after his father, the cheating sod.)
(My ex, I mean. Not Olly.)
(Although I'm deeply suspicious of his performance in the eight times table test.)

**Karl**

Hey! The eight times table test isn't on me...

**Flo**

Unlike Sandra from Procurement.

**Karen**

*He's in the Purple group.*
*The top one.*
There are groups?!
I thought they all got the same?

**Dustin**

*I have no idea how my son managed to come home*
*without his pants . . .*
LOL! Not a problem. I'll wash them and get them back
to you.

**Karl**

Oh God no. Burn them. They're probably communicable.

**Flo**

Just like Sandra from Procurement.

**Al**

Tanya?
We were only playing – everything okay over there?

**Mike**

Relax...
She's probably just had one too many from Hattie's
infamous PTA punchbowl.

**Rosie**

*There are groups?!*
There are.
Purple, Yellow and Green.
To denote different levels of ability.
Theo is in Purple.
The top one.

**Sharon**

*She's probably just had one too many from Hattie's*
*infamous PTA punchbowl.*
OMG – Hattie's bloody punch!
We got so pissed at the Spring Quiz Night we ended
up on the climbing frame at 2am.
Naked.

**Al**

Hattie's the best.
Have you seen what she's done with the library?
What other dinner lady would do that?

**Zofia**

Yeah, it's stunning.
Feeding their bodies and their minds.
Absolute icon.

**Fatima**

*Yes. They are:*
*Incredible*
*Beautiful*
*Terrifying*
*Vicious*
*Intelligent*
*Exuberant*
*Colossal*
*Skilful*
*Adventurous*
*Abrasive*
FFS??!! (Sorry Stella.)
What 10-year-old uses the word 'abrasive' in a sentence??!!

**Karen**

Not Beth.
She's a Green apparently.

**Priya**

Tanya???
Just check in, babe...

**Al**

What 10 year old uses the word 'abrasive' in a sentence??!!
'I just found a really abrasive booger up my nose.'
(And don't sweat it, Karen. We're Yellow and proud!)

**Donna**
*'I just found a really abrasive booger up my nose.'*
Haha!
'This Chablis is a little abrasive when paired with my
pickled onion Monster Munch.'
#TeamYellowForTheWin
#NotAtTheSpellingBeeThough

**Sharon**
Oh Donna, love.
You're gonna fit in just fine...

**Tanya**
Oh my God.
Guys...
I don't know how to tell you this...

**Priya**
Go on?!

**Sharon**
Use your Wow Words.

**Al**
Is everything okay?

**Tanya**
It's Stitchwell.
She's

**Priya**
Satan incarnate?

**Al**
On trend?

**Donna**
Abrasive?

**Tanya**
She's dead.

**Priya**
. . .

**Al**

. . .

**Sharon**

. . .

**Donna**

. . .

**Laura**
Yeah, but the zips are all wrong.

**Laura**
Sorry – wrong group!

**Rosie**

. . .

**Mike**

. . .

**Dustin**

. . .

**Fatima**

. . .

**Flo**

. . .

**Stella**

. . .

**Karl**

. . .

**Petra**
That's so awful.
My prayers are with her loved ones on this darkest of
days.
(The PE top is named, btw.)

# The Flatford Gazette

Tuesday 25 October

## Headmistress Dies In Allergy Tragedy

The headteacher of St Nonnatus Primary School died last night from respiratory complications arising from a severe nut allergy.

Claudia Stitchwell was pronounced dead at the scene after collapsing at a school event in the hall.

'It was horrifying,' said one witness. 'At first she was just coughing, like she had a dry throat. But even after they brought her some water, she kept going. Then she started gasping for breath, before keeling over . . . It was like something out of a horror film. Thank God no kids were there to see it. I'll have nightmares for years.'

A full investigation is now taking place at the school, which will be closed until further notice to allow the authorities to conduct their enquiries. The source of the allergen is unknown, although the severity of Miss Stitchwell's allergy was not.

'I don't get it,' said another parent. 'We have the strictest no-nut policy. A parent once brought a coffee-and-walnut to the Valentine's Day bake sale. Miss Stitchwell locked her in the Key Stage 1 Wendy house, before getting the caretaker to escort her out the playground in a makeshift Hazmat suit made from an Alton Towers poncho.

'Everyone knew not to bring nuts or anything nut-related on to school grounds. I just don't understand how this could have happened.'

Details of a planned public memorial service at St Nonnatus Parish Church will be released in due course. The school has requested, in lieu of flowers and in accordance with the deceased's lifelong campaigning, that donations are made to the St Augustine Moral Correction Camp for Errant Youths.

## Investigation Launched Into Village Fete Corruption

'My marrow conformed to regulations,' disputed winner insists.

## New Kidney Stone Record Set

A patient at Flatford General passed a 14mm kidney stone yesterday in what doctors are hailing as 'a career high'.

# Ben

If there was an award for being in the wrong place at the wrong time . . . I'd still not win it as I'd be at the wrong ceremony.

Lord knows Miss Stitchwell was a challenging person and an even more challenging boss. And that was before . . .

Look, I don't even have to think about it any more.

Not now. Not ever.

It's over.

No one deserves to die like that, clawing for their final breath.

Not even her.

But does her death mean I can breathe easier?

Yes.

Because secrets can be suffocating too.

# Clive

Of all the sins, my favourite is probably *superbia*.

It's not as satisfying as *avaritia*, nor as fun as *luxuria*. But when it comes before a fall . . . it's positively scintillating.

*Superbia*. Pride.

And they didn't come much prouder than Claudia Stitchwell.

Yes, I confess I have sinned.

And for that I have asked God's forgiveness. My transgressions are now His secrets until He calls me for judgement.

Until then, though . . . I may be a sinner.

But, last I checked, *schadenfreude* wasn't a crime.

# Hattie

'For all evils there are two remedies,' Dumas wrote. 'Time and silence.'

Well, in the case of ol' Stitchers, turns out you also needed yer nuts.

I ain't sorry she's gone. Not one bit.

Not after what she done.

But no one need know about that now.

'If you want to keep a secret,' said Orwell, 'you must also hide it from yourself.'

So I won't be saying a word.

To anyone.

Not even to me.

# Kiera

I hated her.

With every atom of my being, I hated her.

I don't just want to dance on her grave, I want to host the grand final of *Strictly Come* bloody *Dancing* on top of it.

She was an Earth-bound demon who deserved every hellish moment of her hideous end. For thirty years, right until the day she died, that witch tormented me.

So the hardest thing about watching her writhing on that floor?

Trying not to laugh.

Everyone knows how I felt about her.

They just don't know why.

My secrets died with Claudia Stitchwell.

And that's where I'm going to bury them.

# STATEMENT OF WITNESS

CJ Act 1967, s.9; MC Act 1980, ss.5A(3)(a) and 5B; Criminal Procedure Rules 2005, Rule 27.1

**Statement of**   Tanya Jones

**Occupation**   Unemployed/Homemaker

**Age of witness** *(if over 18, enter 'Over 18')*   Over 18

This statement is true to the best of my knowledge and belief and I make it knowing that, if it is tendered in evidence, I shall be liable to prosecution if I have wilfully stated in it anything which I know to be false, or do not believe to be true.

**Signed:** Tanya Jones

I am Tanya Jones and I live at the address stated overleaf. I make this statement about the events of Monday 24 October, when I witnessed the sad death of Claudia Stitchwell.

I had been asked, in my capacity as Chair of the PTA, to oversee a special talk to be held in the hall that evening. I spent the day baking and decorating the triple chocolate sponge Miss Stitchwell requested. I cannot stress enough that there were no nuts, nor nut contaminants in my kitchen. I arrived at St Nonnatus Primary School at approximately 3.30pm, dropped the cake in the school kitchen, collected my daughters and escorted them to the library where they and Grace Fisher were to do their homework while we prepared the hall.

I reached the hall around 4pm, where Kiera Fisher was already making preparations for the event. As we progressed, it became clear that we had insufficient plates, napkins and plastic glasses for the evening, so I walked to BuyRite to purchase them. On the way, I ran into Ben Andrews who was on his way to do his grocery shopping – he kindly offered to purchase them for me so I could carry on with the set up.

I returned to the St Nonnatus hall and continued to prepare and decorate with Kiera, where we were joined by Hattie Hughes and Ben Andrews around 5.30pm. The preparations were rather fraught – we spilled a bottle of wine and managed to knock a statue of Jesus into the buffet . . . But, as is always the case, we got there in the end and were ready when parents began to arrive from 6pm, and could help themselves to drinks and snacks if they wished.

At 6.30pm sharp, the event began – Miss Stitchwell was a very punctual lady. We raised a toast to her late father and founder of the school, the Reverend Stitchwell, who has recently passed away. Miss Stitchwell then discussed her plans for the year. It had been anticipated that she would retire as Head, but instead she reconfirmed her commitment to the school and her intention to remain in post for a further five years.

She had been clearing her throat and coughing, but it is always stuffy in our hall. However, it quickly became apparent that it was more serious when she started to struggle for breath – and then she collapsed. I immediately dialled 999 to call for an ambulance. Ben tried to administer first aid, while Clive and Kiera went in search of the on-site EpiPens that are always kept in Miss Stitchwell's and the main office. But it was all in vain. By the time the paramedics arrived, Miss Stitchwell had already died. It was a terrible day for us all.

**Signature witnessed by:** *Robert Alsop*

# PARENTCHAT

Clearer Community Communication

## ST NONNATUS CE PRIMARY

### *Ora et labora*

**Weds 26 Oct**

Mrs Marcia Cox<**M.Cox@stnonnatus.flatford.sch.uk**>

To: <Whole School>

Re: Next Steps

Dear Parents,

Firstly, we hope that you are all as well as can be expected during these dark and difficult days. I would like to draw the attention of our whole community to the support that has been made available to adults and children in light of Miss Stitchwell's sudden, tragic passing. Details of phone lines and support services are at the bottom of this missive and Reverend McAlester has expressly asked me to convey that her doors, arms and ears are always open at the church.

However heavy our hearts, I hope you'll agree that our late Headmistress would be the first to encourage life to go on. And so, in that spirit, we're relieved to report that St Nonnatus Primary will reopen next **Monday 31 October**, following the conclusion of both the police and coroner's investigations at the school.

We thank you for your patience during this period of home schooling and fully acknowledge the impact it will have had on family life, especially coming so soon after the half-term break. However, we remind parents once again that when your child's camera is on during virtual lessons, it is possible for the whole class to see and hear whatever is occurring in the background. Your precaution, discretion and appropriate language would be greatly appreciated, regardless of your views of the *Loose Women*.

We will be holding a Service of Thanksgiving for the life of Miss Claudia Stitchwell at the church this **Friday 28 October at 2pm,** followed by refreshments in the Village Hall. As we have been so painfully reminded, St Nonnatus is a nut-free school and we ask that any food contributions strictly adhere to our allergy policy, on or off-site. You are also politely advised that alcohol will not be served either before or after the ceremony. In light of new guidelines following the distressing scenes at last year's Advent Carol Service, we respectfully ask that alcohol is **not** brought onto the premises, nor that children are asked to conceal it in their school water bottles on their parents' behalves.

After consultation with the governors, it has been decided that **Mr Ben Andrews** will assume the role of Acting Headteacher with immediate effect. Ben's contribution as Deputy Head has been unparalleled and we can think of no safer pair of hands to steer us through these challenging times until the position can be filled on a permanent basis.

Might I also take this opportunity to remind parents to be considerate to our neighbours when parking near the school, ensuring that no driveways are blocked or any access impeded. As the first port of call at the office, I am often the recipient of the frustrations caused by careless parking and I would consider it a personal kindness if these were kept to a minimum this year.

I leave you with the words of Charles Dickens: 'We need never be ashamed of our tears'.

Wishing you all the best,

Mrs Marcia Cox

School Manager
St Nonnatus Primary School

# The Parent Trap

Priya, Al, Tanya

## Friday 28 October
13.02

**Priya**
Hey Tan...
You okay, babe?

**Al**
You beat me to it.
How did it go this morning?

**Tanya**
Urgh.
That's the third time the police have interviewed me.
I don't know what else to tell them.
THERE WERE NO NUTS IN THAT CAKE!!!

**Priya**
It's just standard police procedure, I promise.
I did soooo much of this.
Unexpected deaths are an admin clusterfuck.
We have to tick our boxes.

**Al**
No one is blaming you, Tan.

**Tanya**
Seriously???!!!
EVERYONE is blaming me.

**Al**
No, they're not...

**Priya**
God bless you Al.
But they really are.

**Tanya**
THANK YOU 🙏
(I think.)

**Priya**

People like an easy explanation.

Stitchwell had a nut allergy

+

There were nuts in your cake

=

Your cake killed Stitchwell

**Tanya**

But it's not the right explanation.

I swear it...

**Al**

You don't need to explain anything to us.

We believe you.

No one policed the allergy policy better than you.

I remember when you spotted Tracy Harris's tub of

Celebrations at the summer tombola. Those Snickers

were out of the playground faster than an MP out of a

massage parlour...

**Priya**

True dat.

I've met less conscientious bomb squads.

And your statement made perfect sense.

There's nothing in there that would raise suspicion.

Not to any copper worth a damn.

**Tanya**

*There's nothing in there that would raise suspicion.*

Thank you.

That's a big relief.

Wait a minute...

How do you know?

**Al**

Oh God.

Robocop's on the case again...

**Priya**

*Wait a minute, how do you know?*

Er...

Look.

You don't work in the Met for as long as I did without
developing two things:

1) an instinct for trouble

2) some very useful, if not always entirely above-board
contacts

(On that, next time the kids change the passcode on
your phone, Al, I've got a great guy.)

**Tanya**

What did you do... ?

**Priya**

*Robocop's on the case again . . .*

Deeply problematic language to describe an electric
wheelchair user, Alistair.

But kinda cool, so I'll allow it.

**Tanya**

*1) an instinct for trouble*

And what do you mean?

**Priya**

Okay...

So hear me out...

This whole thing stinks.

**Al**

Here we go...

Is this like Tash Tompkins being a gangland boss all
over again?

**Priya**

It isn't.

(And I don't care how long she's been a Samaritan.
I still think Tash T is dodgy af.)

But remember:

When you've eliminated the impossible...

**Al**

... whatever remains, however improbable, must be the truth.

So go on then, Sherlock?

**Priya**

I think it's impossible that Tanya put nut allergens in that cake.

She's too good a baker.

She's too conscientious a person.

And – sorry Tan – frankly, she's way too anal to make a mistake like that.

**Tanya**

Oh Pri...

Thanks so much.

That means everything.

(I think.)

**Priya**

And as far as we're aware

(autopsy pending)

Stitchwell didn't eat anything else close enough to the meeting to trigger her nut allergy.

You say she was in her office the whole time?

**Tanya**

Yes.

I only saw her come out of her office to get her cake.

She didn't touch anything else.

**Priya**

So (autopsy pending) we can eliminate any other food.

**Al**

So what remains?

**Priya**

The truth.

**Tanya**

Which is?

**Priya**

Someone murdered Claudia Stitchwell.

**Tanya**
WHAT??!!!

**Al**
WTF, Pri?
You've actually lost it this time.
A murder?
In Flatford?
Like anything that interesting would happen here.

**Priya**

Exactly what a murderer would want you to think.

**Tanya**
This is...
You are...
Who would...

**Priya**

Eliminating Tan, there were four other people who had
access to Stitchwell before the event
(listed alphabetically because I'm fair like that):
Ben.
Clive.
Hattie.
Kiera.

**Tanya**
You can't seriously think one of them would actually kill
Stitchwell?

**Priya**

Can't I?
Twenty years on the force and a tenner says I can.

**Al**
I'll take your money.
So first question:
How?
If it wasn't the nut allergy and Tanya's cake... ?

**Tanya**

It was the allergy alright.

I've never seen anything so horrific.

Watching Stitchwell choke like that...

It'll haunt me forever.

**Priya**

Oh I agree it was the allergy.

I just don't think it was Tanya's cake.

Or at least, not how it left Tanya.

**Al**

So you're saying...

Someone deliberately triggered Stitchwell's allergy?

Knowing it would kill her?

**Priya**

There you go, Nurse Bourne.

We'll make a detective out of you yet.

**Al**

Okay.

I can't quite believe I'm going to enable this...

But something did strike me as weird.

**Priya**

Go on... ?

**Al**

So let's say that Tan *did* accidentally put something in the cake.

Used the wrong ingredient.

Almond flour instead of wheat.

Nut oil instead of olive.

That kind of thing.

**Tanya**

But I didn't!

**Priya**

We know babe.

**Tanya**

And anyway, refined nut oils are unlikely to trigger a
response because all the proteins have been taken out.
(I did a course on it after Sue's niece swelled up like a
balloon after eating one of my mince pies.)
I never use nut flours or oils.
I won't even let nuts in the house because I'm terrified
of cross-contamination.
When Sue finally divorces me, I swear she'll cite 'dry
roasted' in the papers.

**Priya**

You see?

Anal.

**Al**

This is precisely my point – you know all this stuff.
To trigger the kind of fatal anaphylaxis that killed
Stitchwell you need actual nut protein in sufficient
quantities.
Ie, nuts, nut powder, specific cold-pressed oils...
So for someone who understands allergies – and Tan,
you do – it would be very hard to do that accidentally.

**Priya**

EXACTLY!

**Tanya**

I just wish there'd been some cake left for them to test.
That would put me in clear, I'm sure of it.

**Priya**

You're a victim of your own success.

And that is inconvenient.

For you, anyway.

For the killer, less so.

**Tanya**

No one liked Stitchwell.
But kill her?
Why?

39

**Priya**

Well that's what we need to figure out.

Who would want to kill her?

**Al**

Who wouldn't?

**Tanya**

Al!

**Priya**

Oh it's true.

Everyone hated her.

Just who hated her enough?

We need good old means, motive & opportunity.

**Al**

The means we know.

Everyone knew about Stitchwell's nut allergy.

It's hereditary – she claims it was what finally bumped off the old Rev.

(Although rumour has it at the hospital that he actually died from complications relating to untreated gonorrhoea...)

Opportunity?

**Priya**

*(Although rumour has it at the hospital that he actually died from complications relating to untreated gonorrhoea . . .)*

This town... we'll circle back to that.

You were there that afternoon, Tan.

You said what you did in your statement.

But what about the others?

**Tanya**

Urgh – it was all a bit of a blur.

But thinking about it...

I think they probably did all go to Stitchwell's office at one point or another...

She was holding a load of meetings.

**Priya**
BINGO!
You don't think she ate anything.
Drinks?

**Tanya**
I'm not sure – like I say, it was a bit chaotic.
But I think Kiera *might* have made her a cup of tea at
some point...

**Al**
Jesus.
I can feel Pri getting her jollies from here.

**Priya**
You're not wrong 🥒.
Anything else?

**Tanya**
Well of course – there was a toast to the late
Reverend.
Clive poured her wine...

**Priya**
Of course!
YOU SEE!

**Tanya**
And Ben poured her a glass of water when she was on
stage.
She kept coughing.
We thought she had a dry throat – but now perhaps it
was the start of her reaction?

**Al**
But that rules Ben out, right?
If she was already reacting, he couldn't have spiked
her water.

**Priya**
Not necessarily.
She could have had a dry throat and then be
poisoned.
Both things could be true.
And Ben is the only one with a clear motive atm.

**Tanya**
What possible motive could Ben Andrews have?

---

**Zofia**
Not surprised.
I heard he turned down the deputy headship at
Shottsford House.
Apparently Stitchwell told him he was a shoo-in for
the Head job when she retired.
I can't believe it, he would have been SO good, I love
Ben . . .

---

**Tanya**
Oh come off it!
You think Ben killed Stitchwell over a job?

**Al**
And let's face it.
She's lovely.
But Zofia is about as reliable an information source as
GB News...

**Priya**
We all thought Stitchwell was retiring.
So Ben must have thought he was a dead cert.
With or without Zofia's rumoured other job.
And believe me.
People have killed for a lot less.

**Al**
Not Ben, surely?
He's such a good bloke.

**Priya**
They usually are.
Unless they're like Clive.
He's sketchy as all hell.

**Tanya**
And Hattie?
You think our lovely dinner lady is a cold-blooded
killer?

**Priya**
I think she knows her way around food.
Which wouldn't be unhelpful.
And Kiera...

**Tanya**
You're just biased because you don't like her.

**Priya**
She's got an attitude problem!

**Al**
How's the view from that glass house, Pri?
But Kiera could definitely kill someone.
Especially Stitchwell.
They go way back.

**Tanya**
Alistair!
That's a terrible thing to say!
Although...

**Priya**
Look – they'll all be at the service this afternoon.
I'll ask my contact for all their statements.
I've got to get ready now, but I'll send them for us to
read as they arrive.
It'll be more interesting than this bloody service.

**Al**
*I'll ask my contact for all their statements.*
Is that even allowed?

**Priya**

Sure.

If we don't get caught.

Let's watch them all today and learn.

SUBTLY!

**Tanya**

I'm dreading this afternoon.

All the evil eyes on me...

**Al**

We got you, babe.

**Priya**

Yeah we do.

They'll have to get past us.

And we're gonna clear your name.

So bitches... ?

Let's do this.

*Priya changed the group name to 'Robocoppers'*

# Hattie

Now I ain't saying I'm no Dostoevsky or nothing – I can't hardly write a cheque, me. But I got my tale to tell. We all do. Every soul on God's green earth is their own book. And when you stick a load of us together you got yourself a human library.

Take this church right now. Here we are, half the folk of Flatford, neatly stacking the pews like novels on a shelf. 'Cept me of course, I'm at the back serving the tea, as God intended. But that don't fit into me metaphor and that's why I'll be sticking to making school dinners and leaving all them fancy words to Dostoevsky. Although I bet old Fyodor never knew his way round a syrup sponge like I do.

Lord knows I ain't done much with me life, but I've read plenty of others, on and off the page. I love nothing more than a good yarn – and we got a bunch of stories here at St Nonnatus. Some'll make you laugh, others weep. A few are true, most are downright fantasy. And I'll tell you this for free: death might have brought us to this church today. But all of life is here.

Take young Priya Mistry. Newcomer here, but she's quite the crime story. Worked up in London as a copper, hunting down all them nasty gangs. But then – plot twist – bullet straight to the spine. She might not be able to use her legs no more, but by Jiminy she's making up for it with the rest of her. Proper firecracker, that one. Moved down here with her little Anya a couple of years ago to be closer to her sister. Priya says she's looking for a quiet life. But I don't believe a word of it. And there ain't no such thing in Flatford to be found.

Her mate Al is more of a romantic comedy, known him since he was a lad here at the school ('97 – used to be an absolute tinker. Once managed to smuggle a ferret into church and set it loose during the psalms – still no idea how he did it). He was a nurse up the local hospital, bloody good one too –

lovely warm hands. But then he fell hook, line and sinker for our Doc Klein and that pair went at it like they didn't know what made a baby. Three kids quick as you like – but two medics and three kiddies don't add up, so now Al is a stay-at-home dad. It's chaos. I don't care what you say, men aren't made for it the way women are. But they seem happy enough.

Oh yes, we got a tale for every taste here at St Nonn's: Domestic Drama (Flo and Karl Davies tearing strips off each other with a divorce what makes them Kardashians look like the Waltons); Romantic Tragedy (lovely Eric Bolton losing his childhood sweetheart, Kathleen, back along – he's been fright-ful lonely since, poor lamb); Rough Justice (Sharon Dooley taking in her grandkids after her son Steve and his partner were sent down for a ten stretch for them rotten drugs); World Politics (Jenna Richardson goes all over the world as a war correspondent – dunno how she stomachs it) and a few downright Mysteries. And I can't get enough of 'em. Flatford has been me whole life. And St Nonnatus Primary School, its beating heart. I've been cooking for the kiddies there for most of my days. And I love 'em all like me own. Well, maybe not all. That Jerry Jenkins ('85 – lousy kid, used to look up all the girls' skirts in PE) was a little bugger. Knew he'd end up the wrong side of the tracks. No wonder he became our local MP.

When it comes to people, though – like every book from the bible to *The BFG* – we'll never all agree which ones are actually any good. And you should never be sure which sto-ries to believe. We'd do well to rate folk like we rate books. Rankings clear for all to see, one to five stars, job done – an anthropological Amazon, if you like. We'll all have our own thoughts, of course. But together we should come out some-where about right.

Take Stitchwell. I doubt she'd have troubled one star on her best day. 'Horrible lead character. Preachy and vile,' would be my write-up, but she was much worse than that. She had all sorts to say about the devil and I believe she had insider knowledge. Her body is still with the coroner, so we don't have a coffin. Shame. I'd've liked something to spit on.

That bloody Clive Baxendale's not much better, 2.3 stars, if that. 'Unconvincing and creepy.' See, a small town like Flatford runs on the favour economy – you scratch my back and so on. But Clive's a flea – all itch and no scratch. Ever since he washed up here a few years back from London, he's kept himself apart – *above*, he'd like to think. Here he is, lurking at the back of the church like mustard gas. The man's oilier than a bloody sardine. What's he smirking at me for?

Ben Andrews is flapping around like a fanny. Everyone else would rate him a 5.0, they love him so. Nice-looking bugger, I'll give him that. Says all the right things – he's everyone's handsome hero. But I'm not convinced. Something about his plot don't sit right with me. And he's Scottish. He's too smooth by half – you should never trust a silver tongue. Virtue talks; goodness acts. I need to see some more chapters before I can submit a review.

Then you got folk like poor old Tanya Jones ('96 – ever such a sweet kid, always tucked her chair in at dinner time and you can tell a lot about a person that way). Lovely woman – woulda been a solid 4.8 until last week. But they reckon her chocolate cake's what done for Stitchwell – musta had nuts in it, they say. Truth is, she's done us all a favour – there's few that'll squander tears on Stitchers. But that don't stop folk judging. The playground ain't just for children. And parents can be the biggest kids of all.

I can see 'em now, giving the poor love the evil eye from their pews. Tanya's had a rough trot lately – she was a big shot lawyer up in Easthampton, our very own Perry Mason, she was. But she's been struggling something awful with The Change, couldn't hold two thoughts in her head, poor love, it came for her far too early. I get it. I had a terrible time with it meself. I used to get awful angry and me bits and bobs wouldn't half itch. One time I nearly laid out old Jim Franklin from down the chemist over a leaking tube o' Canesten, bless him . . . Any road, young Tanya's chambers just chucked her out without a by yer leave. She took 'em to court and everything – but that's the problem when you work as a barrister. The other side's got a helluva defence team. She lost her case, which was proper wrong. And so is what she's getting from folk round here. But no one said life is fair. Not unless theirs is. 'Underrated and undervalued,' I'd say . . .

'Ding dong! The Stitch is dead,' Kiera trills far too loudly, slamming a fresh teapot down next to me. 'Which Stitch? The bitchy Stitch . . .'

I smile. I make no secret of how much I love that girl. Always have, ever since she were a kid at the school herself ('02 – cleverest kiddie St Nonn's ever saw – won some national prize for spelling. I've still got the certificate on me fridge). She's five stars all day long for me: 'Funny and compelling.' Not sure all folk agree, though – Kiera certainly attracts mixed reviews. But all great works of art tend to.

'Hush your noise and let folk pay their respects,' I say, pouring her a cuppa and hoping my quiet might encourage hers. 'It's what we do, you great melon.'

'It's what hypocrites do!' she scoffs. 'She was a stone-cold arsehole! And now her arsehole's stone cold . . .'

'Be that as it may,' I whisper, stirring in two sugars to sweeten her up. 'When death comes this close, folk feel it. They seek comfort together. Funerals ain't really for the dead. And keep yer foghorn down. People are looking . . .'

'Oh dear,' she says defiantly, blowing into her tea. 'Remind me to find a shit to give.'

I smile. She's a terror.

'It's good to see you, gal – how you been?' I ask, giving her a squeeze.

'Don't get me started. It's been a madhouse,' she sighs. 'Taylor's doing my head in. She's rude, ungrateful, disrespect-ful . . .'

'Them genes are a right mystery,' I wink, swatting her with my cloth.

'Matt does nothing, of course,' she moans.

'Apart from cook, clean, look after the girls, work all hours . . .'

'Well, I do all that too,' she snaps. 'But Taylor walks all over him. And she's so entitled. When I think about what my life was like at seventeen . . .'

'. . . and you've worked hard to make sure hers ain't,' I remind her. 'Too hard, perhaps. So take the win. How's my little Gracie? Over the pukes?'

Kiera lights up.

'She's gorgeous,' she says proudly. 'And fine now, must have been a twenty-four-hour thing – Tanya's girls had the same – you know what a petri dish this place is.'

'Poor lamb . . .'

'She was brilliant during home schooling, thank God. How's it been over there?'

Kiera nods towards the school, which backs onto this very church.

'Swarming.' I shudder. 'Coppers, coroners, sciencey fellas – Gods knows who and what. They've been over the place with a fine-tooth comb twice – even went through the ruddy bins! Been spooking the kiddies summit rotten . . .'

'That was good of you to volunteer with the looked-after kids.' She smiles. 'They're lucky to have you.'

'And I them,' I say, thinking of the poor little buggers with no place else to go. 'There's more every year. It's a crying shame. And anyways, what else was I gonna do? Join the bloody circus?'

'Why – are they recruiting a fat lady?' she sasses, earning another swat from the cloth.

She blows on her tea again and her eyes drop. She's deciding whether to say something. She always looks like this when summit's on her mind, always has. I can still see her gangly legs dangling over my school-kitchen units, telling me her wins and her woes. Although there were usually more of the latter, poor kid. Them what do say life is fair sure as hell never grew up in care.

'Hatts . . . ?' she starts, finally dropping her voice to a whisper. 'I really need to talk to you. About . . . that night. We have to . . .'

'No. We don't,' I tell her, staring straight into her pretty green eyes. 'I don't never wanna talk about that night again. It's done, she's gone, I don't ever wanna speak of it. You understand?'

Kiera looks at her tea again. I know that look too. She's feeling guilty.

'Everyone thinks it was Tanya's cake, right?' she asks quietly. 'That's what everyone thinks? No one's saying anything else, are they? What are they saying?'

'I don't give a monkey's uncle what anyone thinks and even less what they say,' I growl again. 'I don't wanna hear it. Stitchwell's gone. Let her rot in her grave. No sense the rest of us wasting more life on her.'

She nods her head and the conversation is over. Good. Best that way for everyone.

'Ladies,' says a voice. 'Might I trouble you for another coffee? A hot one this time, if it's not too vexing?'

I look up to see bloody Baxendale smarming at us.

'Aw, shame. Pot's empty,' says Kiera, folding her arms and nodding at the dry cafetière.

'Then, my dear, might I suggest you go and refill it?' Clive asks. 'Unless you're not actually working today? In which case I can adjust your time sheet accordingly . . .'

Kiera shoots him a look that could turn cream and snatches the coffee pot away. Smart girl. This one's not worth the fight. He turns his gaze back to me. The man makes me want a hot shower and a cold gin.

'I was hoping to see you, Hattie,' he oozes.

'I weren't,' I tell him straight.

'Oh, you do put the fun into funeral,' he leers, his voice and gaze dropping. 'But something has recently come to my attention that I thought I should share with you.'

I feel my blood chill a degree or two. Clive is like shingles. Mainly irritating, sometimes dangerous. You need to tread careful around him. I calm my innards.

'Is it crabs again?' I whisper. 'Because you need to see Jim down the chemist – I'd go meself, but I'm still banned and—'

'Hattie,' he says darkly. 'I know.'

My face is used to keeping secrets – it's held plenty down the years. And it ain't gonna leak now.

But this could be a problem.

'Know what exactly, you great pillock?' I scoff. 'The capital of Burkina Faso? I'm gonna need some detail . . .'

Clive leans forward. He smells good and bad all at once.

'I know . . . that it was really you who made the winning entry at the Harvest Bake Off,' he whispers. 'I've suffered Ella McDonald's anhydrous fruit scones for years . . . That was very kind – if entirely against the rules – for you to help her. And I believe it is Ouagadougou . . .'

I know Clive – he's toying with me. But I'll play along for now. At least until I understand the game.

'Well, I'll wait for them to haul me off in irons,' I tell him. 'Ella's had a rough trot, what with Derek's Alzheimer's and all. Decided he were Benny Hill last week and chased poor Polly the postie round the garden in his Y-fronts. Can't expect Ella to go whipping up some daft scones with capers like that going on at home.'

He smiles. About what?

'I just thought you should be aware,' he says with that punchable half-smirk. 'That I know.'

'Congratulations,' I deadpan as Kiera bustles back with the hot coffee. 'Have a scone.'

'There you go,' she smiles sweetly, filling his cup to the undrinkable brim. 'Scalding hot. Hope you don't burn yourself.'

'Oh, I rarely feel the heat,' he says, sipping his steaming brew and smiling with delight. 'Actually, Kiera, I wanted to speak with you too. Given dear old Douglas's . . . predicament . . . the caretaker job – and house – will shortly be available. It needs some work, of course – bachelor life rarely coexists well with interior design – but I wondered if your husband might be interested?'

'Matt?' asks Kiera in surprise.

'Is that his name?' says Baxendale airily. 'I just thought as you have so many . . . roles . . . here at St Nonnatus anyway, you may as well move in. Your . . . Matt . . . he was a handyman prior to his present position at the supermarket, was he not?'

'He was a construction supervisor in the army,' Kiera says through a slightly clenched jaw.

'Really? Well, I thank him for his service,' says Clive, an eyebrow pointing to heaven. 'I know you're always keen to . . . broaden your financial horizons? Particularly with young Grace off to Shottsford House next year. Congratulations on the art scholarship, by the way. What a pleasant surprise that must have been?'

He smiles like a snake at a mouse. I can feel Kiera bristle next to me. She's proud – and got far too much about her to be cleaning up kiddie piddle for the rest of her days. She's smart as a whip and shoulda got out of this town the second her feet could carry her. Had a place at uni and everything . . . But life ain't worked out that way. And Clive's right. She needs the money.

Or thinks she does.

'Never in doubt,' Kiera replies tightly. 'Not with talent like hers.'

'Indeed,' says Clive, sipping his coffee. 'And won't you make a . . . vibrant addition to the parent community there. I'm not sure any of the other mothers will have met someone with a job before. Let alone three . . .'

'We'll think about it,' says Kiera with jaws that could strain rice, although we all know she'll tell Matt to take it. Gracie's fees might be covered, but private school finds plenty of other ways to make you pay. And you don't look a gift house in the mouth.

'Marvellous,' says Clive, taking another sip before wrinkling his nose. 'On second thoughts, I'll get a decent cup on the way home.'

He wipes his mouth with a tissue and chucks it in the cup, before dropping it hard on the table. He turns on his heel and slithers toward his seat on the front pew.

'Roll on his bloody funeral,' Kiera grumbles, tossing the damp tissue in the bin as Rev McAlester starts the service.

I shush her down, but I can't disagree.

Clive Baxendale's dangerous.

Just like Stitchwell was.

## Robocoppers
Priya, Al, Tanya

### Friday 28 Oct
14.13

> **Priya**
> Jesus, this service is miserable.
> And sooo dull 🌑

**Al**
It's what Stitchwell would have wanted.

**Tanya**
Put your phones away, people are looking.

> **Priya**
> She says. On her phone.
> Oooh – look 👀
> Here's Clive's statement from my... contact.

# STATEMENT OF WITNESS

CJ Act 1967, s.9; MC Act 1980, ss.5A(3)(a) and 5B; Criminal Procedure Rules 2005, Rule 27.1

**Statement of**   Clive Baxendale

**Occupation**   School Bursar

**Age of witness** *(if over 18, enter 'Over 18')*   Over 18

This statement is true to the best of my knowledge and belief and I make it knowing that, if it is tendered in evidence, I shall be liable to prosecution if I have wilfully stated in it anything which I know to be false, or do not believe to be true.

**Signed:**   *Clive Baxen*

Please find herein my account of the tragic events of Monday 24th October, as mighty God is my witness.

For the first two hours after school, I was working in my office. I was interrupted by some kerfuffle in the hall when a statue of Our Saviour was knocked over and smashed the wine. So, just prior to 6pm, I visited the kitchen to obtain a second bottle of Miss Stitchwell's special reserve from her late father's cellars. I opened the bottle in the kitchen, where I exchanged pleasantries with our catering manager, Miss Hughes and our teaching assistant, Miss Fisher.

I was called in to see Miss Stitchwell at around ten past six to discuss budgets for the forthcoming school year. It was a brief meeting – she was distracted looking for a lost bible and in any case Claudia and I were always highly efficient. I returned to the hall in time for the event to begin.

When it became clear that Miss Stitchwell was in respiratory distress, I hastened to her office, where I knew her to keep her personal dose of epinephrine in case of anaphylaxis. I was unable to locate it, so called an ambulance from her office before returning to the hall, where it had become tragically clear my efforts were in vain and Miss Stitchwell had already been commended to the Lord's care.

I remained with Claudia until the authorities arrived, answered such questions as I was able, then briefly visited the church to pray for her before returning home.

**Signature witnessed by:** *Robert Alsop*

# Ben

I don't think I've ever been to a funeral where absolutely no one cried.

There wasn't a damp eye in the house. Even Miss Stitchwell's staunchest supporters, the few that there are, didn't so much as snuffle. Margaret Sutherford, the Year 3 teacher (who has already handed in her notice because I refuse to continue Miss Stitchwell's 'Forgetful Friday', where kids who've forgotten to bring anything to school in the week have to run laps round the playground in lunch break) – even *she* couldn't summon up a sob. I don't want to imagine the pain that my death would inflict on my loved ones. But I hope there might be at least a few soggy Kleenexes to show for my existence.

The reception in the village hall is subdued, but not exactly sombre. They're a cracking bunch of parents here – I like them. The typically bountiful homespun buffet spreads across two tables, though, given everything, it's hardly a surprise that no one has touched a bite. Maybe I should lead by example? Although, looking at Stella McEnzie-Roberts's congealed potato salad, maybe not.

'So,' says Zofia Kaczmarek, sidling up to me, 'is it true that you're going to abolish uniform and let the kids call the teachers by their first names?'

I smile. Zofia is lovely. But she has a mouth the size of Dundee.

'I think today is a time to look back, rather than forward,' I say diplomatically. 'So no new policy from me just now.'

'I knew it!' she squeals, and runs back towards her group of mum chums. News that I'll be letting the kids smoke crack in assembly will be around the school before Stella's potato salad goes in the bin.

A headship. It's what I've always wanted, what I've been working towards. This wasn't how I would have liked to get it, of course, but it's not been the easiest year. This must be where it picks up. Finally.

A couple of kids hare past and my heart misfires. God, I miss my Finn . . .

'Oh, Hattie, could I just—' I call as the school catering manager – dinner lady as she insists we all call her – bustles past. I don't know if she's busy or just ignoring me. Actually, I'm fairly confident I do.

I'm not sure what I've done to offend Hattie, but she's not nearly as warm with me as she is with everyone else. She's a lifer, an institution – she's been there longer than the central heating, over forty years now. Hattie's a wonderful cook – but what I've done to stick in her craw, I have no idea.

'Oh, Mr Andrews?' a welcome voice whispers in my left ear. 'Upsetting the dinner lady *will* result in smaller portions.'

My everything involuntarily tingles at the casual intimacy of the gesture. It's been a while since a woman has been that close to me, casually or otherwise. A long while.

'Something I said?' I ask Kiera Fisher, my colleague and, I think I can say, friend.

'Let's hope not,' says Kiera grimly, laying out the clean glasses she's just brought in from the kitchen. 'Hattie's reading *Hamlet* again . . . and you know what happened to Claudius . . .'

She gestures to my cup of tea. I snort ruefully. Kiera is another St Nonnatus institution, although, dare I say, a more comely one than Hattie or Claudia Stitchwell. My eyes flick guiltily to our late headteacher's stern portrait on the condolence table as I even think it. Kiera's been at St Nonnatus longer than anyone should have been at her age and has been a huge support to me, especially as my TA in Tiger Class. She's funny and smart and direct and I really like her. Not like *that* – she's a colleague, not to mention a parent in what would have been my class this year. I mean, she's not unattractive. Far from it. It's hard to imagine she's changed much since she was a teenager and you'd never believe she's old enough to have one herself – I couldn't when I found out her Taylor is seventeen. But we're colleagues. And she's married. That's all there is to it. Just friends. And colleagues. That's it.

'Did you enjoy the service?' I blurt out, although I have

no idea why. Kiera gives me that lop-sided look that almost makes me glad I'm such an idiot.

'Actually, Mr Andrews, yes,' she says plainly. 'Absolute banger. Best funeral I've been to in ages.'

I swallow my laugh at her callous disregard for her surroundings. As my dad would say, there are no flies on Kiera. I find it incredibly . . . invigorating. And the way she uses my 'teacher' name . . .

She ignores the disapproving looks from a gaggle of Stitchwellites and I force my face to stay neutral as I feel their gaze pass over me. Taking the reins from a long-serving head is never easy. I'm going to need to unite all factions if I'm to get the job permanently.

'Glad to hear it.' I smile and worry that I, a forty-one-year-old man, am actually blushing. I hope she extends the conversation. Seems I'm all out of smooth moves.

'Actually – I need to ask you a favour.' She winces. 'I realise today's not the best time to ask . . . but Grace needs a recommendation letter for Shottsford House. Bitchwell was going to do it, but . . . y'know . . .'

She pulls her finger across her throat with a grin that could turn a man to sin. She's so naughty. I wonder how naughty . . .

Stop it, Ben. Just . . . stop it.

'No trouble,' I tell her. 'I'll do it tonight.'

'You are a legend,' she says, squeezing my arm. It feels . . . lovely. 'By the way, there's a load of condolence cards on the table over there. No one knows who should open them . . . But given there is no family and she had no friends . . . I guess it's over to you, big guy.'

She winks and squeezes my arm again on her way back to the kitchen, the most gorgeous unconscious lilt in her hips as she walks. Is she staying there a bit longer than she needs to . . . ? Oh Christ. I'm like a teenage boy with the Littlewoods catalogue – calm down, Andrews . . .

I'm heading over to the cards when my teacher spidey sense tunes into some slightly raised voices in the corner of the room. Tanya Jones has been cornered by a group of mums, spearheaded by Stella herself. The poor woman looks like she's about to cry. Priya Mistry looks like she's about to kill someone. I should step in. This is my job now. I grab a plate from the buffet and head towards them.

'I'm not trying to upset you,' I hear Stella say as I approach. 'I'm merely speaking on behalf of the few of us who felt that, maybe, it wasn't entirely appropriate for you to come today . . .'

'Then don't upset her,' says Priya firmly. 'Tan has as much right to be here as any of us.'

'I didn't do anything wrong,' Tanya quivers. 'I promise, I didn't . . .'

'It's all right dear,' says Stella, nailing that condescending passive-aggression at which certain mothers and many home secretaries excel. 'Everyone makes mistakes. And we all know you've been . . . struggling.'

'Don't. Even. Go. There,' says Priya, wheeling up menacingly. 'I swear to God, Stella, you back down or . . .'

'Lovely potato salad,' I say, trying to summon sufficient saliva to gulp down Stella's offering. 'How do you get it so . . . firm?'

'Mr Andrews,' says Stella, immediately straightening up. 'How lovely to see you.'

It's funny how most parents immediately go on best behaviour around teaching staff, as though we still wield any kind of power over them. The few that don't, alas, are painfully aware of how little power we actually possess.

I look to Tanya to make sure she's okay. The break in hostilities seems to have given her a moment to gather herself. Priya is holding her hand and shooting daggers at Stella's cronies.

'I realise that this is perhaps not the best moment,' Stella whispers, 'but a few of us are a little concerned about what will happen with Tiger Class this year?'

This drives me potty. Parents like Stella never speak on behalf of themselves, only ever as a spokesperson for an invisible mob. I decide to play dumb.

'How so?' I ask. I didn't think even Stella would be quite this crass at Stitchwell's memorial.

'Well . . . I realise there are many matters for you to deal with,' says Stella, waggling her head as an especially arid piece of potato latches to my oesophagus. 'But your promotion does leave Tiger Class without a form teacher. And given how important Year 6 is, we just wanted to make sure that everything is in hand?'

'Everything will become much clearer this week,' I lie, a little more smoothly than I care to admit. 'Hold your soul in patience, Mrs McEnzie-Roberts.'

A reassuring smile seems to calm her down – or at least shut her up – and she and her acolytes fall out towards the buffet now the seal has been officially broken. I have no idea what to do with the Tigers. Like all schools, we are having a nightmare recruiting. Looks like supply teachers for the time being . . . I look at Tanya. She's shaken.

'Are you okay?' I ask softly, immediately inspiring fresh tears.

'Everyone blames me,' she sobs.

'They don't,' I lie.

'They do,' Priya confirms.

I snort at her directness. She's a character. 'What happened last week was a tragic accident,' I tell Tanya. 'No one is to blame.'

She looks at me hopefully.

'You really believe that?'

I smile.

'Yes,' I lie for a third time. 'Yes, I really do.'

The tears stay in their place. But her face brightens.

'So . . . Ben,' says Priya, staring narrowly at me. I don't know if it's because of her time on the force, or just because she's Priya, but I often feel like I'm being interrogated by her. 'You enjoying Hattie's cooking class? I'm thinking of giving it a go.'

I let go a little. This feels like safe ground.

'Yeah, yeah, it's great,' I reply. 'High time I learned to cook. Of course, I might not make the next few what with . . . everything. But hoping to get back into it asap.'

'That's good to know,' she says quickly. 'So what kind of things do you make?'

'Oh . . . I dunno. I've got a shocking memory . . .'

'Give me an example? Like – what were you going to make the night Miss Stitchwell died? Presumably you remember that one?'

Shit. This is not safe ground.

'I'm not sure . . . It was Chinese spare ribs, I think . . . ? But I might be getting my weeks muddled . . .'

'Mmmm,' says Priya, her eyes belying her suspicion. 'Sounds yummy.'

'I guess I'll never know,' I say, looking around in that way that suggests I'm too busy to stay in the conversation. 'I'd better circulate . . .'

Priya stays a moment more than is comfortable, before taking the hint and wheeling towards the buffet table, accidentally (not accidentally) taking in a few toes from her friend's detractors along the way.

'Thank you,' says Tanya, dabbing her eyes with one of the tissues no one needed at the service. 'Thanks a lot. You've been such a huge support to me.'

I touch her lightly on the shoulder, noting it doesn't conduct the electricity of Kiera's touch. Tanya's had a really rough time since the employment tribunal – no one wants an employee who takes their bosses to court, I'm guessing. And she's been pretty lost. Some people are just born to work. I should know – I'm one of them. But Tanya has been throwing herself into school life in its absence, starting a PTA and generally being a force for good. I wish I could take this worry away for her. She's a sweetheart – she doesn't deserve to have a death on her conscience.

'Why don't you go home?' I suggest. 'You've been here since the crack of sparrow fart and we can tidy up here . . .'

'Speak for yourself!' Kiera huffs, coming up behind me again. 'Some of us want to get home tonight. We've got our own families to pick up after. Your Gracie over the bug now, Tan?'

She squeezes past me carrying a pot of tea, her chest brushing against my back. There's loads of room, was she . . . ? Did she do that on purpose? Jesus – what is wrong with me . . . ?

Is this why middle-aged men take up squash?

'Yes, she's fine now, thank you. And no, of course, I wouldn't dream of . . .' Tanya begins, starting to pick up some cups. Kiera comes back and slings her arm round her. Christ, that must feel good.

'I'm only yanking your chain, Tan,' she says, planting a friendly kiss on Tanya's head. 'We got this. Get out of here. I'm sure Mr Andrews and I can give these witches something else to talk about . . .'

She winks and it lands straight in my groin.

Holy Christ.

I need me a Littlewoods catalogue.

I can feel I'm lingering too long, so I excuse myself and head towards the condolence cards, which have been placed on the table next to Miss Stitchwell's portrait. I find myself having to stifle a totally inappropriate giggle as I see how many are addressed to her. When did they think she was going to open them?

But a few are addressed directly to me, so it feels less intrusive to open those first. I open a white envelope, inside which there's a child's hand-drawn picture of what I think is supposed to be Miss Stitchwell with angel wings, but actually looks like a deranged vampire. Out of the crayons of babes . . .

## Hi Mr Androos

### Im sorry Mis Stichwell is ded.

### Pleese can we play foot ball at play tyme agen??

### Love,

### Milly in Dolfin Class

I feel a surge of powerful hope. Yes, Milly. Yes, you can play football. You're going to be able to do a lot of things you've been denied for too long.

Although I will be talking to Mrs Sutherford about your spelling.

I open the next.

Dear Mr Andrews,

My sincerest condolences with regard to the sad passing of Miss Stitchwell. She was a true original and I can't think we'll see her like again.

In confident anticipation of your forthcoming promotion, I wonder if I might schedule an appointment to discuss my Fabian's reading level? I have felt for sometime it is far below his capable attainment and would like to have a conversation at your earliest.

Warmest regards,
Alan Durant

Parents. Wow, man. I try not to laugh.
I open the last one.
But this one isn't funny.

BEN
I KNOW WHAT YOU DID TO HER.
AND YOU NEED TO PAY.
£10,000 IN CRYPTO.
OR I TALK.

## Robocoppers
Priya, Al, Tanya

### Friday 28 October
15.23

**Priya**
Tanya? Where are you?
I'm so sorry, that was shite.

**Al**
I'm just nipping home.
Casey's locked herself in the bathroom.
Leo told her he had rabies.
What happened?

**Priya**
Bitches be bitches.

**Tanya**
It's okay – I'm fine.
I'm just taking a sec outside before going back in.

**Priya**
Oh screw that.
My sister's got Anya.
We're going down the pub.
We've got stuff to discuss.
Ben just lied to us.

**Al**
About what?

**Priya**
The cookery class.
Sharon takes it too, remember?
Hold on, I'll find it...

> **Sharon**
> I won't be there, Tanya – it's Hattie's cookery class
> tonight.
> Coq au vin, right up my street 😊 😊 😊 !

**Priya**

He said Chinese ribs.

**Al**

How do you remember this stuff?
When you have taken Anya to school on the last three
INSET days?

**Priya**

Occupational hazard.

**Tanya**

That's a bit flimsy, isn't it?
You heard him – he might have got his weeks
muddled.
It's a weird thing to lie about.
And he's a busy man...

**Priya**

Maybe...
But you said you met him on the way to the shops that
night, Tan.
I'd be interested to know what he bought.

**Al**

How the very hell are you going to do that?

**Priya**

I have my ways.
Speaking of which.
Here's Kiera's statement:

# STATEMENT OF WITNESS

CJ Act 1967, s.9; MC Act 1980, ss.5A(3)(a) and 5B; Criminal Procedure Rules 2005, Rule 27.1

**Statement of**   Kiera Fisher

**Occupation**   Teaching Assistant

**Age of witness** *(if over 18, enter 'Over 18')*   Over 18

This statement is true to the best of my knowledge and belief and I make it knowing that, if it is tendered in evidence, I shall be liable to prosecution if I have wilfully stated in it anything which I know to be false, or do not believe to be true.

**Signed:**

Miss Stitchwell came in asking for tea, and helped herself to a piece of Tanya's cake – couldn't even wait for everyone else, the greedy cow. So I gave her the tea and she took it all back to her office.

We didn't have enough of anything we needed, so Tanya went to the shops to get more supplies.

When she returned, she and I carried on setting up until Ben came to 'help' around half five – although he actually just managed to knock over Stitchwell's special wine and drop Creepy Jesus into the cake and sandwiches!

I was called in to see Stitchwell a bit before 5.45pm. Afterwards I went to the kitchen to help Hattie.

The event started at 6.30. When Stitchwell started to choke, I went to the office to get the EpiPen, but couldn't find it.

It was too late anyway – Stitchwell was dead by about 6.45. I was going to help clear up afterwards, but my daughter was feeling unwell, so I took her home.

**Signature witnessed by:**

# Clive

My job is to say no.

As school bursar, every single day I am inundated with requests to dredge the bottomless money well that staff and parents believe finances a school.

The Year 6 parents want ice creams for their end-of-term production. Not budget lollies that can be sourced from the Costco for less than they spend on a cortado – oh no, not for their precious darlings. They want organic clotted-cream gelato from a micro dairy in Shropshire. After all, surely their grotesquely pampered little angels are entitled to Madagascan vanilla?

No.

Our science lead wants a purchase order for £1,000 to pay some failed drama students to come into school and re-enact the discovery of penicillin. Because a generation cemented to screens can't possibly be expected to engage for five whole minutes with the myriad books we have already purchased on the same subject?

No.

Ben Andrews has already hinted at a plethora of new expenditure, designed to modernise a school whose educational raison d'être I am unaware has changed and has been delivered perfectly well for decades within our existing facilities. And it's imperative to move with the times, isn't it?

No. No. No.

Our modern notions of insufficiency are abhorrent. A child not having what they want is a far cry from a child not having what they need. A parent can choose whether to provide the former. I will determine the criteria for the latter.

Today is a perfect example. As a Christian community, we *needed* to administer the proper rites to dearest Claudia in her lifelong place of worship. Her length of service merited that, as do the tenets of our faith. That is what was required. If you *want* to then go and consume soggy quiche and supermarket cocktail sausages in the village hall, that is your choice. And I have chosen to stay in church.

My faith is a private matter. It's not something I share with the champagne congregation, who are only to be seen here annually at midnight mass or at one of the boundless parasitic celebrations that feed off true belief. Christianity is not an Airbnb in Bognor, to be inhabited and vacated at will. A church is not a fetching backdrop for your wedding photos on Facebook, nor for baptising your child to err on the side of spiritual caution. A church is the body of Christ. And unless you are here to thank Him for His sacrifice, then, frankly, you can fuck off.

With the rubbernecking hordes gorging on stale sandwiches next door, I kneel down to pray. I pray for Claudia's peace. I pray for my own. And I pray for forgiveness.

For us both.

When I open my eyes, I see Reverend McAlester smiling at me from a few pews down. I have always been vehemently and vocally against female clergy, but the Lord has nothing if not a sense of humour. I will concede that Katherine (I refuse to call her Katie) is doing a fair job, certainly if the measure is attendance in church. Claudia had no time for her.

'Women should be silent in churches,' she pronounced, quoting Corinthians in a classic moment of contradiction. Claudia wasn't one for female advancement unless that female happened to be her – a fatal flaw of feminism in time immemorial. 'You mark my words, it'll be all tambourines and tampons! That slattern will lead our church over my dead body!'

Well, you were right about one thing, dear.

'Hi, Clive,' says Reverend Katherine, with her usual disregard for rank or propriety. 'How are you holding up?'

I wince. I have no truck with modern parlance.

'How am I holding up what?' I ask her archly.

She smiles as though we're sharing a joke. We are not.

'I know you two were close,' she says. 'I just want you to know I'm here.'

Lord, send me strength.

'I am painfully aware you are there, Reverend; your existence is a matter of visceral visual and audible record,' I point out. 'Unless you wish to debate the finer points of solipsism? But I must confess the day has had the best of me and I would prefer to go home and drink a large glass of Italian red.'

'Amen!' She laughs lightly. I can't decide if she's trying to irritate me or she's just spectacularly stupid. Or both.

'Clive . . . I was hoping we might speak . . .' she begins.

'Then you must be delighted,' I sigh, settling back into my pew with my hands folded across my chest. The reverend wants something from me. I feel it's only fair to prepare her for the likely response. I always know when someone is about to ask me for something – after all, every relationship under the sun is transactional. Nothing is unconditional. Money. Love. Sex. Life. The wages of sin, after all, is death. We all tabulate an unspoken ledger, our lives the futile pursuit of balancing the books. The penance rarely outweighs the transgression. You overindulge for the month of December – you detox for a few days in January. You commit adultery with your secretary – you buy petrol-station flowers for your wife. We are born in sin and can never be clean. But that doesn't stop any of us from smearing a wet wipe around the edges occasionally.

'We've had another referral from StopGap,' Reverend McAlester continues. 'I wondered if you might consider kindly opening your home again?'

Ah yes. StopGap, the church's outreach programme, offering temporary shelter to those with nowhere else to go. I have always supported it, as my duty as a devout Christian requires. 'Be generous to the poor, and everything will be clean for you,' insists St Luke. He clearly never tended a bathroom after a methadone addict did their worst. But inviting the unhoused into my home is my way of doing the Lord's work. And, at present, my ledger needs more balancing than usual . . . But not now. I have important matters to attend to. Matters that require my undivided – and unobserved – attention.

'No,' I say simply, rising to leave. 'This isn't a good time—'

'I can guarantee it's worse for Andy,' she interrupts. 'And I think you'd be a good fit.'

Her tone both irks and impresses me. She's firm – demanding, even. Perhaps our lady vicar isn't all tambourines and tampons after all. I sit back down and nod my acquiescence to hear more.

'It's the usual story,' she says, resuming her fluffy bunny timbre. 'Single guy hard on his luck has fallen between the chasms in the system and found himself on the streets. No drugs, no crime – well, a little bit of hell-raising in his youth, but that's long behind him.'

'In his youth? So he's not a youngster?'

'No – he's closer to your age,' she says pointedly. 'Middle-aged men can be a little . . . more challenging to place. People are inclined to treat the unhoused like pets – they only really want the cute puppies.'

She has chosen her words well and they hit their mark. A man my age on the streets. There but for the grace of God . . .

'How long?' I ask.

'Two nights,' she says, smiling with impending victory. 'Unless you extend the invitation, of course . . .'

I hesitate and it's all the encouragement she needs.

'I saw you praying,' she whispers. 'God is good, of course. But He doesn't half appreciate it coming back the other way sometimes.'

You see? Transactions. Everywhere.

This time she does make me smile. I'm in need of some goodness. She's won.

I nod. The unfamiliar word gains momentum between my jaws.

'Yes.'

'I'll send Andy round,' she says triumphantly. 'I have a feeling you two will hit it off.'

'This is an act of Christian charity, not a sleepover,' I say, re-establishing the tone. 'I will house him until Sunday, then send him on his way.'

'Thank you, Clive,' she says, an irritating smile playing on her lips as we shake hands.

'You're welcome, Reverend,' I say back, ensuring my left eyebrow makes my opinion about the tattoo on her right wrist abundantly clear as I pass.

*

I wend my way back from church to my home on the other side of Flatford. Ours is a typical rural market town, the centre of the universe for denizens of days gone by, the middle of nowhere for us who live here now. I moved here eight years ago, seeking a nourishing slice of bucolic Hardyesque life. But even in the few years I've lived in Flatford, I've discovered one is more likely to encounter an indigestible slice of bacterial Steak Bake. The charming independent outlets that once formed the high street are gone, replaced by the commercial clones that can be found in any town across the land. The market that once offered farm-grown produce and artisanal cheese now proliferates mobile-phone cases and unseemly quantities of Tupperware. I've watched any shop with an iota of pedigree or history steadily close down – the butcher's, the haberdasher's, the deli. When I discovered that I was going to have to purchase my gorgonzola from the cheese counter in Morrisons, I nearly left town. When even that option was denied me, I briefly flirted with self-immolation. Flatford is a town trudging inexorably towards its own decay. But, then again, aren't we all?

I arrive at my gate and walk up the driveway to my home. London money goes a long way in Flatford and my four-bedroom house would be an outstanding example of something I want as opposed to something I need. But the extra space allows me to take in waifs and strays. And it was the devil's work to find anywhere else with sufficient parking for both the BMW and the Bentley, so we all have our crosses to bear. I do, have and will always live alone. Grateful as I am for being part of the Lord's flock, I have precisely zero interest in my fellow sheep. God is always with me and He makes an entirely agreeable housemate. I turn the key in my door and step into the home I have contentedly created: it is elegant, it is expensive and it is empty.

Either Reverend McAlester had prefigured my response, or Andy was already nearby, as barely have I been home five minutes when the doorbell rings. I curse myself for my weakness with the reverend and brace myself for the resulting intrusion. I never know what StopGap will put through my door. I've faced tears of gratitude and threats at knifepoint.

I could be opening my home to a refugee or a rapist. I have long since kept an unlicensed firearm in a locked box beneath the sink as a precaution, procured from one of Flatford's more dubious denizens. The liberal left love to superimpose a narrative of nobility on poverty. But, in my experience, the needy are every bit as likely to be a saint or a sinner as the rest of us. They just can't afford to do either particularly well. I sigh and replace my untouched wine glass. I rejoice in doing the Lord's work. I just wish it kept more sociable hours.

'Y'right?' comes the cheery greeting from the silver-haired man at my front door. 'Clive innit?'

'It is,' I reply imperiously. It's as well to establish hierarchy from the offset. 'You must be Andy.'

'Good to meet you, mate,' he chirps back, walking in without invitation. I draw some swift first impressions. His accent is north of here, although most places are. Liverpuddlian maybe? He smells clean – or at least, not unclean, which is a welcome start. I concur that he is indeed around my age, mid-fifties, although carrying rather less weight and rather more hair than I can boast.

He deposits his large backpack – also clean – in my hallway and puts his hands on his hips as he surveys my home. He whistles slowly.

'Nice gaff you got here, pal,' he says, more judgement than admiration in his tone. 'Big place for a single bloke? You divorced? Or a poof? Don't bother me either way. I'm just made up to have a flushing bog.'

I consider throwing him straight back out on the street. But a light in his eyes tells me that this is a test. He's baiting me to fail. I refuse to give him the satisfaction.

'My house rules are simple,' I state. 'No drugs, no theft, no blasphemy. You will keep your room and my house clean and tidy, or you will be required to leave. Do you understand?'

The light twinkles in Andy's eyes again.

'Gotcha, boss,' he says with a small salute. 'But, Jesus Christ, I was hoping to nick a tenner for some skank.'

I almost laugh despite myself. The man is brazen. He is the recipient of a benevolent act of charity – and yet something in his manner suggests that he is doing me the favour.

But his fearlessness interests me, which is more than most people achieve.

He walks into the lounge and surveys my extensive book collection, running his fingers along their spines. I can't say I care for it. This is not a library. My books are not for public consumption. I haven't read most myself, but they add an air of intellectual gravitas to my room, which feels fitting. Andy removes a tome from the nearest shelf.

'Ni . . . Niet . . . Neo . . .'

'Nietzsche,' I correct him, trying not to wince as he man-handles my pristine leather-bound edition in his oafish paws. But part of my role here is to educate. 'He was a philosopher. A nihilist. Which essentially means—'

'"God is dead. And we have killed him,"' Andy quotes effortlessly, without opening the book from which the words originate. 'Surprised to find heathen attitudes like that festering near a man of God like yourself?'

He turns to me with another twinkle. Tonight is taking a most unexpected turn.

'I can hardly defend the faith if I do not know the devil's argument,' I reply.

'"A casual stroll through the lunatic asylum shows that faith does not prove anything",' he quotes again. The man knows his Nietzsche. '"There cannot be a God because if there were one, I could not believe that I was not He."'

He winks at me before throwing my book end over end and landing it perfectly back on the shelf.

'I'm only having you on, Clivey Boy.' He winks. 'I'm more of a Sartre man meself . . .'

'"Hell is other people?"' I quip back at him with a raised eyebrow.

'"I am condemned to be free,"' he retorts with a smile and a small bow. 'Oooh – don't mind if I do . . .'

He heads over to the kitchen area in my open-plan room – one has little need for doors when you live alone – and starts searching through cupboards until he finds a stemmed glass. He places it heavily down on the counter before helping him-self to some wine from my decanter.

'Excuse me?' I say, flabbergasted by his nerve. 'I'll thank you to take care of that. It's—'

'A half decent Primitivo,' he confirms after a sip, holding the wine to the light. 'If you're going Italian, I prefer a robust Barolo, but it's not bad. Although if you paid more than a tenner for this you've been had, Clive-o.'

He stares at me with amused defiance. Another test.

'It was £9.99,' I reply. 'Delighted you approve.'

A smile cracks his face wide open.

'A man who knows true value,' he says. 'We're gonna get on just fine, Clivey. Now, could you take us to me room? And is it en suite, by any chance? I've got something brewing and it ain't a pint of Best, my friend . . .'

He strolls deeper into my house as though he owns it. I raise my eyes to heaven.

Well played, Lord.

The wages of sin might be death.

But you're repaying mine with Andy.

# Robocoppers
Priya, Al, Tanya

## Friday 28 October
17.02

**Priya**

Al? Where are you?

We're in the Crown.

Come and see us.

**Al**

On my way!

It's cost me an extra tenner and a Dominos for Casey.

(Plus the locksmith.)

But I need a drink!

**Priya**

I'll get them in.

And read this.

Hattie gave an interview rather than a statement.

This is the transcript between her and Bob Alsorp.

He has got to be the worst policeman since Noddy…

# HATITA HUGHES

# RECORDED INTERVIEW

**Date: Thurs 27 October: 4.47pm**
**Duration: 15 minutes**
**Location: 42a Mews Cottage, Flatford**
**Conducted by PC Robert Alsorp**

| | |
|---|---|
| Alsorp: | . . . and then I had to pull it out right there in front of the traffic warden! That'll be a belter for the Facebook page! |
| Hughes: | *[laughter]* You are a one! Right then, Bobby my boy. Let's get this show on the road. I'm due down the bingo. What do you need to know? |
| Alsorp: | Just need to dot the t's and cross the i's *[inaudible]*. Thanks for having me round. I think this thing's working if *[inaudible]*. Right – light's on – let's hope for the best. First thing, need to get the rigmarole done . . . So Hattie, you understand that this is an out-of-custody interview? |
| Hughes: | I do. Although you've been trying to get me in handcuffs for years, Bob Alsorp . . . |
| Alsorp: | *[laughter]* Don't you let my Nora hear you say that, or she'll be next up on a murder charge! You're not under arrest and you are free to leave at any time. |
| Hughes: | It's me own bloody house, Bob. Where am I gonna go? |
| Alsorp: | Fair point. And I also need to caution you that you do not have to say anything, but it may harm your defence if you do not mention when questioned something you later rely on in court. |
| Hughes: | I ain't going to no court, so no problem there. Well, not for this, any road *[inaudible]* . . . |

| | |
|---|---|
| Alsorp: | Don't go telling me that! And anything you do say may be taken down in evidence. |
| Hughes: | Don't you go taking nothing down, PC Alsorp! I still remember you chasing me around you ma's garden in the buff when we were nippers! Don't need to see no more of your little truncheon. |
| Alsorp: | *[laughing]* You mind your lip, gal! Now, can you tell me what you remember of Monday night? |
| Hughes: | Well, I'll hardly forget it in a hurry . . . It were a right bloody mess. I met with Stitchers— |
| Alsorp: | For the tape, the witness is referring to Claudia Stitchwell . . . |
| Hughes: | Yeah – her – and she wanted to chat about menus for the term. No idea why. I ain't listened to a bloody word she's had to say about it for twenty year and I ain't gonna start now. She'd feed those kiddies gruel if it were down to her, the mangey old bat— |
| Alsorp: | Stick to the facts, Hattie. |
| Hughes: | That is a fact! Plain as the spots on your arse, Bob! Anyhoo, I'd been preparing egg sarnies – I don't care what no one says, everyone loves an egg sarnie – and the tuna vol-au-vents (my own recipe). And, I'll tell you this for free, your boys can check every inch of my kitchen – you'll find more nuts in a convent. Anyway, I was putting out me savouries and Tanya was putting out her cake – bloomin' Stitchwell turns up and nicks a bloody great slice before we've even finished laying out, the greedy cow – when dopey Andrews tripped over his own feet, knocking St Stitchwell's special brew over and dropping Creepy Jesus in me vol-au-vents and Tanya's lovely cake! |
| Alsorp: | Daft sod! Handsome lad, though. Reminds me of me back in the day. |

Hughes: Ha! You've always had a face like a bad dream, Bob Alsorp. Even your own mother used to put a blanket over your pram when you were a babe. Said you looked like *[inaudible]*.

Alsorp: You're yanking my plank!

Hughes: My lips to God's ears. She told my ma – and you know what that pair were like, thick as thieves . . . Anyways – the vol-au-vents were a gonner, so I had to make some more. The cake was a mess, but I fixed it up and Kiera came to help me clean up (although she made more a mess, smearing it all over me face, the daft mare) and we did a half-decent job even though *[inaudible]* so I sent her to take Stitchers a cup of tea. I went back to sorting out me vol-au-vents, before Clive turned up banging and slamming around my kitchen like an oaf, trying to find the rev's poxy wine. Apparently, madam was in a right state – couldn't find her pa's bible for the opening prayer, so I went to the office to help her look. Turned out it was in the wrong drawer, the dozy mare, so I calmed her down. She made me wait while she guzzled down her cake and tea and sent me on my way.

Alsorp: What time would you say this was?

Hughes: I dunno, don't wear a watch do I? But not long before the thing started? Quarter past six maybe? But I wasn't going to the speech – I heard enough of the old witch all day long, so I cleaned up and buggered off home to *[inaudible]*.

Alsorp: Can anyone confirm what time you left?

Hughes: No, you great melon . . . Actually, I did run into Kiera's Matt on me way home, who brought me my handbag what I'd left in his shop like a proper dumdum. Gave me my bag and I went on my merry way. It was Monday. Corrie weren't gonna watch itself . . .

Alsorp: Right – interview terminated at *[inaudible]*. Thanks, Hats, appreciate your time. It's all a bloody nonsense . . .

Hughes: You're telling me! And if you want to investigate summit, why not that tenner you owe me from the footie sweeps down the Crown? I'm adding interest if it ain't in my purse by the weekend, you *[inaudible]* . . .

Alsorp: It's a fair cop! Thanks for this, Hats – especially when you're the last person who's gonna bump off old Stitchwell! It's not like you're gonna *[inaudible]*. Now how do you switch . . .

# Kiera

This wasn't The Plan.

I clearly remember The Plan. The Plan was to run out of Flatford the second I finished school and head straight for the golden streets of London. Upon abandoning my art degree because my first exhibition was such a critical and cultural triumph, I was going to live in a creative commune before committing to both Heath Ledger and Orlando Bloom in a pagan hand-binding ceremony, lavishly but tastefully photographed for *Hello*.

The Plan was to live a life of free love, expensive tastes and artistic expression.

And yet here am I, scraping egg salad into a bin liner.

I am constantly cleaning up someone else's mess. As a teaching assistant, any child can leak anything, anywhere, at any time – I clean it up. As a lunchtime supervisor, the hall is left looking like the bottom of a monkey cage every day – I clean it up. My family wreaks all manner of physical and emotional mess – I constantly clean it up. The Plan might be a distant pipe dream, but I'd love, however briefly, for someone to just clean up after me. Surely, it must be my turn to make a bloody great mess?

But, for now, I'm having to clean up after Stitchwell.

Again.

'Guess everyone's allergic to a Nonnatus buffet now,' I sigh, grabbing my third plate of couscous. 'Although if you've survived Rachel Shylone's coronation chicken you'll outlive the cockroaches . . .'

'Oi, don't be chucking all that away – there's folk'll eat it!' says Hattie, snatching the dish out of my hands. 'Throwing good food away's a sin . . .'

'All right, Bob Geldof,' I say, backing away as she aggressively scrapes leftovers into her own bewildering array of Tupperware. Hattie lets nothing go to waste, whether it is offered or she simply nicks it. She's been in a filthy mood since the church. 'What's boiling your piss?'

'Don't matter none,' she grunts, thumping spoonfuls of coleslaw into a tub. 'I just wanna get out of here is all.'

'Suits me,' I sigh. 'I'll do a last sweep.'

I love Hattie – she's been like a mum to me, which is more than anyone else has managed.

But, Jesus, she's a mardy cow sometimes.

I leave the kitchen, expecting the hall to be empty. But I'm not unhappy to see that Ben's still there, ripping through the pile of condolence cards. In a school full of Christians and cardigans, he's been a very welcome addition to the mix. Dynamic people make dynamic teachers and he can rightly claim to be both. And he's not so awful to look at for six hours a day . . . certainly beats the hell out of Trevor Elson who teaches our Year 5 and has a mullet from the year 1985 (which was also the last time I suspect he used mouthwash). Ben's classically tall, dark, handsome but with trendy stubble and glasses. Oh, and that gorgeous Scottish lilt . . . Urgh – who am I kidding, I fancy the crap out of him. Don't get me wrong, I love my Matt. But I kinda love who I am around Ben. I'm younger. Sexier. I'm the girl who had The Plan. And I've missed her.

'Are you feeling suitably sorry for your loss yet?' I ask, creeping up behind him and whispering in his ear. I know I shouldn't. But I love to play with him. I watch to see the response it creates in him, if any. Do I still have it? Or has 'it' been washed, ironed and folded so many times it's sitting at the back of the cupboard with my skin-tone bras and tummy-holdy-in knickers?

Ben smiles, but it's strained. He's not playing. Yet.

'Did you . . . did you see who left any of these?' he says, rifling through the envelopes.

'Well, Mr Andrews . . . the standard clue is the name written inside the card,' I point out. 'But I'm sure Dolphin Class can teach you about basic letter-writing. They covered it last term in Year 2.'

I wait for him to lob my sass back at me – ours is a thrilling game of taunt tennis and I love it when he pulls my pigtails. But, again, just the strained smile.

'What's wrong?' I ask him. 'Is it . . . bitchface?'

I feel him tense as his ex-wife clouds his mind. Six months ago, Ben's wife Elena upped and left him, taking their son, Finn, back to Scotland with her. I found him the day after they left, crying in the art supplies cupboard, and he bared his soul. Rumour is that there was someone else involved – but why anyone would leave this sweet, kind and . . . well, frankly, shit-hot . . . man for one of the other dropkicks out there, I wouldn't know. I do know that she's been an arsehole since they split, making it as difficult as possible for him to see Finn and generally rubbing as much salt as she can in the wound she has created. She always was a snooty cow. I never liked her. He could do so much better.

'Er . . . yeah,' he says softly, gathering the cards up. 'It doesn't get any easier.'

'I bet,' I say gently. 'Can I help?'

He sighs, takes off his glasses and raises those soft brown eyes. They lock with mine. I feel all kinds of thrills. Keep it together, woman. It's just a crush. It'll pass. They always do.

'Thanks,' he says, running a weary hand through his hair, 'but I'd better get home. So much to do for Monday.'

'You'll be great,' I tell him, and I mean it. After so many grim years of the Stitchwell regime, Ben is just what St Nonnatus needs. A little tenderness and love. As do we all.

'Thanks,' he says again, putting his left hand on my right shoulder. 'Truly.'

My head turns to the fingers resting lightly there. I have this overwhelming urge to tilt my cheek to rest on them, to invite them to cup my face, to pull me into the chest that's straining against his shirt buttons and . . .

Oh FFS, Fisher.

No more *Bridgerton* for you.

'If I'm not disturbing you,' comes Hattie's shrill command, 'the kids' bogs are dripping in piss. Get to it, gal.'

At the sound of her voice, Ben snaps his hand back like it's been burned. I smile. That's not the response of a guiltless man. Although, in the wrong mood, Hattie could make Mother Theresa feel like Miss Hannigan.

'Sorry, Hattie,' he smiles. 'I'm distracting her. "Listen to many, speak to a few."'

Bless him. He's even quoting *Hamlet* to cosy up to her. Good strategy . . .

'"One may smile and smile and be a villain,"' she grumbles back at him, shuffling back to the kitchen.

Maybe not.

'See you around, Mr Andrews,' I grin. 'I've got a hot date with a J Cloth and some Jif . . .'

'Try to keep your personal peccadillos out of your work, Mrs Fisher,' he smiles back with a wink. 'See you on Monday.'

'Not if I see you first.' I wink back. I hear his breathing catch as I turn away and make sure my hips have a swing as I leave.

I know I shouldn't need it.

But some days it's nice to have it confirmed.

Oh yes, Kiera Fisher.

You still got it.

Despite the Turner Prize entry that was the village hall toilets, I head home feeling like a sex kitten.

A feeling that survives roughly five seconds after crossing the threshold of my house.

'MUM! You said you'd washed my black crop top – where the hell is it? I'm going out!'

'MUM! What's a simultaneous equation? Taylor won't help me!'

'MUM! Tell Grace to sod off out of my room and stick her equations up her arse!'

'MUM! Tell Taylor to put two pounds in the swear jar! And she still hasn't paid for calling you an effing B last weekend! So that's four pounds!'

'MUM! Tell Grace to make it a fiver and FUCK OFF!'

I sigh and peer into the front room and see my husband sitting peacefully with a cuppa and his feet up in front of *Pointless*.

Oh, the irony.

'Hi,' I say sarcastically. 'Not sure if you're aware, but our daughters are auditioning for foster care upstairs . . . ?'

'Anna Scott!' he shouts in his loudest Bolton brogue at a mousy man called Ashley, who is trying to think of Julia Roberts's characters with ten or more letters in their name. 'Get in! Y'right, gorgeous? I'm telling you, love, I should go on this. I'd bloody clean up.'

'That's nine letters. And only if you think you can squeeze it in between your doctorate and your *Men's Health* cover shoot,' I mutter, picking up the remnants of his toast. 'Have you fed the girls?'

'Nah,' he says. 'Taylor's gorit in her head she's not pescatarian this week, so won't even eat bloody fishfingers now. And Grace reckons she's allergic to vegetables and, bugger me, life's too sodding short, so . . . Tess Ocean! I'm telling you, Kier – I could win us a piggin' fortune on here! Oh no, hang on – that's nine and all.'

Oh, Matt . . .

Matt was never part of The Plan. But then, to be fair, neither was anyone in this household. I wasn't part of my parents'. Taylor wasn't part of mine. Grace wasn't part of Matt's. What's the collective noun for accidents? A 'whoopsie'? Because that's us. A family of accidents. Happy ones, mostly. But when you find yourself pregnant at seventeen, The Plan needs a whole lot of revision. And when a fit Northern squaddie swaggers into town from the local army camp a few years later, treats you like a queen and promises to take care of you and your kid, that felt like a pretty solid edit.

I trudge towards the kitchen, trying to devise a homemade gastronomic feast for our family that is wholesome and tasty while being both vegetable-free *and* vegetarian.

'Pesto pasta?' I shout to Matt, who is guffawing at Ashley's answer.

'Erin Brockovich?' he mocks. 'Yeah, pal – no one will have thought of that . . . Don't worry about me babe, I'm on lates.'

'Since when?' I groan back. 'I thought the manager was supposed to set the rota?'

'I do,' he calls back, 'but Freida needs a hand.'

'We all know where Frieda wants your hand,' I call back. 'And it ain't in the World Foods aisle.'

'Give over,' he says, as he always does when I challenge him about the co-worker who has been shamelessly making a play for my husband for over a year.

I put the pasta on to boil and set the table for me and the girls. Matt meanders into the kitchen and puts his arms round me at the stove. I wriggle free. I'm busy.

'So I had an interesting day today,' I tell him.

'Did Stitchwell poke 'er hand up through the dirt like Carrie?' Matt says, clawing at me.

'That would have been less surprising,' I sigh, batting him away. 'Baxendale's offered you – well, us – the caretaker job at St Nonn's.'

'Yer what?' he says, his shaved head wrinkling in confusion. 'Me, picking up Twix packets off the playground for a living? No, ta.'

'We'd get the caretaker's cottage,' I point out. 'We could rent this place – give us some money for Gracie's school fees . . .'

'What's the point of that scholarship if we still have to pay summit?' he asks for the millionth time.

'The point is to pay the seventy-five per cent of the fees we still can't afford,' I reply, for the millionth time.

'Kier – we don't have twenty-five per cent. We don't have two per cent.'

'Which is why this job could be the answer to everything!' I cry, trying to keep my voice down while wanting to shake him. 'What's keeping you at BuyRite? Apart from Frisky Frieda?'

'Give over,' he says again. 'I'm happy there. I've got mates. I like it.'

'Well, we don't always get to do what we like,' I say more bitterly than I intend. 'But, if you want to do what's right by your daughter, you'll take an easy job and a free house.'

He sighs. 'I'll think on it,' he says. 'But it'll cost ya . . .'

He reaches for me again with a horny grin. I duck out of his arms. I don't have time for this. Sex after fifteen years together goes on the same list as washing the net curtains and dehumidifying the loft – I will get round to it. Eventually.

'Thanks,' I say graciously, even though we both know this means I've won. There's nothing Matt won't do for Gracie. For any of us.

'Grace! Taylor!' I call up the stairs. 'Dinner!'

A slow stomping suggests that my teenage daughter has actually responded to a request. She appears in the doorway defiantly, wearing what barely amounts to a red bra and a black Band-Aid. I laugh.

'Not in this lifetime,' I tell her. 'Go and change.'

'Oh my GOD!' she huffs. 'I told you, I'm going out!'

'Since when?' I ask her. 'It's a school night.'

'Matt said I could,' she says smugly. I stare at Matt, who shrugs and wanders back out of the kitchen. Argh . . . Matt is, by and large, a great stepdad. He's been in Taylor's life since she was four and he loves her like his own. But she's got him wrapped round her finger like a Claire's Accessories ring – I make a note to have the umpteenth conversation about discipline.

'So yeah. I'm going. Out.'

'Where?' I reply, too tired for the fight tonight. 'Got a shift at the strip club?'

'You are SO lame,' she withers at me, reaching for her bag. 'I don't need dinner – I'll eat out.'

'Not so fast,' I say, snatching her bag, and my only leverage, out of her reach. 'Who are you out with?'

'Why do you care?' she snarls.

'Because I can't afford your bail. No names, no bag.'

She freezes as her teenage ire reboots.

'Just my friends. You know. Friends. Some of us have some . . .'

Wow – teenagers know where to sting.

'Like who?' I ask. 'Jools? Tilly?'

'Jesus Christ, Mum! How many times!' she rages, like she's Tom Cruise and has Jack Nicholson on the stand. 'If you're talking about SEBASTIAN, *they* are non-binary, so stop using their dead name!'

'Sorry . . . sorry – still getting my head around it,' I sigh. 'And Tilly? Can I still call her that?'

'Yeah, sure. If you want to infantilise her and not allow her reclamation of her birth name? Her name is Matilda, Mother. But she's changing it by deed poll next year to Leif to reflect her cultural heritage.'

'Er . . . don't Karl and Flo come from Swindon?'

'Oh my GOD, do you want to be a bit more racist?' she outrages. 'Leif is descended from the Vikings? It said so in that DNA kit her nan gave her for her birthday? So shall we stop white-washing her much?'

Wow. How do the youth get it so very right and yet so very wrong?

'Got it.' I nod. 'Much as I admire your generation's dedication to personal identity—'

'Good,' she snarls.

'. . . if you think you're leaving this house dressed like Vivian Ward – *that's* ten letters – you're making a big mistake. Big! Huge!'

I do my best Julia Roberts impression. But, like so much of my creativity, it's wasted here.

'Are you, like, having a fit or something?' my teenage daughter disdains.

'Change. Or stay home. Your choice,' I tell her, returning to the pasta.

'OHMYGODYOUARESUCHAFREAK!' she says in a monosyllable of outrage as she storms upstairs to don actual clothing. 'And who the fuck is Vivian Ward?'

'Six pounds!' Gracie shouts down.

'Home by nine!' I shout as I dish up mine and Gracie's pasta. 'Gracie! Pasta! Now!'

'I'm off, babe,' shouts Matt from the hallway. 'Be back round midnight. Love ya.'

'Don't wake me,' I shout back as the door shuts behind him. The devolution of 'goodbye' is one of a marriage's sadder declines. First you can't leave without shagging against the door. Then some passionate snogging to send you on your way. Tender words of love are next, with ardent demands to see each other soonest. Then, before you know it, you're just hoping that someone remembers to pick up bum wipes on the way home.

Grace hurtles into the kitchen, her glasses steaming up as she peers into her pasta.

'Hey, Mum,' she grins, racing over to give me a hug. I honestly think it's only Gracie and the cat who would notice if I never came home. And, in truth, I'm sure Tinkerbell would gladly move in with Mrs Hodgkins next door. But Grace still seems to like me. She's such a great kid – and deserves all the good things. Which is why she's going to get them. No matter what the cost.

She grabs her pasta and runs out again.

'Hey! Where you off to?' I call after her. 'I thought we could have tea and watch *Only Connect* together?'

'I can't,' she calls back. 'I'm doing homework with Verity – she's on the phone – byeeee!'

I hear her bedroom door close and look at my solitary bowl of pasta.

Screw it.

I open the fridge and throw the last of the wine I said I wouldn't drink this week into a glass, before scooping up my bowl and settling myself on the sofa with both. I pick up the remote and flick to my viewing pleasure with a smile.

And there it is.

Come on then, *Bridgerton*.

Let's be having you.

# Robocoppers
Priya, Al, Tanya

## Friday 28 October
20.46

**Priya**
Thatss was fun in pub.
I love yooooiiuuu two.

**Al**
Pri – you hold your booze like a sieve.
But fun night, girls, thanks!
See ya Stitchers.
You absolute bitch.

**Tanya**
These statements...
We need to talk.

**Priya**
Yeshh!
Letsss be detectivists!
I'm the best at detectiving.
Heres Ben's thingy.
I siad thingy!

# STATEMENT OF WITNESS

CJ Act 1967, s.9; MC Act 1980, ss.5A(3)(a) and 5B; Criminal Procedure Rules 2005, Rule 27.1

**Statement of**   Benjamin Andrews

**Occupation**   Deputy Headteacher

**Age of witness** *(if over 18, enter 'Over 18')*   Over 18

This statement is true to the best of my knowledge and belief and I make it knowing that, if it is tendered in evidence, I shall be liable to prosecution if I have wilfully stated in it anything which I know to be false, or do not believe to be true.

**Signed:**   *BXAndrews*

I am Ben Andrews of 52 Landsdowne Lane, Flatford, and this is my recollection of the events of 24 October.

The first day back is always fraught and this had been no exception. Immediately after school ended, I drove to the local supermarket BuyRite to do my shopping, encountering Tanya Jones on the way and Hattie Hughes in the store, with whom I returned to school in my car.

I got back to St Nonnatus around 4.45pm and did some paperwork in my office. A little after 5.30 I went to the hall to help with preparations for the drinks night – but there was an incident when I slipped and fell, so I returned to my office to fix the Jesus statuette that had been damaged in the fracas. I met Miss Stitchwell in the main office, where she was tending to some admin, and she asked to see me. I went to her office shortly before 6pm, where she informed me of her intention to remain in post. I congratulated her and went outside to greet parents as they arrived.

The evening began promptly at 6.30pm, but it became clear quite quickly that Miss Stitchwell was unwell. I gave her some water to ease her cough, but her condition quickly deteriorated. I am our designated First Aider and I administered resuscitation, but it was sadly too late. The ambulance and police arrived shortly thereafter and I stayed on site until approximately 9pm to help them with their enquiries.

**Signature witnessed by:** *Robert Alsop*

# PARENTCHAT

Clearer Community Communication

## ST NONNATUS CE PRIMARY

*Ora et labora*

**Flatford FC**
Eric

**Mon 7 Nov**
08.30

**Eric**
Hi everyone!
Wanted to leave it a respectful distance, but...
As promised (threatened!) I wanted to start
a group for the footie!
(Only masochists need apply!)
Me and the girls are going Saturday
– I can get guest tickets!
Should be a good one – we're playing Westmouth
Wanderers, our old nemesis!
Need to know by Wednesday lunchtime if
you're up for it!
See you there I hope!

# PARENTCHAT

Clearer Community Communication

## ST NONNATUS CE PRIMARY

### *Ora et labora*

**Monday 7 November**

**Mrs Marcia Cox<M.Cox@stnonnatus.flatford.sch.uk>**

**To: <Whole School>**

**Re: Week commencing 7 Nov**

Dear Carers,

We have all been so delighted to see how well the children have settled back into school this past week.

Mr Andrews has asked me to pass on his gratitude for all the lovely messages and feedback he has received and reminds everyone that his morning clinics will continue between 9–9.30 every Tuesday and Thursday. We will however need to instigate an appointment system owing to the sheer volume of meetings – please use the link at the bottom of this letter if you'd like to book in. We also respectfully request that language is kept to an appropriate choice and volume, as Mr Andrews's office is within earshot of Bumblebee class. On a related note, we apologise again for the unfortunate incident in assembly last week and assure you that the Year 1 children were supposed to be singing '*The Duck Clucked in the Muck*'.

We are glad that so many of you are availing yourselves of the suggestion box in reception and can announce that, after tallying the votes, the new school goldfish will be named 'Fishy McFishFace'.

In response to some early feedback, we will be instigating the following measures with immediate effect:

- As per the salutation in this letter, we will now refer to 'carers' rather than 'parents'. It has been pointed out that not every adult in our community is a parent and we want St Nonnatus to be an inclusive space. We are always happy to address you by your preferred prefixes or pronouns and this feels like an excellent opportunity to introduce our new lunchtime supervisor, Jedi Master Bernard.

- Mr Andrews is undertaking a comprehensive review of all behavioural policies, but will be removing the 'bon' and 'mauvais' points system from today. There will no longer be Forgetful Fridays, nor any other sanctions for forgotten homework or reading diaries. We understand that life can be hectic and things fall through the cracks. However, we do ask that the children arrive promptly to start their day at 08.45. Awaiting the conclusion of an episode of *Paw Patrol* does not constitute an acceptable reason to be late.

- While we ask that the correct uniform is worn at all times, there will no longer be a formal distinction between 'boys' and 'girls' uniforms. Children and their carers may elect whichever of the clothing list best suits their needs. In a similar vein, while we all understand the morning rush, we do ask that carers dress appropriately while on school premises. While we discourage it, if sleepwear is to be worn at drop-off, it is to be done so in such a way that conforms with our safeguarding requirements.

- As mentioned in assembly last week, for the remainder of term, we will be trialling allowing children to bring in a packed lunch if they wish. We understand that not every child wishes to eat school dinners and may benefit from having lunch provided for them from home. Please fill out the attached form if you wish to supply your child's lunch, remembering again our allergy and healthy eating policies. In response to several similar questions about the new lunch policy, the school will not accept orders from Deliveroo on your child's behalf.

May I remind you again about parking considerately during the morning and afternoon drop-offs/collections? Access to our neighbours' drives and the church car park are to remain unobstructed at all times and the zigzags are for emergency use only. And, for clarity, 'reformer Pilates at nine' does not an emergency make.

I leave you with the words of D:Ream: 'Things Can Only Get Better'.

Wishing you all the very best,

Mrs Marcia Cox

Office Manager
St Nonnatus Primary School

# Tickly Tiger's Diary!

Date: Monday 7 November

This weekend I went home with: Amelia

Tickly Tiger and I had so much fun this weekend! On Friday we went out for curry at Naan Taken because Dad didn't have time to go to the shops and Tickly ate a whole plate of poppadoms! Then we all FaceTimed Mum because she's in Overseas on a holiday where she doesn't eat anything and Daddy told her everything was under control and she had to relax. But could she just tell him where she kept the dishwasher tablets, marmalade, fabric softener and the hoover? Mummy said she was REALLY enjoying her break and might never come home!

We would have been able to stay up really late because Dad was too busy to put us to bed, but Daisy-May said she wanted Tickly and I wouldn't give him to her and she broke my Lego Friends house so Dad said that was ENOUGH, he was tired from having to do so much, and we had to go to sleep.

On Saturday we went to Primark because Dad's been too busy to do the laundry and we needed some clothes. We had a real adventure when Daddy couldn't find us and we got to go to the special office and Tickly could watch all the people on the little televisions! Then we went to Starbucks for lunch and I had a ham and cheese toastie because Daddy was too busy to make one at home.

Then my Granny and Grandad came to take us to Mr Blister's Soft Play to help Daddy out. I played with Elijah (who was there with his Aunty and cousins because his Mummy will be in Overseas for ages so his Daddy was WAY too busy to take him) and Aleksander (who was there with his mummy, who wasn't too busy to take him, but was too busy chatting to her friends to remember to take him home). And then – best thing ever – Granny and Grandad decided to take me and Daisy-May for a sleepover to give Daddy a break!

Granny cooked a roast dinner with apple pie and even made some to take home so Daddy didn't have to cook. We had so much fun playing noughts and crosses and snakes and ladders until I got a bit sad and we FaceTimed Mummy again to make sure she was actually coming home because I really miss her. And I really need some clean socks.

# PARENTCHAT

Clearer Community Communication

## ST NONNATUS CE PRIMARY

*Ora et labora*

### Year 6 Tiger Class

click here for group info

### Tuesday 8 Nov
9.43

**Stella**
Hello everyone.
I hope this finds you well.
I just wanted to see if anyone else shares
any of my concerns
with regard to this week's newsletter?

**Flo**
The parking?
Absolute nightmare.
Did you see Emma Mullins last week?
Parked her 4 x 4 in the way of a funeral cortege!
Told the undertaker she'd be back after she'd dropped
off Euan's toilet roll model of Stonehenge!

**Dustin**
What is wrong with these people?!

**Zofia**
But isn't Marcia a legend?
I heard she's a black belt in ju-jitsu.
Must come in handy at that reception...

*Sarah has joined the group 'Year 6 Tiger Class'*

**Sarah**
Hi everyone!
New phone, new number, same old me!

**Sharon**
Hi Sarah!
Haven't seen you for ages!
All well?

**Sarah**
Just crazy busy – kids, house, work, the usual.
Lost my phone, losing my mind…
What have I missed?

**Jenna**
Just sliding in – my turn to go off for a few weeks!
New assignment in Myanmar.
Mike's in charge (sort of…)
Back soon x

**Al**
You are astonishing, Jenna. Please take care.

**Mike**
*Mike's in charge (sort of . . .)*
She's not wrong.

**Tanya**
*What have I missed?*
Where do we start?!
Coffee soon?

**Sharon**
*You are astonishing, Jenna. Please take care.*
And so say all of us. God speed, sweetheart.
We'll look after Mikey while you're away 😊

**Laura**
You need to use the green bags, they're the best.

**Laura**
Sorry! Wrong group!

**Stella**

Yes, the parking is frustrating.

But I was referring to other aspects.

The clothing, chiefly.

Although I'm also not happy to see we still have the

supply teacher in this week.

**Sharon**

*But I was referring to other aspects.*

You mean them politely asking Jimmy Platt to keep his
mouse in the house?

I've paid subscriptions to see less than that man
shows in his PJs at drop-off.

**Rosie**

*Although I'm also not happy to see we still have the*
*supply teacher in this week.*

I quite agree.

This Ms Tayke hasn't got a clue.

She put Theo on the Green table for Maths last week!

(Theo's on the Blue Table.)

(The top one.)

**Stella**

No.

I meant the degendering of our uniform policy.

**Fatima**

That wasn't my take.

It's just about choice, no?

Khadija is loving wearing trousers.

(And I suspect so is everyone else who isn't seeing her
flashing her knickers in the playground every time
she's doing cartwheels.)

**Al**

I agree.

The trousers are much more practical for the girls.

Especially in winter – so much warmer.

**Jennie**

Does anyone know how to get loom bands out of the U-bend?

**Rosie**

*I meant the degendering of our uniform policy.*
I'm with you Stella.
The girls in trousers is one thing.
But I can't imagine Theo collecting his certificates in celebration assembly in a skirt.

**Priya**

Why should that make a shit of difference?

**Stella**

*I'm with you Stella.*
Thank you Rosie.
I was hoping to raise my concerns with Mr Andrews.

**Tanya**

Hey everyone! Few things...
Just to say that I've allocated Tiger Class the bar for the Xmas Fayre!
I must be losing my mind!
1) If you could sign up for shifts on the Doodle poll, that would be great.
2) Don't forget that the Xmas cards need to be in this week.
3) The last payment for the Year 6 residential at Radford House is due by Monday.
4) Don't forget to put in your secondary school applications – deadline is end of the month xxx

**Sharon**

What would we do without you, Tan?
Thanks love xxx

**Priya**

*I was hoping to raise my concerns with Mr Andrews.*
What possible concerns can you have about children wearing clothes?

**Petra**

*3) The last payment for the Year 6 residential at
Radford House is due by Monday.*

Oh God, thanks – I had totally forgotten.

Archie must have left the form in his trousers...

(btw – has anyone seen his trousers?)

**Donna**

*2) Don't forget that the Xmas cards need to be in this
week.*

Oh no. 😕

You do the Christmas card thing here too?

Finley drew a pink snowman last year.

It looked like a penis.

My aunt Christine nearly choked when she opened it...

**Mike**

Does anyone have this week's spellings?

(I have no idea which group Jacob's in.)

**Al**

Oh don't fret, Mike.

Ben's got rid of the groups.

Everyone gets the same spellings now.

(Still no bloody idea what they are, though.

Millie decided to give Maisie's book a bath...)

**Mike**

And what's everyone going to do about the lunches?

I barely have time to get breakfast down them, let
alone make bloody lunch.

But Jacob says everyone is doing it?

**Karl**

I hear you.

Ollie is dead keen.

Although less so when I explained that two kit kats
and a bag of Monster Munch did not qualify as a
proper lunch.

**Flo**
Neither does a Gregg's pasty and a knee-trembler in
the stationery cupboard.
But you and Sandra managed.

**Rosie**
*Everyone gets the same spellings now.*
Everyone?
Even those in the Purple Group?
The top one?

**Priya**
Even them.
So this is how revolution feels...

**Stella**
*What possible concerns can you have about children*
*wearing clothes?*
I appreciate that my views aren't in tune with
modern thinking.
But I think that the late Reverend would be spinning
in his grave at the thought of boys in skirts at the
school he founded. And so would Miss Stitchwell.

**Al**
*It looked like a penis.*
That's hilarious!
They used to do the xmas cards with pictures from the
nativity play.
Leo looked like he'd been taken hostage by a terror cell.
Dressed like a donkey.

**Petra**
Has anyone seen Archie's trousers?

**Sharon**
*But I think that the late Reverend would be spinning*
*in his grave at the thought of boys in skirts at the*
*school he founded. And so would Miss Stitchwell.*
HA!
Trust me, there was no bigger fan of skirts than the
randy Rev...
He'd chase anything in one!

**Stella**
That's a terrible thing to say.
He was a very loving pastor.

**Sharon**
Oh sure!
He loved half the bloody town!
Talk about tending your... flock.
He had a massive affair with my Aunty Pat.
And she was just one.
He was at it with Mary Smith who used to run The
Crown, Joanie Hughes in the bakery, Connie Rogers
when BuyRite was the haberdashers – and he cleaned
up at the camp when the boys were on deployment.

**Al**
Wow.
Love thy neighbour...

**Sharon**
Oh yeah.
That man was full of the Holy Spirit.
He could've fathered half the town!

**Sarah**
And yet it was Miss Stitchwell that had a baby on the
wrong side of the blanket.
The fabled Stitchwell Love Child.

**Zofia**
Stichers?
Surely not?
That woman never got laid.
But tell me more...

**Sarah**
That's the story I was told.
Apparently she fell in love with a squaddie, got
knocked up.
He went back to America.
Baby was spirited away by the church.

**Sharon**

I've heard tell of the Stitchwell Love Child too.
Local rumour's been doing the rounds forever.
Sounds about right – them sort's always hypocrites.
It'll all be in her black book.

**Stella**

I refuse to give your scurrilous gossip the time of day.
But if anyone would like to join me in raising concerns
I shall be seeing Mr Andrews this week.

**Flo**

*4) Don't forget to put in your secondary school*
*applications – deadline is end of the month xxx*
Oh God – I can't believe they're going to secondary
next year!
They're so tiny!
Is the gang staying together?
Is everyone going to Flatford High?

**Al**

Yup

**Sharon**

We are.

**Rosie**

Theo is sitting the 11+ for Westmouth Grammar.

**Priya**

*It'll all be in her black book.*
?????

**Sharon**

Stitchwell's diary.
Legend has it she kept everyone's secrets in it.
Including her own.

**Zofia**

I heard she kept it in a hidden compartment in her
desk.
And it contained the colonel's secret recipe.

**Donna**

*Is everyone going to Flatford High?*
I guess... we only just started this school!
Is it any good?

**Karl**

Yes, our Tilly is there.
As are Kiera's and Leanne's girls (they're BFFs).
We're happy enough with it.

**Sharon**

Better than it used to be.
Back in the Stitchwell era...

**Zofia**

Stitchwell taught secondary?
I assumed she'd always been at St Nonn's?

**Sharon**

Oh no – both Stitchwells plagued Flatford High
originally.
The Rev taught fire and brimstone, she taught Year 13.
Taught a few on here – Al, Kiera, Tanya, Sarah, Karen,
my Steve.
Miserable bastards there too.

**Al**

*Stitchwell's diary.*
It's a myth.
We broke into her office once to find it.
My mate told me we'd find out who killed JFK.

**Karen**

*Miserable bastards there too.*
Oh God, they really were.
Would have been the worst teacher there if it weren't
for Mr Pandy...
Do you remember Handy Pandy, Sarah?
Such a leching perv...

**Sarah**

He was disgusting.

Deserved every second of that heart attack.

**Donna**

That's appalling.

What did the school do?

**Mike**

*Is it any good?*

Our eldest Bea is in Year 10 – she's doing alright.

**Karen**

*What did the school do?*

Ha!

I was there in the early nineties.

There was no 'Me Too' then.

More like 'Your Fault'.

Hideous 'asking for it' narrative.

**Sarah**

And Stitchwell was chief storyteller.

**Karen**

Totally.

I'd hoped things would be different for my daughter.

But…

**Mike**

Funny you should say that.

We have some concerns.

Has anyone seen this Themis thing?

**Tanya**

*Theo is sitting the 11+ for Westmouth Grammar.*

Good luck!

We took one look at the papers and couldn't answer a single question!

Figured that if we couldn't, wasn't fair to push Verity through it!

**Zofia**

*As are Kiera's and Leanne's girls (they're BFFs).*
I hear Taylor's become a bit of a live wire.
Been getting into trouble.
I wonder if that's why Kiera's going private for Grace?
You know she got an art scholarship to Shottsford
House?

**Flo**

*Has anyone seen this Themis thing?*
No.
Should I have done?

**Mike**

Hold on – I'll try to find it...

**Rosie**

*Figured that if we couldn't, wasn't fair to push Verity
through it!*
We're not 'pushing' Theo through anything.
He wants to sit the test and we're supporting him.

**Tanya**

Sorry Rosie – that wasn't what I meant at all.
I was just making a joke about how stupid we are.
No offence intended.

**Mike**

Here it is.
So these posts keep appearing on social media, from
an account called Themis.
Apparently it's to warn girls about inappropriate
behaviour from the boys:

# THEMIS

## The Goddess of Justice

### Unnerves the pervs

The Goddess is back! And this time she's dishing out some retribution to football captain Kyle Norris in Year 12, who thinks it's okay to send unsolicited dick-pics to girls via Airdrop! Well I've got news for you, Kyle – NO ONE WANTS TO SEE YOUR TACKLE!

But the Goddess is a benevolent judge. So seeing as how you're so keen to demonstrate what you've got up front – I'm gonna share it with the stands! Click the link below if you want to see how Kyle tries to score off the field (you'll need your binoculars). And if you want to see how he scores on it . . . well on his current form, you'll be waiting a while.

So Kyle – and anyone who thinks this kind of attack is fair game – KEEP YOUR BALLS TO YOURSELVES!

Goddess 1.

Pervs 0.

Love,

Themis

Xxx

**Flo**

Jesus... That's a worry.

**Mike**

I've got to say... I'm glad someone's calling it out.
One of Bea's friends got sent this.
The school said there was no proof who did it.
She was in Year 8.

**Karl**

What are Flatford High doing about it?

**Rosie**

*I was just making a joke about how stupid we are.*
I see.
I just tire of being made to feel like a pushy parent.
Just because I want the best for my son.

**Leanne**

*Apparently it's to warn girls about inappropriate
behaviour from the boys:*
Themis is complete shit.
I know Kyle.
He ain't done anything.
You shouldn't spread it around.

**Petra**

Does anyone have a spare Christmas card form?

**Sharon**

Why – has Archie lost his? 😄

**Petra**

No, for once!
But he did just draw Santa stabbing Rudolph with a
candy cane.

**Priya**

*Just because I want the best for my son.*
And we all don't?

**Mike**

*You shouldn't spread it around.*

I wasn't trying to gossip, truly.

I was expressing my concern about the school.

If it's true, this kid needs to face consequences.

If it's not, someone needs to find who is spreading falsehoods.

**Al**

*But he did just draw Santa stabbing Rudolph with a candy cane.*

HA!!!

I'll buy Archie's!

**Rosie**

*And we all don't?*

This is what I mean.

This isn't 'us' and 'them'.

It's an educational choice.

The grammar system is a fair and meritocratic way of nurturing academic excellence.

**Donna**

*I'll buy Archie's!*

Brilliant.

Perhaps we could start our own niche line of inappropriate Christmas Cards?

**Leanne**

*If it's true, this kid needs to face consequences.*

I just told you.

It ain't true.

Kyle lives in our block.

He tried to overdose on aspirin after that shit was posted.

**Priya**

*The grammar system is a fair and meritocratic way of nurturing academic excellence.*

Er... not really, though, is it?

You're tutoring Theo.

Which costs money.

And will help him pass the test.

Not everyone has that option.

So if you can afford it, you have an advantage.

**Stella**

Everyone is entitled to their opinion, Priya.

I'll be speaking to Mr Andrews about the spelling groups too.

And William will also be sitting the 11+.

**Priya**

Will he be wearing a skirt?

**Flo**

*He tried to overdose on aspirin after that shit was posted.*

Jesus... was he okay?

**Sharon**

*Perhaps we could start our own niche line of inappropriate Christmas Cards?*

We're in!

Matthew's just drawn an angel.

With massive boobs.

**Al**

Haha 😂!

We've got our own cottage industry!

'Have a Tiger Class Christmas.'

'Putting the X-rated into your X-mas cards.'

**Leanne**

*Jesus . . . was he okay?*

Yeah.

His mum was keeping her vitamin c in the aspirin pot.

Turned his piss bright green, but he was okay.

This shit destroys lives.

113

**Rosie**

*So if you can afford it, you have an advantage.*
Or you work extra shifts to pay for it, like we do.
It's our choice.

**Priya**

I'm just pointing out that not everyone has the choice.

**Rosie**

And what precisely am I supposed to do about that?

**Tanya**

Guys... this is my fault.
I made a stupid joke and I apologise.
Let's just drop it now, eh?

**Mike**

*This shit destroys lives.*
I'm sorry for your friend.
But so does predatory behaviour from boys.
Who become men.
And perpetuate the cycle of violence.

**Priya**

*Guys . . . this is my fault.*
It's not your fault, Tan.

**Stella**
Nothing ever is, is it?

**Priya**

What's that supposed to mean?

**Tanya**

Please – both of you.
Stop now.

**Leanne**

*But so does predatory behaviour from boys.*
Not if they've done nothing wrong.
And girls abuse all this Me Too bullshit to spread lies.

**Mike**

We'll have to agree to differ.

**Leanne**
Whatever.

**Eric**
Hi Everyone!
Does anyone have this week's spellings?!

# Ben

The thing about being a headteacher is that no one actually knows what you do.

Turns out, me included.

I came into this job – the teaching profession, in fact – thinking that my role would be to improve the life and education of the kids in my care.

Ha.

Hahaha.

Hahahahahahahahaha!

On my first day, I got a call from Lucy Ellis, the head of Flatford High.

'Congratulations,' she said. 'You're now a shit umbrella.'

I thought she was kidding.

This past week has largely been spent sitting in this windowless box in a blur of curriculum spreadsheets, budget meetings, governors' reports, self-evaluation, safeguarding training . . . the list is endless.

And that's before you get to the parents. I mean . . . carers.

I really wanted to have an open-door policy to ring in the changes.

But I'm beginning to understand why Stitchwell's was bolted shut.

Uniform. Lunches. Discipline. Playground disputes (between the adults, as much as the children). Staff gripes. Homework. Worship. Bloody goldfish. There is not a single aspect of school life that doesn't attract myriad opposing views – and somehow I have to navigate a line between them all.

'And so you see,' I hear Bruce Laycock saying as I tune back in to his monologue. 'I think in a world where we should be constantly mindful of the language we use around disordered eating, for the whole class to be reading a text that simultaneously glamourises binge eating while also conveying some deeply problematic fat-shaming messaging is a big concern.'

'Uh-huh.' I nod earnestly, resting my chin on my inter-locked fingers. He's been talking so long, I can't even remember what his complaint is. 'Remind me again, what have the Badgers been reading?'

Bruce huffs distastefully at the thought.

'*The Very Hungry Caterpillar*,' he pronounces.

'I see,' I say, just as the phone rings. 'Will you excuse me a moment?'

'Hi,' says Marcia, right on time. 'This is the phone call you asked me to make to get rid of him.'

'Okay, thanks for letting me know. I'll be right there,' I reply, grimacing apologetically at Bruce as I put the phone down. Marcia is an absolute brick. This place would fall apart without her. Apparently, she used to be a marine and did two tours in Afghanistan. She must miss the peace and quiet . . .

'I'll let you get on,' says Bruce, rising to leave. 'Thank you for listening to my concerns . . . Oh, by the way – do you need a lift in the mornings?'

'Er – no? Why do you ask?'

'Oh – we live a couple of streets down from you – I've noticed you walking in for the past few days. Just wondered if your car was in the garage or something. It's no trouble . . .'

Jesus. Does nothing go unnoticed in Flatford?

'Ah – just trying to keep my step count up, keep the middle-age spread at bay,' I lie, patting my stomach. 'But that's very kind of you. And mind how you go. My door is always open . . .'

'Sure, well, thanks, Mr Andrews. See you on your walk home!'

I smile and close the door firmly behind him. Lord, give me strength. And some chocolate cake, ice cream, a pickle, Swiss cheese, some salami, a lollipop . . .

The phone rings again.

'Thanks, Marcia,' I say genuinely. 'He's gone . . .'

'It's not that,' she says, an edge of concern in her voice. 'I've got a call for you—'

'Oh Christ – not Ofsted?'

My everything clenches. Claudia deferred Ofsted last term so we're due any minute – and it's the last thing we need. The call will come twenty-four hours prior to the inspection on a Monday to Thursday morning after 10.30am. It's Wednesday And it's 10.36am . . .

'No,' she laughs gently. 'We live to fight another day.'

I audibly exhale. Thank God for that.

'But, Ben,' she says warmly, 'it is your son.'

My heart runs cold. What's . . .

'Thanks, Marcia,' I say quickly. 'Put him on.'

There are an endless few seconds while the line transfers.

'Finn?' I urgently enquire. 'Finn? Are you there, pal?'

A few little breaths confirm that he is.

'Hi, Daddy,' he says brightly.

'Hey,' I say, relieved he's not crying. There have been a lot of those calls over the past few months. 'What's up? Where are you? Why aren't you at school?'

'Mummy said I didn't have to go today,' he reports.

I pause for some internal censorship.

'Is that so?' I ask. 'Are you poorly?'

'No,' he says. 'I just told her I was sad about your divorce and she said I could stay home.'

The familiarly noxious blend of anger and guilt courses through my body. Divorced parenting is nothing if not a curdling emotional cocktail.

'I see,' I say. 'Well, you don't sound very sad.'

I can almost hear him shrugging.

'I'm not,' he says. 'I've got the day off school.'

I try to keep my breath and temper even.

'So . . . what's been going on?' I ask him.

'Not much,' he says, already sounding distracted by something else. 'Oh yeah, except I got on the football team!'

'No way!' I cry. 'That's amazing!'

'I know,' he says. 'My first game's on Saturday – are you coming?'

And there it is. Shaken and stirred. Here I am, simultaneously proud beyond words and gutted beyond belief. I'll miss my boy's first game. I won't be cheering on the sidelines.

I won't be shouting at the ref. Another cobblestone on his path I've missed.

'It'll be really good,' he urges, sticking the blade a little deeper. 'And you can meet Don . . .'

'Don?' I ask, my instincts sharpened. 'Who's Don? A friend of yours?'

'Finn?' I hear in the background before he can reply. 'Finn, what are you doing with my . . . Oh for . . . Give me that!'

'But, Mummy – I was just telling Daddy . . .' he protests.

'I'm telling you, Finn – give me the phone!' Elena barks at him. I hate the way she speaks to him sometimes. I want to hold him so much . . .

'It's okay, son,' I say, hoping the hug comes through my voice. 'We'll talk soon. Do as your mama says.'

I hear the phone being handed over. I feel like the Very Hungry Caterpillar on Saturday night.

'Ben, you have to stop disrupting him like this,' she snaps. 'We agreed – phone calls on Tuesday and Thursday nights and once on the weekend.'

'He called me!' I protest. 'What am I supposed to do? I thought something had gone wrong – something with you or him or . . .'

'We're fine,' she says, offering no further information.

'Elena . . . he needs to go to school,' I ask. 'He needs routine. He's playing you up . . .'

'Oh, you know that, do you?' she spits. 'You were up with him at 1am and 3am and 5am this morning sobbing his little heart out, were you? Just like he did on Monday? Just like he's been doing since we moved here? With only me to comfort him . . .'

'Well it's a little tricky to hands-on parent from four hundred miles away,' I snap back. 'You decided to move back to Inverness—'

'No, I didn't,' she interrupts darkly. 'You decided for both of us.'

I take a breath. I'm not going round this carousel again.

'Who's Don?' I ask, making little effort to sound casual. She hesitates too long.

'A friend,' she says.

'I got that,' I reply. 'Whose friend?'

'Don't you even dare!' she shouts. 'You have no right—'

'I have every right!' I try not to shout back. These walls are like rice paper. Marcia has the confidence of the confessional, but I'm sure she's already heard too much. 'If you're introducing random men to my son—'

'He's not your son,' she says, going straight for the jugular. 'He's mine.'

Only out of concern for Marcia and the Bumblebees' hearing do I not emit a roar of frustration. This – *this* is always Elena's ace. And she's never afraid to play it. How different the conversations were ten years ago.

'You'll be the baby's dad in every sense that matters,' she cajoled back then. 'We'll finally be a family. Kids need love, not genes . . .'

The product of a loving adopted family, I knew she was right. But I've always felt . . . genetically untethered. I thought having a baby of my own might fix that. Not being able to father a child biologically then was a breathtaking blow to my masculinity. Not being allowed to father one emotionally now is a sucker punch to my soul. Elena was happy to use donor sperm when she needed it. Just like she's been happy to use a donor father until she didn't.

'I am his father,' I try to say evenly. 'If it affects you, it affects him.'

I don't know how Elena manages to make silence sound angry. But she's a pro.

'Bit late for you to remember that now.'

Elena's on a mobile; she can't slam her phone down.

So I do it hard enough for the both of us.

'For fuck's sake!' I try to say quietly as there's a sharp knock at my door. That's the other thing about this job. There is never a bloody second to breathe . . .

My mobile pings a text. I snatch it up. I'm guessing it's Finn again . . .

I glance at the screen.

It's not Finn.

I wish it were.

I have some feedback for you . . .
£10K isn't enough.
Not for what you did.
Same price. Same account.
This week.
Or I talk.

Oh shit.

How does this guy have my number? I sold the car – I paid the last one. How the hell am I going to come up with . . .

'I do hope I'm not interrupting anything,' comes Clive's unctuous voice. I turn with as genuine a smile as I can muster and it is returned, as it always is, with his signature sneer. He's a weird guy – can't get a handle on him. I usher him inside, hoping that the sweat patches under my arms aren't visible.

'Not at all, you're bang on time,' I say, taking my seat and gesturing for him to do the same. 'How are you?'

'Good news first,' he says without ceremony. 'I have filled the vacant caretaker position. He's fully vetted and very experienced. He starts tomorrow.'

'Oh great,' I say, genuinely relieved. The agency cleaners have been costing us a fortune.

'Did you read the forecasts I sent you?' he asks. 'The governors will require your budget monitoring report by month's end.'

'Yes and yes,' I reply, picking up the neatly bound report – I'll say this for Clive, he's certainly diligent. 'And on that . . .'

I have no idea how to say this. There isn't an umbrella big enough for this shitstorm.

'The forecasts make for grim reading,' I begin.

'Indeed,' says Clive, looking curiously delighted. 'Claudia was undergoing a review of all extraneous expenditure. She had some thoughts on cuts.'

He removes a crisp piece of paper from the folder beneath his arm. I read the bullet-pointed list. It's brutal.

'No, we can't lose any more SEN support staff,' I say, shaking my head. 'We're so stretched already.'

'All educational needs are special,' he replies. 'We can't give preferential treatment.'

I bristle, but say nothing. Supporting a child with a learning need is hardly preferential. But I'll save the fight – they'll still get their funding.

'Rationing the heating and lighting?' I scoff. 'We can't do that.'

'You've seen the cost of gas and electricity,' he sighs. 'We don't get paid more just because the prices are rocketing.'

He's irritating, but he's right. Our budgets are set and that's that. Higher or unexpected costs come out of the same pot. Which means that something else can't. I put the paper down.

'I've been speaking with the governors and they raised an issue that I'd like to discuss with you,' I say, not looking at him. 'We need to cut staff costs. Teaching staff are out of the question – as it is we need to recruit new teachers for Tigers and Dolphins and we'll need cover for Amy Burgess in Owls when she goes for her surgery next term.'

'Yes – I'd heard that we're subsidising staff members to have cosmetic surgery . . .'

Jesus. Christ.

'Clive . . . Mr Baxendale,' I say as evenly as I'm able, 'Amy is having reconstructive surgery following her mastectomy.'

He shrugs.

'I wasn't aware that two breasts were a requirement for teaching, but I suspect I'm out of touch . . .'

Wow. This guy . . .

'Anyway,' I continue before I put his head through the wall. 'The teaching budget is sacrosanct. So we have to look elsewhere for staffing cuts. Now, don't get me wrong – you are a highly valued member of the team.'

'But an expensive one,' he says with a nod. 'I anticipated this might be a conversation.'

'You did?'

'Of course,' he condescends. 'I am the school bursar. No one has a clearer overview of school finances than me.'

'Well, that's very . . . objective of you,' I say. 'And I just wanted to sound you out to see if, given everything, you might want to . . .'

'Fall on my sword?' he says.

'Not at all.' I smile, although that's precisely what I'm hoping he'll do. He's a middle-aged bloke, clearly not short of the readies – I'd hoped he might jump at the chance of a severance package. 'I just wanted to see . . . how you saw your future here?'

He smiles like the Cheshire Cat taking a selfie.

'Extensively.'

Brilliant. There goes that idea . . .

'But of course, Headmaster.'

'Clive – please call me Ben.'

'Ben. Please call me Mr Baxendale,' he shoots back. 'This is a school. Not a rugby club.'

'Duly noted,' I say, and feel my fists clench under the table.

'Well . . . Headmaster . . . there is another substantial cost-saving that could be made. Look at the final item on Claudia's list.'

I open the paper again and read Stitchwell's final suggestion.

'Oh, you're not serious,' I say, putting the list down.

'Something has to give,' he says, his eyes gleaming. 'I'm afraid this job is all about difficult choices. Headmaster.'

'The kids and parents – I mean, carers – will take to the streets,' I promise.

'We have to cut costs,' he says, standing up. He has clearly decided this meeting is over, even if I haven't. 'And this one makes the most sense. As it happens, I have a meeting scheduled today. I could . . . test the waters?'

He leers at me again. He's not weird. He's an arsehole.

I sigh and look out of where a window should be. I can't create money that isn't there. And I really don't fancy dealing with this one myself.

'Okay,' I say quietly. 'But Cl– Mr Baxendale. Tread softly. And if this isn't going to work we'll need to revisit this conversation.'

I can almost see him strapping on his hob nails.

'Of course,' he smiles.

He turns to leave just as a thought occurs to me.

'Oh – and I'm going to need to see the school bank files as part of my prep for the budget meeting.'

He stops. Without turning round, he speaks again.

'Why?' he asks, the smile gone from his voice. 'All the figures are in my report.'

'I know,' I say. 'But for my own due diligence – and with Ofsted imminent – I just need to lay eyes on them. Money-laundering thing. No photocopies, they have to be the originals.'

His back remains turned to me. He pauses.

'Of course, Headmaster,' he says as he walks towards the door. 'Leave it with me.'

The door shuts behind him and I'm glad. I close my eyes for a moment. Today is going to kick off.

Fabulous.

I turn to the computer to tackle the mountain of emails in my inbox when the phone rings again.

'Tell me I haven't summoned Ofsted?' I ask Marcia nervously.

'You're still in the clear,' Marcia replies. I don't know how many more of these mornings I can take – my blood pressure must look like a pinball score. 'But I have Delia Ellens here, Joseph's mum? She'd like to talk to you about why her Jamie was told that it was Venus in the night sky, when he's always believed it was the spirit of his late grandmother?'

I bang my head on the desk as softly as I am able.

'Send her in,' I say as brightly as possible. 'It's always a privilege to interface with parents.'

Marcia snorts down the line.

'Don't you mean carers?' she whispers.

# Hattie

Packed bloody lunches!

Packed bloody lunches!

The damn sauce of the man!

I've been feeding kiddies for four ruddy decades at St Nonnatus and there's never been any talk of packed bloody lunches!

Even Stitchers knew the value of a hot meal in a little un's belly.

But not Mr Sushi Roll. Noooo – he's got his own fancy Nancy ideas.

It's a ruddy outrage. I looked inside little Zac Phillips's lunchbox to see what I'm up against. The lad's lunch? A cold slice of pizza. I ask you.

'Power is given only to him who dares to stoop and take it,' said old Dostoevsky. 'One must have the courage to dare.'

Well, I dare, Ben Andrews. And I'm stooping to sticky toffee sponge for pudding. Let's see how many bloody packed lunches there'll be after that.

It's break-time and I'm storming through school to the library. Library . . . it's a grand name for a disused classroom that wasn't big enough for these modern class sizes, but it serves the purpose. And Kiera made it look lovely with all her paintings and whatnot on the wall, clever girl. They're lovely to look at – all characters from all kinds of books. And they cover up the damp patches beneath, so win-win.

You see, when I do a job, I do it right. Forty years ago, I pledged to feed these kiddies and that's what I've done. But they don't just need full bellies, they need full minds. And I know better than most – I had neither. So, like any kid starved of anything, the moment I could, I gorged on both – and my sturdy frame is bought and paid for, thank you very much.

I ain't never really been out of Flatford. ('Cept that time I went up to London for a Michael Ball concert what I won in the Easter raffle – he weren't half bad. He's no Donny

Osmond, mind, but who is?) But I seen the world through the pages of me books. I have my favourites, of course – *Count of Monte Cristo* and *Crime and Punishment* will be in the box with me when they put me six feet under. The only book Stitchers cared about was the ruddy Bible and I ain't convinced she read that right. But I fought my corner for this little library and so here we are. And I'll defend it like the bloody Somme.

'Hey, Hattie,' grins Verity Jones, one of my Year 6 librarians, Tanya's eldest. 'I came early to try to get ahead, but the door's locked?'

Bugger. I left the keys in the kitchen. Can't be arsed to go all the way back there, so . . .

'You ain't seen this, right?' I say to her as I pull a paring knife out of my apron.

She shakes her head earnestly. Bless her little heart.

I stick the knife in the door and jimmy the lock. Learned that from a book and all – though these doors are all so old you could pick the locks with an ear bud. And it's worth it to see Verity's little face as the door opens and I tip her the wink. She heads in and immediately takes charge.

'So I'm going to reshelve the weekend returns, sticker all the new arrivals and I've sorted the wish list into alphabetical order for you,' she says, presenting me with a piece of paper, typed and everything – these kiddies are so smart these days.

I smile. She's a proper chip off the old block. She'll be running the country one day. Or dictating it, could go either way with that one.

'Thank you, my lovely,' I tell her with a cuddle as I look down her list. Phew. That's a lot of books. Ben's given me a few quid more than Stitchers did, but it'll never cover this lot. Still, I'm a resourceful woman. There's charity shops and second-hand sales. And failing that, Sticky Steve ('84 – head chorister at the church – his '*Pie Jesu*' coulda made the devil repent) can nick 'em from Smiths. He owes me for the weekly banana bread during his last stretch.

Kids come in all shapes and sizes, but there's a certain sort that loves a book. They're always good kids – although all kids are good at source; it's the bad stuff that happens to 'em what queers the pitch – and they always have big hearts.

I reckon books do that. All them words and ideas get into you and, with nowhere else to go, they swell your heart and grow your mind. I never met a reader I didn't like. And most of the people I can't abide don't read. It takes a certain kind of folk not to be open to someone else's words. They're called closed books for a reason.

I leave Verity to her bustling and look around the room as my regulars file in. It's amazing what a few second-hand beanbags and cushions can do. Kids don't just come here for books – they come here for sanctuary. The playground's a scary place for some and they take shelter in the library. I love my little bookworms. Whatever else is going on, they're safe here with me.

'How you getting on with *The Goldfish Boy*, Omar?' I ask the little lad already engrossed in the tatty armchair.

He raises a thumb, but won't unglue his eyes from the page. I'll take it as a good sign. His ma, Mariam, lost a baby late in the day into her third pregnancy last year. I can't tell her how sorry I am, given I don't speak Arabic and all – but this book'll help her boy. That's the other thing books can do. They're medicine for the soul.

I do a bit of sorting and tidying and cuddling until the bell rings for the end of play.

'All right, you little lovelies – back to class,' I tell them. They all duly file out without question. That's the other great thing about bookworms. They always do what they're bloody well told.

I'm about to shut up shop – I got a sticky toffee pud to deploy – when I hear a little sniff. You don't work in a school for forty years without knowing the sound of a little un crying. So back I go – and there's little Jacob Richardson sobbing his heart out behind the non-fiction.

'Hey now,' I say, getting down to the floor, which is no mean feat, let me tell you. 'What's all this about?'

He wipes his snotty nose on the back of his hand before realising he ain't got nowhere to put it. I offer up my apron with a smile and he makes good use of it. I've got others and they've all seen worse.

'I'm scared,' he sobs. 'About my mum. I saw the news. The

place she's gone – Ryanair – has got a big war. There's loads of bombs. What if one of them gets her? What if she's hurt? What if she dies . . . ?'

The poor little mite melts into tears again. I pull him in for a big old cuddle. I saw the news too. There's been 'intense shelling' in Myanmar, where his ma, Jenna, has gone to report. It ain't safe for no one. I can't fathom why a mother would put herself in harm's way like that, but none of mine, I suppose.

'Now listen here, young Jacob,' I tell him. 'I'm older than Father Christmas and if I've learned one thing in this life, it's that I'm not a big fan of "what if". It's a terrible business! "What if" lets tomorrow steal today and I ain't having none of it! I'm a much bigger fan of "I know". So what do we know here? Have you heard your ma has been hit by a bomb?'

He shakes his soggy little head.

'Right! Then today you know she's all right,' I tell him. 'So why don't we say that? Go on, say it with me.'

He shakes his little head.

'Go on,' I cajole. 'I've got some spare custard at lunchtime says you can do it.'

He pants snottily into my armpit.

'I know she's all right,' he says, sniffing.

'Well, how's about that, then?' I say brightly. 'That's a bit better, innit? Much better than all that stuff what hasn't happened and might not never?'

He nods a bit.

'And I tell you something else I know,' I say, rooting around in my pocket for the biscuits I always keep for this very purpose. 'I know that I have this packet of bourbons waiting for my mid-morning cuppa. And I know I shouldn't eat them, what with my big ole bum and whatnot, so do you know what I'm going to do with them?'

'No,' he whimpers.

'I know you need to eat 'em for me,' I whisper, handing them over.

His little eyes light up. He hesitates.

'But Mr Andrews want us to be a Healthy Eating school,' he says. 'He told us all about it in assembly. We have to eat five vegetables a day. So I'm going to eat five peas at lunchtime. Biscuits aren't healthy.'

'Is that so?' I ask. 'Well Mr Andrews is forty-one. I'm fifty-seven. I've been eating bourbons all me life and I've already lived sixteen years longer than Mr Andrews. So who knows more about the health benefits of biscuits, him or me?'

He grins.

'You do,' he says, taking the top biccie and shovelling it in sideways.

I smile to meself. 'When reason fails, the devil helps,' said Mr Dostoyevsky. Any argument works best with those what want them to be right.

'I know,' I whisper to him, giving him a squeeze. 'Now gobble them down you and get your little backside back to Tigers. That seven times table ain't gonna learn itself.'

He duly obliges, stands up and gives me a big hug.

'Thanks, Hattie, you're the best,' he says, skipping off back to class with a belly full o' biscuit. That's the thing about kids. Their moods are like tropical rainstorms: they pass over quick enough.

I shut up the library and go back to the kitchen to see to lunch. I've not been in five minutes when I hear the door go and Kiera's skinny bum pops up onto the side.

'Ain't you got nowhere better to be?' I tell her, swatting her off with a cloth.

'Love you too,' she says back, blowing a kiss, the cheeky mare. 'Tigers are doing their Maths test, Owls are out at play, so I've got a break.'

'Nice for some,' I say, stirring my custard.

'So . . .' she begins, 'we've decided to take the caretaker job.'

I raise an eyebrow, though I can't say I'm surprised. Even if the last thing Kiera needs is to get more stuck in this place.

'We?' I ask. 'Or you?'

'Same net result,' she grins. 'And I've just seen the uniform list for Shottsford House. A blazer alone is a hundred and fifty quid! I don't own anything that costs a hundred and fifty quid! My bloody wedding dress didn't cost a hundred and fifty quid! Come to think of it . . . my whole wedding didn't cost a hundred and fifty quid . . .'

'You didn't have such expensive tastes back then,' I mutter.

'Oi!' she cries, swatting me back. 'What's that supposed to mean?'

'All's I'm saying is that you're spending a lot you don't have,' I tell her. 'You spoil those girls. All them fancy clothes and latest phones. Kids don't need all that.'

'Pffff,' she scoffs. 'You have that conversation with Taylor . . .'

'And this Shottsford House business—'

'Hattie, don't . . .' she warns. But I ain't never been scared of Kiera Fisher, woman or girl, and I ain't about to be starting now.

'I bloomin' will,' I insist. 'Little Gracie done ever so well with her scholarship . . . but are you sure a posh gaff like that is the right place for her?'

'Yes,' she says, her mouth puckering like a monkey's arse-hole. 'It's the best. She's the best. So it's the right place.'

'It's the most expensive,' I point out. 'That don't make it the best.'

'You've seen what Flatford High has done to Taylor,' she glowers. 'I'm not seeing Gracie go the same way.'

I throw my cloth on the side.

'Flatford High ain't done nothing to Taylor,' I correct her. 'She's just the same as any kid that age – gobby, rebellious and a pain in the arse. Like every seventeen-year-old girl under God's blue sky, you included, missy. You can't buy your way outta that . . . What about all o' Gracie's friends?'

'She'll make new ones,' Kiera sighs. 'Better ones.'

'Richer ones, you mean?' I shoot back. 'Ones that she won't be able to keep up with? That she'll always feel like the poor relation to? I already stopped you from making one stupid mistake with Stitchers. High time I stopped another—'

'That's enough!' Kiera hisses, and I know I gone too far. 'Thought we were never speaking of that again? And you don't know anything about raising kids, Hattie. You can't learn that in a book.'

'Oh, I know plenty, gal,' I remind her. 'You don't have to know how to sail to see when the ship's sinking.'

'I'm fine,' she spits. 'We're fine. Just . . . just keep your nose out of it!'

She strops out of the kitchen and the door flaps behind her. Kiera's got a right hot head on her, but she won't stay mad – she never does. She'll be back in a bit, we'll pretend nothing happened and the world'll keep on turning. But she doesn't get that mad unless she knows I'm right. And I am.

People like to throw spinsterhood around as a weapon, when I reckon it's the only sane choice. I saw my ma done wrong by men all her life. My pa didn't want nothing to do with either of us and I watched her scrap and scrimp and struggle until she died too soon. They don't put poverty on a death certificate. Yet it's killed more folk than cancer.

And as for being alone . . . well, that were my choice too. Never got all the fuss about sex. I tried it once with a man and once with a woman and weren't tempted to give it another go. Felt much the same about crayfish, as it goes. I've been happy with myself and by myself. Folk have never understood it. Back along, they didn't have a name for what I am. These days, I 'spect there's seventeen hashtags and a flag.

'Hattie,' slicks that greasy toad, Baxendale, oozing into my kitchen. 'Is now a good time for our chat?'

I huff loudly.

'No worse than any other,' I grumble, checking on me spuds. I want him to think I don't care. However much I do.

'Excellent,' he says, and I don't need to be looking at him to know he'll be grinning like a clown. 'As you will be aware, the school finds itself in . . . a challenging financial climate.'

'Shame we ain't got a decent bursar, then,' I heave, draining me taters.

'In times such as these, difficult cuts must be made,' he says. 'We old-timers are expensive, Hattie. There are cheaper alternatives to us both.'

I snort.

'Can't imagine they get much cheaper than you,' I mutter, popping my spuds back in the pan.

'So I just wanted to gauge your interest in early retirement,' he smarms. 'It would be an . . . elegant solution to a complex problem.'

I point my masher right at him.

'Retire!' I cry. 'I'm only fifty-seven years old!'

'Hatita Hughes, you are sixty next month,' he says. 'I have your National Insurance details on your staff record.'

I say nothing. Bloody number-cruncher.

'What of it?' I mutter, starting to mash.

'Perhaps I'm not being clear,' he says, moving closer. 'One of us has to go. And I find myself in somewhat . . . reduced circumstances. So it's not going to be me.'

'And you think it's gonna be me!' I laugh. 'Let's see you find someone to do my job! We can replace you with a bloody calculator . . .'

'Oh, Hattie, you are entirely irreplaceable. I wouldn't even try,' he says with a smile as sincere as a dead kipper. 'But, seeing as you ask, on my desk there are some projections for an external catering company. They cost a fraction of what you do—'

'Because the kiddies will get a fraction of the food!' I roar. 'They'll turn up with their trays o' crap and the kids won't touch a bite.'

'Well, then, Mr Andrews's trial of packed lunches is timely indeed,' he continues. 'Our school budget is in deficit. Cuts need to be made.'

'Well, make 'em somewhere else,' I snap. 'You get rid of me, I'll kick right off! I'll rile the parents up something rotten! You'll have a riot on your hands!'

'I don't think you will,' he says, leaning against one of the units. 'I think you'll announce that you're going to retire and go ever so quietly and graciously.'

'Well, you got a truckload o' thinks coming!' I laugh. 'I ain't going nowhere, boy.'

'I beg to differ,' he says. 'You see, Hattie. I know.'

'Yeah, yeah, yeah – I fiddled the Harvest Bake Off, that's hardly gonna get me sent to Alcatraz, innit . . .'

'No, Hattie,' he whispers. 'I *know*. Claudia – may she rest in peace – was kind enough to divulge the contents of your final meeting with her.'

I feel my fingers start to shake. I grip the masher. Hard.

'Is that so?' I grunt. I'm gonna let him spill first – he might yet be bluffing.

'It is,' he replies. 'I know that she too was planning to get rid of you.'

I stop mashing. Bugger me. He does know. I throw down my cloth and turn about.

'Well, ain't that grand?' I tell him.

'It is rather.' He snorts like a bloody schoolgirl. 'So I know. I know about you and the reverend . . .'

A sudden clattering at the door saves me from explaining why I've dropped me masher.

'I'm . . . I'm so sorry,' cowers Tanya Jones, her feet surrounded by cake tins.

How long's she been standing there?

'So you should be – you nearly gave me a bloody coronary!' I say with a cheery smile, strolling over to help her pick them up. 'You're fine, lovely – what can I do for you?'

'I just came to return your cake tins – and to thank you for your mum's Victoria sponge recipe. It is by far the best I've ever made,' she grins. She's a sweet girl.

'And she'd be glad to hear it,' I say, taking the tins from her. 'How you travelling, love?'

'I'm okay,' she says and clearly isn't. 'Apologies again for interrupting – Hattie, Mr Baxendale . . .'

She backs out me kitchen like her bum's on fire.

I look back at Clive. This needs sorting, quick smart.

'Whatever you think you know about me 'n' Stitchwell senior, you have no proof.'

'Don't I?' he counters. 'You resign. Or I start talking.'

Bugger. Bugger, bugger, bugger. Let's try calling his bluff.

'Go on, then. I ain't got nothing to be ashamed of,' I lie again. 'I don't care who knows.'

'Oh, I think you will,' he chuckles like a bloody schoolgirl. 'After all, it's a powerful motivation for murder . . .'

'*What?* What you jabbering about now?'

He leans in.

'You knew Claudia better than anyone,' he says. 'You fed her daily. You could have got the allergens into her any number of ways. One word to Bob Alsorp about the reverend and . . .'

I grit my teeth. He's got me over a barrel and he knows it.

'If you go to the police now, you'll have withheld evidence,' I bluster. 'You'll be in a whole heap of trouble . . .'

'Not as much as you'll be in,' he rightly points out. 'And I would only be doing the Lord's work if you had any part in Claudia's tragic death . . .'

Enough of this. Time to fight fire with fire.

'And why would you wanna do that, Clive?' I say. 'You need to shine the light away from you? I heard you two that night. You were screaming blue murder at her. You go snitching, I will too.'

'A professional disagreement is not a crime,' he says slickly, although I fancy I've rattled him. 'But I think the authorities would take a rather dimmer view of the information you've withheld.'

'I ain't done nothing . . .'

He eyes up me copy of *Hamlet*.

'The lady doth protest too much, methinks,' he whispers.

'We are arrant knaves all,' I quote back. 'Believe none of us.'

Daggers are stared. Now I ain't scared of no one. But, like I say, Baxendale's a dangerous player. He needs to be taken out of the game.

'You have my terms,' he says. 'Do with them what you will.'

And, with that, he turns on his shiny shoes and buggers off.

I look out the kitchen window, at all the little ones running around the playground. This school has been my life. I'm not even sure what my life is without it.

And I have no intention of finding out.

Clive Baxendale, you just declared war.

And let me tell you, boy.

I fight dirty.

# PARENTCHAT

Clearer Community Communication

## ST NONNATUS CE PRIMARY

*Ora et labora*

### Flatford FC
Eric

### Weds 9 Nov
14.02

**Eric**
*Need to know by Wednesday lunchtime if*
*you're up for it!*
No takers?
Not to worry!
Another time!

# Robocoppers
Priya, Al, Tanya

**Thurs 10 Nov**
09.39

**Tanya**
Hey guys 🖐.
You still on for group playdate after school?
By which I mean 'justifiable wine before six'.

**Al**
Sorry babe 😔
Just back from the doc's.
Millie's got Hand, Foot and Mouth.
Caught it off the bloody babysitter.
We're in quarantine.

**Priya**
Noooo!
I've got so much I need to talk to you both about!
(Not least that you have to find a new babysitter, Al,
your Casey is a liability.)
I've been studying the witness statements again and
thinking about the stuff we discussed last week.

**Al**
'We discussed'
You mean, your crackpot theories that Tan and I
tolerated over croissants?

**Priya**
Yes.
Like I say.
Discussed.
I have thoughts.

**Tanya**
😑
Like?

**Priya**
In their statements, both Clive and Kiera reference
going to look for epipens, but neither can find them.

> The event started at 6.30. When Stitchwell started to choke, I
> went to the office to get the EpiPen, but couldn't find it.

> When it became clear that Miss Stitchwell was in respiratory
> distress, I hastened to her office, where I knew her to keep her
> personal dose of epinephrine in case of anaphylaxis. I was
> unable to locate it, so called an ambulance from her office

**Al**
OK. That is weird.
I did a lot of outreach with local schools around allergy
safety.
And given Leo's lactose intolerance, I wanted to be
sure St Nonn's was covered.
Clive and Kiera were right – there should always be
two doses on site (in case one doesn't work).
That's really remiss of the school not to have them to
hand.

**Priya**
I don't think the school is to blame.

**Tanya**
Whyever not?
They really should be on top of that stuff.

**Al**
Absolutely – the authorities will hang them out to dry
over this.
And rightly so.

**Priya**
So ask yourselves?
Why haven't they?

**Al**
We all know you're going to tell us.

**Priya**
I *might* have had a look at the preliminary findings
from the investigations at the school.

**Al**
Of course you have.

**Tanya**
Of course you have.

**Al**
Jinx!
Go on then...

**Priya**
I won't bore you with the whole thing – I'm still wading
through it.
But for one thing (sorry Tan) all the food Hattie made
that night came back allergen-free.
There were samples left of everything (not surprised
given the menu – egg sandwiches and tuna vol au
vents 🤢?!)
So even if Stitchwell did eat some of Hattie's food, it
didn't kill her.
But check this out.

---

And in accordance with governmental guidance, two doses of
epinephrine were found on site: one in the first-aid box in the main
office, one in Claudia Stitchwell's desk drawer.

---

**Tanya**
Huh?

**Al**
So they were both there?!

138

**Priya**

Yup.

And there's no record of them being used, nor thrown away – the cops went through the bins, nothing in the report about finding an epipen.

So that leaves us with two options:

1) One/both deliberately didn't find them.
2) Someone had already moved them.

**Tanya**

Or 3) They just didn't see them.

It was incredibly frantic that night, Pri.

People were screaming and running around.

Stitchwell was choking to death in front of us.

You could be forgiven for being in a panic.

**Al**

I agree.

People do all kinds of weird things in traumatic situations.

The adrenalin can impair all kinds of systems.

And like Tan says, just plain old fashioned panic plays its part.

**Priya**

I'll buy it for a dollar with Clive.

That pen was found in Stitchwell's desk drawer.

It could have got hidden.

And we know Stitchwell had been rummaging around looking for the lost bible.

(More on that later.)

**Tanya**

Oh God.

There's more?

**Priya**

So much more 🕵

But let's stay with the pens for now.

So Clive can't find it in Stitchwell's messy drawers.

**Al**

**Priya**

But Kiera couldn't find it in the first aid kit??!!!
She's a trained TA.
And doesn't strike me as someone who panics in a crisis.

**Al**

True.
We all saw her when Freddie Burrows choked on a Lego head at the summer picnic.
She was cool as a cucumber.

                                                          **Tanya**
                           But Pri... you're not exactly her biggest fan.
                           So maybe your judgement is a little coloured?

**Priya**

I can't stand the arsey cow.
But I'm looking at this as a detective, not a mum.
And it doesn't look good.
Unless...

**Al**

2) *Someone had already moved them.*
That's where you're going with this, right?

**Priya**

Maybe.
And, if Clive and/or Kiera didn't deliberately miss them.
That leaves Ben and Hattie.

**Al**

I just can't see either of them being that malicious.
And even if we go with Ben being pissed about the job...
We still have zero motive for Hattie.
Why would she kill Stitchwell?

**Priya**

She has a pulse?

**Tanya**

Oh God.

Okay.

So, I've been wondering if I should tell you this.

**Priya**

Well you have to now.

**Al**

Don't do us dirty like that, Tan!

**Tanya**

Look.

You know I'm not entirely on board
with this conspiracy theory...

**Priya**

You mean 'murder investigation'.

I don't do conspiracy theories.

**Tanya**

... but I heard something weird at school yesterday.

**Al**

*I don't do conspiracy theories.*

Oh sure!

Just ask Tash Tompkins!

I can't believe you asked her if she had any unspent
criminal convictions at the Macmillan coffee morning!

**Priya**

There was context.

We were talking about DBS checks.

**Al**

You know full well she doesn't need one for a bloody
bake sale.

Anyway, sorry Tan.

What happened?

**Tanya**

Right.

If I tell you – Priya, you are not to take it and run with it.

Promise?

**Priya**
Of course.
I am a pro, you know.
I can keep it in my pants.
(Metaphorically at least 🥒)

**Al**
😭

                                                              **Tanya**
                                                                  So...
                                          I walked in on Hattie and Clive today.

**Al**
Oh GOD!
They weren't at it, were they?

**Priya**
😭 😭 😭 😭 😭 😭 😭 😭 😭 😭 😭 😭 😭 😭

                                                              **Tanya**
                                                                   No!
                                     But they were having a bit of a tiff.
                                       And Clive said something weird.

**Priya**
Go on??!!

                                                              **Tanya**
                                                                   In.
                                                                Pants.
                                                           Remember?

**Priya**
Yes yes yes.

**Al**
What did he say?

                                                              **Tanya**
                            He said: 'I know about you and the reverend'.
                                        And it sounded... threatening.

**Priya**
WHAT?!

**Al**
Nice pants you've got there.
🌰🌰🌰🌰🌰🌰🌰🌰🌰

                                                    **Tanya**
                                    Do you think it's significant?

**Priya**
ARE YOU SHITTING ME??!!

**Al**
Does that answer your question, Tan?

**Priya**
Okay, I'm adding that to the list...

                                                    **Tanya**
                                                    What list?
                                            There's a list?

**Al**
Of course there's a list.

**Priya**
You're damn right there's a list.
How did Hattie react?
To Clive's comment, I mean.

                                                    **Tanya**
                            Honestly, I couldn't really say.
                    I was so shocked I dropped her cake tins.
                                    But 'know' what?

**Al**
Eugh? So Hattie and the Rev were at it? 🤮 🤮 🤮
I mean, disgusting as it is, the Randy Rev was at it
with half the town.
If Clive is threatening Hattie with it, it's embarrassing,
but hardly a motive.

**Priya**

I agree – there must be more to it than that...
Speaking of this wildly dysfunctional town.
Did you see that stuff on the group chat?
About the Stitchwell love child?
And the black book?
Any proof that either exist?

> **Sarah**
> And yet it was Miss Stitchwell that had a baby on the
> wrong side of the blanket.
> The fabled Stitchwell Love Child.

> **Sharon**
> Stitchwell's diary.
> Legend has it she kept everyone's secrets in it.
> Including her own.

**Tanya**

No proof of either as far as I'm aware.
Persistent local gossip, though.

**Al**

Also, we don't know that Clive wasn't lying.
Or winding Hattie up.
He's such a prick.

**Priya**

This could also be true.
But Hattie was the last person to be alone with
Stitchwell prior to the event:

> slamming around my kitchen like an oaf, trying to
> find the rev's poxy wine. Apparently, madam was in
> a right state – couldn't find her pa's bible for the
> opening prayer, so I went to the office to help her
> look. Turned out it was in the wrong drawer, the
> dozy mare, so I calmed her down. She made me

**Priya**

She specifically mentions going into Stitchwell's drawer.

She could have taken the EpiPen then.

**Al**

Okay... I'm going to join you on the crazy train for a minute:

So Hattie's our murderer.

To silence Stitchwell over something to do with her secret fling with the Rev.

She takes the EpiPen.

She knows that Stitchwell is going to have the reaction.

Because she's the one who has somehow administered the nuts to her (although not with her food as that's been given the all-clear)?

She takes it from Stitchwell's desk under the guise of looking for the bible?

Then somehow returns it afterwards so the authorities find it.

**Priya**

With you so far.

**Al**

So riddle me this...

What did she do with the other one?

**Tanya**

Exactly!

There were two pens.

I'm just reading the statements back.

No one places Hattie in the school office at any point.

So even if she nicked one pen.

There's no evidence she took the other.

**Al**

Which kinda makes it unlikely she only took one.

I think Clive's shit-stirring.

Or trying to throw suspicion elsewhere.

I wouldn't be surprised if he knew Tanya was there today.
And said something on purpose.
I wouldn't put anything past that man.

**Priya**
You're both missing a third explanation.

**Al**
You're a paranoid cynic who needs something else to fill her days?

> **Tanya**
> Behave!
> Go on, Pri.

**Priya**
You're right – there's no evidence that Hattie went to the office.
She also claims she left school before Stitchwell died, so wouldn't have had the chance to put it back if that's true.
We know Clive was in Stitchwell's office, but there's no evidence he was in the school office at any point – although he is unaccounted for more than the others earlier in the evening.
But Ben goes through the school office to reach his own – twice: once to do paperwork, once to fix the Creepy Jesus statue (you two need to fill me in on this).
And Kiera goes there after Stitchwell's reaction.
So theoretically either of them could have taken it and later returned it.

**Al**
So what about Hattie and Stitchwell's pen...?

> **Tanya**
> Oh God.
> I know how this thread pulls out.
> Hattie couldn't be in two places at once.
> So she would have needed an accomplice.

**Priya**

Bingo!

And who do you think she's most likely to work with?

**Al**

We're back with Kiera.

So now you're saying we don't have one murderer in
our rural primary school.

We have two?

**Priya**

I'm just saying that anything is possible.

So what's with the statue?

They all mention it at some point?

**Al**

Oh yeah.

Creepy Jesus!

                                                        **Tanya**

It's that horrible crucifixion that Miss Stitchwell always
insisted on having out.

It's been freaking kids out for decades.

**Al**

It really is hideous.

Although it had its uses.

We used to hide sweets in it.

If I'm going to hell for anything, it's for taking sherbet
lemons out of Jesus's arse.

                                                        **Tanya**

*I'm just saying that anything is possible.*

It is.

But you have to concede another possibility.

You're wrong about this.

And that it was just a horrible accident.

**Priya**

Perhaps.

Look, I gotta go, I'm off to BuyRite.

**Al**

Try not to arrest any suspicious looking pensioners.
Or dodgy girl guides.

**Tanya**

Or Tash T.
The poor woman's going to take out
a restraining order.

**Priya**

If it spares us from her bloody awful brownies at the
next bake sale.
Next time we're looking for a murder weapon...

**Al**

You are a nightmare.
But we love you.
Laters girls.

**Priya**

Xxx

**Tanya**

Love you guys
Xx

# Clive

One of the many ways in which I was in complete accord with dear Claudia was the power of paper. My late colleague trusted nothing digital, keeping meticulous written records and never owning, nor relying upon, any technology. She never used a computer, never possessed a mobile phone. Everything was entrusted to good old-fashioned hard copy. Having been delegated as her executor, it's certainly making her estate hard work, as is the reverend dying intestate shortly before her. Clearly, she inherited her administrative diligence from her mother – the dear reverend didn't even leave a will. But at least everything is written down, clear as day. No corrupted files, no opportunity for tampering. Just clear, honest records.

However, that particular knife can cut both ways. Paper trails are beyond contestation – and that's their problem. They are clear, honest records.

And now Ben Andrews requires them for the financial review.

I'm pacing around my office considering his request, as I have been for much of the past twenty-four hours. Upon his appointment, St Ben elected to forgo Claudia's large office that adjoined mine, surrendering it to the Special Educational Needs department so yet more children can be given bespoke attention we can neither afford nor justify. He retained his cupboard next to the main office – I will be staying put. This is my fortress and I will not surrender it. Only a fool gives up an advantageous position in war. And, in war, the ends can justify the means.

With this in mind, I go to my filing cabinet and remove the bank documentation Andrews requested yesterday. Statements, withdrawal slips, countersignatures . . . it's all there, written in black and white. The headmaster must of course be provided with all the financial information he requires.

It just can't be this.

I walk across my plush carpet.

And deposit all of it in the shredder.

The files are still whirring through the blades when there is a knock at my door. I switch it off and kick it beneath my desk.

'Enter!' I command. I always feel it is as well to be foreboding from the off.

The door creaks open to reveal Kiera Fisher standing defiantly on the threshold. Her face is a permanent invitation to combat and I'm always delighted to engage. As a relative newcomer to this community, I missed her time at the school. But Claudia assured me that she was an utter wastrel. Like me, Miss Stitchwell didn't give any credence to the bleeding-heart tears with regard to her upbringing in care. She was lucky to have somewhere to go; many aren't. I understand she got herself in the family way at secondary school and never sat her A levels. The resultant spawn is mired in original sin and creating some more of her own if local gossip is to be believed.

'Mrs Fisher,' I say with an insincere joviality. 'How may I help you?'

'It's about the job,' she says, incredibly rudely.

'And which job would that be?' I ask, returning to some imaginary task on my desk. There are myriad ways to assert dominance if you know them. And I know them all.

'The Professor of Neuroscience,' she quips. 'I thought that Rainbow Class would really benefit from both my doctorates?'

For reasons that are the Lord's to know, I find her insolence irksomely arousing. The Almighty enjoys sending temptation in troublesome female form. Eve. Delilah. Liz Truss. All alluring. All dangerous.

'Sarcasm is the lowest form of wit, my dear,' I say, trying to banish my degenerate desire to take her over my knee.

'Oh, I've met lower,' she says, walking in without closing the door and slumping inelegantly into the chair across from my desk. 'So I've thought about it – and we'll take the caretaker job.'

'Will you now?' I reply, picking up a pen and writing some nonsense on a piece of recycling. 'How very gracious of you.'

'I know – I'm St Nonn's answer to Maria von Trapp . . . So when do we start? When will the house be ready?'

I try not to let my smile betray the fun I'm about to have. 'No.'

I say nothing further. Pauses can be so much more powerful than words. She puts her arms on the desk and leans forward, exposing a sinful, if delightful, view of her décolletage.

'Go on, then, Clivey,' she whispers, like the serpent in Eden. 'Give us a clue. However you want. Charades? A haiku? Through the medium of interpretive dance . . .'

I put the pen down and remove my glasses. I stare straight into her pert yet impertinent face.

'I'm afraid, Mrs Fisher, the position is no longer available.'

I let my words hang between us. Her cheeks start to colour like a ripe plum.

'What do you mean?' she says darkly.

'Precisely what I just said,' I sigh, replacing my glasses. 'There is no vacancy. For a caretaker. Nor a neuroscientist. Good day.'

I return to my pretend work, knowing full well she won't leave. I can't imagine how irate she is. But I'll certainly be reflecting on it privately later.

'You offered it to me,' she growls. 'At Stitchwell's memorial.'

'I think you'll find that a) I merely gauged your interest and b) we had that conversation on Friday 28 October. Today is Thursday 10 November. Nearly two weeks have passed,' I point out. 'You have not spoken to me about it since, so I – entirely reasonably – assumed you weren't interested.'

'Matt can't just change job without making arrangements. This affects all of us,' she spits. A fleck of her saliva lands on my paper. I wipe it away slowly with my index finger. 'You'd know that if you had a family.'

'And I can't have the wheels of our school grinding to a halt because of your indecision,' I retort. 'You'd know that if you had a significant role.'

'You know my family needed that job!' she cries. 'And you know that Matt would have been bloody good at it!'

I nod. Both statements are, indeed, factually correct.

'So why won't you let him have it?' she rants on. 'The school needs a caretaker . . .'

'It does,' I interrupt. 'Which is why I have filled the position.'

I go back to writing an imaginary note. Lord, forgive the pleasures of the flesh . . .

'What?' she rages. 'You gave it to someone else? Who?'

'Someone who actually needs a job,' I say coolly. 'Someone to whom life hasn't been nearly as kind as it has to you.'

'Oh please,' she spits again. 'You think life has been kind to me?'

'Yes,' I answer plainly. 'Yes, it has. You have a roof over your head and – as you were so quick to point out a moment ago – a family around you. Some people are blessed with neither. You'd do well to remember your privilege. And learn how to cut your cloth.'

I can't resist. I look up to find her seething, her chest swelling invitingly with each outraged breath. After an unpromising start, today is proving most generous in its bounty.

'But . . . but . . . we have a mortgage to pay! Bills! Kids . . . stuff!' she babbles. 'It never ends! I've got no idea how I'm going to pay for Grace to go on the residential next month . . .'

Our Heavenly Father. You are too kind.

'Oh, now. With that I can help you,' I say, teasing a piece of paper out of my in-tray. 'Our new headmaster has increased the budget – from where I don't know – for our Hardship Fund, to ensure no child misses out on any such opportunity through financial restrictions. Personally, I feel that if parents can afford twenty B&H, they can save up for their progeny to go on a residential trip. But these decisions are not mine to make. You are of course welcome to submit an application.'

She accepts the paper tentatively and reads it.

'So . . . I can apply?'

'Absolutely anyone can apply,' I confirm. 'The form is a little laborious. I'd be happy to help you with some of the longer terminology should your major life disadvantages inhibit you? Although I must say you speak very eloquently for one of your . . . educational attainment.'

'That's too kind,' she says, standing up and leaning over the desk like Eve proffering the apple. 'Especially from someone whose main "educational attainment" was probably a B for buggery at your posh boarding school. Screw you, Clive.'

She extends her middle finger before sauntering out like a hussy, leaving the door wide open behind her.

'Just say the word, dear,' I mutter as I return to my computer with a smile that finds its way to every extremity. Today is turning out to be truly glorious. The Lord is good.

But back to business.

I turn to my computer, pull up a private browsing page and enter in the terms of my search. I am so absorbed by the results that I nearly have a coronary when a lone voice invades my silence.

'Wotcha, boss,' Andy chirps, dropping himself into my chair and his bag onto my floor. I note he never travels without it. Such is the lot of the itinerate soul, I suppose – if you're used to moving at short notice, you want your worldly possessions with you at all times. 'I dig your digs. Seriously rocking the Scrooge and Marley vibes.'

In the nearly fortnight Andy has been staying with me, not a day has passed where he hasn't surprised me. Last week, he fixed a persistent issue with my hall wiring. That night, he sat at the church piano and bashed out a passable *Für Elise*. His conversation ranges from Everton to evolution, he's a veritable gourmand (his osso bucco could tempt a man to hell) – and today he drops a Dickens reference. And yet he cannot be relied upon to consistently flush a lavatory.

He certainly livens the place up – which is why I have elected to extend his invitation until such time as the caretaker cottage is fit for human habitation. And yet I still don't entirely understand the nature of the transaction between us. His side of the sheet balances up well – in just over ten days he's acquired a place to stay, a steady job and no amount of expenditure – the cost of the veal in the osso bucco alone brought tears to my eyes . . .

And yet I paid it.

So what am I getting in return?

'I presume I'm too late to illuminate you as to the etiquette of the knock?' I say.

'Open door, open invitation,' he grins, leaning back and threading his fingers behind his head. 'You want privacy, porn or a poo – shut the door, lad.'

I roll my eyes. He is incorrigible.

'Are you ready to begin?'

'Born ready,' he beams. 'Never afraid of a day's graft.'

I await his gratitude for my bestowing the caretaker role upon him. It doesn't come.

'Well, come along, then. I'll introduce you around,' I tell him. 'And might I remind you that I have placed my faith and reputation on the line to secure you this post? Please ensure you are worthy of them.'

'Oh sure,' he says with a mocking bow. 'Wouldn't want to besmirch a fine upstanding fellow like yourself, Mr B.'

'I'm glad to hear it,' I say, awaiting the punchline. Andy is rarely sincere for long.

'But word to the wise, chief,' he whispers as I stand, 'if you wanna decent forgery, I can hook you up better than Google ever will.'

This is a joke for which I do not care.

'Whatever do you mean?' I say stiffly.

'None o' mine,' he says casually, gesturing to my computer screen with a wink, 'but if you're after a hooky bank statement, you need a word with my mate Bootleg Barry . . .'

# Kiera

Fuck you, Clive.

I really needed that job. Properly, massively, actually needed it. My house costs more to heat than Buckingham bloody Palace, I don't have next month's mortgage in the bank and I have to pay the rest of the deposit for Grace's place at Shottsford House this term, or we forfeit the scholarship. And to have to go with my begging bowl to Clive bastard Baxendale for Grace's residential . . . But I'll do it. There's nothing I wouldn't do for my girls.

Nothing.

So screw you, Baxendale. And screw you too, Hattie. If you're happy with your nothing life in this nothing town with your nothing ambition, have a fucking cookie. I'm not. And I'm not seeing my girls trapped in this shithole like I've been. If that's spoiling them, then I don't give a fuck. Screw St Nonnatus, screw Flatford and SCREW EVERYONE!

I'm alone in the art cupboard, inside the main hall – it's the only place I can get some peace. I say art cupboard – there's hardly anything in it now – years ago we used to have coloured paper and glitter and crepe. Now Pritt Sticks have become more precious than palladium – yeah, the government can go screw itself as well. It's just . . . It's all just so unfair . . . AAAAAAARRRRRGGGGHHHH!

In my rage, I kick what looks like a big rock, only to discover that it is in fact made from papier-mâché, which promptly implodes at my feet.

'Fuck!' I grunt as I think of all the work I'm now going to have to do to salvage this poor kid's prized art and make it look like they did it. 'Fuck, fuck, fuck . . . !'

I push the door to the cupboard open to get some air – it's stifling in here. But, as I open the door, it becomes clear I'm not alone.

'You've been spending too much time with Year 1,' comes

the only voice I actually want to hear. 'You're picking up on their potty mouths.'

I laugh – partly because I think it's funny. But mostly because I don't want Ben to see me being a psychotic freak.

'You've come to beg for forgiveness?' I ask, pointing to Creepy Jesus in his hands.

Ben winces at the hideous statue.

'In a manner of speaking,' he says, putting it back on the table and walking towards the cupboard. 'I noticed in assembly the other day that I glued his crown of thorns on wonkily. I was hoping to fix it before anyone noticed.'

'Too late,' I say, pointing to the sky. 'The all-seeing one knows your sins.'

'I hope that God has better things to watch than my shonky DIY,' Ben smiles. 'There's *The Traitors* for one . . .'

'I wasn't talking about God,' I whisper, moving back into the cupboard. 'I was talking about Stitchwell.'

This time he doesn't laugh. That probably wasn't in the best possible taste. And I should be more careful.

'You okay?' he asks gently, moving into the cupboard and pulling the door to before hesitating. 'Okay if I shut this? I've just read thirty-six Powerpoint slides about making female colleagues feel at ease. Here, I've been practising my least domineering face. How is it? Does it make you feel easier?'

He sticks out his bottom lip and widens his gorgeous eyes. He looks absurd. Absurdly hot. But absurd.

I laugh. In truth, the thought of being in this small space with Ben makes me want to be as easy as all hell.

'You're a natural,' I quip. 'And you're right. It's probably as well the Bumblebees don't hear me. If you think the "clucking duck" song was bad, just wait until you hear their rendition of *We're Going on a Bear Hunt.*'

This time he does laugh. We're back. And he's just what I need right now.

'Having a day, are we?' he says, leaning against the shelving and folding his toned arms. I've always had a thing for men's arms. And Ben's are, of course, perfect. Lightly tanned, muscular, strong. It mystifies me that men persist in sending unsolicited pictures of the least attractive part of their bodies.

Send me a sexy forearm and you've got a shot. A ropey selfie of your balding Mr Snuffleupagus and you're always going to lose out to *Poldark* and a couple of AAA batteries.

'And a half,' I say, trying to pause the soft-porn reel of what Ben could do to me in a secluded stationery cupboard with his Pritt Stick . . .

'Anything I can do?' he offers. He takes a step forward and a colourful range of possibilities crosses my mind. We are thrillingly close. I tuck a strand of hair behind my ear coquettishly and make my eyes as big as possible. I know I shouldn't. But I need this today. I need . . . something.

'That depends, Andrews,' I say, huskily I hope. 'What else have you picked up from those PowerPoints?'

It's meant as a joke – mostly. But it somehow reacts with the atmosphere to become an unequivocal come on.

Shit.

I've gone too far. He's my boss. I've made it weird, shit, shit, shit . . .

But he laughs that gentle laugh, looks at the floor and then locks his eyes with mine.

'I think the best lessons are learned through practice, don't you?' he says softly.

Jesus Christ.

I'm hornier than a herd of rhinos.

We stand there, frozen. No one is laughing now. We're here. It's that moment. The one that has been fermenting for months. One move from either of us and we go through the looking glass. I want him to cross the threshold. And I don't trust myself not to do it. He's looking to me for any sign of invitation, any licence to throw his bloody PowerPoint in the trash, envelop me in those sexy arms and pin me up against this shelving right now. I want him. I want him so much. Our lips move closer. Closer. So close . . .

Bollocks!

My ringtone shatters the silence and the moment. The girls love to mess with my phone and it appears they've been at it again. I'll tell you this much. They never get interrupted by the Crazy Frog in *Bridgerton* . . .

I pull my phone out of my back pocket and groan. I feel

Ben stand down. It's probably as well. No good would have come from that.

Even if I might have.

'Shit – it's Taylor's school,' I lie, clearing my throat. 'I'd better . . .'

'Of course,' he croaks with a sheepish smile. 'You know where I am if . . . You know where I am.'

He opens the cupboard door and the harsh strip lighting of the hall casts an ugly sheen on the moment as he hurries away.

I wait until he's out of earshot and answer the call I've been ignoring for days. I can't avoid it forever.

'Yes,' I say stiffly.

'Mrs Fisher?' comes the condescending tone on the end of the line, as if he doesn't know who he's just phoned. 'I hope you're well. It's Nigel Carter here from Savings First Bank. We've been trying to get hold of you.'

'Congratulations,' I sass. 'You succeeded.'

He laughs out of his nose. 'I trust you're having a good day. Did you receive our letter? Or, indeed, letters?'

He deliberately over-pronounces the plural, the prick.

'I did,' I reply archly. 'Which has made it increasingly difficult to have good days.'

'Then you are aware you are in mortgage arrears?' he says, not waiting for my response to continue. 'Here at Savings First, we have a range of support available for any of our customers experiencing financial difficulties.'

'Do they include not having interest rates higher than my knicker size so that working people have a decent chance of making repayments?'

Nasal Nigel laughs through his nose again. Did I mention he's a prick?

'I see from your file that earlier this year you took a payment holiday? And requested to be transferred to an interest-only product?' he says, as if we don't both know that's the case. 'But you have missed the past two months' payments regardless.'

'Look . . . it's just been a really expensive time,' I say, trying to keep the panic out of my voice. 'You know what it's like – food, fuel, school fees – everything's so expensive right now . . .'

'School fees? You're educating your children privately?'

Nigel leaps on my stupid tongue slip like a hungry lizard. Why did I say that . . . ?

'Child, not children,' I say, like that's going to make it better. 'And it's just the deposit at this stage – most of it will be covered by her scholarship.'

'Mrs Fisher,' he says, without a hint of amusement in his nostrils, 'you are £986 in arrears. If this money is not credited back to your account within fifteen days, we will have no alternative but to issue a claim for possession of property and commence court proceedings—'

'Wait . . . what the hell?' I shout 'You're going to repossess our house? We've not missed a single repayment in ten years before now!'

I can't keep the panic out of my voice. Matt and I nearly killed ourselves to get the deposit together for that house – and these days we wouldn't get near it. I thought we had the caretaker cottage coming our way, so I didn't pay this month . . . I can't lose my home. I just can't.

'We are authorised to take whatever steps are required to bring your account with us back into credit,' he says, not one hint of sympathy in his voice.

'Steps like throwing little girls out onto the street?' I say dramatically. 'Does that square your account, you heartless git?'

Nigel pauses and I hear him slowly exhale at the end of the phone.

'At least they'll have their education,' he says unpleasantly. 'Good afternoon, Mrs Fisher.'

The phone goes dead and I clock the time – I need to get home. I leave the papier-mâché where it is and make a mental note to sort it tomorrow. Yet another mess I have to clear up.

Although, thinking about that dangerous moment with Ben . . . to be fair to Nasal Nige, that call might just have stopped me from making an even bigger one.

*

Grace does clubs most nights after school, so when I get home only Taylor has beaten me to it. As I switch the oven on for tea, I can hear she's in her room with her best mates, Tilly, Jul— Sorry . . . Sebastian and Tilly. Sorry . . . Matilda. Sorry . . . Leif? The three of them have been thick as thieves since primary and they all spend more time in my house than their own. None of them have it easy – Tilly's (screw it) mum and dad, Karl and Flo, are going through a shitty divorce after Karl left them for his colleague, the git . . . My mind flits to Ben. But that's totally different – I haven't done anything. Yet.

Sebastian's mum, Leanne, is a low-level junkie/dealer who has inexplicably managed to persuade social services to let her raise her kids. Leanne came up the hard way too – we were briefly in the same care home. Which is why I have precisely zero sympathy for her. You can use your past as an accelerant or as an excuse. Mine has made me more determined to make a decent life for my kids. Leanne has used her past to justify the shitty one she gives hers. So Seb's always hung around mine and I've been happy to have them. They need a safe space to be. I know I did.

'Hi, girls!' I chirp, walking into the council tip that serves as my teenage daughter's bedroom. 'Shall I get the pizza on?'

'MUM!' Taylor screams, whipping her phone out of sight, as if it's not permanently glued to her appendages. 'How many times? Bloody knock! And we're not all girls, FFS! *And* Sebastian is gluten intolerant! Could you get one sentence any more wrong?'

'Sorry,' I say as Sebastian jumps up to give me a hug. 'I will get my head around it. Takes this old mouth a while to learn new words.'

'Don't sweat it, Kier, we love you,' says Sebastian from inside my arms. I don't think they get very many hugs at home, so I'm happy to issue double when they're here. And it's not like Taylor ever wants one. 'And, Tay – don't be such a bitch to your mum.'

'I really like your hair,' I say, admiring Sebastian's new, shorter crop. It doesn't seem like five minutes ago I was French-braiding these three in their princess dresses. 'And I've never seen this outfit before – someone's been on a shopping spree! You won the pools?! It all really suits you.'

'Oh my God!' Taylor huffs. 'Could you be any more bloody obvious? Well done, Mum. Have a medal from Stonewall—'

'Tay!' Sebastian chides again. 'Thanks, Kiera. And don't worry about the pizza – Mum said she'd cook tonight.'

I try to smile. Leanne often says she'll cook. I'm not sure how often it actually happens. But at least she's buying her kid some new clothes. She must have grown some sense of shame. Or upped her prices.

'I'm in!' Tilly pipes up. 'Mum took the microwave off Dad because he didn't pay for my guitar lessons. And he's doing keto and I cannot eat any more meat.'

'No worries,' I say as Sebastian skips back to the girls. 'I'll bring it up.'

'Thanks!' say the two children upon whom I didn't waste fourteen hours and a perfectly good vagina to bring them into this world.

'Oh – and, Taylor – we need to talk about your Shakespeare coursework,' I say, hoping that her friends' presence will either prevent a scene or provide witnesses. 'I got an email from Mr Geary this morning. He's not happy . . .'

'That's because he's too busy looking at porn on his phone to teach us properly,' Taylor reports.

I hope to God this is teenage hyperbole. I don't get a chance to ask.

'I'll help her!' Sebastian chirps like a happy budgie. 'I'm a bit of a Shakespeare geek – I love *The Two Gentlemen of Verona*.'

'You are such a nerd,' says Taylor with a grin, throwing a cushion at her friend.

'Better than a dropout,' Sebastian laughs, chucking it back.

I try to smile at their bants as I back out of the room. But the truth is that Taylor *is* dropping out. As soon as I've got Gracie sorted, Taylor's next on the hitlist. Perhaps they do a massive sibling discount at Shottsford . . .

By the time I get downstairs, Matt and Gracie are coming through the door.

'Hey, baby!' I cry as she runs past me on the stairs. 'How was tap?'

'Good!' she calls back. 'Got a maths test tomorrow, gotta revise, bye!'

'There's something wrong with that bloody kid,' says her father with a grin. 'Why isn't she off smoking and snogging with the rest of the kids? No good can come of all this maths, I tell ya.'

'Maybe if you'd spent more time on maths and less time smoking and snogging you'd have made more of yourself,' I scoff, throwing pizzas in the oven. I wince as the words come out. That was crueller than I intended. Matt's another one who seems happy with a small life. It was comforting when we first met. But these days? My mind drifts back to the art cupboard . . . No. Stop it, Fisher. It's not Matt's fault he's not Ben. It's not fair to punish him for it.

I turn round and give him a kiss to make amends, trying to push the thought of Ben's arms out of my mind.

'Mmmm,' he says when I pull away. 'I might not've been any good at Maths. But I weren't half bad at Biology. Fancy studying later?'

'Period,' I lie quickly. If Matt had any actual grasp of biology, he'd know it's been only two weeks. But his Maths really isn't that good. 'Sorry, babe.'

'No worries,' he says with an amiable smile. 'It's me birthday soon. Can't wait to unwrap my pressie . . .'

He pats me gently on the bum as he goes to hang his coat up. I try not to audibly sigh. Urgh. Birthday sex. Why can't men just be happy with an Amazon voucher and a mid-week madras? I do love Matt. I still like Matt. But I can't often be arsed to sleep with Matt. It's not that the sex isn't good – far from it. Many women would be grateful to have a man who is as insatiable for them as Matt is for me – when the girls went to his mum's in the summer, Mrs Hodgkins next door thought we were being burgled. But we've been together a long time and things are bound to taper off amongst the daily grind. Sex with my husband these days is like the Christmas tree on the fourth of January – it's just not as exciting as when he first put it up.

'I spoke to the bank today,' I announce as he returns to the kitchen and opens a beer. 'It's not good.'

'Babe . . . we can't keep fannying around this,' he says, taking a sip. 'If the caretaker job ain't there – thanks for that phone call by the way, Foghorn Leghorn, me eardrums are still ringing – it's simple. Poshford House or the mortgage. We can't do both.'

'So what's that supposed to mean?' I snap at him for committing the crime of telling the actual truth. 'We just chuck Grace into Flatford High and let her rot?'

'She ain't gonna rot – she's a good kid,' he says. 'She'll do fine anywhere.'

'She's going to do better at Shottsford House! You don't understand—'

'Yeah, I do,' he says calmly. One of things that drives me crazy about Matt is that he never loses his temper. 'I get that you want the best for our kid—'

'Well done. Have the maths prize,' I spit.

'But that's our job, not any bloody school's,' he says. 'And killing ourselves for summit else we can't afford is just . . .'

'Just what?' I shout, happy for the excuse to have a go at him. 'Just good parenting? Just aspirational? Just makes sense?'

'Just fucking nuts,' he says plainly. 'Grace is a good girl. She works hard. She'll get to where she wants to go any road. You know that really.'

'No, Matt! No, I don't!' I yell, sick of having this conversation on repeat. 'I know that I don't want her stuck in this dead-end town! I know that I don't want her to go to Flatford High! I know what that place does! I sent them a good kid last time, for fuck's sake. Look what happened there!'

'Wow,' comes the quiet, dark voice behind Matt.

Shit.

Shit, shit, shit.

'Tay . . .' I sigh. 'I didn't mean it like that. You know I didn't . . .'

'I was just coming to see if the pizza was ready,' she says, a horrible, hateful sadness in her eyes. 'But look what happened there.'

She turns round and stomps back upstairs. There's no point in going after her. It'll only end up in a screaming match.

'Brilliant. Well done,' I snarl at Matt.

'What the bloody hell have I done?' he asks, choking on his beer.

'It's fine – I'll sort it out,' I grumble as the oven pings. 'Just for a change.'

I throw the pizzas onto plates and attack them with the pizza wheel.

'Take this up to the girls . . . people . . . humans – argh!' I shout. 'I'm going for a walk.'

I push past him and grab my coat. I know it's not his fault – I know it's not anyone's fault – but I'm sick of impossible choices. I've made enough lately . . .

'Mum,' I hear a little voice peep as I yank open the door. 'Where are you going?'

I turn to see my little Gracie looking worried at the top of the stairs. I give her a reassuring smile and blow her a kiss.

'I just need some air, baby,' I say. 'It's been a long day and I'm in a bad mood.'

'It's late,' she says nervously. 'Don't be long.'

'I won't,' I promise, and I'm glad of the reminder. Because if it wasn't for my Grace, right now, I'd probably just keep on walking.

I try not to slam the door as I head out into the darkness. It's cold and drizzling and suddenly this feels like a stupid idea. I don't want to go back in. But maybe a little drive would clear my head? I'm just figuring out how to slope back in to get the keys and keep my dignity intact when I notice a note on the windscreen. If it's Mrs Hodgkins moaning about us not putting our bins back, I'm going to go round there and tell her where to stick her composting . . .

Shit.

It's not Mrs Hodgkins.

The handwritten note has clearly been here for a while – the ink has started to run in the rain. Yet I can understand it perfectly. I look around in case whoever left it is nearby to relish my response. But the street is empty.

Empty except for me and this single word.
A piece of paper that simply reads:

# CHEAT

# The Flatford Gazette

Friday 11 November

## Good Samaritan Goes Bad

Local charity worker Natasha Tompkins was convicted yesterday of running an organised-crime ring through her extensive charitable endeavours.

Tompkins, 44, of Chestnut Drive, appeared in Westmouth Crown Court yesterday, charged with illegal money lending, money laundering, possession with intent to supply Class A drugs and a supply and production penalty following the largest seizure of prescription drugs in the force's history.

Known amongst the local criminal fraternity as Tash 'The Stash', Ms Tompkins had reportedly been running her illegal enterprises for many years.

'She was a smart one, all right,' said an associate who wished to remain anonymous. 'Found channels none of the rest of us could touch. The Stash used church groups, food banks, soup kitchens – you name it, all a front. She used to shift a load of horse through the village fair. If you asked for her 'special sponge mix', you could bet your a**e you were gonna get baked.'

'Tash could spot a hole in the market like no one – and she knew her customers,' another anonymous source revealed. 'A lot of her clients were the middle-aged yummy mummy crowd, so lately she's been making a killing selling black market HRT for women who can't get a prescription. You saw all those women sobbing at her trial? You can be expecting plenty more of them.'

Tompkins was sentenced to seven years' imprisonment. She was also fined £10,000, which the Flatford branch of the Women's Institute have pledged to finance with a kickstarter campaign.

## Council Defends Library 'Regeneration' Plan

'It'll still have books as a Tesco Metro,' pledges council chief.

## Local Centenarian Signs Up For London Marathon

'Maybe this'll do the ****ing trick,' says the 104-year-old novice runner.

**Robocoppers**
Priya, Al, Tanya

**Friday 11 Nov**
07.12

**Priya**
IN YOUR FACE BIATCHES!!!

---

# The Flatford Gazette

Friday 11 November

### Good Samaritan Goes Bad

---

**Al**
It is WAY too early for this...
Is it too much to hope you're going to spare us the smug?

**Priya**
Told you so!
Tash Tompkins is a crime boss.
And someone killed Claudia Stitchwell.

**Al**
God help us.

**Tanya**
I had no idea Tash had been arrested.
(Although where the hell I go for my extra Oestrogel now, I have no bloody clue.)

**Priya**
I'm glad one of us is on the case...
So while I was at BuyRite yesterday,
I got chatting with Matt Fisher.

**Al**
Kiera's fella?

**Tanya**
He's such a lovely guy.

**Priya**
Sure.
Bit gullible.
But nice enough.
And lousy taste in partners...

**Al**
Claws away, dear.

**Priya**
You know how Ben went shopping on the
night of the murder?
Guess what he bought?

```
43857    Champagne                            28.99
33858    Luxury chocolate ice cream            2.99
76400    BuyRite Special Selection Brie        2.69
49594    Red wine                              8.49
2435     Durex Intense                        11.00
10349    BuyRite Basics Bleach                 0.79
6893     Masking tape                          1.69

         Thank you for Buying Rite!
```

```
                    BUYRITE
           Buy more, pay less, buy rite!

Mon 24 Oct                                    16.11

58432    Rice Wine Vinegar                     2.90
59382    Soy Sauce                             2.75
50293    Groundnut oil                         2.00
981233   Pork ribs                             5.62
00293    Cornflour                             2.45
8762     Garlic                                0.24
59203    Chinese 5 Spice                       1.10
8350     Spring onions                         0.55
5023     BuyRite Basics Chicken stock cubes    1.00
19845    BuyRite Basics 50 Paper plates        2.50
19473    BuyRite Basics 50 Paper cups          7.50
19029    BuyRite Basics 1ply Napkins           1.00

         Thank you for Buying Rite!
```

**Al**

Wow.

He was planning one helluva night in...

Condoms AND bleach...

**Priya**

Ben's is the second one, you fool.

What do you notice?

**Tanya**

His Chinese ribs were going to be really shite with that stock.

Always make your own.

**Priya**

Stand down, Delia.

He said he 'wasn't sure' about the recipe in class that week.

The recipe he bought all the ingredients for.

So he lied.

**Al**

How did you get this?

**Priya**

Told Matt I was doing a freelance article for the Gazette about supermarket security.

Got him to show me how they can track who was in store and what they bought.

The picture's a bit crap, I had to take it quickly.

Told Matt I thought I saw Alexander Armstrong in the Pet Care aisle.

But you take my point.

**Al**
Yes, we know.
Groundnut oil.
Ie, peanut oil.
Are you sure it's Ben's?

**Priya**
It's in the right time window.
And corroborates with the cookery class he thought he
was going to.
And the stuff for the welcome evening.

**Tanya**
Just because he bought it.
That doesn't mean he used it.

**Priya**
You're right.
But even if it wasn't him, we have the
potential murder weapon on site.
Someone could have taken it to lace
Stitchwell's food or drink.
And therefore someone had the means.

**Al**
But only if they knew he had it?

**Tanya**
Exactly.
Why would anyone know what Ben had in his
shopping?

**Priya**
Because they saw him buy it.
Remember the statements?
Hattie went to BuyRite around the time Ben was there.

**Tanya**
So did I.

**Priya**
You left before he went in.
He confirms that.

**Tanya**
Glad I'm not under suspicion!
Pri?
Pri?
I'm not under suspicion right?

**Priya**
Of course not, you idiot, I'm just reading the
statements back.
Hattie doesn't actually mention going to the shop.
But Ben gave her a lift back.
And she does refer to leaving her handbag there.

**Al**
*Ben's office is right by the main office.*
So anyone going into the office could have seen/
nicked his shopping.

**Priya**
True dat.
And we still don't know what it was
Stitchwell ate or drank.
Tan – where was your cake?

**Tanya**
On the table, everyone could see it.

**Priya**
I mean before that.
When you got to school?
Where did you put it?

**Tanya**
Oh – in the kitchen.
You don't think it was my cake again, do you?

**Priya**
Not in the condition it left you.
But if it was in the kitchen for, what, two hours?
Someone could easily have tampered with it.

**Al**
With Ben's nut oil.

**Priya**
Precisely.
Damn your cake for being so good.
We really could have done with a piece...

**Tanya**
Alright Poirot.
I need to get the girls to school.
Drinks at The Crown later?

**Priya**
You bet your sweet ass.
It's Friday...

**Al**
Sorry girls.
Nomi is on the graveyard shift.
And our sitter has mocks.
Which is weird, as I'm sure she left school last year...

**Priya**
Bummer...
We could bring the party to you?

**Tanya**
YES!

**Al**
YES!

**Priya**
It's a date!
Laters bitches.
And did I mention...?
I WAS RIGHT!
xxx

# PARENTCHAT

Clearer Community Communication

## ST NONNATUS CE PRIMARY

*Ora et labora*

**Monday 14 November**

**Mrs Marcia Cox<<u>M.Cox@stnonnatus.flatford.sch.uk</u>>**

**To: <Whole School>**

**Re: Week commencing 14 Nov**

Dear Guardians,*

We are very much looking forward to our inaugural Love Day on Friday and we will be exploring the theme of love across the school this week.

Firstly, we'd like to show our love to those in our broader community who might be in need. All week, we will be accepting donations of dried, tinned and other non-perishable food items at the office, as well as bathroom and kitchen products to donate to the Flatford Food Bank. We remind everyone that all donations should be unopened and unused and **must** be legal to supply and consume.

On Friday, we invite the children to dress up in any way that celebrates our theme of love. As with all dress-up days, we ask that costumes are tasteful and age-appropriate. For clarity, as with World Book Day, any costume based on the *Fifty Shades of Grey* series will not be deemed suitable.

We also want our children to understand and respect love in all its forms. As part of your child's education at St Nonnatus, students will now be taught Relationships and Sex Education (RSE) alongside health education. The aim of RSE is to give young people the information they need to help them develop healthy, nurturing relationships of all

174

kinds and all teaching materials are appropriate to the age and emotional maturity of our pupils.

For Love Day on Friday, Year 6 will be covering the non-statutory themes of conception, pregnancy and birth, gender identities and LGBTQ+ relationships. This is the only aspect of RSE from which your child may be withdrawn, Please speak to Mr Andrews if you'd like to discuss this.

The online appointment system for Parents' Evening will open tonight and, following feedback, meetings will take place in person this term. Please bear in mind that the slots are strictly five minutes each and should you wish to discuss your child's achievements, challenges or recent holiday to Torremolinos in more detail, you should make a longer appointment on another occasion. We welcome any contributions for sustenance – it's a long night for our teachers.

While we are aware that most of our community adheres to the Polite Parking Principles we have outlined in previous newsletters, we continue to have complaints from our neighbours about the minority that need to reflect on their choices. We remind you again that our neighbours' driveways are not to be blocked at any time. This includes parking on the driveway and is not exonerated by putting a five-pound note and an assurance you'll only be 'whipping around BuyRite' on their windscreens.

I leave you with the happy news that our supply Tiger teacher, Ms Tayke, is expecting a little cub of her own! She has decided to take her maternity leave with immediate effect so we will announce the new Tiger teacher in due course.

I leave you with the words of the Beatles: 'All You Need Is Love.'

Best wishes,

Mrs Marcia Cox

Office Manager
St Nonnatus Primary School

* Further to community feedback, we have updated our terminology to 'guardians' as it was strongly felt by some that the term 'carers' belonged to a specific group of individuals with caring responsibilities and was not to be appropriated more generally. At St Nonnatus we always strive to ensure every voice is heard and we thank you for using the Feedback Box. Although whoever attempted to return their 'Jesus Hates You' mouse mat to Amazon via this means may wish to reclaim it from the office.

# Tickly Tiger's Diary!

Date: Monday 14 November

This weekend I went home with: Ollie

Tickly and I spent Saturday at my mummy's house. We turned the whole house into a blanket fort and played The Floor is Lava which was the best! Mum made my favourite lunch for Tickly (sausage and mash and beans) with chocolate ice cream with sprinkles, marshmallows and squirty cream for pudding. Then she let me take Tickly out on my bike to the park and pushed me on the swings for more than 20 minutes! Then we went for hot chocolate and cake at my favourite cafe. That night we turned our front room into a cinema and watched Jumanji: Welcome to the Jungle (even though it's a 12!) with a pizza that the man brought in a box and we made our own popcorn and had a box of Celebrations. We didn't go to bed until 10 o'clock!

On Sunday, we went to my dad's flat, but we didn't stay there long because he took us to Splashworld and we went on all the waterslides, even the Dragon's Revenge where you're supposed to be 13, but my dad fibbed so we could go on it. Then he took us to Laster Blasters, before a game at EpicBowl (Tickly and I got to play on all the machines too) and then we went to Mr Blister's Soft Play and I got a slushie and maybe a verruca. Then it was lunchtime, so we went to Burger World and I got to make my own ice-cream at the ice cream factory! In the afternoon we went to the cinema to see Spiderman Into the Multiverse in 3D and we got to sit in the big cinema with the seats that go back and Dad bought me popcorn with all the sweetie toppers.

On Sunday night Tickly looked after me when I was sick all over Daddy's new car.

# PARENTCHAT

Clearer Community Communication

## ST NONNATUS CE PRIMARY

### *Ora et labora*

### Year 6 Tiger Class
click here for group info

### Monday 14 November
11.42

**Zofia**
Yay for Love Day!
I've had a thought...
Thought it might be cool to coordinate Tiger class?
We could all do different colours of the rainbow 🖋?

**Al**
That's such a great idea!
Bagsie yellow.
Maisie got a hideous dress from her grandmother and
we've had no idea what to do with it.
She looks like a daffodil, bless her.

**Donna**
Orange please!
I've got a T-shirt left over from World Flag Day at
Finley's last school.
We got Armenia ▬.

**Tanya**
This is so lovely, Zofia.
We can do any colour.
The girls still fit in their Pride outfits, so we're covered!

**Jennie**
Does anyone know how to get pencil lead out of an
ear canal?

**Karen**
Is Sasha's mum on here?

**Karl**
Hi guys.
I don't quite know how to put this.
Is anyone else finding that things have started to go...
missing?

**Donna**
My sanity?

**Sharon**
Me pelvic floor?

**Flo**
My husband?

**Fatima**
*We could all do different colours of the rainbow 🌈?*
Lovely thought.
We'll do green.
Khadija is going to be in Peter Pan at the Arts Centre
this Christmas

**Annie**
*Is Sasha's mum on here?*
Here I am 👋
Everything okay?

**Zofia**
Thanks for all your enthusiasm!
Do we all just want to choose?
Or shall I divide the class into groups?

**Karen**
*Khadija is going to be in Peter Pan at the Arts Centre*
*this Christmas*
Oh wow!
We're coming to that – we'll know the star!

**Stella**
*Do we all just want to choose?*

William won't be in school on Friday.

**Fatima**
*We're coming to that – we'll know the star!*
Not exactly.
She's a tree.
But no such thing as small parts, eh?

**Karen**
*Everything okay?*
Hi Annie! 👋
I just wanted to get your deets.
Beth is having her birthday party and wants to invite Sasha.

**Priya**
*But no such thing as small parts, eh?*
Depends what kind of tree 🌲 🌲 🌴 🌳 🌴 🍄

**Mike**
Does anyone have this week's spellings?

**Karl**
*My sanity?*
Not sure I have any left.
(And will have at least 50% less after the divorce.)
No, I mean... stuff?
The kids' stuff?
Ollie keeps coming home without... things.

**Petra**
Is it his PE sock?
Because Archie now has three.

**Jane**
*Beth is having her birthday party and wants to invite Sasha.*
Sorry Karen, could you send me the deets too?
Phoebe's lost the invite!

**Tanya**
*William won't be in school on Friday*
Oh bless him – orthodontist again?

Verity's in after Christmas, she's dreading it.
Sue watched *Moonraker* with her and now V's
convinced she's going to look like Jaws.

**Stella**
No.
We are withdrawing William for the day.
I don't want to fall out with anybody.
I respect everyone's lifestyle choices.
But we will not be participating on this occasion.

**Zofia**
May I ask why?

**Mike**
Question for the Flatford High crowd:
What did you do for this bloody Year 10 work exp
placement next term?
Who the hell wants a 16yo knocking around their work!
And have you seen the latest from Themis?
Apparently one of the male teachers watches porn on
his phone during class…

**Stella**
*May I ask why?*
They are children.
We don't think it's appropriate.

**Donna**
*She's a tree.*
Better than an Armenian flag.

**Priya**
*We don't think it's appropriate.*
What are you worried about?
William might decide he likes orange socks?

**Karen**

*Phoebe's lost the invite!*

Hi Jane.

So...

We're doing one of those Bear Building Parties?

It's crucifyingly expensive.

Would have been cheaper to take them to Disneyland!

So we've only invited five – sorry!

**Flo**

*What did you do for this bloody Year 10 work exp placement next term?*

Tilly and her mates all did it at St Nonn's.

Taylor worked in Rainbows, Seb in Year 6 and my Tilly did admin.

(Her younger brother has put her off kids for life!)

And yeah, I saw the Themis.

I hear Mr Geary's been suspended.

**Rosie**

*Is anyone else finding that things have started to go . . . missing?*

No.

Theo always returns with all his belongings.

Except for the M&S hoisin duck wraps he likes for lunch!

Such mature tastes!

**Stella**

*What are you worried about?*

Like I say, I respect your choices.

I only ask that you respect mine.

**Dustin**

Plant-based diets and dolphin tattoos are choices, Stella.

Sexuality, not so much.

**Tanya**

I think the idea is just to celebrate love in all its forms.

**Mike**

*Tilly and her mates all did it at St Nonn's.*
Oh that's genius! That would make life so much easier.
Mind if I nick the idea?
And I'm glad to hear it about Geary.
Go Themis.

**Stella**

*Sexuality, not so much.*
There – you said it.
It's about sex and sexuality.
They are too young.
Already I hear them throwing around terms they don't
understand.

**Al**

Then let's help them to understand.

**Stella**

We are a Christian school.
I am a Christian.
And a lifelong member of St Nonnatus congregation.
The late Reverend preached no sex before marriage.
And I would like my boys to adhere to his teachings.

**Jane**

*So we've only invited five – sorry!*
Ah.
I'd just assumed.
Because Phoebe had Beth at her waterpark party at
Splashworld in the summer.
(Platinum package.)

**Fatima**

*Ollie keeps coming home without . . . things.*
We've had stuff go missing from a lunchbox too.
It was just a few quid for the food bank donation,
but still.
Do you think one of the kids is behind it?

**Flo**

*Mind if I nick the idea?*
Course not!
Happy to help.
And yeah re: Geary.
It's rough justice.
But at least it's justice.

**Tanya**

*Do you think one of the kids is behind it?*
It would be tricky.
The lunchboxes are put on trolleys and kept by the office.
Only staff have access.

**Sharon**

*The late Reverend preached no sex before marriage.*
That's true.
He tended to wait until after they were married.

**Stella**

Don't speak ill of the dead.

**Sharon**

I'm not!
You forget, you young whippersnappers.
I've lived in this town all me life.
I knew Claudia Stitchwell woman and girl.
And let me tell you, she weren't always such a prig...

**Sarah**

#StitchwellLoveChild

**Zofia**

Stitchwell the slapper!
There's an image...

**Stella**

This is baseless and scurrilous gossip and I'll play no
part in it.
And as for 'Love Day'...
We're all free to make our choices.
This is ours.

**Priya**
*Only staff have access.*
Do you think it could be one of them?

**Tanya**
*Do you think it could be one of them?*
Down, girl 🕵.
And we don't know if anyone's stealing, tbf.
Kids lose stuff all the time.

**Priya**
*We're all free to make our choices.*
But Stella...
Your choice is excluding your son.
And more than a little offensive to this inclusive group.

**Sarah**
Does anyone know anything about this Andy bloke?
The new caretaker?

**Zofia**
He's working at the school?!
I thought he was there for some charity thing?
He's homeless – he used to busk outside BuyRite.

**Stella**
*And more than a little offensive to this inclusive group.*
INCLUSIVE???!!!
You think this group is inclusive?

**Al**
Come on Stella.
Everyone is invited to everything.
And all are welcome on here.

**Laura**
I liked the premise.
And the plot twists really took me by surprise.

**Laura**
Sorry! Wrong group!

**Stella**

*Everyone is invited to everything.*
*And all are welcome on here.*
So how 'inclusive' do you think this group is to those
who don't speak English?
And all your nights out are at the pub!
How 'included' do you think people who don't drink
alcohol feel?
Or families who can't afford a meal out?
My interfaith community group *is* inclusive.
We have translators. We help people access services.
We make sure children have everything they need for
school.
They could teach this group a lot about inclusivity.

**Priya**

So long as they're not gay, bi, trans, queer...

**Stella**

I repeat, I have no issue with any adult's sexuality or
gender identity.
I just don't want my son exposed to conversations he's
not old enough to understand.

**Zofia**

But you're making him too young to understand.
He just isn't.

**Stella**

He's my child.
It's my decision.

**Priya**

Well one day, all our kids will make decisions without
us.
I'd rather they were fully informed about consent and
contraception when they do.

**Stella**

And that is your choice.

186

**Priya**

It is.

**Rosie**

*Does anyone know anything about this Andy bloke?*
Yes.
He's part of the church's StopGap programme.
He's a very decent man in need of some Christian
charity.
Theo has already invited him to our house for Sunday
lunch.
He's so thoughtful like that (even if we are busy for the
next three months).
Perhaps others could demonstrate a little generosity of
spirit?

**Karl**

It's the generosity of lunchbox I'm worried about.

**Sarah**

It's unfortunate timing.
New guy turns up.
Things immediately start going missing.

**Karl**

Precisely.
I mean, I'm sorry if he's down on his luck.
But stealing from kids is low.

**Flo**

Sure.
Just ask your Sandra.
She nicked you from ours.

**Rosie**

*But stealing from kids is low.*
There's absolutely no evidence he's stealing from
anyone.
And this kind of idle chit-chat is pejorative and unfair.

**Priya**

It is suspicious though.

**Al**
You think everything and everyone's suspicious!

**Priya**
Because they are 👀.

**Karl**
Maybe we should set a trap?

**Donna**
The Parent Trap?

**Sharon**
Mousetrap?
We could catch the perp under a massive cage!
That's been dropped by a shoe kicking a bath!

**Karl**
I'm serious!
I'm going to put £20 in Ollie's lunchbox.
See what happens.

**Rosie**
You're all being ridiculous.
And very unkind.

**Karl**
Perhaps.
But if there's a thief in our midst, we deserve to know.
We have to keep the children safe.
(And their M&S hoisin duck wraps.)

**Annie**
*Because Phoebe had Beth at her waterpark party at*
*Splashworld in the summer.*
Phoebe had a birthday party?

## Robocoppers
Priya, Al, Tanya

**Monday 14 November**
12.13

> **Tanya**
> Pri?
> You okay?

**Priya**
No!
I'm pissed off!

> **Tanya**
> Appreciate you going into bat 🏏.
> But it's just not worth it with Stella.

**Al**
Don't stress.
We all know Stella is holier than a pair of old tights.
And we all know she's wrong.

**Priya**
I'm not pissed off that she's wrong!
I'm pissed off that she's right!

**Al**
Huh?

> **Tanya**
> What?

**Priya**
Stella's right.
We do exclude people.

> **Tanya**
> Not intentionally.

**Priya**
Tan – we both know that's not good enough.
The next coffee morning we should do what she says.

Get a translator, have it at someone's house so it's
cheaper.
Make sure we invite the parents who don't normally
come.

**Tanya**
We could...

**Priya**
Oh God.
Or... ?

**Tanya**
Or maybe... instead of doing what she said.
We could do what she does.

**Al**
How so?

**Tanya**
She said about her interfaith group.
Perhaps we should support that?
Rather than set up our own thing in competition.

**Priya**
I hate religion.

**Al**
I'm sure it takes a pretty dim view of you.

**Tanya**
You see?
Already something in common!

**Priya**
I hate you.
Both.
Not least because you're right.
I'm also going to talk to Clive about upgrading
Parentchat.
Most of these things have a translation subscription?
Could open it up a bit?

**Al**
Great idea.
Interesting about Stitchwell's slaggy past...
Kind of supports the Stitchwell Love Child theory.

**Priya**
You see – religion.
Don't do as I do, do as I say.

                                              **Tanya**
                    If she was forced to give up a child.
                Maybe that explains why she was so angry.

**Priya**
Or maybe she has a very angry abandoned child...

**Al**
Here we go...

**Priya**
I'm serious.
So if Stitchwell had a kid young...
It would be an adult now.
Didn't Kiera grow up in care?

                                              **Tanya**
             You think Kiera could be the Stitchwell Love Child?!
                        Now you are speaking in tongues!

**Priya**
It's not such a stretch.
She stayed local.
Axe to grind.
Statistically, you're most likely to be murdered by a
family member.

**Al**
Or exasperated friends.

**Priya**
Don't bother.
I've got files on you both.

**Tanya**
I wish that was a joke...
Right, I'm going to reach out to Stella's group.
I think it meets on Thursdays.
I'll rally the troops.
So see you both there?

**Priya**
I'll get onto Clive.
Let's do the Lord's work 🙏 .

**Al**
God help us.

# PARENTCHAT
Clearer Community Communication
## ST NONNATUS CE PRIMARY
*Ora et labora*


**Flatford FC**
Eric


**Tuesday 15 November**
09.24

**Eric**
Hey Everyone!
Big Game this weekend – away to Easthampton!
The last one was an absolute cracker!
The girls and I thought we'd make a day of it, best fish
and chips around!
So a few spare seats in our van if anyone wants!


12.35


**Eric**
Last knockings!
Let me know!


14.58


*Laura joined the group 'Flatford FC'*

**Eric**
Oh hi Laura love!
You up for some footie?

**Laura**
Sorry! Wrong group


*Laura left the group*

**Eric**
No worries!
Busy lives!
Take care all!

# Clive

'Ah, the bounty of liberal guilt,' I say as I survey the cornucopia of donations for this absurd 'Love Day' upon arrival at the school.

'Liberal guilt tastes better than hunger,' Andy muses as he picks up a jar. 'Although what the feck someone who can't afford a sliced white is going to put with their artisanal sweet onion marmalade is anyone's guess . . .'

'It's bourgeois fly-tipping,' I scoff. 'People merely offloading the excesses of their gluttony and claiming it in the name of charity. Charity isn't charity unless it costs you something.'

'Is that what I am?' Andy grins at me. 'Am I your artisanal sweet onion marmalade?'

'You're a pain in my artisanal,' I quip back as we arrive at my office.

I insert the key to unlock my office door. Andrews's open-door policy is an affront to personal privacy and I shan't be participating. But my door is already unlocked. This is most irregular. I always lock my door. For very good reason . . .

'Oh, Clivey,' Andy whispers in my ear as we walk into my office. 'Someone been geggin' in your dodgy dealings . . . ?'

'I must have forgotten to lock it,' I say, still fairly confident I did not. 'Now go and do your job. And shut the door behind you . . .'

'Yes, boss,' he calls out with a mocking salute, swaggering off down the hallway towards the kitchen and leaving my door wide open. The man is immune to closing doors, front, back and, most disconcertingly, lavatorial . . . But I can't help but smile behind his back as I close it on his behalf. Perhaps I'm being paranoid. I've been somewhat distracted lately – not least by Andy. And I refuse to let it spoil my chipper mood. We've just been out for a bite and I'm feeling replete with blessings and breakfast.

Last night when I returned home from a late governor's meeting, Andy had prepared the most beautiful seafood linguine – I didn't even have to buy the ingredients. This makes me deeply dubious about their provenance, but what the eye can't see, the heart can't grieve . . . And so this morning I took him out to 'Toast', some kind of temporary, cash-only establishment of his choosing (Andy calls it a 'pop up', I call it a 'tax dodge') where he entreated me to try something titled 'smashed avo on sourdo'.

Quite why this Lauraceae had to be subjected to such violence was beyond me, but I admit it made a refreshing change from my usual sliced grapefruit and a hard-boiled egg. Those who customarily cohabit will be inured to the simple pleasure of dining *a deux*. I had almost forgotten the convivial delight of sharing a table with another human, discussing trivialities over toast. And how invigorating it can be when that other person introduces you to new things – I confess to being a little set in my ways. I've never considered myself a lonely person – I have always enjoyed, preferred indeed, my own company. But, rather like avo on sourdo, perhaps one doesn't know what one's missing until it is placed in front of you. So overall my experience at Toast was a pleasant enough way to spend an early Wednesday morning. Although I will require rather more persuading as to why I was unable to order a simple coffee without a working knowledge of Italian and fourteen assorted milk alternatives.

My office phone rings.

'Yes,' I reply curtly. I see no need for extraneous greetings at this point in the day.

'Mr Baxendale,' Marcia from the office replies, remembering as she always does that staff should be addressed by their full title and surname. 'Your nine o'clock is here.'

'Send them down,' I say, referring to my desk diary to see who has the displeasure.

Ah, Priya Mistry. Interesting character. Her background is in law enforcement, but I could see a future for her in the secret service. Or the Cosa Nostra – she has an air of clandestine authority that would work well in either field. I'm not easily disconcerted. But Ms Mistry has retained an air of interrogation that I must be mindful to tread around carefully.

There is a knock on the door and, atypically, I get up to

open it. When she joined us two years ago, Ms Mistry asked for several modifications to be made to allow her electric wheelchair access to our Victorian building. I refused to finance most of them, so this extra effort feels like a fair concession.

'Priya,' I say brightly (parents should be addressed by first names only). 'What a pleasure to see you this fine morning.'

'Blimey,' she says, wheeling past me suspiciously – she does everything suspiciously, 'someone's had their Weetabix.'

I smile to myself as I think of my pummelled avocado. Its effects are clearly palpable.

I return to my desk chair and lean forward in a show of interest.

'How is young Anya settling in?'

She raises an eyebrow.

'This is her second year, Clive,' she deadpans. 'She's been here longer than most of her teachers.'

This is why I don't fritter time away on small talk. And I'll even overlook the lack of correct address. That avocado is playing havoc with my sense of propriety.

'So glad. What can I do for you?'

'I'd like to submit a request for a translation upgrade for Parentchat,' says Priya, removing some paperwork from her bag and handing it over to me. I skim it, but I already know it will have been filled in correctly. Priya Mistry has a rare and pleasing eye for details.

'Translation software?' I summarise. 'To what end?'

'As our community diversifies – and not before time, might I add, Flatford is as monochrome as a magnolia paint chart – it's becoming clear that certain of our parents . . . er, carers, er guardians . . .'

'I believe today's terminology is "supporting adults",' I say with the incline of my eyebrows that such nonsense deserves.

'Yes – they are unable to access much of the school communication as they do not speak sufficient English.'

'I see,' I say, leaning back in my chair and preparing my 'no'. 'So . . . you're asking the school to subsidise the decision made by certain families to migrate to a country in which they do not speak the language?'

'I suppose I am,' she says with a dangerous smile. 'Although I'm not sure how much choice you think the Kovalenko family had when they left Ukraine. Or Mariam Darwish when she travelled here heavily pregnant after her husband was killed in Syria. In fact, now I think about it, I'm not sure Adel's trip here from Afghanistan was a Disney cruise . . .'

She's lucky I'm in a good mood. As such, I'm prepared to consider her point.

'I think there are broader applications that justify the cost,' she continues. 'The software can also be used in the classroom for students and will even live translate online meetings, which would enable families without much English to access home learning and virtual meetings, as well as making school life more accessible to anyone who is Deaf or hard of hearing . . .'

She drifts off and I note her eyes wandering across my desk to Bootleg Barry's handiwork. Andy's useful local knowledge, it has transpired, extends beyond Toast. She can't possibly know what they are, but I'm uncomfortable with her being even faintly aware of their existence.

'Sorry,' I say with faux mortification, 'such a mess.'

I sweep the statements into a folder and put them in my drawer. Away from Priya eyes, if you will . . . I smile at my internal joke. I'm, as they inaccurately say, on fire today.

'What did I miss?' Priya asks in her clipped way.

'Sorry?' I ask, my mind still celebrating my *bon mots*.

'The joke?' she says. 'Or whatever just made you smile. An odd response to a serious conversation, Mr Baxendale?'

The smile drops from my face. Priya Mistry also has an inconvenient and invasive eye for details. Come along, Clive. Stay alert.

'My apologies, it's a busy time,' I say smoothly, looking back over her proposal before folding it up and returning it to her. 'And this is a considerable extra item of capital expenditure that I can't possibly justify to the governors with budgets as they are.'

Priya looks at me coolly before removing another piece of paper from her bag.

'Is that so?' she says. 'And yet, with this software, the school would be able to accommodate more children for whom English is not their first language. 'Children who receive a not-insignificant government subsidy. I've done some rough sums.'

She hands over a printout of a spreadsheet. I mentally check her calculations. They are meticulous. She is right – the cost of the software would be amply covered by just one additional EAL pupil. Any more and we'd be in profit.

'I see,' I tell her, putting her paper to one side. 'Now you're talking my language.'

And there I am again! This must be how Oscar Wilde felt. Although if Ms Mistry understood my joke, she's not sharing it.

'So?' she asks impudently.

'So,' I reply deliberately. 'I will have to run a full cost analysis – but, in principle, it sounds like an excellent enhancement to our school community.'

'Or an excellent enhancement to your school coffers?' she not incorrectly surmises.

'Virtue is its own reward,' I tell her.

'And no good deed goes unpunished,' she quotes back. What does she mean by that? What does she know . . . ?

'What the actual FUCK, Clive?'

The volcanic verbal eruption at my door frame makes us both startle and enquire after the source of the interruption.

'You all right, Kiera?' says Priya, with no small degree of amusement. 'Has Clive cut your crayon budget?'

'Screw you, Priya,' she snaps. 'Clive – I need to talk to you. Now.'

Her unprofessionalism makes me positively tumescent with rage.

'As you can see, Mrs Fisher,' I veritably spit at her, 'I am in a meeting with a parent . . .'

'Oh, don't mind me,' Priya says, reversing her wheelchair and heading for the door. 'I'm done. You're all hers. Bye, both.'

She wheels out of the room to a scowl from Kiera, who slams the door shut behind her. I want to stand up, but I find myself presently unable.

'Might I remind you, Mrs Fisher,' I remonstrate with

Kiera, 'that we are required to hold ourselves to the highest possible standards of professionalism at all times at St Nonnatus and that offensive outburst is—'

'You turned her down,' she says, slamming a form down on my desk. 'You turned my Grace down for the hardship funding. Why?'

I peer at the paper, although I know exactly what it is. I've been bodily anticipating this discussion from the moment I signed it.

'Firstly,' I say more calmly, 'I didn't turn Grace down for anything. You submitted the application. It is you I am declining.'

'Why?' she asks again. 'On what grounds?'

'You said it yourself,' I respond. 'It is a Hardship Fund. Respectfully, your family's income does not meet our definition of hardship.'

'Your "definition" was made before it cost £80 to fill a bloody car with petrol! Before our gas bill tripled! Before our mortgage nearly doubled! So – *respectfully* – you can stick your sodding "definition" up your arse!'

She is practically panting with ire. It's delicious.

'Mrs Fisher,' I say glacially, 'do you recall the conversation we had last February about teaching assistant salaries?'

'The one where I told you that your zero-hour contracts were bordering on infringing modern anti-slavery laws?'

'The very same,' I reply with a smile. 'And, courtesy of your rabble rousing amongst the support staff, you were all put on salary last March. Am I correct?'

'You know you are,' she seethes.

'So you now earn a salary of eighteen thousand pounds per annum?'

'Your point?'

I pause for as long as I can without disgracing myself.

'In order to be eligible for consideration for the Hardship Fund, at least one . . . supporting adult . . . must be earning seventeen thousand pounds or under.'

'*What?* Since when?' she rages.

I smile at her like Eve's serpent.

'Since last March.'

Her chest heaves and her hands twitch.

'You said anyone could apply,' she glowers.

'And I was entirely correct,' I point out. 'But I didn't say everyone was eligible. You need to learn that you can't break all the rules—'

'What's that supposed to mean?' she interrupts. I've hit a nerve. Good. I drop my voice to a low whisper. It's a touch dramatic, but the circumstances call for it. I lean towards her.

'You know very well what I mean,' I tell her. Even though I'm not at all sure she does.

Her fingers curl. I think she's going to slap me.

What a delectable proposition.

After a few heaving breaths, she calms herself and lifts those limpid, defiant eyes to me.

'You'll get yours, Clive,' she finally glowers. 'If I have to give it to you myself.'

She turns on her heel and storms out of the door – where she nearly trips over Priya Mistry, who has clearly been eavesdropping outside.

'You okay, Kiera?' Priya goads. 'You seem a little . . . het up?'

'Get out the damn way!' Kiera yells at her. 'And mind your own fucking business!'

'I would have done,' Priya grins, looking straight at me. 'But someone wouldn't finance wheelchair-accessible doors . . .'

# Kiera

I am so bloody furious there's no way I can go back to class. The Tigers are learning about the suffragettes and no one wants to hear my opinion on men right now. I storm through the corridors, trying not to hit anything or anyone. That man is fucking evil. Who takes pleasure in denying a little girl a school trip? What is wrong with him? What have I ever done to him? Apart from the odd petition, constant denigration and maybe, just maybe, when I was pissed at last year's staff Christmas party, slipping an anonymous photocopy of my arse on his desk?

I'm so enraged I storm round a corner . . . and slam square into Ben.

'Er . . . no running in the corridors, Mrs Fisher,' he chides, holding my shoulders to help me regain my balance after rebounding off his astonishingly solid chest. 'You're lucky we're not doing *mauvais* points any more . . .'

One look at my face informs him I'm not playing today.

'Kiera?' he says softly, his face full of concern. 'Are you okay? Look, I've been meaning to talk to you about last week. I'm so sorry if I—'

'It's Clive,' I interrupt. 'He's rejected Gracie's application for the Year 6 residential and I've got no idea how I'm going to . . .'

I stop. I can feel the heat of tears and I'm not doing this in front of Ben.

'Hey,' he says softly. 'I'm so sorry to hear that.'

'I'm gonna kill him. I'm gonna bloody kill him,' I rage.

'Well, that's a lot of *mauvais* points,' he smiles. I feel myself softening. That smile . . . 'And listen – Clive doesn't have the final word on all these things. Leave it with me. I'll see what I can do.'

I melt into his concerned, caring face.

'Really?' I ask him.

'Really,' he confirms with a wink. 'But I need you on playground duty. Khadija and Anya have started a chapter of Women's Lib, which largely involves imprisoning the boys under the climbing frame for their contribution to the patriarchy . . .'

I laugh. But then I think of that note.

# CHEAT

Someone's watching me. I have to be careful.

'On my way,' I say as Marcia rushes towards us. The way that woman covers ground is astonishing. But maybe not surprising in a former parkour champion.

'Oh God,' says Ben. 'Ofsted?'

'Stand down,' she smiles.

'Thank Christ,' Ben sighs. Ofsted is the tax audit, or megapixel camera, or eighties TV presenter of the education world. Not something you ever want looking at you too closely.

'Kiera – it's you I'm looking for,' she says kindly as Ben takes a quiet step backwards. 'I've got a phone call for you.'

'Oh, I'm so sorry, Marcia – I forgot my mobile at home. If it's Matt asking what to get for dinner, tell him it's Fridge Surprise tonight.'

'No,' she says with a smile. 'It's Lucy Ellis from Flatford High.'

Shit. The head. Taylor.

'You go,' says Ben before I even have to ask. 'I'll go and liberate the lads. I hope everything's okay.'

I'm already racing towards the office before he can finish.

'Hello?' I say quickly as I snatch up the office phone. Calls from the school are never good. Especially from Taylor's.

'Hello, Mrs Fisher – Mrs Ellis here, Taylor is fine,' says the Flatford High headteacher smoothly. She must make this call twenty times a day – she's a pro.

'Phew!' I say with faux relief. If she's physically fine, that means something else is wrong. Secondary schools rarely call with good news.

'I'm afraid to say there's been a bullying incident,' she says. 'We're going to need you to come and collect Taylor.'

'Shit – sorry – I mean, oh my God – is she okay?' I garble.

'As I said, she's fine,' Mrs Ellis reassures. 'But I'm going to need you or your husband to come in.'

'Of course,' I say obediently. 'I'll be there in ten minutes – leaving now.'

'Drive safely,' she says, reminding me that Matt has the bloody car today. 'We'll see you shortly.'

I race through the drizzle to Flatford High School, another institution in which it feels like I've been imprisoned for a lifetime. St Nonnatus has at least tried to modernise in the past twenty years – FHS doesn't even pretend. It knows that no one from here will ever amount to anything, so there's little point in investing in either its buildings or its students. To say it's a bog-standard comprehensive would be deeply unfair to a lot of bogs.

I desperately didn't want Taylor to come here. I tried to prep her for the 11+ so she could go to Westmouth Grammar. But she didn't get in, even after I appealed. Tay doesn't haven't Grace's artistic talents, isn't sporty and has the musical sense of a spoon, so a scholarship to Shottsford House wasn't an option. When she started here, she was in all the top sets, winning prizes and doing really well. Every day I looked forward to her bringing home some certificate or accolade. Now I just pray she doesn't bring home a positive pregnancy test or crabs. I only managed to avoid one . . .

But if she's being bullied, maybe that's why she's being so difficult? Hurt people hurt people, right? And you can bet your ass I'm going to hurt whoever's been hurting my little girl. Because somewhere, underneath the acne and attitude, I know she's still there. My Tayta Tot. My baby girl. Empty nesters bemoan their kids leaving home, but the truth is you lose them long before they leave. Screens. Friends. Crushes. Shopping centres. There are any number of things competing for your teens' attention, and they have one helluva marketing campaign. I remember wishing when she was tiny that she'd let me have a moment's peace. And now I'd give anything for her to demand I take her to the park, or that I watch her favourite show, or we make cupcakes together.

Although it is quite nice having a wee by myself.

I wind easily through the school's nondescript corridors to the head's office – the layout also hasn't changed in twenty years, so I can find the route on autopilot. I knock, but the door is ajar and I can see Taylor sitting in one of the chairs with her arms crossed defiantly. She's putting on her game face – she gets that from me – but her eyeliner is smudged. She's been crying. A woman around my age is sitting across the room with what must be her son. They both look rough as fifty bears. Life has given me every excuse to look and act like crap, so I have no time for anyone else not making the effort. The woman's barely got dressed and her son's uniform is filthy. So that's the little shit, is it? Brace yourself, sunshine. You picked on the wrong kid.

'Mrs Fisher, thank you for coming,' says Mrs Ellis, gesturing to the empty chair. 'Do have a seat . . .'

Vicky Pollard is straight off her chair and in my face.

'WHAT THE HELL'S YOUR LITTLE SLAG DOING MAKING UP SHIT ABOUT MY NATE?' she yells, jabbing her finger in my chest.

I've been told a few times that I have an anger problem. I don't have any problems with my anger.

But this bitch is about to.

'Get your hands off me,' I snarl, pushing her away. I lived a lot of places growing up and evolution teaches you to fight back pretty fast. 'And you say one more thing about my daughter and you'll be eating your dinner through a straw.'

'Don't you fucking freaten my mum!' says darling Nate, knocking back his chair and getting right up in my grill. 'Someone needs to teach you and your gobby slut to keep your filthy mouths shut!'

'You touch her, we'll end you both!' Taylor screams, lunging at him.

It's not really the time nor place.

But kinda nice to note that my daughter still wants to do something with me.

'Everyone! Enough!' Mrs Ellis barks. 'Any more of that language or behaviour and I will be calling the police!'

This isn't the first of these situations she's dealt with in this school, so I know she means it – Marie Tintell spent a night in the cells after laying out Jason Forbes's dad in the car park over his son's Instagram posts. This rough bint isn't worth it.

And the last thing I need right now is attention from the police.

I stare Vicky Pollard down and wait for her to back off. I'm not going to start a fight. But I'm not ending it either. She curls her lip at me and drops back into her chair, pulling her son with her. I smile reassuringly at Taylor and we both take our seats.

'Now,' says Mrs Ellis with a calming breath, 'there has been a serious breach of the school's anti-bullying rules and we are all here to try to find a constructive way forward.'

Pollard scoffs, but I don't take the bait. Let her look like an arse. By the time I'm done here, her Nate's going to be out of this school faster than you can say, 'Do you want fries with that?'

Mrs Ellis draws a breath.

'As everyone is aware, we have recently had to amend our bullying policy to include cyber activity, such is the extent of the challenges we are facing from unacceptable behaviour online.'

I give Nate a look that could set concrete. I hope he understands it. It's saying, 'Anything you've sent a picture of to my child does not leave this building with you today.'

'We keep impressing upon our students that not only is anything posted online subject to the same laws around defamation and slander as any other media,' Mrs Ellis continues, 'but that the impression left by these words – technically and emotionally – is entirely indelible.'

'She's a fucking liar!' Nate's mum rages again, pointing at Taylor. 'My boy ain't done nuffin!'

'Wind your neck in,' I tell her, 'or I'll do it for you.'

'Both of you!' Mrs Ellis snaps in a cautionary tone. 'Final warning.'

Vicky Pollard gets back in her box. I look over at Taylor.

She's staring doggedly forward. She gets that move from me too. What has this shitbag done to her? I admire her standing up to him, but why didn't she tell me?

Mrs Ellis pulls out a phone and places it on the desk. It's Taylor's . . . Why?

'We have been investigating a social media account that goes by the name of "Themis",' Mrs Ellis continues. 'It has been broadcasting incendiary allegations about a number of students and staff and has caused a great deal of upset.'

Oh shit. Themis. I've heard about this. Lots of people are talking about it, even kids at St Nonn's. And this rancid chav has been posting about my girl?

This is serious. Enough already.

'What the hell did you say?' I spit at him. 'Because I will come after you with the police, lawyers, Satan incarnate himself if you've been—'

'Mrs Fisher,' Mrs Ellis speaks over me, 'I'm afraid you've misunderstood. Taylor is not the victim here. Nathan is.'

But . . . what . . . ? I look at Taylor, who is still refusing to turn my way. But it's a red rag to Vicky Pollard.

'Yeah – that shut you up, dinnit, you mouthy cow!' she rants. 'Your little tart has been saying that my boy's been taking pictures of all the girls' fannies—'

'"Upskirting" is the term, Ms Roberts . . .' Mrs Ellis interjects.

'Yeah, well, whatever – he ain't done it. My Nate's a good boy. He's got a trial with Easthampton Rovers – he's gonna be in the Premiership; he's going places. And this shit sticks! The club saw the post and called him in! He ain't done nuffin!'

Taylor mutters something quietly. I'm sitting next to her and even I can't hear it.

'You have something to say, Taylor?' Mrs Ellis asks firmly.

'Tay?' I ask.

Taylor looks hatefully at Nate.

'I said,' she growls, 'yes he has. He's been upskirting all of us. He doesn't even try to hide it. He even comes into the girls' toilets – says he's a "tranny" like Seb and no one can stop him – then he takes pictures under the cubicle doors. It's disgusting.'

'You little perv!' I hiss at Nate.

'He ain't no perv!' his mum screams. 'Your girl's a lying little—'

'Taylor, this is a very serious accusation,' Mrs Ellis shouts over us all. 'Why haven't you raised it through official channels?'

'Because what's the point?' Taylor shouts back, raising her hands. 'What did you do when we complained that Kyle kept showing us all his dick? Or when we tried to tell you that Mr Falston keeps staring at our tits? Or when Ryan Smith told Olivia Jacobs that he'd post naked deepfakes of her online unless she sucked him off! We have told you all of this! No one DOES ANYTHING!'

I still can't speak. I'm Taylor twenty years ago. In this school. In this state. How has nothing changed?

'Taylor, none of these allegations have been proven and I can assure you that I would have treated them with the utmost gravity if they had,' Mrs Ellis says. 'But what we are discussing right now are the damaging claims made on Themis. And Ms Roberts has reason to believe that you are responsible for them.'

'They all know it's her,' Nate's mum chimes in. 'She and her freak mates . . .'

I look to my daughter for clues. Taylor holds her nerve, but I can see her fingers trembling.

'And so, Taylor, now your mother is here, I'm going to ask you formally,' Mrs Ellis says quietly. 'Are you responsible for Themis?'

There is a long, long pause. I try to hold her hand, but she snatches her fingers out the way.

'No,' says Taylor quietly.

'What a crock of shit!' Mother of the Year pipes up. 'Prove it! Unlock her phone! Make her show us what's on there!'

I don't know what to say. I don't know if Taylor is innocent. And if she isn't I sure as hell don't want it played out in this room. What should I do . . . ?

'Fine,' Taylor shoots back suddenly, taking the decision away from me. She's looking Nate's mum straight in the eye. 'I will.'

'Thank you, Taylor,' says Mrs Ellis, sounding relieved. 'I'm sure that's the most efficient way of clearing all this—'

'But only if Nate shows us all what's in his photo library.'

Vicky Pollard looks at her beloved son triumphantly. But it's a short victory.

Because Nate looks like he's going to crap himself.

And there it is. The little creep.

There is a stand-off that would make a spaghetti western weep. I don't know if Taylor is Themis or not.

But I'm not sure I've ever been prouder of her.

'Just leave it, Mum,' Nate mutters eventually, standing up. 'Let's get out of here. She's not worth it. She's just a psycho lezzer.'

'No, I'm not,' says Taylor, a treacherous tear leaking down her face. 'You're a sick, predatory arsehole. And I hope you get what's coming to you.'

'Whatever . . .'

Nate walks towards the door, leaving his mum as lost for words as I am.

'So . . . am I to understand that you are withdrawing your complaint against Taylor?' Mrs Ellis asks her.

'S'pose,' she replies, dragging herself towards the door. 'But you stay the fuck away from my boy.'

'You tell him to stay the fuck away from our bodies,' Taylor shoots back.

'Before you all leave,' Mrs Ellis says in a tone and at a volume that gives none of us a choice, 'let me be abundantly clear. If all parties are agreed, we will leave this here. But if I catch wind of any of the behaviour discussed in this room today, the perpetrators will face immediate exclusion and I will be referring them to the police. Do you understand?'

No one says a word.

'Do. You. Understand?' Mrs Ellis barks.

'Yes, miss,' Taylor and Nate both mutter back.

'Good,' she replies. 'I suggest you both go home now and regroup – I'll see you at school tomorrow.'

We all walk out of the office, but I instinctively hang back. I'd go there with Roberts. But I don't have the energy today. We eventually get outside and Taylor starts to stride off towards home.

'Hey!' I say, practically jogging to catch up with her. 'I think we need to talk, don't you?'

'Leave me alone!' Taylor shouts back, freely crying now.

'Taylor! Tay!' I shout after her. 'Why didn't you tell me any of this? How long has this been going on? Is it you? Are you Themis?'

This stops her in her tracks. She turns to me, her face a blotchy collage of burning rage and liquid eyeliner.

'And what if I am?' she says. 'What do you care?'

'What does that mean?' I ask her. 'Of course I care! I care if you're getting hurt! I care if you're getting in trouble! I care if—'

'Oh, please,' she says bitterly. 'You don't care about me! No one does . . .'

'How can you say that!' I shout after her, my own tears starting to flow. 'You're my Tayta Tot! You're my baby girl! You're my greatest joy!'

'You mean I'm your biggest mistake!' she shouts back at me. 'I'm the reason you're stuck in this stupid town in your stupid job with your stupid husband! I'm the kid you never wanted! And I'm why you never got the life you wanted! That's what you think!'

'Tay . . . no,' I beg her. 'You've got it all wrong! You're everything . . .'

She stares at me with a hatred I never thought my own flesh could produce.

'No I'm not,' she spits. 'I'm not Grace.'

And, with that, she spins on her heel and storms away.

I chase around Flatford for hours trying to find Taylor. But, if you want to, it's possible to hide, even in this small town. By the time I get back to St Nonn's, the school is deserted, everyone long gone. I head straight for Ben's office. I know he'll still be there – he works crazy hours.

'Hi,' I say, knocking softly on the door. 'I'm sorry I've been gone all day . . .'

'Don't even think on it,' he says, jumping up to greet me. 'What happened? Are you okay? Is Taylor okay?'

I take one look into his worried face. And I burst into tears.

The whole sorry saga comes dribbling out in a snotty soliloquy, my heart spilling into his office and his Kleenex. Eventually, my words exhausted, I breathlessly start to pull myself together. This is mortifying.

'I'm so sorry,' I sniff. 'I'm so embarrassed.'

'Hey,' he says softly, handing over another tissue. 'Hey – it's okay. No need to be embarrassed. I've had a few good sobs in this place myself over the past few months, believe me.'

'I bet,' I sob harder, trying to steady my breath. 'The break-up must have been so hard.'

'Christ, I don't even have time to cry about Elena,' he says. 'Have you tried to talk to Hattie about the sugar content of her treacle tart? The menace that woman can convey with a garlic crusher . . .'

I laugh and the emotional pressure valve is released. I dab at my eyes and hope that my mascara hasn't run. I've been putting more effort into my make-up lately. I don't want to blow it all now.

'Look,' he says, coming round the desk and perching in front of me. Christ, he smells so good. 'I wish I could take it all away for you, Kiera. But let me at least help with one thing. I have been looking into my headteacher's discretionary funds. Grace won't miss out on the residential. Not on my watch.'

I go to argue with him, to say I don't need it. But I do. Grace does. Hattie keeps saying I need to accept help. And this time I really do. So instead I start to cry again.

'That's . . . You're . . . Ben, I . . .' I stutter, new tears breaking loose.

'Oh, Kiera,' he says, standing up and pulling me into a hug. 'Come on, now. It's all going to be okay, I promise.'

He wraps those strong, gorgeous arms around me and it's the first time I've felt safe in I don't know how long. Something about the way my small frame fits inside his broad one, something about the way he's holding my head so gently, yet so protectively, something . . . something primal takes hold. This man is going to take care of me. And Christ knows I need it.

We stand there for I don't know how long, until the hand that has been supporting my head starts to gently stroke my hair. It feels tender and loving and . . . oh, so goddamn sexy. I daren't move. I don't want to break the moment. I don't want him to stop. I want to go through the looking glass . . .

'Is this okay?' he whispers, and I nod my head against his chest. I unfurl the arms I've been crossing against myself and gently wrap them round him, slowly pulling our bodies into alignment. My contours start to mould into his and I feel every part of our bodies connect. Our arms. Our chests. Our hips . . .

Christ on a bicycle!

The man's harder than a Russian Wordle . . .

I peel my head away from his chest and look up into his face. I must be a mess – but his eyes don't say so. He smiles down at me and rubs his thumb gently along each cheekbone, wiping away my tears.

It's so beautifully intimate.

It's so fucking hot.

The thumb travels down my cheek, tracing the side of my face until it reaches my mouth. He runs it lightly over my bottom lip and it's the sexiest thing any man has done since Mr Darcy fancied a quick dip. I open my mouth, drawing his thumb between my lips so I can flick it lightly with my tongue and graze it with my teeth . . .

'Ow!' he gasps, drawing it away sharply.

'Oh God, I'm so sorry – what did I do?' I panic. Am I that out of practice? Did I bite him?

He pulls the thumb to his own mouth and sucks it with a smile.

'Paper cut,' he laughs softly. 'I was helping the Ladybirds make paper chains today.'

We look at each other.

And burst out laughing.

It's actually a relief. We might be heading for Wonderland. But we're still Kiera and Ben.

We let the laughter run its course before the tension beneath it pulls taut again. He looks at me with a smile.

'So. What now?' he whispers.

He's putting the ball in my court. He's offering me the choice. He's giving me the way out.

And I know what to do.

I touch his arm.

I walk towards his door.

And I turn the key in his lock.

I move to go to him, but his eager steps have already devoured the space between us and I'm back in his arms in two seconds. I tilt my head up to him – our eyes lock again . . . and then he meets my lips with a kiss that I thought only existed in the movies.

By Christ I've missed kissing. I mean real, proper snogging. Like matching underwear and morning breath protocols, kissing doesn't survive long-term love. I love it. It is the bruschetta of the sexual menu – if the chef can make something this exquisite for a starter, you know you're in for a great main course. And based on this I'm ordering the chateaubriand. Ben's kiss is passionate and longing and feels so good . . .

Shit.

I had tuna for lunch.

What if I have Billingsgate breath?

Would it be weird to ask him for a Smint?

But if he's bothered he's not showing it. Our kissing is ferocious now, but his lips instinctively mirror mine in every movement, our mouths hungrily melding as his hands explore my curves, running beneath my right thigh before he pulls my leg with sexy urgency round his hip, pressing himself closer into me. I have never wanted anything as much as I want this man right now.

Except maybe that Smint.

He tears his mouth from mine and starts kissing the length of my neck. Oh holy Jesus. My neck is the undisputed most erogenous part of my body. Nigel Farage could nuzzle it and I'd go back and vote for Brexit. Foreplay with Matt these days is a bag of chips and a power cut, but this . . . this is truly electric. I throw my head back and moan as Ben's mouth works its way down me, kissing and nibbling gently along my collar bone, his fingers starting to work the buttons of my blouse as he pulls it off my shoulders . . .

Oh crap.

What bra am I wearing today?

Not that it makes much difference. All my underwear is older than the cast of *High School Musical*.

Bugger, it's a really shitty skin-tone one. I picked it because it doesn't show through my white blouse, but it's the colour of cold tea and . . .

All right, then.

He's taking it off anyway.

I feel his hands work at the clasp. It feels so good to have his fingers on parts of my body that can't wait to surrender their secrets to him . . .

'Er . . . it's a bit stiff,' I tell him as he struggles with the ancient hooks.

'You're telling me,' he whispers sexily in my ear, demonstrating his point with a gentle nudge of his pelvis. I feel like I should be doing something – he's putting in most of the leg work here. So I start on the buttons of his shirt, kissing the bronzed, smooth skin revealed with every button. I yank the shirt out of his trousers and run my fingers lightly around his waistband, eliciting a soft moan as he continues to work at my bra. I pull the shirt off his shoulders – but between him still struggling with my bra clasp and my having neglected the buttons on his cuffs, we end up slightly . . . stuck.

'Seriously – is there a passcode or something?' he asks with a smile in his voice as we stand there clumsily intertwined. I giggle softly, reach behind my back and unclasp it in a single motion as he takes off his shirt.

Dear God, the man is gorgeous.

Buff, muscular, tanned.

I'm going to have sex with the Highlands answer to the Hemsworths.

I'm living my best *Bridgerton* life.

He gently peels off my bra straps and steps back to look at me. I suddenly feel shy. Other than my doctor and our window-cleaner, no man except Matt has seen my boobs since my twenties. And, frankly, they're not quite where I left them. Two pregnancies and thirty-four years on the clock haven't been kind. What was once at quarter past three is now more like twenty-five past five . . .

'You're so beautiful,' he gasps. And for a moment I believe him. He reaches out to me again, slowly this time, and scoops my head back to his for a kiss that could make a girl see God. Our naked chests graze against one another, denoting the point of no return. The looking glass is now the rear-view mirror. His fingers move gently down from my shoulders and . . .

Oh thank God.

Finally.

A man who understands that female nipples don't function like an X-box controller.

Our kissing is becoming more urgent again and his hands travel down my spine until he has swept me up and is carrying me towards his desk, my legs wrapped round his. We kiss tenderly until he places me down and . . .

'Jesus!' I shriek as something very cold bites the back of my thigh.

'What? What is it? You okay? Did I do something wrong?' Ben gabbles in a panic.

I snort. And remove his stapler from my left bum cheek.

We laugh again. This is how sex should be. Intimate and sexy and funny and . . .

'I'd better just move these spreadsheets,' he says, pulling a file out from under my other buttock. 'Oh – and this health-and-safety stuff . . .'

He starts clearing his desk and I hover there awkwardly.

Okay. This isn't how they do it on *Bridgerton*.

We smile shyly and he starts kissing me again. He's so damn good I briefly wonder how many women he's been with. I mucked around a bit as a kid, but I've only actually slept with three men. Barney Johnson at the Year 11 prom, Taylor's dad and Matt. And it sure wasn't like this with any of them.

Oh God.

He's pulling down my trousers. We're moving to DEFCON 1.

I return the gesture, unbuckling his belt and easing my fingers under the elastic of his boxers. I – carefully – pull them down his legs and oh my God the man is . . .

'Shoes,' he whispers, his pants and trousers now around his knees. 'I need to take my shoes off.'

'Me too,' I giggle, my own trousers stuck round my hips. We both tend to the practical matter of removing our own footwear. And I can now confirm that there is no sexy way to take off your shoes.

This is also not how they do it on *Bridgerton*.

We both pull off our shoes and socks (why the hell aren't I wearing sexy hold-ups or something that doesn't make me feel like I'm getting changed for PE?) and we stand in front of each other. Ben is totally naked, thank the Lord – I am one pair of knickers away from divorce proceedings.

Ben puts his hand on the small of my back and draws me to him again. He leans his forehead on mine and whispers down to me.

'Do we need anything?' he asks.

I look seductively south.

'I think you've got it covered,' I husk back at him. He laughs his soft, sexy laugh.

'I mean . . . do we need protection?' he qualifies.

For some weird reason, my mind goes straight to the yellow ponchos we have to wear when cleaning up puke. It takes me a moment to realise he's talking about contraception.

'Oh – I'm on the pill,' I tell him. This feels like an awkwardly administrative conversation to have topless. 'And . . . I don't have . . . anything. Nasty, I mean. Unless you count the occasional bout of thrush, but that's more of a Lycra thing . . .'

What the . . . SHUT UP, KIERA!

'Okay,' he smiles with no small relief. He gently leans me back against the desk and his fingers hook into my knickers. He pushes them down my legs, dropping to his knees to follow their course, as he kisses his way down my belly and . . .

Shit, shit, shit!

When was the last time I had a bikini wax?!

I remember the beauty therapist was pregnant . . .

And I think her kid just started nursery.

Oh Christ.

I must look like Cousin Itt doing a handstand.

But, again, if it bothers Ben he doesn't show it. And several of the most erotic, orgasmic minutes of my life follow. When I'm so turned on I'm not sure I can stand, Ben stands back up, pulls my leg around his hip again and looks deep into my eyes . . .

'Are you okay?' he asks, running the thumb over my cheek again.

I nod. I am incapable of human speech.

I just want him to . . .

Oh.

Oh my God.

Ohhhhhhhh.

Holy Jesus and all the saints in heaven . . .

Now this . . .

This is exactly how they do it on *Bridgerton*.

# PARENTCHAT
Clearer Community Communication
## ST NONNATUS CE PRIMARY
### *Ora et labora*

**Year 6 Tiger Class**
click here for group info

**Thursday 17 Nov**
14.24

**Stella**
Hello everyone.
I just wanted to say...
It was so lovely to see so many of you at the interfaith
community group this morning.
Really appreciate your time and donations.
They'll make a real difference.

**Tanya**
Absolute pleasure.

**Priya**
Really enjoyed it.
You're doing some incredible work.

**Al**
Sorry I couldn't make it.
My sitter's aunt died.
Again.

**Sharon**
Lovely morning, darlin.
Nice to meet some new faces.

**Zofia**
Loved it.
And I'll get those Polish children's books to you.

**Annie**

I've got a bag of clothes that Sasha has hardly worn.

**Karl**

And I'm talking to my work about donating kitchen equipment.

**Karen**

I've already spoken to our rabbi – he's happy to host the group at the synagogue when the church roof is being repaired.

**Stella**

This is all wonderful, thank you so much.
And I was just wondering?
Does anyone have some orange socks William could borrow for tomorrow?

# Hattie

'Hattie, you're going straight to hell,' smiles Al Bourne as he helps me 'rehome' some of the contributions for Parents' Evening tonight into the food bank pile.

'Well, at least I ain't taking these crappy biscuits with me,' I say, pulling a pack o' 'No Frills' custard creams out of the charity box and swapping them for some posh florentines. It's a sin, folk donating food they'd never eat themselves. No money don't mean no taste. And offloading crap ain't generosity.

'Oh Christ,' he says, holding up a plate of grey-looking cake slices. 'Rosie's made her choco-banana bread again. I don't know what she puts in it, but last time I ate a slice my intestines ended up like the M25 at rush hour.'

'Give that here,' I whisper, and slide it straight into the bin.

'Hattie!' he cackles. 'You can't do that! She's going to expect to see it tonight!'

'And she will,' I say, grabbing kitchen equipment like a marine assembling a rifle. 'The secret is mayonnaise – works a treat. And still keeps you regular as clockwork. If I learned one thing in my nearly sixty years on God's green Earth, it's how to make a bloody moist cake in no time whatsoever. You just watch me . . .'

'Wait a minute,' he says, looking at me with the same cheeky look he's had since he was a lad. 'Nearly sixty? I thought you were fifty-seven . . . ?

'Well, maths never were your strong point,' I mutter, fuming to have let that cat out of the bag.

'HATTIE!' he roars like a great melon. 'We have to celebrate! What are you going to do?'

I whip up my batter like it's the devil himself, before putting in a great slug of cocoa. Stitchers wouldn't let the kids have chocolate, so every time I put it in a pud it's a nice way to raise two fingers to her.

'I'll tell you what I'm gonna do,' I tell him. 'I'm going to come to work, like I always do, do my job and not pay the blindest bit of mind . . .'

'Your birthday's 17 December,' he says, looking at his phone. 'Oh wow – that's the Christmas Fayre!'

'Like I say,' I tell him, mashing bananas, 'I'm going to do my job. It's a day like any other. Sun'll rise, go back down again and both me and the whole wide world will be one day older.'

He smiles and says no more about it.

'Does it make you think about retiring?' he asks. 'I mean, this place is a lot. Although I can't ever imagine you not working . . .'

'Well, I bloody can!' I tell him, chucking the mixture in a tin. 'I've been working all me life! I was putting loaves in Ma's oven before I could walk! And I been here woman and girl! I can't wait to put me ruddy feet up! I'm off to Vanuatu!'

'Sorry – what now?' he asks with a grin.

'Vanuatu,' I repeat, setting the oven timer. 'Island in the South Pacific. I read about it in the *Economist*. Middle of sodding nowhere. Just me, a palm tree and a pool boy.'

'Sounds heavenly,' he whispers. 'I might run off with you. Whaddya say, Hattie – you and me drinking out of coconuts on the beach?'

'Can't think your Naomi'd think much of that!' I hoot. 'Can you imagine! That'd give 'em something to talk about! A handsome bugger like you running off with a school dinner lady who's old enough to be your ma!'

'It'd make a nice change from spellings and socks,' he sighs. And this time he ain't joking.

'How is your missus?' I ask. 'Ain't seen the doc around for weeks.'

'You and me both,' he says, his eyes trying to smile. 'Sometimes I think the only way we'll get to spend time together is if I have a heart attack . . . and with my lot that isn't entirely unlikely . . .'

'Oh, hush your mouth,' I tell him. 'You got lovely kids – and I've seen enough to know the difference, believe you me. Your little Leo came up to the hatch the other day and told me I made the best spaghetti bolognese in the world.'

'Bloody traitor!' he cries, adding another box to the pile. 'He said that to me last week!'

'He'll go far,' I laugh, putting the banana bread in the oven. 'There. That'll be done inside the hour. And I'll even ice it like crap so no one knows it ain't Rosie's.'

Al puts the boxes down and comes over and gives me a big old cuddle.

'You are this school, Hattie Hughes,' he says. 'Don't go running off to Vanuatu just yet, eh?'

'I promise,' I sniff, a daft tear coming to my eyes. I can't bear the thought of leaving this place neither.

So I'm gonna make damn sure I don't.

'Oh, get yer mitts off,' I tell him, batting him away. 'Save it for the pool boy. Now get on the business end of that crate and we'll—'

'What's goin' on here, then?' that fool boy Andy pipes up behind us, making me jump near out of my skin. 'You pair up to no good?'

'Hey, Andy,' Al chirps, and I don't join him. I don't like Andy. Something don't sit right about him. He don't belong here.

'Whaddya want?' I ask bluntly. 'We're busy.'

'Just came to see if I could lend a hand, like,' he says, waving his hands about like a bloody hypnotist. 'It's chaos here today.'

'Don't know how you tell the difference,' Al says with a great soppy grin on his face. 'But thanks, mate. Would you mind—'

'We're just fine, thank you,' I say quickly. 'Why don't you go take your . . . help . . . someplace else. It ain't needed here.'

I can feel Al looking at me, but I don't look back. I got an instinct about folks. This boy's gonna cause trouble.

'Receiving you loud and clear, chief,' says Andy, and I can hear the daft grin on his face. His voice lowers to a whisper. 'But, if you are raising hell, let a lad in. I can spot a villain a mile off. And you, Hattie Hughes – you're all kinds of naughty. And I like it.'

I shake my head as he slinks off.

'What was all that about?' Al says, swatting me with a cloth. 'Not like you to be so . . . off.'

'I don't trust him,' I say plainly, because that's the best way to be.

'Well, you're not alone,' sighs Al. 'The knives are out for him with the Tiger parents, poor sod. I think he seems lovely. The kids love him . . .'

'Kids don't know this about that and nor should they,' I remind him. 'But, whatever he's selling, I ain't buying it.'

'Got the memo,' says Al, restacking the crates as the kitchen door thunders open again.

'Ow! What the . . . ?' rages Kiera as she storms in and walks straight into a crate. We ain't spoken since her blowout last week and she won't apologise for it now. That's just the way with her. You have to let her burn out like an oil fire. She means no harm.

'Hey, Kiera,' says Al amiably. 'You okay?'

'No I'm bloody not!' Kiera shouts, grabbing her foot. 'I think I just broke my bloody toe . . .'

'Oh, babe,' Al says, genuinely sympathetically. 'Look – jump up on the side and take your shoe off – I'll have a look. The chances are, you probably just—'

'I don't need your pity,' she snarls – and there's the problem with Kiera straight up. Proud as a peacock. And constantly getting in her own bloody way, the daft mare.

'Oh, okay,' says Al, poor lad. 'Listen, Hatts, I'm really sorry, but I've got a meeting at Flatford General, so . . .'

'You go on, boy,' I say, patting his arm. 'You've been a big help.'

'Anytime,' he smiles back. 'See you, Hatts. Er, bye, er, Kiera.'

He skulks out, giving Kiera a wide berth.

'Well, that was downright silly,' I tell her, cos I ain't afraid of her moods. 'You've upset that nice boy. Whatever's eating you ain't his fault – you owe him an apology . . .'

'Maybe,' she mutters, in some small suggestion that she might see sense. 'It's just a crap day.'

'How so?' I ask, throwing her a cloth to help me with the drying up.

She sighs and picks up the mixing bowl.

'We've put our house on the market.'

'WHAT?' I shout, spinning round. 'Why would you go and do something daft like that?'

'I can't do it, Hattie!' she shouts, angry tears starting to spring. 'I can't do it all! I can't work all the hours God sends! I can't pay the mortgage! I can't give my girls what they deserve! I can't keep running to stand fucking still! I can't . . .'

'Hey now, come on there,' I say, grabbing some kitchen towel and taking it over to her. 'This is no good. You can't go getting yourself all het up like this. Come on now . . .'

I take her into my arms like I've done so many times over the years and let her have a good old snotty sob. There's nothing quite like it. The oil fire starts to extinguish.

'Now then,' I tell her, standing in front of her. 'Tell me what's what and let's see what we can do. You can't sell your home. You've both worked so hard for it . . .'

'I don't have a choice,' she sniffs. 'We just can't make the payments. We were struggling with the interest only, but now they've taken us off it . . . And the bills and the girls and the food . . . It's never-ending.'

I hesitate before my next words. But she needs to hear them.

'You do have a choice,' she says. 'You just don't wanna make it.'

'Not this again!' she shouts. That girl's fuse is shorter than a ruddy birthday candle. 'Gracie IS going to Shottsford House! I'm not going to pull her out now! Not after all the promises I've made! Not after all her hard work! Not after everything I've done to . . .

She pulls herself up short. She don't finish the sentence and I don't want her to. The poor mite clambers back off the ceiling and draws a decent breath.

'I'm just saying . . . Gracie is going to Shottsford House. And that's the end of it.'

I shake my head. There's no reasoning with the woman when she's like this.

'Are the girls okay?' I ask. 'About the house?'

She shifts uncomfortably.

'I haven't told them,' she says. 'No point until there's something to tell. Once we know for sure the house is sold and what we can afford to buy, then I'll give it to them all in one go.'

I nod – there's sense in that, at least. Bad news ain't no tastier in small portions. Best to swallow it down in one lump.

'I'd better go – gotta get ready for Parents' Evening,' she says, dropping down off the counter and heading to leave. I grab her hand as she walks past.

'It all comes out in the wash,' I promise her softly. 'You just see if it don't.'

She nods her head weakly, the fight all gone outta her. It's no wonder. She's been fighting all her life. Fighting for a seat at the table. Fighting 'The System', if there even is one – it certainly didn't care when a young girl got knocked up by a man who shouldn't've been near her . . . Fighting to keep her baby. Who can blame her for running out of punches?

But I love that girl.

So I'll keep on fighting for her.

There's a gentle knock on the open door.

'Sorry to interrupt,' comes Marcia's gentle tones. I can see why she trained as a priest, she woulda been good at it. 'But, Hattie, Clive was wondering if he could have a word?'

I roll my eyes to the heavens, as if He's gonna help me.

'You go,' says Kiera, blowing her nose. 'I can finish up here.'

'Good girl,' I tell her, giving her a squeeze on my way past. 'Thanks, Marcie love . . . what does His Lordship want?'

'No idea,' says Marcia sympathetically. 'But he said it was urgent.'

'Urgent my arse,' I mutter, flinging off me pinnie and stomping down the corridor to his office, like I don't know exactly what Clive Baxendale wants to talk to me about . . .

I arrive at his door, pummel on it and let meself in without invitation.

'Hattie,' he says with that daft grin of his. 'Thank you so much for making time for me.'

'You've got one vegetarian lasagne and half a banana loaf,' I tell him. 'So you'd better make it snappy.'

'Then I'll get straight to the point,' he says, sitting back in his chair. 'Earlier in the week, I became aware that someone had entered my office without my permission.'

'Dear life,' I say. 'Bring back the gallows . . .'

'Furthermore,' he continues, his voice hardening, 'since then I have become aware of certain . . . documentation going missing from my office.'

'Sounds like you need a better filing system, Mr Baxendale.' I smile at him. 'Perhaps you should start with A. For, you know, arsehole . . .'

'Don't mess with me, Hattie,' he suddenly hisses, like a serpent striking. 'I know you broke in here. Give me one good reason why I shouldn't have you immediately dismissed.'

'Oh, I can give you more than that,' I tell him, leaning forward meself. 'In fact, I can give you fifty odd thousand. After all, that's roughly what you've nicked from the school, innit? Give or take.'

For the first time in a decade, Clive Baxendale doesn't know what to say.

Bugger me, that feels good.

'This is defamatory nonsense,' he says. He's bluffing, sounding me out. I'll play. 'You have absolutely no proof.'

'Funny thing living on your own, ain't it?' I say to him. 'It's the evenings what get to me. Only so much telly you can watch. I've read all me books twice. So I like jigsaw puzzles, me. I find they're a super way to while away the hours, piecing something together, little bit at a time . . .'

I gesture towards his empty shredder.

'Amazing what you can make from all them little pieces,' I tell him. 'Paints quite the picture.'

He takes a breath. I've got him.

'What do you want?' he asks, and it's the only thing he can say.

'My job,' I tell him plainly. 'You're good at moving money around – and I got the paperwork to prove it. You find the money to keep me on – and I'll have a pay rise while you're at it. I'm long overdue.'

'I want those papers back,' he says.

'And you'll get 'em,' I tell him. 'But, like I say to the

kiddies, if you can't behave yourself, you ain't getting no pudding. So I'll be holding on to them for now. Just until I know you can be a good boy.'

He glares at me like I've just boiled his spuds. Good.

'Well now, I must tend to me lasagne and I'm sure you've got lots to be getting on with too,' I say, pulling myself out of his chair. 'Although if I might make a suggestion?'

'Go on,' he says through a jaw that could strain spaghetti.

'You might want to get yourself some decent security,' I whisper with a wink. 'That lock was as easy to pick as me front teeth . . .'

# Ben

I would never wish to underestimate the damage done to so many lives, economies and mental and physical wellbeings during the pandemic, nor return to that strange half-life we all lived for so long.

But, bugger me, I miss virtual Parents' Evenings.

I'm less than an hour in, already running twenty minutes over and have no idea how I'm going to return my cheek-bones to their natural position.

'. . . and so you see, Mr Andrews,' Leslie Harlow blithers on, seemingly oblivious to the irate line of parents behind her whose appointments are getting later by the inanity, 'given that Luke knows all of his times tables, is clearly light years ahead of his peers and is socially very advanced, I can't help but think he'd fare better in the Year 5 top maths group.'

Leslie is one of the many middle-class parents vicariously trying to prove her own self-worth through her children's successes. She used to be a C-suite financial officer and tries to negotiate her child's education like a multi-million-pound merger. I smile back at her. My face hurts.

'Mrs Harlow,' I begin, 'I will have to wrap this up as I have other families to see tonight, but the fundamental issue about moving Luke from his present maths family remains the same as it was when we discussed it in the summer.'

'And I still don't understand it!' she huffs. 'Luke is clearly attaining at a high Year 5 level!'

'But he's still only in Year 2,' I point out as my phone buzzes in my pocket. 'Excuse me a moment . . .'

I'd not normally have my phone at Parents' Evening, but I've been fielding calls from Finn all day. I thought he might feel more in touch with me if he had his own phone (Elena has let me know her views in visceral Celtic terms) – but no good deed goes unpunished. I pull out my phone. It's not Finn. And I try not to smile with any part of my body at the message.

**Kiera**
You look so sexy tonight.
Can I make an appointment for later . . . ?

We've not been able to speak much since my office on Wednesday, so our phones have been doing a lot of the work for us. It's sexy as hell. I can't wait to be alone with her later. I've been thinking of her constantly. I haven't felt like this since . . .

I force my eyes and attention back to Leslie Harlow.

'Sorry – it's my son, it's his first football game tonight, he just scored . . . So, Mrs Harlow, while I'm sure Mr Bitt can find Luke work that will stretch him, it just wouldn't be practical – nor fair – on Luke to put him with children three years older than him.'

'But if you'd just—' she begins, and I'm saved from making the point for the umpteenth time by Priya Mistry aggressively running into her chair.

'Oi! We've been waiting here for fifteen minutes!' she says stroppily. 'Appointments are five minutes long! Perhaps you could get your Luke to do the maths for you?'

'Well, I never . . .' says Leslie, but it has the desired effect and she storms off.

'Hey, Priya,' I say, relieved for a sane parent. 'This won't take long. Anya's doing great.'

'Oh yeah,' she says dismissively, 'I know. Far as I'm concerned, every day she's not pregnant nor in prison, I'm winning, so . . .'

I laugh.

'Well if you're happy, I'm running seriously behind, so . . .'

'There was one thing I wanted to ask you,' she interrupts. I knew it couldn't possibly be that simple. 'Anya was really fascinated by the Love Day stuff today. she's come home all excited about genetics and characteristics passed on from one generation to the next – she's decided to do a project in her spare time.'

'Oh wow, that's great,' I say and I mean it. The feedback from Love Day has been mixed to say the least. Apparently Sasha McCall isn't speaking to her dad for 'putting your peanuts in Mummy's wee-hole', so we clearly need to do a bit of follow up.

'Yeah, so, on that,' says Priya, looking me straight in the eye, 'my aunt is boring her down the phone with fifty-seven generations of Bangladeshi heritage as we speak. But Anya was wondering about your parents? You see, I'm not really in touch with her dad, so she was hoping to feature a man in the project? Are you very like your folks?'

I'm used to parents having no boundaries about my private life – Rosie Thompson stopped me on a jog over the weekend to ask for Theo to get harder spellings – but this is next level. And, as ever with Priya Mistry, the very fact she's asking the question makes me profoundly uncomfortable.

'Erm . . . I'm probably not the best example,' I tell her. 'I was adopted.'

Dropping the A-bomb is usually enough to activate social embarrassment and prevent further enquiries. But not with Priya.

'I see,' she says, as if we're in an interview. 'And are you in touch with your birth family?'

'No,' I say, trying not to be irritated about her crossing a line I shouldn't have to draw. 'I have never felt the need. My parents are lovely. And that's always been enough.'

Surely that must stop her?

Nope.

'Interesting,' she says. 'What brought you to Westmouth? You're a long way from home in Inverness?'

Now I'm worried. I never told Priya I lived in Inverness. How does she know that?

'Look, Priya, I'm very happy to support Anya with her project – that's great,' I say, 'but tonight I've really got to . . . Excuse me.'

I feel my phone buzz again. This time, it is Finn.

**Finn**
Daddy? Daddy please please fone me.
I'm sad.

Oh God. There it is, the dagger to the guts.
'You okay?' Priya asks.

'Fine,' I tell her, stuffing the phone back in my pocket. 'But I'm so behind. Do you mind if we . . . ?'

Rosie Thompson herself barges in, sparing me the rest of the sentence as Priya wheels towards her next meeting. What was that all about?

'Ben – we haven't made an appointment – it's clear Theo is excelling,' she boasts, putting a slice of cake in front of me. 'So I just want to say what a great job you're doing. And you must try my choco-banana loaf. I don't want to brag, but I think it's the best one I've ever made . . .'

I look down at the slice of cake. Rosie's baking could plug the Hoover Dam.

'I'll look forward to it later,' I say, putting the slice of con-stipation to one side as Kiera sashays towards me with a tray of teas and coffees.

'Something to whet your whistle, Mr Andrews?' she says with a devastatingly cheeky glint in her eyes.

'Thank you,' I say, taking a much-needed coffee.

'My pleasure.' She beams back. 'You let me know if there's anything else you need.'

She wiggles away. God, I want her. My phone buzzes again. I hope it's her . . .

It's not.

> I haven't had my money.
> One way or another.
> You pay.

Jesus . . . where does this guy think I can spirit up ten grand from . . . ?

'Mr Andrews,' comes Stella McEnzie-Roberts's clipped tones, 'I want to talk to you about the boys' spiritual devel-opment. We strongly feel that, since Miss Stitchwell's tragic demise, the religious aspects of the children's education have been somewhat neglected in favour of—'

A huge clatter explodes, bringing the buzzing hall to a shocked silence.

'You did that on purpose!' I hear Kiera yelling, and see Clive standing smugly next to a swamp of smashed crockery and tea and coffee.

'You should watch where you're going, my dear,' he says archly. 'Now run along and clean it up.'

'You're all right, love,' says Andy, who's been helping her dish out the drinks. 'I'll grab me mop and it'll all be sorted . . .'

'You are an absolute prick!' Kiera yells at Clive, and I jump to my feet. The whole hall is looking and I know I should be thinking about this as Kiera's boss. But all I can see is the woman I adore being treated like shite by Clive and I just want to . . .

But, before I can reach Kiera, Hattie appears out of nowhere and ushers her out of the hall, practically carrying her back to the kitchen. I walk over to Clive.

'Everything okay here?' I ask him. He looks insufferably pleased with himself.

'You just can't get the staff, can you?' he says slickly. He really is a colossal prick.

'Ben – sorry to interrupt,' says Mike Richardson. 'I don't want to take up a whole appointment, but I was wondering if my Bea could do work experience here next term. I understand that you had other students here last year and—'

'Oi! Wait your turn! Some of us've been here nearly an hour!' Leanne Phillips shouts out from my line, which seems to have doubled in size again. She never normally comes to Parents' Evenings . . . Why is she here tonight? My heart is thumping. My phone buzzes again.

**Finn**
Daddy. Daddy. I don't like Don. Hes mean.

Shit. I have to call him. I go to dial his number.

'Oh – so you got time for a phone call, then!' Leanne yells across the room. 'Nice to know your priorities.'

Leanne is the last person I need to upset – she's trouble. But Finn . . .

'Jeez – calm down,' says Karl Davies from further back in the line. 'The man's doing his best . . .'

'What's your problem?' says the man with Leanne, who I don't recognise. 'You wanna have a go, mate? You talk to me.'

Christ alive.

I put the phone down and head over.

'Okay, everyone, let's keep it calm. I'm sorry we're running so behind, but—'

'But you have to give the most time to all these posh bints – yeah, we get it mate,' says the unknown quantity.

'We haven't been introduced,' I say firmly to him. 'But I'm going to have to ask you to check your tone and language, friend. This is a primary school. Please be mindful of how you're behaving around the children.'

'That's rich,' he snorts. 'Coming from you, you jock nonce . . .'

I am so gobsmacked I can't even form a thought, let alone a word.

'Hey! You're way out of line,' says Karl Davies.

The man takes off towards him.

'I told you once,' he snarls, shoving Karl backwards. 'Mind your fucking mouth!'

'That's enough!' Barney Brock says firmly, getting between Karl and this prick. Barney's a fitness instructor, former army man and a right big bugger. 'Stand down – you're out of order.'

'Stay out of it, you poof!' Leanne shouts back. 'Leave my Lewis alone!'

'What the hell did you just say?' Barney's husband Dustin cries out. 'Sounds like it's not just the kids who need a lesson in tolerance on Love Day . . .'

'Right, that's enough, everyone!' I say firmly. 'I'm calling time – let's all go home and cool down.'

'But what about my meeting!' Leanne shouts. 'I need to talk to you about my Zac! Or aren't you interested in my kids no more?'

'I will reschedule everyone's meetings, but this event is over!' I try to shout over the growing fracas.

'This is bullshit,' says Lewis, kicking my table across the room.

'Okay, pal, you're out of here,' Barney roars, grabbing his arms and saving me from giving this man a decent hiding here and now.

'Get off me, fag!' screams Lewis as he kicks and writhes in Barney's massive grip. 'I bet you're loving this, you perv! I'm gonna report you for assault!'

Lewis has no chance against Barney's hulk. But before he is wrestled out of the hall he manages to lash one more kick at the buffet table, which is, as ever, overseen by Creepy Jesus. The crappy folding table collapses at the blow, sending cake, coffee and Christ all clattering to the ground.

Creepy Jesus rolls across the hall floor and falls apart.

And out of him drops a half-empty bottle of BuyRite groundnut oil.

## Robocoppers
Priya, Al, Tanya

**Friday 18 Nov**
20.14

> **Priya**
> Where are you pair?
> Trying to find you at the Crown!
> Groundnut oil?!
> WTF???!!!!

**Al**
Sorry – Naomi got called into surgery.
Casey broke up with her boyfriend.
So had to dash home.
But...
Holy shit.

**Tanya**
I'm halfway home too – absolutely knackered after the
clean-up.
We had to call Bob Alsorp over that Lewis's little
outburst.
We handed over the bottle at the same time.
There could still be an innocent explanation.

> **Priya**
> Oh COME ON, Tan!
> What more do you need?
> A bleeding knife through Stitchwell's skull?!!

**Al**
I have to agree with Priya, babe.
(Terrifyingly.)
Coincidence is one thing.
Groundnut oil up Creepy Jesus's arse is another.

**Tanya**
Fair.
I just... I still can't believe it.

**Priya**
I can.
So we have our murder weapon.
And it's the same brand Ben bought at BuyRite.

**Tanya**
So Ben did it?

**Al**
Not necessarily.
Just because he bought the oil doesn't mean he used it.

**Priya**
Exactly.
But he still has a motive – the job.
And I think I know Hattie's.
When I was in Clive's office on Weds,
I saw a few things.

**Tanya**
You mean, you snooped at a few things.

**Priya**
Not mutually exclusive.
So for one thing...
Clive had a load of quotes on his desk from catering
companies, predating Stitchwell's death.
I think Stitchwell was trying to get rid of Hattie.
#motive

**Al**
Another person prepared to kill for a job at St Nonn's?
I think you're overestimating staff job satisfaction.
#paranoid

**Tanya**
Although...
That school is Hattie's life.
I can't imagine her taking that kind of thing lying down.

**Priya**
Exactly.
And if Stitchwell also knew about this thing with the
Reverend...

**Al**
You're getting ahead of yourself.
Hattie isn't going anywhere.
I talked to her about it just today, before the hospital.
And just because Clive knows something, doesn't
mean Stitchwell did.

**Priya**
Solid point.
But I... spotted something else.

**Tanya**
*I talked to her about it just today, before the hospital.*
Hospital????
Are you and the kids okay?
And I think the word you're still searching for, Pri is
'snooped'.

**Priya**
Potato/patata.
Clive had some dodgy bank statements on his desk.

**Al**
*Hospital????*
We're fine.
I was visiting an old colleague for a catch up.
Dodgy how?

**Priya**
They were forgeries.
I'd know Bootleg Barry's work anywhere.
Skilled forger.
If massive dyslexic.
So unless the school banks at 'HBSC'...

**Tanya**
Why would he need to forge school bank statements?

**Priya**
Precisely.

**Al**
So motives:
Ben = pissed off about his job
Hattie = pissed off about her job (and/or trying to cover up something to do with Rev Stitchwell)
Clive = cooking the books (Stitchwell knew? Threatening to out him?)
Kiera = ???

**Priya**
= she's Kiera
(And maybe the Stitchwell Love Child?)
I saw her in Clive's office and she was pissed.
The girl's got rage.

**Al**
Oh Jesus – I saw her today too.
Filthy mood.

**Tanya**
I think her and Matt are having money troubles.
Their house is on the market.

**Priya**
I might have... accidentally overheard the conversation on Weds.
Clive turned Grace down for the hardship fund.
So Grace can't go on the residential.

**Tanya**
On no!
That's horrible!
Why don't we see if a few of us can have a whip round?

**Al**
Oh come on, it's Kiera.
She's proud as a priapic peacock.
She won't have a bar of it.

**Priya**

Erm...

Sorry to play devil's advocate.

**Al**

No you're not.

**Priya**

But I think Clive's got a point.

If she can afford that posh school she can send

Grace on the trip.

**Tanya**

I suppose it's just priorities.

These are tough times.

**Priya**

But we have another candidate for

the Stitchwell Love Child.

Ben.

**Al**

What?

**Priya**

He's adopted.

Right age.

Right place.

And he didn't look nearly as surprised

at that oil as he should have done.

**Tanya**

ENOUGH!

Just got home.

My brain hurts and I'm tired.

Going to bed.

Have great weekends both xxx

**Al**

You too, babe.

I'm off too.

Casey's talking about joining a convent.

**Priya**

At least then she might actually be able to babysit.

**Al**

Good point 👍

Put it down, Pri.

Have a good weekend x

**Priya**

You're no fun any more...

## Priya Mistry

## Friday 18 Nov
20.43

**Al**
Pri?
You still there?

**Priya**
The bar is open.
So here I shall remain.

**Al**
I need to talk to you about something.
Didn't want to raise it in front of Tanya.
I lied about why I was at the hospital today.

**Priya**
Shit – you okay?

**Al**
I'm absolutely fine – it wasn't medical.
Well, not exactly...

**Priya**
Al, you're scaring me...

**Al**
Sorry...
The inquest won't be for months.
But I wanted to get hold of Stitchwell's
autopsy report.
See if we could put Tan's mind at rest,
if Stitchwell didn't eat the cake.
So I pulled in a favour from a mate who
works in pathology.
Owes me for a very discreet STI treatment...

**Priya**
You sly dog!
I love it.

**Al**

I am spending WAY too much time around you...
But it's not what I hoped.
Here's the relevant bit:

---

**Gastrointestinal Findings**

Oesophagus:

The oesophagus is intact throughout with no signs of injury, tears, or abnormalities.

Stomach:

The stomach is not distended and maintains its normal size and shape.

Approximately 400 millilitres of dark-coloured fluid are present within the stomach. Analysis detected the presence of alcohol in this fluid.

Approximately 200 millilitres of undigested food material are observed. The consistency and appearance of this material are consistent with cake-like substance, as reported to have been consumed shortly before death.

These findings are consistent with the reported circumstances and timeline of events leading up to the individual's demise.

---

**Priya**

Okay.

So the cake is there.

Still doesn't mean it was the cause.

There's fluid there too.

If we're assuming the groundnut oil is the culprit

The murderer could have put it in her tea, water or sherry.

**Al**

Absolutely.

But doesn't rule it out.

Which I was hoping it might.

**Priya**

Me too, matey.

**Al**

And here's the other thing.

So let's have a working hypothesis:

Someone spiked Tanya's cake with the oil

**Priya**

That's where I'm at.

**Al**

Two things:

1) That's pretty indiscriminate.

Stitchwell isn't the only person with a nut allergy at St Nonn's.

This murder feels very personal.

To potentially hurt someone else as collateral damage feels deranged.

**Priya**

I agree.

That's the act of a maniac.

Although crimes of passion tend not to be very organised...

That said, the murderer didn't have to spike the whole cake.

Just the piece that Stitchwell ate.

That makes more sense.
However (just checking something...)
Yes.
Stitchwell got her own cake.
Both Hattie and Kiera's statements back that up.

> every inch of my kitchen – you'll find more nuts in
> a convent. Anyway, I was putting out me savouries
> and Tanya was putting out her cake – bloomin'
> Stitchwell turns up and nicks a bloody great slice
> before we've even finished laying out, the greedy
> cow – when dopey Andrews tripped over his own

> Miss Stitchwell came in asking for tea, and helped herself to a
> piece of Tanya's cake – couldn't even wait for everyone else,
> the greedy cow. So I gave her the tea and she took it all back to
> her office.

**Priya**
I still think they could be in it together.
They even use the same insult.

**Al**
Even if they are it would be a helluva bit of luck
to spike the right bit.
And come on, you know Hattie.
She'd never risk a child picking up cake that
could hurt them.

**Priya**
True.
What's the second thing?

**Al**
For there to be sufficient nut protein to kill
Stitchwell as quickly as it did
There would have to be a LOT of oil on that cake.

**Priya**
That groundnut oil bottle was over half empty...

**Al**

Exactly.

The murderer would have had to have absolutely
doused the cake – or slice – in oil.
You don't think Stitchwell would have noticed a piece
of cake with most of a bottle of oil in it?
It would have slid off the plate.

**Priya**

Hmmmm.

These are both good (bad) things.

Perhaps we need to look at the liquids.

Although your constitution point applies there too.

Surely Stitchwell would notice tea/wine/water
swimming in a bottle of oil.

**Al**

Yup.

Bloody hell.

This detective thing is hard.

**Priya**

Wait till they start shooting at you.

**Al**

I dunno.

I've had every bodily fluid chucked at me and then
some.

**Priya**

What you and Naomi do in your private time...

**Al**

Ha!

Chance would be a fine thing.

I'm not sure we've been in the same room
for the past six months.

**Priya**

You guys okay?

**Al**

I'll tell you if we see each other!

It'll be fine.

I just miss her.

And work.

I REALLY miss work.

Being there today reminded me how much I love it.

**Priya**

Oh babe.

I hear you.

I would never have left the force through choice.

**Al**

You were obviously a great copper.

**Priya**

And you a great nurse.

I can throw some warm piss at you to make you feel
better 💦?

**Al**

You say the sweetest things.

**Priya**

TALK TO YOUR WIFE!

I'm sure she'll understand.

All the kids are at school now.

Perhaps there's another way?

**Al**

Perhaps.

But I'd miss them too.

Devil and the deep blue sea...

**Priya**

Welcome to every mother's dilemma since Eve decided
to open an apple shop...

**Al**

I honestly don't know how you've done it
all on your own.

**Priya**

'Complete absence of any alternative' was a big
motivator.
I gave Anya's dad the option to be a father.
And he took it.
But with his wife and kids.
So it's always just been her and me.

**Al**

Well you've done a fantastic job.
Anya's absolutely awesome.

**Priya**

I think so.
But don't tell her.

**Al**

It'll be our secret.
What should we do about Tanya?
With the report, I mean.

**Priya**

I think you were right not to tell her.
There's nothing there that will make her feel better.
Let's see how things play out for a while.
The groundnut oil bottle is with the police.
That might shed some light.

**Al**

Okay.
Thanks babe.

**Priya**

Anytime.
And Al?

**Al**

Yup?

**Priya**

TALK TO YOUR BLOODY WIFE!!!

# PARENTCHAT

Clearer Community Communication

## ST NONNATUS CE PRIMARY

*Ora et labora*

**Monday 21 November**

**Mrs Marcia Cox<<u>M.Cox@stnonnatus.flatford.sch.uk</u>>**

**To: <Whole School>**

**Re: Week commencing 21 Nov**

Dear Parental Responsibility Providers,*

We hope this finds you really well and getting your brains buzzing for our annual Family Quiz Night on Friday! This is always a real highlight of the St Nonn's social calendar and our enormous thanks as always to the PTA volunteers who work so tirelessly to pull it all together. We're really looking forward to a fun and friendly night. In that spirit, we remind you that the adjudicator's scores are final and that we would appreciate no disputing of the results on the night, in the car park afterwards or during class assembly in the coming weeks.

We also remind you that we will be offering flu immunisations next month for those who wish for their child to be vaccinated – you can find more information and give your consent for these in the link below. We remind you that these are offered by the local health authority, so any concerns about safety, efficacy or potential monitoring by extra-terrestrial lifeforms will need to be taken up with them.

We're delighted to report that we have recruited a new teacher for the Tigers – Ms Rose Sild. Some of you might remember Miss Sild when she did her student placement with us last year (and those of you with even longer memories might remember her from her time as a pupil at St Nonn's!) – she is now fully qualified and very excited to be starting her first teaching post with our lovely Tigers.

I'm sorry to say that the issue with inconsiderate parking continues and so you might have noticed that we have placed cones along the zigzags outside the school gates and around our neighbours' driveways. To be clear, these are for the **prevention** of parking in these areas, not reservation. We will continue to remove any names attached to the cones, which, I must also point out, are not hats.

I leave you with the words of Jeremy Paxman: 'And it's goodbye from me. Goodbye.'

Best wishes,

Mrs Marcia Cox

Office Manager
St Nonnatus Primary School

* In response to further feedback about our terminologies, we have once again changed our policy as many felt strongly that the term 'guardians' excluded those with biological and legal care duties towards their children, as well as confusing children who thought this meant their parents now had moral obligations to defend the galaxy. We continue to listen.

# Tickly Tiger's Diary!

Date: Monday 21 November
......................................................................
This weekend I went home with: Archie
......................................................................

*Hi - Petra here - sorry, Tickly Tiger got a bit lost on his adventures with Archie! We'll bring ~~one~~ him in later in the week when I can find ~~one~~ him xxx*

# PARENTCHAT

Clearer Community Communication

## ST NONNATUS CE PRIMARY

*Ora et labora*

## Year 6 Tiger Class
click here for group info

**Monday 21 Nov**
10.24

**Dustin**
Hi everyone.
Does anyone know if the flu vaccine is a needle?

**Al**
Hey D – no.
It's a nasal spray.
Very unobtrusive.

**Dustin**
Doesn't it, like... give them flu?

**Al**
Shouldn't do.

**Priya**
Always bloody does though.

*Borys has joined the group 'Year 6 Tiger Class'*

**Borys**
Це клас Іванни? Я в правильному місці? Переклад працює?
*Suggested translation: Is this the class of Ivanna? Am I in the right place being? Does working this?*

**Priya**
Oh Borys – hi!
Everyone – the school has installed the translation
software!
(Clive bought the cheapest one, of course, the
skinflint.)
But does it actually work, Borys?

**Dustin**
Hi Borys!
Welcome!

**Tanya**
Great to see you Borys!
Verity has loved playing with Ivanna.
Please let me know anything I can do for you.

**Jennie**
Does anyone know how to fix an accordion?

**Boris**
*But does it actually work, Borys?*
Начебто працює. Слова йдуть у дивному порядку.
Але я розумію. Чудово мати можливість з вами
спілкуватися. В мене є питання.
*Suggested translation: Maybe. Your strange order are
words coming in. But understanding I can.*
*Communication with you is wonderful. I must be asking
a something.*

**Sharon**
Ask away, love.
It must be a big shock coming to Flatford all the way
from Ukraine.
You've been through so much.
We're all here for you.

**Al**
Absolutely.
Anything we can do to help?

**Felicity**
Hey everyone!
I'm BACK!

**Borys**
Щиро дякую. Я поки ще навчаюсь. Але я дещо не
розумію.
*Suggested translation: Thank you muchly so. Learning
is very much here. But understand one thing I cannot.*

**Tanya**
What do you need?
Doctor's surgery?
Help with forms?
Local tips?

**Borys**
Ні, дякую. Але, будь ласка, підкажіть – які слова
задали цього тижня для тренування правильного
написання?
*Suggested translation: Thanking, no. Please, but – what
are this week for the spellings?*

**Leanne**
*Very unobtrusive.*
Before you put any of that poison shit in your kid
I suggest you read this: www.droptheact.org

**Sharon**
*I'm BACK!*
Hello Flick love!
How was it?
You didn't run off with a Turkish waiter, then?
Now we just need Jenna home and we've got a full
house!
You on here Mike? How's she getting on?

**Karl**
Hi everyone.
Sorry to be the bearer of bad tidings, but...
I put that money in Ollie's lunchbox last week.
It got nicked.

**Tanya**

*Suggested translation: Thanking, no. Please, but – what are this week for the spellings?*

I'll put a copy in Ivanna's bag, Borys.

So everyone... a little bird tells me...

Hattie turns 60 the day of the Xmas Fayre!

I thought it would be nice to do something really special for her.

**Zofia**

Oh I love Hattie so hard!

Yes, yes, yes! We're in!

By the way – did anyone else hear?

My mate works in the solicitor's office that's dealing with Stitchwell's will.

Apparently, she was absolutely loaded!

And a relative has come forward and claimed the lot!

**Al**

*I suggest you read this:*

I respect that vaccines are everyone's choice.

But Leanne – I've just read this.

And from a medical perspective?

It's very, very misleading.

**Mike**

*You on here Mike? How's she getting on?*

Kind of you to ask, Sharon.

Comms are pretty hard.

But last I heard she'd scored an interview with a key rebel leader.

Which cost me about three nights' sleep...

**Priya**

*And a relative has come forward and claimed the lot!*

Does your mate happen to know who?

**Fatima**

*It got nicked.*
Yes!
Khadija (stupidly) took her phone in.
Put it in her lunchbox for safekeeping.
By lunchtime it was gone.

**Felicity**

*You didn't run off with a Turkish waiter, then?*
More likely to run after one – I'm starving!
I've eaten about 20 calories a day!
But I've lost half a stone!
And I feel great!
(If hungry.)

**Sharon**

*Which cost me about three nights' sleep . . .*
Dunno how you do it, Mike love.
But she always finds her way home.
Thinking of you all xxx

**Zofia**

*Does your mate happen to know who?*
She doesn't.
I reckon it's the Stitchwell Love Child.
Come to cash in.
And who could blame them?

**Dustin**

*I thought it would be nice to do something really special
for her.*
Great idea – count us in too.
What did you have in mind?

**Rosie**

*I respect that vaccines are everyone's choice.*
Are they?
I think if you want to put your child in a social setting
you should have to vaccinate them.
Otherwise it's not fair on everyone else.

**Donna**

Oh God.

Has anyone seen the home learning?

How the hell do you make a Chinese lantern?!

**Mike**

*Thinking of you all xxx*

Thanks Sharon.

Looking forward to a few bevvies at Quiz Night on Friday!

**Sarah**

*It got nicked.*

Us too.

We've lost money and a game console.

Who takes the lunchboxes to the hall?

**Sharon**

*I reckon it's the Stitchwell Love Child.*

Well good luck to them if so.

Very least they deserve.

**Karen**

*I think if you want to put your child in a social setting
you should have to vaccinate them.*

I think with the big ones – MMR etc, then maybe?

But flu?

It doesn't seem worth it to me.

**Priya**

*I've eaten about 20 calories a day!*

Flick!

Good to have you back, matey!

Coffee soon (low cal)?

And Tan – that's a great idea re: Hattie.

And CHINESE LANTERNS? WTF?!

**Leanne**

*It doesn't seem worth it to me.*

Read what the MMR does.

Gives your kid autism.

**Karl**

*Who takes the lunchboxes to the hall?*
Andy.
I think it's time to have a word with Ben.

**Tanya**

*What did you have in mind?*
I thought maybe we could make some kind of book?
Get the kids to write about her?
Add in our own memories?
The Book of Hattie?

**Al**

*Read about what the MMR does.*
*Gives your kid autism.*
Okay, that's not just misleading.
That's dangerous.
That study was discredited years ago.

**Felicity**

*Coffee soon?*
Totes!
Weds after drop-off?
(We can try to make Chinese Lanterns together ☺)

**Leanne**

You're not gonna bully me out of my views.

**Al**

I'm not bullying you.
I worked as a healthcare professional for twenty years.
When you see the consequences of these decisions –
deafness, blindness, sterility – you feel a bit differently
about them.

**Leanne**

*You feel a bit differently about them.*
And if you saw what the Covid jab did to my dad
You'd feel 'a bit differently' and all.
It killed him.

**Flo**

*The Book of Hattie?*
What a lovely idea.
Maybe Kiera could do the cover?

**Al**

*It killed him.*
I'm so sorry for your loss.
And I don't know the circumstances of your father's
death.
But vaccination is not only safe in the vast majority of
instances.
It's vital.

**Leanne**

*But vaccination is not only safe in the vast majority of
instances.*
*It's vital.*
WTF???
Are you trying to tell me you know more about my
dad's death than I do?!!!
You arrogant prick!

**Dustin**

Leanne... Al...
I was only asking the question.
Let's all agree to disagree.
We're all just trying to do the best for our kids.
On a different note – does Adel have a parent on here?

**Al**

*We're all just trying to do the best for our kids.*
Yes.
By keeping them safe.

**Leanne**

*We're all just trying to do the best for our kids.*
By not filling them full of toxic shite.

**Tanya**

*Maybe Kiera could do the cover?*
Great thought!
You see how great this group can be!
When we all work together...
(Don't forget to sign up for shifts at the Xmas Fayre.
Atm, the bar is being run by myself, Priya and Al.
And no good can come of that!)

**Rosie**

*By not filling them full of toxic shite.*
Are you telling me that your Zac is entirely
unvaccinated?
He hasn't had any childhood immunisations?

**Stella**

*On a different note – does Adel have a parent on here?*
Adel is in the care of the local authority.
He arrived in the UK from Afghanistan as an
unaccompanied minor.
His last foster family emigrated.
So he's now at Rainbow House.

**Leanne**

*Are you telling me that your Zac is entirely unvaccinated?*
Yeah.
And he's never ill.

**Rosie**

Then I'm sorry, but I'm going to have to rescind his
invitation to Theo's Splashworld party.
It wouldn't be fair on the other children.

**Karen**

Oh come on Rosie, that's a bit rough.
They've all been in the same class for years.
I think if Theo was going to catch bubonic plague it
would have happened by now?
We don't do the flu jab either.
Just doesn't seem as important as the other ones.

## Dustin

*He arrived in the UK as an unaccompanied minor.*
Oh my God.
I had no idea.
He doesn't have any family here?

## Rosie

*We don't do the flu jab either.*
There's a difference between spreading flu and
spreading measles.

## Jane

*Then I'm sorry, but I'm going to have to rescind his
invitation to Theo's Splashworld party.*
Just wondering?
Did Theo enjoy Phoebe's (platinum package) party?

## Stella

*He doesn't have any family here?*
Not that we've been able to locate.
He apparently travelled across Europe from
Afghanistan quite alone.
We work with him through the church – lovely child.

## Annie

*Then I'm sorry, but I'm going to have to rescind his
invitation to Theo's Splashworld party.*
Theo's having a party?

## Dustin

*We work with him through the church – lovely child.*
He really is.
I'll reach out to Tom at Rainbow House.
He was Simeon's key worker when he was there.
Thanks Stella.

## Leanne

*Then I'm sorry, but I'm going to have to rescind his
invitation to Theo's Splashworld party.*
Screw you.
And screw this group.
You're all a bunch of stuck-up pricks.

You have no idea what really goes on.
Fuck you all.

*Leanne has left the group.*

**Donna**
Um, just to say...
There's a great Chinese Lantern tutorial on You Tube if
anyone needs it.

## ST NONNATUS CE PRIMARY

### *Ora et labora*

**Flatford FC**
Eric

**Tuesday 22 November**
09.24

**Eric**
Hi guys!
Gonna wind this group up!
Thanks for your time!

*Donna has joined the group 'Flatford FC'*

**Donna**
No!
Wait!
I'm so sorry!
I've been so busy with the move.
Soooo much paperwork...

**Eric**
You poor love!
I remember it well!
Absolute shocker!

**Donna**
You're not wrong!
I keep meaning to message you, but I don't have a phone!

**Eric**
Wow!
No phone!
That's very modern of you!

**Donna**
Or very ancient of me!
(Also keeps my bastard ex at bay 😈)
So I can only use these groups at my laptop.
Which I keep losing under boxes!
But anyway…
Finley and I would love to come to a game!

**Eric**
Oh!
Really?

**Donna**
Totally!
We used to love going to watch Skipton Town.
I say love…

**Eric**
Haha 😄
Oh yes!
Local league isn't for the faint hearted!
So you're a Northern lass?

**Donna**
Yorkshire born and bred.

**Eric**
Me too!
I grew up in Grassington.

**Donna**
Oh wow!
Then we're practically neighbours!
What brought you down South?

**Eric**
Love!
(My late wife was from here.)
You?

**Donna**
Hate!
(It's as far away as I can get from said bastard ex.)

**Eric**

So... Saturday then?
We're at home (their ground double booked with the
car boot sale).
It's the Rington Rovers.
So we might actually win!

**Donna**
Result!
Where and when shall we meet?

**Eric**
Well – I don't want to take up your Saturday?

**Donna**
It's you or washing Finley's PE kit...

**Eric**
Ha!
Well the girls and I always go for lunch
at The Crown first.
They do a great pre-footie menu.
And you're gonna need your strength if
you're going to be a Flatford supporter!
We go around 1ish?
Fred always keeps us a table
– I can make it for five of us?

**Donna**
It's a date!

**Eric**
Oh!
Great!
Right!
Well that's smashing!
See you Saturday!

**Donna**
Looking forward to it!

**Eric**
Me too, Donna!
Lovely to chat!
Really smashing!

## Robocoppers
Priya, Al, Tanya

### Weds 23 Nov
11.41

**Priya**
Oh my God!!!!
Both of you!
I have something HUGE to tell you!

**Al**
Bloody hell Pri.
We're already meeting for coffee after school.
I haven't even had my second tea yet.
I'm not ready for you...

**Priya**
This can't wait.
Tanya!
I've got a piece of your cake!!!

**Al**
Er... happy for you babe.
Her lemon drizzle is off the charts.
But I still need that tea.

**Priya**
Not that cake you arse.
THE cake!
Stitchwell's cake!

**Al**
WHAT?
FUCK!!!!
HOW????!!!!

**Priya**
Flick!
I've just got back from coffee with her.
Do you remember?
She went on a detox holiday the night of Stitchwell's
death? Hold on....

> **Felicity**
> I'm on my way Tanya!
> But I'm not staying long – I'm off tomorrow!
> And if I'm not eating for a month, I'm doing it with your
> cake in my guts!

**Priya**
Well before she went, Hattie gave her an extra bit to
put in her freezer for when she came home!

**Al**
That tracks.
Hattie's such a feeder.
My freezer is still full of leftovers from the Harvest
supper.
I have no idea when I'm going to eat 15 portions of
chicken chasseur...

**Priya**
Well now Flick is so full of bloody wheatgrass enemas
she doesn't want to eat cake.
So she offered it to me!

**Al**
SHIT!
What are you going to do?

**Priya**
Give it to the police, of course.
(After I've had the bit I've kept tested.)
(Got a mate who is looking at it for me now.)

**Al**
Of course you do...
But this is incredible!
Tan – this is exactly what we need !
Tan?

**Priya**
You there, babe?

**Tanya**
I'm here.
Making a Chinese lantern.

**Al**
This is everything!
This could prove your cake had nothing to do with it!

**Tanya**
Sure.

**Priya**
You okay, Tan?
Kinda expected a happier response?

**Tanya**
Sorry.
I'm really grateful for your efforts.
And you're right – it could prove I had nothing to do
with it.
Or...

**Priya**
Or what?

**Al**
Tan?

**Tania**
Or it could prove the complete opposite.

**Al**
Oh my love...

#### Priya
I don't understand.
You know there were no nuts?

#### Tanya
I think I know...
But my brain has been so, so foggy lately.
Yesterday I couldn't find my car keys.
The day before, the actual car.
I know what I think I did.
But my hormones are all over the shop.
What if I... made a mistake?

#### Al
Listen to me Tan:
You didn't.
You've had a shit time.
It's no wonder you are second guessing yourself.

#### Priya
But you're still you.
You had nothing to do with this.
And even if the sample tests positive for nuts.
Doesn't mean you put them there.

#### Tanya
I hope so. And I suppose it's better to know one way
or the other.
But Pri?
Can you tell me first, before the police?

#### Priya
You don't have to ask.
I should have the results in a few days.
You'll be the first to know.

#### Tanya
Thank you.

**Priya**

But back to actually who did do this...
We need to remember the first rule of any crime:
Follow the money.
Did you see Zofia's post the other day?

---

**Zofia**

Oh I love Hattie so hard!
Yes, yes, yes! We're in!
By the way – did anyone else hear?
My mate works in the solicitor's office that's dealing
with Stitchwell's will.
Apparently, she was absolutely loaded!
And a relative has come forward and claimed the lot!

---

**Al**

Zofia again?

**Priya**

Even a stopped clock is right twice a day...

**Tanya**

And she is right.
I'm so sorry (foggy brain again).
I meant to tell you that.
Sue's office is dealing with the estate.
It's true. Stitchwell was minted.
And a relative has come forward.
(No, I don't know who.)

**Priya**

Damn it!
But I agree with Zofia:

---

**Zofia**

*Does your mate happen to know who?*
She doesn't.
I reckon it's the Stitchwell Love Child.
Come to cash in.
And who could blame them?

---

**Priya**
You say 'a relative'.
So it has to be the Stitchwell Love Child.
Who else could be related to either of them?

**Al**
Ha!
Good luck with that!
You heard Sharon back along:

> **Sharon**
> Oh yeah.
> That man was full of the Holy Spirit.
> He could've fathered half the town!

**Priya**
But we know that only Ben, Kiera, Clive or Hattie killed
Stitchwell.
So it has to be something to do with one of them.
And it's the Stitchwell Love Child that interests me.
Ben shut me down at parents' evening.
Couldn't get any intel.
Who was Kiera's dad?

**Tanya**
No idea.
She grew up in care.
The church found her foster families.

**Priya**
The church?
When the Rev was in charge?
How convenient...
I have had another thought.

**Al**
Of course you have.

271

**Priya**
We've talked about Hattie and Kiera
being in it together.
You say they're very close.
What if it's more than that?
What if they're related?

**Al**
Wait... what?
You think Hattie could be Kiera's mum?

**Priya**
Just positing a theory.
It would explain Clive's 'I know about you and the
Reverend' remark.
But there's another fatherless child in this gene pool too.

**Tanya**
I can't believe I'm going to say this.
But the same thought has crossed my mind.
Taylor Fisher?
Kiera's daughter?

**Priya**
Bingo.
I know Kiera was still at Flatford High
when she was pregnant.
Do you know who the dad was?

**Al**
It was all very hush hush.
One minute Kiera is an A-grade student.
The next, she's out on her arse.

**Priya**
And Rev Stitchwell taught there, right?

**Sharon**
Oh no – both Stitchwells plagued Flatford High
originally.
The Rev taught fire and brimstone, she taught Year 13.

**Priya**
We know he was a ho.

**Al**
Oh Jesus.
The Rev would have been old enough to be Kiera's
father.
Grandfather.
He would have been in his sixties 🙎

**Priya**
Stranger things have happened.
And Kiera was a vulnerable girl in
the care system.
But if he is Taylor's father...
It would give Kiera a powerful motive
to kill Bitchwell.
Sounds like a lot of money there.
And Stitchers was the only barrier
between it and Taylor.

**Tanya**
I still can't get my head around any of them being
killers.
But first I need to know I'm not.
Not gonna lie – I'm freaking out about this cake
sample.

**Priya**
We got you, Tan.
It'll all be okay.
And for the love of Christ.
What would you charge me to make
a sodding Chinese lantern?

# Kiera

'Did you remember bleach?' I ask Matt.

'Er . . . dunno, love,' he pants back.

'I'll pick some up tomorrow.'

'Sound.'

Some moments pass. I look at our bedroom ceiling.

'That crack's got worse,' I tell him.

'I'll . . . get . . . some . . . rendering . . .' he grunts.

'Good. Because that couple's coming round for a second viewing and . . .'

'Kier?'

'Yup?'

'Do you reckon you could, y'know . . . focus a bit—'

'I am focused!'

'. . . Because I'm trying to give you a right good shagging here.'

Oh yeah. That.

'Sorry,' I whisper. 'You're doing great. Really.'

'Loving this purple patch,' he grins mid-thrust. 'Haven't done it this much since that weekend in Weston-super-Mare!'

I try to smile. He's right. I'm guilt-shagging. I feel like slightly less of a massive arsehole if Matt is somehow a net beneficiary of my affair with Ben. My mind wanders back to Ben's office last week . . . That thrill. That intensity. That climax . . .

'You see,' groans Matt, who is apparently still here. 'Now you're getting into it!'

'Oh yeah,' I moan, thinking of Ben's lips on my every-where. 'It's incredible . . .'

'Innit?' he roars.

'Shhhh!' I say, thinking of the girls, who are due home any moment. 'And . . . hurry up.'

'Oh God, Kier, I'm so close,' he moans. 'So close. So close . . .'

'Great. Get closer,' I say, thinking of the therapy bill should my daughters arrive home and find us having a nooner.

'I'm nearly there,' he announces with a strained voice. 'Go on, Kier – do . . . do the thing.'

'No, no – you'll be fine . . .'

'Please, Kier! I'm so close! Get me over the line . . .'

Oh God. The Thing. Of all the kinks in all the world . . .

But we're in a hurry.

Needs must.

'Matt Fisher,' I whisper in his ear. 'For one million pounds . . . Who was the second president of the United States? Was it a) Thomas Jefferson b) James Madison c) . . .'

'No time!' He strains. 'It's ah . . . ah . . . ah . . . John Adams!'

'You're saying . . . d) John Adams?'

'Final answer!' he squeals.

'Matt Fisher,' I say, glad his eyes are closed so he can't see mine rolling. 'You've . . . just won ONE MILLION POUNDS!'

I sing the ascending chords of the *Who Wants to Be a Millionaire* theme tune . . .

And we are Game Over.

After a few shuddering gasps, he rolls off and lies in a breathless heap on the bed next to me.

'That were banging,' he pants when he's capable of speech. 'Did you, er . . . ?'

'Oh yeah,' I lie. I think back to threatening the structural integrity of Ben's office last Wednesday. How can grown men need confirmation of female climax? Orgasms are an NHS dentist – just because you don't see many of them doesn't mean you don't know how they work. And don't get me started on the waiting times for both . . .

Hey ho.

There's always Fastest Finger First.

We hear the door go and I leap out of bed and throw Matt's trousers at him.

'Get up!' I hiss at him. 'The girls are back!'

'What?' he says, still in the afterglow fug. Post-ejaculatory male incompetence only confirms to me that men weren't supposed to survive mating. Evolution clearly intended for them to sow their seed, then be eaten by a sabre-toothed tiger and let us get on with it in peace.

'Get dressed,' I whisper as I hear footsteps trudging up the stairs. Oh God, why did I wear skinny jeans? It's like getting toothpaste back in the bloody tube.

'Mum, you in—' says Taylor, bursting into my bedroom, her own stringent rules about knocking apparently not valid here. 'Oh. My. God . . . GROSS!'

'What? What is it?' Gracie squeals behind her. 'Let me see!'

Taylor looks at me like I've just annexed Poland. She backs out before her sister can enter.

'Mum's waxing her bits,' I hear her say behind the closed door.

'Eeeuuuggh!' I hear Grace squeal gleefully. Not the ideal cover story, but probably less therapy required than the truth.

Also a pertinent reminder to actually wax my bits.

My phone lights up on the bed and I snatch it away before Matt can see it – not that I need to worry. He's still reacquiring basic motor skills. This phone has become like a live grenade since Ben's office. It could go off at any moment. But I just love his messages . . .

**Ben**
Can't wait to see you tonight.
You looked so beautiful today.
I want you.
Bxxx

I supress an audible groan at his simple sensuality. A single text has nearly achieved in one minute what Matt couldn't for the past twenty.

And not an American president in sight.

'What a day,' says Matt, coming round and grabbing me in his arms. He's so . . . everywhere. 'An afternoon delight AND a quiz night!'

'Are you sure you want to come?' I say, trying to dissuade him for the umpteenth time this week. 'I'm going to be helping Hattie at the bar and the kids couldn't care less.'

'Give over . . . Gracie's up for it,' he says. 'And it'll be good to do summit as a family. It'll be fun.'

I smile my assent. Ten days ago, I would have completely agreed. But last week I was Kiera Fisher: frustrated wife and mother.

This week, I'm Kiera Fisher: sex kitten.

I think of Ben and an involuntary bolt of desire runs through me. I'm going to have to be careful tonight.

But not too careful.

Matt snatches me from my less-than-honourable thoughts with a swift pat on the bum before walking towards the bedroom door.

'Right, you bloody rug rats!' he bellows with all the satisfaction of a man whose oats have been sewn. 'We leave in ten. Shake yer fannies into action.'

'Yay!' says Gracie.

'Sod off,' I hear my eldest shout. 'I'm not going.'

'You bloody well are if you want a lift to that poncy shopping mall in Easthampton Saturday!'

Silence. Well played, Matt.

'I'm only going if Seb goes.'

'No – you're fine, it's a family thing,' says Sebastian quickly. Can't blame them for wanting to dodge the draft.

'Shut up, Sebby – you're coming,' says Taylor in a whisper that only a mother could hear. 'Mum's running the bar. We'll nick some beers.'

'I really don't . . .'

'Sebastian's coming!' Taylor declares, before the bedroom door is slammed.

'Final answer,' Matt winks at me as he walks downstairs with a swagger.

My phone rings in my pocket and I both hope it is and isn't Ben. It isn't – we've snatched a few phone calls, but he knows not to call me at home.

It's our estate agent.

'Archie – if you've called to tell me that they've pulled out of this viewing after I took the afternoon off to clean, I'm going to—'

'Not at all, Mrs Fisher,' says Archie, who is younger than most of my stretch marks. 'I've got some good news. We've had an offer!'

This is good news. I think . . .

'Go on,' I say cautiously. 'Is it that couple who wanted us to get a priest to certify the house isn't possessed, because I just don't have the bandwidth—'

'No,' he laughs. 'This is a new bidder. Full asking price. Cash buyer – they're moving for family reasons and want to move fast. Really fast – their solicitor has already been in touch.'

'Wow,' I say, not sure how I feel. 'Okay, well – let's go.'

'You don't want to talk it over with your husband?'

Oh good. Casual sexism. That's the best one.

'No, Archie,' I tell my embryonic estate agent. 'I don't need to ask my husband if we're accepting a full price cash offer on our house. But thanks for checking.'

'No problem!' he says brightly. 'We'll hit the go button on that, then! Speak soon – and congratulations!'

He hangs up and I wait for the relief to flood over me. I look around my bedroom. All the details that have been irritating me for years – the fraying wallpaper we put up wrong, the patchy carpet we could barely afford, the chintzy curtains we inherited – suddenly seem like birth marks on my babies, distinctions that I love. This house was everything – it represented everything I didn't have. It's my home. And now someone else is going to live in it.

I shake it off. This is the right thing to do. For everyone.

Now all I have to do is tell them that.

Quiz Night is always popular and, even arriving at the hall early, it's starting to fill up. Al Bourne is at the front in a sparkly jacket as quizmaster and the teams are assembling around their tables.

'Where the bloody hell've you been?' asks a harassed Hattie behind the makeshift bar as I fight through the thirsty parents to give her a hand.

'Sorry,' I mutter, throwing my coat off. 'It's like herding cats – you know that . . . Yes, what can I get you?'

I drop straight into the familiar routine of service with a smile, dishing out bottles of supermarket beer or ladles of Hattie's lethal bloody punch. I take a small glass for myself.

'Christ alive!' I splutter. 'They'll all be under the table by the music round.'

'Job's worth doing, it's worth doing right,' says Hattie, flipping the lids of six beer bottles in a few seconds flat.

I take another sip and feel the warm confidence of booze hitting my bloodstream. I look around the room for Ben. As if reading my mind, my phone buzzes in my back pocket.

**Ben**
Come to my office.
I have to kiss you.
Now.
Bxxx

'Here you go, kid. Think that's the last of 'em,' says Andy, slamming down a massive crate of beer and pulling a bottle from it. 'Don't mind if I do . . .'

'Well, that's not gonna be nearly enough, rate this lot are putting it back. Don't leave that there, you great lug,' Hattie chides, gesturing for the inoffensive crate to be moved somewhere equally as unobtrusive. 'And you want that – you can bloody well pay for it.'

'You're a hard taskmaster, you,' says Andy with a wink, opening his beer regardless. 'Tell you what – I'll work for it. Kiera – why don't you go play quiz with your fella – I've pulled a few pints in me time. I can cover you here, babe.'

I look over to where Matt and Gracie are filling in the picture round. Taylor's sitting with a face like a smacked arse next to Sebastian, who looks like they're at a funeral.

'SUELLA BRAVERMAN!' Matt yells out triumphantly before Grace shushes him down.

I don't really want to play with them.

But I know someone with whom I do.

'I'm sure we've got some more Prosecco in the PTA cupboard,' I lie. 'I'll go take a look.'

'Don't be long about it,' Hattie scolds. 'We need all hands to the—'

'Who wants some Sex on the Beach!' Andy yells, to the cheers of the parents.

But I'm gone before Hattie can finish her moan. I walk

through the empty corridors. Everyone is in the hall – there's no bugger around. I reach Ben's door and my heart starts gyrating.

I knock.

'Mr Andrews,' I rasp.

'Come in,' comes the soft, sexy reply. I can hear the smile in his voice.

I gently push the door open and lean against the door frame. He's perching on his desk holding a red rose. I don't know whether to kiss him or have his babies.

'Were you expecting someone else?' I ask, walking in and closing the door behind me.

'I was hoping for Ted who mows the football field,' he grins. 'But you'll have to do.'

I run to him like a giddy teenager and jump into his waiting arms. My legs wrapped round his waist, we kiss with the passion of fresh lovers, desperate to become familiar ones. It feels so natural and right and . . . good.

'When we get downgraded by Ofsted because the head-teacher can't stop thinking about the sexiest TA on the planet, I'm holding you personally responsible, Ms Fisher,' he whispers in my ear.

'Holding me where?' I whisper back, before nibbling his earlobe. He groans. So he likes that, check. 'And don't worry, Mr Andrews – I'll give you a great ranking . . .'

He laughs and carries me across the room until I'm backed up against the wall. He's pushing against me and we're both getting out of control, our hands yanking at each other's clothes until we're half dressed and wholly aroused. I know we shouldn't – I know this is reckless and stupid and wrong . . .

But I'm going to do it anyway.

I'm wearing a short skirt and hold-ups – lesson learned – so it's little trouble for Ben to hoick my skirt over my hips.

'Oh my God,' he groans as I throw my head back and wait for ecstasy to unleash . . .

But, instead, there is a knock at the door.

The door I forgot to lock.

'Headmaster, I need to talk to you about . . .' says the

intruder as Ben and I freeze, mostly naked and entirely compromised.

Oh hell no.

Of all the people.

Not him.

'My apologies,' sneers Clive, not even allowing us the dignity of dressing ourselves as he lingers in the doorway. 'I can see you're . . . otherwise engaged.'

# Hattie

'Who wants some Sex on the Beach!' Andy shouts to the ruddy great roar of pissed-up parents.

The man's a born fool. He's only been here two minutes and he's already turned our perfectly decent bar into some kind of ruddy Tom Cruise film, chucking drinks around like an alcoholic juggler.

'Keep your voice down – there's kiddies here,' I grunt at him, handing a miserable-looking Annie McCall a glass of lukewarm Sauvignon Blanc as she gazes enviously at the bloody great cocktail Jane Brightman has just been handed by Handy bloody Andy.

'Sorry, boss,' he grins, looking anything but as Jane shoves an extra tenner in the donations jar.

'You're brilliant,' slurs Mike Richardson already three sheets to the wind. 'It's normally all flat beer and cheap fizz at these things. Touch of class you are, Andy.'

'Much obliged, chief,' says Andy with a little salute. 'But you must try Hattie's punch – it's the biz . . .'

Mike takes one look in me punch bowl and another back at Andy.

'I'd rather have Sex on the Beach,' he slurs back.

'Do you do Sex in the Office Car Park?' Flo Davies shouts as Karl reaches the front of the line. 'That's more Karl's style . . .'

'I'll do Sex Anywhere You Want, gorgeous.' Andy winks as the line cheers him on and he chucks the cocktail shaker we ain't shifted in four raffles up to the ceiling.

Flashy git.

'And you can put that back and all,' I say to the little thief behind my back.

'Oh, come on, Hatts,' young Taylor strops. 'Mum lets me at home.'

'Happy for you both,' I tell her straight. I've known Taylor since she were a bump. I can tell her what's what. 'But I ain't letting you here.'

'Whatever,' she sulks, but doesn't leave.

'Why don't you come see me no more?' I ask her as Andy lobs his ruddy shaker through a hula hoop. 'You too grand for your old Hattie now?'

'Sorry,' she says, and, to be fair to the girl, she does look a bit guilty. 'I'm just busy.'

'Doing what, I wonder?' I ask. 'You keeping your nose clean, missus? You'll put grey hairs on your mother's head, you will.'

'Fat chance.' She pouts. 'She'd have to notice I exist first.'

I put down my cloth – the whole line's queuing for bloody Andy now anyway – and turn round to her.

'Now that won't do,' I tell her quietly. 'Your ma has worshipped the bloody ground you walk on since the day you were born. She's sacrificed a lot for you and—'

'And what?' she flashes back, fire in her eyes. 'I didn't ask her to get knocked up when she was my age! I didn't ask her to ruin her life for me! I didn't ask her to—'

'And yet she did it anyway, you ungrateful little bugger,' I tell her. 'And she didn't ask for none of it, neither. Your ma had nothing growing up, same as me. And, like me, she's had to fight for every scrap – including you. Your pa was no use and there were plenty that wanted her to give you up. Said she was too young. Said she didn't have nothing to offer you. And I watched that girl – same age as you are now – fight for what was hers. Fight to give you the very best she could. Fight to give you everything what she never had.'

Something seems to have broken through. The pout drops.

'She . . . she was going to give me up?'

'No,' I correct her. 'She was never going to give you up. Despite the whole wide world – the social, the doctors, the bloody Stitchwells trying to get their claws on you for the church. But your ma weren't having none of it. So next time you decide to give her the lip, you'd do well to remember that, missy.'

For a moment, she looks like the little one who used to bake brownies in my kitchen. These teenagers can put on all the slap they like, but they can't hide the little girl underneath.

'Whatever,' she says again, and goes to leave. I hold her hand and slip her a bottle of beer from behind the bar.

'Share it with your friend.' I wink. 'And behave yourself.'

'You're the best, Hatts,' she says, giving me a kiss. Yes, it's cupboard love, but I'll take it all the same.

I go back to the bar to find I do have a customer after all.

'Do you have a Picpoul, lightly chilled?' Clive drawls.

I grab a plastic cup and slop him out a piss-warm Sauv.

'Gracious,' he drawls, picking it up and holding it to the light. 'It's like being back at the Savoy.'

'Not playing the quiz, Clive?' I ask him. 'I thought you enjoyed games?'

'Oh, I do,' he replies. 'But I like it when they're a bit more challenging. Although with a gun to my head I couldn't tell you who played Peggy Mitchell in *EastEnders* . . .'

'BARBARA WINDSOR!' Kiera's Matt yells out, to Grace's horror.

'Dad! Shurrup!' she says, slapping him on the arm. He grins. He's good people, is Matt. I'm a big fan. I turn back to Clive.

'Isn't Andy a character?' he says. 'Such a breath of fresh air.'

I look over to where the buffoon is balancing a bottle on his head to the delighted cheers of the parents.

'So's a draught,' I tell him. 'Don't mean I wanna be near one.'

Clive laughs. Or as close to a laugh as he can muster.

'Do you know, I've been reflecting a great deal on our chat last week,' he says.

'Really?' I say, wiping down the table. 'I ain't given it another moment's thought.'

'I realise now – I've been handling this whole business quite the wrong way,' he says. 'Negotiating with your . . . past . . . is a terrible way forward.'

'Bloody hell,' I remark. 'Don't you learn a lot at quiz night? Clive Baxendale has a bloody conscience. Who knew . . .'

'No, no, no – your past isn't the right table for our . . . negotiations,' he says. 'Perhaps we should discuss . . . the future.'

So that's his game. I got this base covered.

'You go jabbering about Stitchwell, and Bob Alsorp'll have a bunch o' bank statements on his desk before the sun is up,' I promise him with some eyes that mean business. Cos they do.

'You're right,' he says. 'And on that score, my dear, we are assured mutual destruction. And who wants that? No, no, no – let's let dear Claudia rest in peace.'

His eyes glimmer and my heart deadens. What's he about?

He leans in to whisper.

'So seeing as it's Quiz Night, here's a question for you: how did young Grace get that scholarship to Shottsford House?'

I try not to let my relief show. So it ain't about Stitchers. Good.

'Well, that's not too hard – I saw her lovely picture meself. That were talent and bloody hard work,' I tell him. 'You should try them. One of 'em, at least.'

'Interesting,' he says. 'You saw Grace's work? Well then . . .'

He pulls out his phone and starts tapping away. He pulls up an image of a painting.

'Much as I'd like to help you with your interior decor, Clivey—'

'You don't know this picture?'

'Never seen it a day in me life,' I say, bottling up. 'Now if you don't mind . . .'

'And yet *this* is the work that was submitted for Grace Fisher's application to the Shottsford House Art Scholarship,' he whispers. 'So I'll ask you again – how did she get it?'

'LARGE HADRON COLLIDER!' Matt shouts out again.

But that ain't the answer.

And I wish I didn't know what were.

And I really wish it weren't that Kiera did it for her.

You stupid, stupid, girl . . .

'And so you see I find myself in quite the moral quandary,' says Clive. 'If I reveal this to Shottsford House, young Gracie will lose her place. And as for Kiera . . . I think you'll find this constitutes fraud. The courts take a very dim view of this kind of conduct. You remember that college business in America . . . So, remind me, how are your plans for retirement?'

The bastard.

He's got me. Even if I play my ace, that'll be no good to Kiera and Gracie. And Clive Baxendale bloody knows it.

'Coming along nicely,' I tell him. 'Between my investment portfolio and my stock options, I should be looking forward to a grand old time.'

The sneer is back.

'I look forward to the official announcement on Monday,' he says. 'But you'll have to excuse me. I need to drop in on our esteemed headteacher – I have some paperwork for him to witness. Don't ever offer to be an executor, Hatita. Claudia's estate is endless, although a little easier now I've finally found her copy of her father's will. Indeed, I've been wading through all of Claudia's papers – such a meticulous record keeper. Would you believe I can now prove that the Stitchwell Love Child isn't just local folklore . . .'

If he wants a reaction from me, he ain't getting one.

'Fascinating,' I scoff, cleaning up the bar. 'I suppose she wrote it all down in her little black spell book, did she?'

'She didn't need to,' he whispers. 'Because her father kept the birth certificate . . .'

'Come on, Hats – let's be having your punch,' says Priya from behind Clive. 'Everyone's still got their kit on.'

Didn't see her there. She's good at that.

'I'm taking up far too much of your time,' says Clive. 'No rest for the wicked. Farewell.'

I watch him slink off – it's a wonder the man don't leave a trail o' slime behind him.

'You all right, love?' I ask Priya, pouring her a punch and one for me nerves. 'Ain't seen you around so much.'

'Oh, you know me, they seek me here, they seek me there,' she says, necking hers and handing the glass back for another. I join her, to be polite and all. 'I'm a woman of mystery.'

'Ain't we all,' I tell her. She's looking at me funny. Can't say as I like it.

'Can I ask you something?' she slightly slurs.

'No law against it,' I say, filling her glass for the third time.

'What's he like?' she whispers, gesturing towards Andy.

I let my face give the answer.

'I see,' she smiles. 'Because you know that stuff has been going missing?'

'Stuff's always going missing, my love,' I laugh. 'It's a primary school. Kiddie could lose a bloody kidney in here.'

'Some of the parents think he's on the nick. You've got good instincts,' she carries on. 'Do we have a problem?'

I look over at Andy then back to Priya.

'Yes,' I say honestly. 'I think we've got a problem.'

'That's what I thought you'd say.' She winks, hiccoughing slightly. 'Oh shit – the music round, nineties pop – that's my jam. See ya!'

I watch her wheel back to her team – she's playing with Tanya, Borys the Ukrainian lad and Rose Sild the new Tiger teacher ('10 – nice girl, speaks Portuguese of all things). There's no such thing as a casual question from Priya. What's she up to?

But I have other things to worry about. I turn back to Andy – he's now titting about juggling glasses to a slack-jawed line, you'd think none of 'em had ever been to the circus . . .

Enough.

'Come on now,' I grumble at him. 'We've got a line to serve.'

'Right you are, chief,' he says, catching the glasses one inside the other to a round of applause. 'Who's next?'

Folk just keep on coming for the next twenty minutes or more – me serving them in seconds, Andy taking a bloomin' age, pulling coins out of kiddies' ears and making tenners disappear. I bet he's good at that.

'Where's Kiera got to?' I tut. 'We need more fizz. How long does it take to get some bloody Prosecco?'

'Maybe she can't carry it – she's knee-high to a grasshopper that one,' he says. 'Do you want me to go and give her a hand?'

'I'll go,' I mutter as another parent tells him to keep the change from a twenty. I'll give him his due – he's coining it in. 'You hold the fort.'

'Roger that,' he grins, winking at me. 'Don't go getting yourself into too much trouble, gorgeous.'

'Oh, hush your hole,' I mumble as I waddle off in search of Kiera.

The PTA cupboard is right over the other side of the school, out the back near the playground. I walk through the empty corridors, the ones that have watched over me practically my whole life. I love this place, every ruddy brick of it. And I can't believe I'm being forced out of it by Clive bloody Baxendale. But I'm not going quiet. I'll think of something.

The door to the PTA cupboard is shut fast – Kiera ain't been here, the lazy bugger. I open it up and spot the missing fizz – I'm just hauling it back out the door when Kiera comes hurtling towards me. And she's in a right two and eight.

'What's going on here?' I ask her, making the daft mare near jump out of her skin. 'You fermenting the bloody grapes yourself? And I need a word with you . . .'

She turns her streaky face to me. She's been crying.

'Oh my love, what's going on?'

'Hattie . . .' she sobs. 'I've done something really stupid . . .'

'I know all about it, gal. What do you think you were doing, cheating like that?'

She stops dead.

'How do you know?' she says.

'Clive,' I say grimly. 'We got to work out what in the bloody blue blazes we're gonna—'

'But . . . but Clive only just . . .' she splutters. 'He's still there . . .'

'Still where? What you blithering about, woman?'

'He's with Ben!' she wails. 'Clive knows! He knows about me and Ben!'

What's she . . . ?

Oh mercy . . .

'You daft bugger,' I say, the pieces falling into place as she dissolves in tears. I put my arms round her. They're not happy. But they're still there. The silly bint. I let her cry herself out for a minute.

'What you doing messing around with that smooth git? He's a wrong un, I tell you. I can feel it,' I chide her. 'And what the bloody hell has Clive got to do with the price of fish?'

'He just . . . he just walked in on us,' she says. 'When we were . . . When we were . . .'

She breaks down completely and I don't need her to fill in the blanks. Oh Lord . . .

'What if he tells Matt?' she starts to sob. 'What if the girls find out? What if I lose my job? Shit, Hattie – what am I going to do . . . ?'

'Where is he now?' I ask plainly. 'Clive, I mean.'

'Still in the office with Ben. Said they needed to talk.'

'I bet he did,' I say, peeling her off me and holding her at arm's length. 'Now here's the thing with Clive – knowledge is currency. And he'll wanna spend it. All's you need to know is the price. You have to strike a deal. He'll want something – he always does. So give it to him.'

'You . . . you think so?'

'I know so,' I tell her. 'I've met a lot of Clive Baxendales in this life. You have to play them at their own game.'

I pick up my crate of Prosecco. I'm gonna need the lot meself at this rate.

'I'd best get back, folk'll be missing me,' I say. 'You pull yourself together and you go see Clive. You've got yourself out of bigger scrapes than this, gal. You got it. You're a survivor, Kiera Fisher. Now go and survive.'

She pulls her shoulders back and wipes her eyes.

'Atta girl,' I say. 'Come find me when you're done.'

She nods and her lips purse in determination. I leave the cupboard with the drinks and head back to the hall, my mind ablaze.

Kiera might have been as daft as a dopey brush, but I ain't. And I need to play smart. For both our sakes.

I might not win no quiz tonight. But when it comes to the Game of Life?

Hattie Hughes is a bloody champion.

# Ben

'Well, well, well.' Clive practically drools as Kiera slams the door behind her. 'Full marks for staff engagement . . .'

I cannot believe I've been so stupid. I try to gather my clothing and my dignity as he sits watching me from my desk.

'Look, Clive,' I start, in the vain hope that a little reason might make this go away, 'I appreciate that this is an unfortunate situation, but I just want to assure you—'

'Oh, spare me.' He practically yawns. 'Whatever sins of the flesh you and that adulterous little hussy get up to behind closed doors are no concern of mine. We're all adults here.'

I breathe a silent sigh of relief, while wanting to lay him out for talking about Kiera like that.

'Glad to hear it,' I say, 'but I am sorry – that was unprofessional. It won't happen again.'

He fixes me with a narrow stare. 'Yes, it will,' he says plainly.

'It really won't,' I insist. 'We both got carried away and this is our place of work and—'

'Yes. It will,' he proclaims. 'After all, it's happened before.'

My chest tightens.

'What's that supposed to mean?' I ask him.

He leans in over the desk. 'You know perfectly well what *that* means,' he whispers. 'I know all about your . . . indiscretion last year. Did you know she's here tonight? I would have been less surprised to see you two having an . . . appraisal.'

Fuck. Double fuck. Double, triple fuck, fuck, fuck . . .

A penny the size of Penzance finally drops.

'It's you,' I tell him. 'You're the one sending me the messages. You're the blackmailer.'

'And you're fortunate I am,' he says, not even bothering with the slightest hint of denial. 'I honestly thought my demands were rather reasonable. Far cheaper than losing your entire career.'

'That's my private business,' I remind him. 'What I did was foolish. Nothing worse.'

'Oh, I doubt our governors would agree,' he says. 'And, given that you've sent me twenty thousand pounds over recent weeks, I don't think you really do either. Your wife certainly seemed to take a pretty dim view. And Claudia was positively outraged . . .'

Fuck. She told him. There is nothing to be said. He's right. And he knows it.

He leans back in his chair and presses his finger pads together in an arch.

'Claudia clearly rated you,' he continues. 'After all, she went to no small measures and expense to ensure you could remain here – a substantial pay-off, a watertight NDA . . . I always wondered why you turned down the job at Shottsford House, but now I know – Claudia bought you. She did so like to own people. And you were hers. You would have had to do whatever she wanted. For life. Her death must have been frightfully convenient for you . . .'

There's little point in denying it. So I don't.

'But now, Headmaster, I own you. And I'll be needing you to take care of a little something for me.'

'What do you want?' I ask darkly.

'As you may be aware, prior to my appointment here, I worked in the city – I was an investment banker,' he says. 'An incredibly good one, in fact – made a great deal of money, although the thrill of the chase wore off after a while.' His eyes twinkle. 'You know a little of that.'

I say nothing in the hope it moves this along. I need to find Kiera. I need to make sure she's okay.

And I really need to make sure she hasn't said anything to anyone.

'And so I moved down here into my big house and took this job to fill my days,' he continues. 'But once a money man, always a money man – and when I arrived here, I saw an . . . opportunity to utilise my skills again.'

I don't think I want to know where this is going. And yet I absolutely have to.

'Schools turn over vast sums of money – millions every

year,' he explains unnecessarily. 'That kind of seed capital is very hard to come by. As soon as I saw the books, I knew I could put it to much better use.'

'Better use for who?'

He leers.

'For me. And it's "for whom".'

It's been a while since I gave a man a good kicking. But this guy . . .

'And so I began . . . rearranging . . . school funds into a savings account. I could use the funds for my own purposes, then recredit the school with the original amount plus interest before the year's end. It was a win-win situation. The school made money too.'

'Just not as much as you.'

He shrugs with a horrible smile.

'Well, I was doing all the hard work,' he says. 'But, like I say, Claudia was a meticulous woman—'

'And she found out,' I say, putting the pieces together. 'She was blackmailing you.'

A laugh emits from his nose, until it takes over his whole spindly body.

'Blackmailing me? Claudia?' he laughs. 'Good Lord, no. Claudia didn't want to punish me! She wanted in on the deals!'

FFS.

Of course she did, the miserly bitch.

'It was wonderful – with her on board, it was so much easier to move the money around!' he says gleefully. 'You should never invest your own money – but we were on to such a sure thing that I started taking capital from my home, as did she. We put all the money into a joint account so we could each take it out without incurring tax or suspicion. Before she died, there was over a million pounds in it! We were going to be rich!'

'So what happened?' I asked.

His face goes dark.

'The night of her death, Claudia called me into her office and told me that she had withdrawn all the funds. In cash,' he growls. 'She never trusted banks – she was an under-the-bed kind of a girl. "There's no honour among thieves," she told me without a hint of apology. She'd taken all of the money. Including what we'd borrowed from the school, leaving me twenty thousand pounds out of pocket with a fifty-thousand-pound hole in the books.'

'So what did you do?'

'What could I do?' he says.

'You could kill her,' I point out, clutching at one of my few straws.

He grins at me.

'We both know I didn't do that,' he says. 'But Claudia knew I couldn't report her anywhere – I'd only implicate myself. She saw it as just desserts for my sins and in that regard, at least, she was right.'

I shake my head. This place . . .

'Why are you telling me this?' I ask. 'You know that Ofsted are going to be crawling all over our accounts at some point – how on Earth are we going to explain that kind of shortfall?'

He smiles horribly.

'We're not going to have to,' he says. 'Because you're going to fill it.'

I'm taking a sip of water and I nearly choke.

'How?' I say. 'How the fuck do you think I'm going to find fifty grand? I've given you everything I have!'

'Well, the good news is that as of this evening,' he leers, 'that has ceased to be my problem.'

We both know what he's saying. He's holding two smoking guns. I can at least try to disarm one.

'There's no law against having a relationship with a colleague,' I attempt.

'I don't think her husband's going to care about the legal implications, do you?' he retorts. 'I can't think you want to put your little Jezebel in that position? And, even if you do, there's still the . . . other matter. Perhaps I should go out there now and have a word with her . . .'

Fuck. Fuck, fuck, fuck.

'There's no law against that either,' I point out.

He spits an unpleasant laugh.

'Do you think that's how everyone here will see it?' he sneers. 'Or any future employer? You might not face the

Courts of Justice. But the Court of Public Opinion would condemn you in a heartbeat. And, like you said, it's a terribly good motive for murder . . . which reminds me, however *did* that bottle of nut oil get inside that statue? It was in your office that night, was it not?'

He grins triumphantly at me. But I have one card to play.

'You're right – they're still investigating Stitchwell's death,' I say, 'and if you throw me under the bus, pal, you're coming with me.'

'Are you threatening me?' he laughs.

I stand up. I'm a big bugger and I don't like to throw my weight around, but I'll make an exception for this wee prick.

'Aye,' I say. 'I am.'

He stops laughing. Good.

'I'm glad we've reached a mutual understanding,' he says as he stands to leave. 'If you need me, I'll be in my office. I take it all back. Quiz Night is providing all manner of answers . . .'

I stay there, stone-faced, until he leaves. The door shuts, my bravado collapses . . . And I punch the wall.

'FUCK!' I roar, not caring for a moment who can hear me. How could I have let this happen? How could I have been so stupid? How could I—

A knock at the door stops my ravings. I rush over to open it. Kiera must have come back and . . .

'Mr Andrews?' says the visitor.

'Hattie?' I say, confused to see her. 'Er . . . how may I help you?'

'May I come in?' she asks, barging past me. 'It's a bit delicate, see.'

Oh Christ. I'm too late. Kiera's told her – I know they're close . . .

She sits down uninvited.

'Now I'm not one for tittle tattle,' says one of the bigger gossips in Flatford, nay, the planet. 'But when I see something that just ain't right, I need to speak up.'

'Okay,' I say nervously.

'Cos it's not on, not in a place like this what God's watching over,' she continues. 'And I know you ain't gonna wanna hear it, but I'm gonna say it no mind.'

'I see.' I brace myself.

She lets out a deep huff.

'That Andy's a rotten, dirty thief.'

It takes me a moment to untangle her actual words from my predicted ones.

'I'm sorry?'

'I know – everyone thinks the sun shines outta his bum-hole,' she says, crossing her arms. 'But I've had my suspicions for a while and now I'm sure. There's stuff's been going missing from the kiddie's lunchboxes . . .'

Oh, thank Christ. A simple criminal allegation against one of my staff. This I can handle.

'A few parents have spoken to me about this,' I start, trying to calm my heart and breathe, 'but there's no actual proof, Hattie . . .'

'But tonight I've been working that bar with him,' she says, 'and he's been pocketing tenners all night.'

Relieved as I am we're having this particular conversation, I could really do without this right now.

'That's a very serious accusation, Hattie – are you sure?'

'Does the pope shit in the woods?'

Oh Christ. I don't have the energy for this . . .

'I'll talk to him on Monday – he has a right to put his side of the story across . . .'

'Well, that's just brilliant, innit?' she says. 'Give him time to nick all the PTA money and do a bunk with it! How are you going to prove it then, you great melon . . . ?'

'Hattie, I—'

'No,' she says firmly. 'You need to catch him red-handed. With his hand in the cookie jar. You need to confront him now. Tonight.'

I rub my sore knuckles. Andy seems like a decent guy to me. I don't want to embarrass him. This smacks to me of middle-class prejudice. Lord knows I've seen that in action before . . . But, then again, if he is the honest bloke I think he is, it might just make it all go away . . .

'Fine,' I say, standing up. 'Let's get this sorted once and for all.'

I open the door for her and we head down the corridor.

The quiz is in full swing when we reach the hall – Hattie's punch has been doing its worst and many of the parents are absolutely rat-arsed. I look around the quizzers and my heart thumps.

Clive's right.

She's here.

I look away before I can meet her eyes. She's done enough damage already.

I take a breath and steel myself for the next shit shower. Andy's behind the bar chucking bottles around like a pro – how is a guy this talented in so many things living rough? This is going to be hideous. But this is the job.

I tap him on the shoulder.

'Andy mate,' I say quietly, 'could I have a quick word?'

'Sure thing, chief,' he says, flipping a bottle and whipping off the cap on the table, much to the delight of Sharon Dooley, who looks like she could swallow him whole.

'I got this,' says Hattie, practically elbowing him out of the way to get to the bar. 'What can I get you, love?'

Andy grabs his rucksack – he never leaves it unattended, I've noted – and saunters out into the corridor.

'What can I do for you, mate?' he asks cheerfully.

On a night where I don't exactly feel great about myself, I've never felt like more of an arse.

'Andy – I'm really sorry to ask,' I begin, 'but we've had a spate of items going missing from children's bags . . .'

His sunny faces clouds over. It's not a look of anger. It's worse than that. It's . . . it's defeat.

'So it's gotta be the dodgy homeless geezer, right?'

'That's not how I think of you,' I say. 'And I don't think you've done anything wrong.'

'Pretty words, boss,' he says. 'But the fact we're having this little tête-à-tête tells me different.'

I look pleadingly at him. But there's only one thing to do.

'An allegation has reached me tonight about money being taken behind the bar,' I say. 'I don't give it any credence, but the easiest way to resolve it, is . . .'

'Whaddya need?' he says with a heavy sigh. 'Turn out me pockets like the kids?'

He spares me having to ask him to do exactly that, by turning his pockets inside out. There is nothing there.

'Happy?' he says, now starting to look angry.

My eyes flick to his trusty bag.

'You're not serious,' he says. 'You gonna do a cavity search and all?'

'Andy, I'm so sorry,' I tell him. 'I really don't want to have to . . .'

'Aw – just do it,' he says. 'It's you or the bizzies.'

He throws the bag to me and I hesitate. This feels so intrusive.

'Go on,' he says, leaning against the wall. 'You ain't the first. You won't be the last.'

I open it up. The few contents are neatly arranged. I pull out a book. It's *Wuthering Heights*.

'Me mam's,' he explains. 'Fancied being an author. Thought it were written by Kate Bush, though, which weren't a great start.'

I put it gently to one side with an apologetic smile. I quickly go through the rest. A rolled-up sleeping bag. Some tea. A shabby hot water bottle. Gloves. Two changes of clothes. A well-thumbed crossword book. Three biros. A library card. It's not much to show for a life. And yet it is everything.

Enough already.

I start putting it all back, furious with myself that I've let these people get in my head. This man's just trying to make his way, as are we all.

'Andy, I'm so sorry,' I begin, trying to stuff the sleeping bag back in the rucksack. 'This has been . . .'

I accidentally drop the sleeping bag. It slowly unrolls.

And inside are two mobile phones, a games console and about £200 in cash.

# Clive

One of the many ways in which I admired Claudia was that she understood the power of information. At school, she kept immaculate written records – expenditure, correspondence, attendance. She reflected this same precision in her personal life, keeping detailed records on everyone she encountered in the browning pages of a leather notebook – her fabled black book. This book contained everyone's secrets and had the power to disprove their lies. In the wrong hands, it would be a very dangerous weapon.

Which is why, on the night of her death, I ensured it fell into mine.

I'll confess that my motivation wasn't entirely altruistic – despite our uneasy friendship, I too had a detailed entry in the black book, information that will now never see the light of day if Andrews plays his part, thank the Lord. I should, of course, take it straight to the authorities. But the authorities don't always recognise the power of information. I, however, do. Claudia's black book is both my salvation from my past sins and my insurance against any future ones. Not to mention an insight into just how much sinning is going around. I leave the headmaster's office a happy man. The Lord has found a way to ease my burden and in His grace go I.

And I might not win the quiz tonight. But I'm officially fifty thousand pounds to the good. Andrews will pay. He has no choice.

I return to my office with a lightness in my step. It's been a most satisfying evening. My job is secure. My reduced circumstances greatly improved. I even got a glimpse of Kiera's alabaster thighs . . . Oh, why not.

I pull out my bottom drawer, where I keep my celebratory whisky. I've earned it.

I'm just enjoying a small nip when there's a knock at my door. I tense – has Andrews come to make good on his threat?

But, when the door opens, it's an entirely different kind of danger.

'Can I come in?' she asks, atypically.

I sit back and inhale deeply.

'I don't know, Mrs Fisher,' I reply. 'Can you?'

I see her jaw twitch, but her usual impertinence is gone. I can't decide whether I prefer this or not. But it certainly feels like some kind of victory.

'Clive . . . about what you saw . . .' she begins and I raise a hand to stop her.

'Fear not,' I say. 'Lover boy has elected to spare your blushes. 'Your sordid little secret is safe with me.'

She closes her eyes and looks relieved.

'Thank you,' she says, and her earnestness almost moves me.

Almost.

'That said,' I continue. 'There are a couple of . . . other matters I should like to discuss with you. Will you take a seat?'

She moves cautiously into the room and sits down gingerly. Gone is the swagger of the impudent tart. She looks cowed. Vulnerable. Scared, even.

It is sinfully arousing.

'I think it's time you and I had a very honest conversation,' I tell her. 'And I confess I've not been entirely truthful with you. I'm hoping that tonight's . . . revelations . . . might herald a new dawn for our relationship.'

'Go on,' she says uncertainly. She's right to be suspicious.

'The night we lost our dear Claudia,' I begin, 'do you recall me entering the kitchen as you and Hattie were cleaning up after the statue debacle?'

'Vaguely,' she says, still on her guard.

'Well, I must confess, Mrs Fisher, one of my vices has always been nosiness. I'm a frightful snoop,' I whisper. 'I'd actually been at the door for some time. Which is when I saw you. I saw you put something in Claudia's tea. A tablet of some kind I believe?'

I have to give it to her, she takes it like a champ. Only the faintest colouration to her cheeks denotes any response at all.

'It was a sweetener,' she blatantly lies.

'Claudia didn't take sugar,' I remind her.

'I realised that afterwards,' she says. 'Which is why I poured it away and made her a new one.'

'I see,' I tell her. 'Now that I didn't witness. What a shame.'

'Hattie did,' she says quickly. 'I have an alibi.'

'Oh, come now, my dear,' I chortle. 'There's no need for high-sounding words like that – if I were going to report you to the authorities, I'd have done so long ago. I'm sure there's a perfectly innocent explanation. None of my business.'

I smile. Because this time I am telling the truth. I remain unconvinced that anyone murdered Claudia Stitchwell. I know I didn't. But the very spectre of its possibility is proving incredibly useful.

'Good,' she says. 'What was the other matter? You said there were a couple?'

'An excellent eye for detail,' I begin. 'Just like our dear departed Claudia. As you know, she never trusted technology – she relied on written correspondence only.'

Kiera nods. She has no idea where this is going. Excellent.

'However, she was aware of the importance of detail – of keeping proper records,' I say. 'You're too young to remember carbon paper – we relied on it back in the day. But the old ways can be the best. And, while tending to Claudia's personal effects, I found copies of every letter Claudia ever wrote.'

I watch the colour drain from her face. I pull open my top drawer.

'Including her final one.'

I hand it over to her. But a single glance at the intended recipient, Margaret Porter, Head of Shottsford House, and she knows precisely what it says.

'You can keep that if you like. I have a copy at home,' I tell her as I see her fingers twitch to destroy it.

Her jaw locks.

'It was you,' she says plainly. 'The "cheat" note. You put it on my car.'

'And, judging by tonight's little performance, wasn't I prescient?' I rejoice.

'What are you going to do?' she asks.

'Well, that very much depends on you, dear,' I say, the bouquet of possibilities blossoming in front of me. 'I know you destroyed the original the night of Claudia's tragic demise. But this is a certified copy in her handwriting. The message could still be conveyed.'

She replaces the piece of paper carefully on the desk. She raises her eyes and bolts them to mine. They're red and slightly puffy. She's been crying. I have an overwhelming urge to taste her tears.

'What do you want?' she says plainly. I have to admire her for not even attempting to defy or justify her actions. It would be a shameful waste of both our time.

I try to push the sin from my mind. But it's been there a long time and has grown weighty. I think of her stocking-sheathed thighs, wrapped wantonly around Andrews, the little slut.

'Payment,' I tell her simply. 'I want you to pay for what you've done.'

'I don't have any money,' she says. 'You know that.'

'Well then, my dear,' I say quietly. 'I suppose the question must be . . . what are you prepared to give me?'

Most of my moves thus far have been purely for self-preservation. Hattie was to keep my job. Andrews to repair my finances. Claudia would have appreciated this and I've only done what anyone would do given my position. It's just business.

But Kiera Fisher?

This is purely for pleasure.

It would have been base to articulate my meaning and, given my audience, it isn't required. She exhales through her nose and stares at me again. The granite is back. Thank the Lord. This would feel so wrong if it weren't. She stands slowly and pushes the chair back with her thighs – those thighs . . . She walks to the door and turns the key in the lock, checking the handle for confirmation we won't be interrupted. She's learned one lesson tonight already.

And I'll be delighted to teach her another.

She pauses at the door – she knows she can still walk out of it; I'm not a violent man. And there's no victory in snatching something. It's so much the sweeter if it's presented to you.

Kiera returns to the desk and stands awkwardly. She's awaiting instruction. I can barely breathe for the anticipation. I've thought of this moment many times. But in the sinful flesh it is so much more than I could ever have hoped for. This is wrong. Wicked. Bad.

And I am powerless to stop it.

'What do you want . . . me to do?' she finally asks. She truly is the Whore of Babylon, quite prepared to prostitute herself for her own gain. I'm disgusted.

Exhilaratingly so.

I stand up and move slowly round the desk and perch next to her. I cannot touch her. That would be a sin. She's another man's wife, not that she seems to have been aware of that tonight. The seventh commandment: You Shall Not Commit Adultery. Mrs Fisher has broken a sacred law. And for that she should be punished.

I lean forward and feel her shudder.

'Put your hands on the desk,' I tell her.

'What are you going to do?' she asks, not unreasonably, I suppose. I smirk – I'll confess, it is a smirk – and walk round her to the other side of my desk where my stationery sits neatly in an oak pot. I remove my wooden ruler – I do so like things to be precise – and I run my fingers along the length of it.

'I'm going to give you something you should have had a long time ago,' I tell her.

'And what's that?' she asks.

Her lips are puckering in shameful rage. I will cherish that until my dying day.

'Some discipline,' I tell her. 'Put. Your hands. On the desk.'

I watch her struggle. I think the little slattern would rather have surrendered her body. But I want something far more precious.

I want her obedience.

I gesture towards the door to remind her that it remains an option open to her. She flicks her eyes towards it, but appears to eliminate the possibility. I can almost feel her teeth grinding. She looks at me like Satan himself is staring at her . . . and bends forward, slamming her palms on the desk.

'Further,' I whisper. 'Reach further.'

She slides her hands robotically across the desk, until she's almost inclined ninety degrees. I can make out the trim of those stockings through her skirt, the slut. I swallow down my excessive saliva.

'You've been wicked,' I tell her, as I was told so many times at school. 'And now you must pay.'

She doesn't move. There's no crying, no begging, no whimpering. She is resolute and strong. It's infuriatingly erotic.

I stare down at her, bent over my desk. I yearn to touch her, to run my finger along her spine, to feel her skin pucker at my touch. But that would be a sin. And I'm here to make her atone.

I grip the ruler in my hand and stand alongside her.

'You ready?' I ask, although it matters not either way. She doesn't respond. She doesn't have to. I was never consulted.

I lower the ruler with a trembling hand. I've been on the receiving end of this treatment many times, at school and since. But I've never administered it. And I like to do everything proficiently.

I pull the ruler back . . . and bring it down smartly on her behind. She jars – but I think more through shock than pain. My aim is not to hurt her. It's to teach her. I bring the ruler down again.

'You are wicked,' I repeat through clenched teeth. 'You are a wicked, wicked girl.'

I spank her again. And again. I'm building a steady rhythm of justice, a blow every two seconds in line with the ticking of my grandfather clock. She is motionless, taking the punishment as a sinner should. I know she's not penitent. I know she'll never be clean. But I'm doing the work of the Lord.

'Wicked,' I pant, speech deserting me as the sweat begins to bead on my forehead. 'Wicked, wicked girl . . .'

The blows are coming faster now, every second at least and my neat rhythm has gone all to hell. I imagine the skin beneath the ruler blooming beneath the rod, those wanton stockings wrapped round my hips, the taste of those pert lips on mine as we sin over this desk and . . .

It is done.

I pause breathlessly for a moment before returning the ruler to its rightful place. I walk back round the desk, mop my brown and sit hastily down.

'You may leave,' I tell her by way of dismissal. I can't look at her. Everything is a transaction. And the price of sin is shame.

I hear her move wordlessly to the door and I hear it closing behind her.

I clasp my hands.

I drop to my knees.

And I pray for the Lord's forgiveness.

'And I'm telling ya, I'd never nick off the kids . . .'

I hear the furore before I see it – it is rare for Andy to raise his voice, so it rather stands out. As I turn the corner, there he is, standing with Andrews, his personal effects littered on the floor around them. The Quiz Night is coming to an end in the hall.

'WINNER WINNER, CHICKEN DINNER!' I hear Matt Fisher bellow down the mic.

What little he knows.

'You have to understand, Andy,' Andrews says in that patronising tone of his, 'this doesn't look good.'

'Course it doesn't!' Andy replies. 'Because that's what you're supposed to think, you pratt!'

'You're saying that someone planted these things in your bag?'

'Look, mate – not to brag,' Andy says, an exasperated hand on his hip, 'but if I were gonna nick off you, you'd never see it coming. And I'd not be bloody stupid enough to keep it on me.'

'What's going on?' I ask, striding briskly up to them.

'We have a . . . situation,' Andrews says. 'There have been reports of certain items going missing – I've just found them in Andy's bag.'

I look at Andy, who just shakes his head. I urge him to

fight. But this is a man who has fought enough. He knows the war is lost. And it is deeply, profoundly unfair.

So I will fight the good fight for him.

'This is palpably absurd,' I tell Andrews. 'This is clearly a set-up . . .'

'All I know is that some personal items have been stolen and they've been found in Andy's possession,' says Andrews, the ineffectual idiot. 'I'm sorry – but I'm going to have to refer this to the police. And, Andy – I'm afraid I'm going to have to suspend your employment here until further notice.'

'Mr Andrews,' I say, with no small menace in my voice, 'I cannot allow this farce to continue . . .'

'Course you are, pal,' says Andy, stuffing his belongings into his rucksack. 'And I'm sure the feds'll be ever so considerate to the homeless guy with the kiddie phone in his bag. I'm outta here.'

'That's probably for the best,' Andrews simpers.

'Whose best?' Andy asks him.

'No – Andy – wait,' I tell him, an unfamiliar panic rising in my chest. 'There has clearly been a misunderstanding. The headmaster just needs a moment to consider his response. Don't you, Mr Andrews?'

I look at Andrews in a way that can leave absolutely no doubt as to my meaning. He returns my gaze with steel in his eyes. He's angry. Very, very angry.

'And I'm sure the school business manager knows that we are obliged at all times to act in accordance with the law,' he shoots back, his fingers twitching. 'I'm sorry, Andy. I wish you well. Truly I do.'

'Yeah, whatever,' says Andy, slinging his backpack over his shoulder. 'Time to move on anyhow . . .'

'No . . . Andy . . . wait!' I tell him. 'Let's . . . let's just go home. I can find you another job . . . You don't need another job – you can stay with me. It'll all be well . . .'

Andy turns and stares at me.

'You're a decent bloke, Clive,' he says. 'But you need to go and find your own life. Mine's already spoken for.'

And with a single-fingered gesture of farewell, he storms out of the door.

I spin on my heel. I am ablaze with fury.

'You spineless, vengeful bastard,' I hiss at Andrews. 'You did that on purpose. And you're going to pay . . .'

'Now look here, pal,' he says, squaring his considerable frame up. 'I've taken about as much I'm gonna take from you tonight. You've said your piece. Now get out of my face. Before I make you.'

There is so much more I want to say. But discretion is the better part of valour. I'm never going to win a fist fight with this brute. And, besides, I have other weapons at my disposal. I back away. Andrews stands down – Priya Mistry is first out the hall, laughing drunkenly with Tanya Jones.

'Oi, oi!' she slurs in our direction, pointing an unsteady finger. 'I hope you lot weren't conferring out here! *Mauvais* points for the lot of you!'

'Glad you had fun,' says Ben as she starts to wheel away, before turning sotto voce to me. 'Go home. I've had enough for today. We all have. Let's just take the weekend to cool down and—'

'CLIVE BAXENDALE, I'M GONNA BLOODY BRAIN YOU!'

I barely have time to register the threat before I'm enveloped by large amounts of Hattie. She's pummelling at me with her sizeable fists, raining wrathful blows down on me. I feel hair removed and my nose bloodied before she's yanked off me like a wild animal.

'Hattie!' Tanya says, holding her back. 'What on earth are you—'

'You ask him!' she shrieks. 'You ask him what he did to Kiera! I always knew you was a creep, Clive Baxendale. But I didn't have you down as one of them sex attackers!'

'*What?*' I cry. 'I did no such—'

But my protestation is quickly silenced.

By a large Scottish fist to my face.

It is a while before I am back home. Tending to my bleeding nose took some time, especially as I was offered no assistance from Ben, nor Hattie, nor the two parents who witnessed the assault. Them having an inkling of the events in my office is inconvenient, but this is tomorrow's problem – after I go to the police. Andrews isn't getting away with violence and with no actual evidence of my financial situation it would just look like tit for tat.

For tonight I have more pressing concerns. I have been driving the streets of Flatford for over an hour trying to spot Andy. People think that the homeless are everywhere. But when they don't want to be found they are truly invisible. I leave a few messages with a few people and hope that he heeded what I said and made his way home. Because in these short weeks it has become his home. Our home. And it won't feel like a home without him.

But, as I pull up on my driveway, I'm struck by an overwhelming relief. Praise be! The prodigal son has returned!

Even if he still can't shut a wretched door . . .

I veritably leap out of the car and run into the house. It's dark, but I don't even pause to put on the light. I just want to find him.

To find Andy.

To find my friend.

'Andy! Andy!' I call into the darkness. 'Andy – I'm so relieved you . . .'

Argh – this is ridiculous. It's dark and I can't see a damn thing. I fumble around at the base of a lamp and turn it on, the luminous eruption particularly invasive after the pitch black.

But as my eyes adjust I wish they hadn't.

My house has been ransacked. Furniture overturned, vases smashed, papers strewn across the floor . . .

And my own gun is pointing straight at me.

I'd always hoped that the last words I'd hear would be from Psalm 23.

*The Lord is my Shepherd.*

*I shall not be in want.*

*Even though I walk through the valley of the shadow of death.*

*I will fear no evil.*

But it isn't to be.

Instead, I am to be commended to the Lord's care with a parting shot every bit as violent as the one that shortly follows it.

'Fuck you, Baxendale. Rot in hell.'

# The Flatford Gazette

Saturday 26 November

### Local Bursar Pays Ultimate Price

The community of St Nonnatus Primary School was left in shock last night by the violent death of their business manager, Clive Baxendale.

Mr Baxendale (57) was pronounced dead at his home in Arcadia Mews, apparently the victim of an armed burglary. Neighbours report hearing gun shots at around 11pm, immediately alerting the authorities.

The police are keen to speak to Andrew Duggan (55, no fixed address) who was recently known to be staying with Mr Baxendale and who hasn't been seen since before the attack.

'We urge Mr Duggan to come forward to assist us with our enquiries,' Constable Robert Alsorp appealed. 'If anyone has seen or has any information regarding the whereabouts of Mr Duggan, we ask that you contact us in confidence, rather than approaching him directly. He may be armed and dangerous. Although to give the fella his due, he made one helluva Bloody Mary.'

An anonymous tip-off to the *Flatford Gazette* suggested that Mr Baxendale's involvement in illegal financial dealings might have been responsible for his death. St Nonnatus Primary declined to comment when approached.

Mr Baxendale will be laid to rest in a private burial next week. He leaves no family.

## Local Library Gets Reprieve

The council has reversed its controversial decision to close Flatford Library. 'You can't put a price on community,' says council chief in a far-ranging speech that includes cuts to the youth centre, a raft of council tax increases and the abolition of free cinema tickets for pensioners.

## Lucky Gambler Wins Record Casino Jackpot

'Reckon I'll get me boobs done,' says new millionaire, 59.

## Robocoppers
Priya, Al, Tanya

### Saturday 26 Nov
### 07.34

**Al**
Fucking hell...
I can't sleep for thinking about Clive.

**Tanya**
Me neither... it's just too awful.

**Priya**
Shhhh.
I was sleeping perfectly well until you bastards woke me.
What did Hattie put in that punch... 😵

**Al**
Behave.
I mean, the guy was an arsehole, but...

**Tanya**
Do you think... ?

**Al**
What?

**Tanya**
I'm spending too much time with Robocop.
But do you think it's connected to Miss Stitchwell?

**Al**
I don't know what to think.
The most exciting thing that used to happen in Flatford was the new Costa.
And now we're like gangland LA...
Come on then, Flatford's answer to Poirot?
I'm sure you have views...

**Tanya**
So presumably we can knock Clive off the suspect list
now?

**Al**
Well… not entirely.
Just because he's dead doesn't mean he didn't do it.
Indeed, could be dead because he did.

**Tanya**
Really?
You think anyone cared about Stitchwell enough to
avenge her?

**Al**
No.
But they might have hated Clive enough.
Or he knew too much…
Jesus.
I'm even starting to sound like Pri…

**Priya**
SHHHHHHHHHH!
I'm dying.

**Al**
Oh Christ!
You say her name and she appears!
Like the Candyman.

**Tanya**
Or Sue's mum.

**Al**
Get an egg butty down you, you'll be fine.

**Priya**
👿👿👿👿👿👿👿
I'm awake now.
So thanks for that.
And you're both right.
I do think Clive's death is related to Stitchwell's.
And it also doesn't mean he didn't do it.

**Al**

Andy?

The evidence doesn't look good.

**Priya**

The evidence looks too good.

Murder is rarely that neat and tidy.

And there was all that kerfuffle in the hall...

**Al**

Yeah... what was all that about?

**Priya**

Not 100% clear.

My razor-sharp instincts are a little... dull this
morning.

**Al**

I missed it.

Matt Fisher was on his third victory lap of the hall.

**Tanya**

*My razor sharp instincts are a little . . . dull this
morning.*

You mean you can't remember, you boozehound?

🍷 🍺 🍸 🍹

Well I was driving, so I can tell you exactly what
happened:

Andy was accused of taking the kids' stuff.

Ben fired him.

Clive defended Andy.

Hattie then comes charging over accusing Clive of
assaulting Kiera.

Ben punched Clive. Hard.

**Al**

Jesus... is Kiera okay?

**Tanya**

I tried to call last night.

No answer.

**Priya**
Bloody hell.
Why do I always miss the good stuff?

**Al**
PRIYA????

**Priya**
Oh FFS, not Kiera, that's hideous.
And one helluva motive.
(Fully justified.)

**Tanya**
I agree.
I want to believe in the law.
But if Clive attacked Kiera, he got what was coming to
him.

**Priya**

But the question is – who gave it to him?

**Al**
I need a coffee.

**Priya**
I need three.
Fancy meeting up this morning?
We could even go to Costa if you like...

**Al**
IN!
(Casey had a row with her mum, so she's staying over!)

**Tanya**
I can't, I'm taking Verity to ballet.
But Pri?
You will let me know as soon as you hear something?
About the cake?

**Priya**
The very second.
We're going to be a step closer to the truth.
Hang on in there.
And now I'm off to vom xxx

# PARENTCHAT

Clearer Community Communication

## ST NONNATUS CE PRIMARY

*Ora et labora*

### Monday 28 November

**Mrs Marcia Cox<<u>M.Cox@stnonnatus.flatford.sch.uk</u>>**

**To: <Whole School>**

**Re: Week commencing 28 Nov**

Dear Guiding Adults,

You will doubtless have seen from the local news coverage that we have suffered another tragic loss in the St Nonnatus family.

Last Friday night, our business manager, Clive Baxendale, was cruelly taken from us. In the years he had been at our school, Mr Baxendale had made quite the impact on our community and was a diligent and committed member of staff. As the circumstances surrounding his death are still under investigation, we ask that people refrain from public comment until the details are a little clearer, as we are keen to avoid false and potentially damaging claims circulating across various media.

But, once again, we must find our strength and a new way forward through these dark and difficult days. To that end, a few notices:

To quell speculation, the Year 6 Tigers residential at Radford House will go ahead as planned tomorrow. We are confident that Mr Baxendale would have wanted the trip to proceed – no one understood the Blitz spirit, nor a non-refundable deposit, better than he. Please have your Tigers ready at school for a 7.30am departure. Unfortunately, Miss Sild will not be joining the trip as she has decided to leave teaching for calmer professional waters. I'm sure you'll join me in wishing her well in the Air Force.

We are experiencing increasing problems relating to mobile phones in school. We have noticed a sharp decline in social interaction during playtimes, not to mention some anti-social behaviour relating to social-media misuse. (Please check that your child's phone content is age-appropriate. For your information, 'OneNightFriend' is not a bedtime story app.). We are therefore implementing a new policy. Children arriving with phones must hand them in to the office at the start of the day and are not permitted to have them back until school finishes at 3.20pm. Should a child urgently need to communicate with their guiding adult, or vice versa, you can make contact through me in the school office. I remind everyone once again that this is for exceptional circumstances only and matters pertaining to dinner choices, *The Great British Bake Off* or preferred leggings from the Next sale do not qualify.

I leave you with the words of Winnie the Pooh: 'You're braver than you believe, stronger than you seem and smarter than you think.'

Best wishes,

Mrs Marcia Cox

Office Manager
St Nonnatus Primary School

# Tickly Tiger's Diary!

Date: Monday 28 November
..............................................................................................
This weekend I went home with: Ivanna
..............................................................................................

I love Tickly Tiger! Archie must have given him
a bath because Tickly Tiger used to look a bit
dirty and he smelled liked beans. But this week
Tickly Tiger was clean and fluffy and his left
ear had even grown back!

We had fun. Not on Saturday morning – on
Saturdays we have to go to another school to
learn English. My sister and I can speak it quite
well because we've been in England for nearly
nine months. But I think grown-ups aren't as
good at school as children are and my mummy
and daddy can still only ask if you have any
sisters and where the train station is. And there
isn't a train station in Flatford, so it's not very
useful. They're trying very hard though, so I'm
going to ask Mr Andrews if they can have a
sticker for effort.

After English school, my mummy wanted to go
for a traditional English meal. So we had a balti
and some pakoras at Naan Taken. It was yummy!
Then I went to the park and played with Phoebe
and we are now best friends and Phoebe says I
can come to her next Splashworld party
(platinum package)! My mummy and Phoebe's
mummy Jane used Google translate to talk to
each other, which was very funny as it kept using
the wrong words and they ended up talking
about parsnips! And Jane gave my mummy this
week's spellings and some of Phoebe's old
clothes and toys for my sister Yana, so my
mummy gave her a big hug. They didn't need
Google translate for that.

On Sunday we went to church and Tickly and I asked God to look after our family in Ukraine. William was there with his family and we went to Sunday School and had three biscuits! After church, my daddy tried to make Yorkshire puddings (again), but they exploded in the oven (again), so we had a McDonald's instead. Then we watched Arsenal v Man City, which was very exciting! It turns out my daddy does know quite a lot of other English words! But I can't write any of them down in Tickly Tiger's diary.

# PARENTCHAT
Clearer Community Communication

## ST NONNATUS CE PRIMARY
*Ora et labora*

### Year 6 Tiger Class
click here for group info

**Monday 28 Nov**
10.42

**Petra**
Has anyone seen Archie's trainers?
I'm trying to pack for Radford House.

**Fatima**
I can't believe it's still happening.
I thought they'd cancel.
Mark of respect.

**Zofia**
I spoke to Ben A this morning.
He's determined.
Thinks it will be really good for the kids.
He's such a great guy.

**Jennie**
Does anyone know a decent cranial osteopath?
For cats?

**Jane**
I think Ben's right.
I don't agree with the phone thing, though.
They're just making them forbidden fruit.

319

**Stella**

*I think Ben's right.*
I don't.
A senior member of staff has died.
I think a period of mourning would be more appropriate.

**Annie**

*I don't agree with the phone thing, though.*
Me neither.
Sasha hates the playground.
She just wants to sit quietly and play games.

**Petra**

Archie had one.
For less than a day.
Don't miss it.

**Priya**

*I think a period of mourning would be more appropriate.*
Hard disagree.
They're kids. There has been too much real life around
lately.
Let them be kids and escape from it all for a while.
The phone thing makes sense to me.
There's so much trouble on social media.
We wouldn't let them have knives at school...

**Sarah**

Did anyone see the piece in the Gazette?
What 'financial irregularities' do you think Clive was
dabbling in?
Do you think the school's in trouble?

**Rosie**

*There's so much trouble on social media.*
I agree and I'm all in favour.
We don't allow Theo to have any social media.
He'd rather read a book.
I think that's why his spelling is so strong.

**Zofia**

*Do you think the school's in trouble?*
I don't think it's anything to do with the school.
I think it's Andy.

**Karl**

Me too.
Dead suss.

**Stella**

This an ongoing criminal investigation.
And we've been asked not to speculate.

**Sharon**

Absolutely.
So I'm going to keep my views on Stitchwell's killer
striking again to myself.

**Stella**

Sharon!

**Sharon**

Alright, mum...


*Mariam has joined 'Year 6 Tigers'*

**Mariam**

ه‍ل اذه الشيء مفتوح؟ لقد
عملت للتو على كيفية
استخدامه!
*Suggested translation: This thing is on? I am working
its function!*

**Priya**

Yay Mariam!
So glad you found us!

**Mariam**

أنا انا أيضًا! الآن هل ل‍ه الآن هل يدل ى أي
شخص جاء هذا الأسبوع؟
*Suggested translation: As well am I! Now is anyone
having of the spellings of the week?*

**Borys**

*We don't allow Theo to have any social media.*
Ви мама Theo?
*Suggested translation: You are mothering of Theo?*

**Laura**

Does anyone have a monkey wrench I could borrow?

**Laura**

Sorry! Wrong group!

**Rosie**

*Suggested translation: You are mothering of Theo?*
I am.

**Borys**

Тоді тобі потрібно сказати своєму синові, щоб він
перестав фотографувати свою дупу.
*Suggested translation: Then you needs tell your son to
not making pictures of the arse.*

**Rosie**

I beg your pardon?
I think the translation app isn't working.

**Borys**

*I think the translation app isn't working.*
Ні, додаток працює. Він @Tmanbumbum?
*Suggested translation: It is. He is @Tmanbumbum?*

**Dustin**

Ah.
We've seen those pics too.
Didn't realise it was Theo or I would have said.
(Privately.)

**Karen**

I've just checked Beth's phone.
There's a whole lot of @Tmanbumbum.

**Rosie**

This is absolutely outrageous!
Theo would do no such thing!

**Sharon**
Rosie – did you go for that posh rug in the end?
The one from John Lewis?

**Rosie**
Yes – what does that have to do with anything?

**Sharon**
Cos you can just make out it out behind @Tmanbumbum's
left arse cheek on a post in October. Oooh – I think I can
see Tickly Tiger's tail now I look at it. And a perfect
spelling test...

*Rosie has left the group*

**Priya**
Now that's something new for Tickly Tiger's diary...

**Dustin**
Is anyone else freaking out about them going on this trip?
It's the first time away from home...

**Sharon**
Aw love.
Simeon will be fine!
He'll have the time of his life!

**Dustin**
Who said anything about Simeon 😟?

**Al**
They'll have the best time.
(And I'll watch out for them – I'm going too for medical
support, yay!)
But I do wonder who's going to teach Tigers when
they're back?

**Zofia**
I heard it was going to be Ben 👍.
Love him!

**Tanya**
Oh my days...
Everyone – I've got some terrible news.

**Sharon**
Oh Christ.
Stitchwell's risen from the dead?

**Stella**
Sharon!
That's in appalling taste.

**Sharon**
I usually am.
What's up, Tanya love?

**Tanya**
It's about Jenna Richardson.
The media crew she was travelling with in Myanmar?
It's been involved in some kind of explosion.

**Priya**
Oh my God...

**Flo**
That's awful.

**Karl**
I'm so sorry.

**Stella**
Thoughts and prayers.

**Al**
Is Jenna okay?

**Tanya**
We don't know.
All that we know is that she was definitely travelling with them.
And that two of the crew are dead.

**Dustin**

I just...

This is awful.

What can we do?

How is Mike?

**Tanya**

In pieces, as you can imagine.

I thought about doing a food and childcare rota?

So he can just focus on finding out about Jenna?

**Felicity**

Just catching up...

But count us in.

I'll take dinner tonight.

**Zofia**

And I'll do it tomorrow.

Is Jacob still going on the trip?

**Tanya**

As far as I'm aware.

Mike thinks it'll be a good distraction.

**Karl**

Then I can pick him up and take him tomorrow.

Jacob and Ollie are tight as.

It'll be good for him to have a friend.

And we can take Bea to Flatford High too.

**Flo**

Good idea, K.

I'll go round and see if I can help pack for the trip.

Must be the last thing on Mike's mind.

**Sharon**

And when they're back I'll have him, Riley and Ollie round for the weekend.

Bit of a sleepover – give Mike some space.

**Priya**

I know someone who works in... doesn't matter.

I'll see what I can find out about Jenna.

**Mariam**

أي يوم جمعة يمكنني أن أتناول العشاء في.

*Suggested translation: Fridays I am doing dinner every time.*

**Dustin**

We'll do any dinner any night.

**Stella**

Us too.

**Al**

Just point me where you need me.

**Karen**

Ditto.

**Borys**

Ми теж.

*Suggested translation: Us and.*

**Tanya**

You guys are the best 🖤.

**Sharon**

We're Team Tigers.

And we take care of our own.

(Just like Stitchwell and Clive's killer.)

**Stella**

SHARON!

**Sharon**

Sorry... 😈

# PARENTCHAT

Clearer Community Communication

## ST NONNATUS CE PRIMARY

*Ora et labora*

### Flatford FC
Eric, Donna

### Tues 29 Nov
09.35

**Eric**
Hey Donna!
Well that was an early start!
Good to see the Tigers off.

**Donna**
So many tears!
But the parents will get over it...

**Eric**

I'm so sorry, in all the drama I haven't had
a chance to say
I had a really wonderful time with you
on Saturday.
(With Finley of course!)

**Donna**
Oh me too!
Pub lunch AND a curry for dinner!
What a treat – can't remember the last time I was out
that late!
Or talked so much – I hope I didn't bore you!

**Eric**
No!
No, no, no!
No, not at all!
You were... smashing!

**Donna**
Well thank you!
You too.
I had such a great time with you.
(With Finley of course!)

**Eric**
I'm so glad to hear it!
So, I was wondering...
If you might like to go out again?

**Donna**
Absolutely!
When's the next game?

**Eric**
Oh.
Saturday week!
There should be loads of tickets

**Donna**
Fab!

**Eric**
That'll be grand.
But I also wanted to see...
If you maybe...
Another time...

*Borys has joined the group 'Flatford FC'*

**Borys**
Це група для футболу?
*Suggested translation: Is this the group where the
football is participating?*

**Donna**
Hi Borys!
Yes it is!
Welcome!

**Eric**
Borys.
Hi.
So glad you found us.

**Borys**
Це гарна новина! Я люблю футбол! Коли наступна
гра?
*Suggested translation: This news is great! The football
is loving me! When next game is happening?*

**Donna**
It's a week on Saturday!
Come along!

**Eric**
Um...
I'll have to check if there are tickets...

**Borys**
Ми б залюбки! Ми з Іванною великі фанати
Арсеналу. Флетфорд схожий на Арсенал?
*Suggested translation: We'd love to! Ivanna and I are
huge Arsenal fans. Are Flatford like Arsenal?*

**Donna**
Ha!
You'll hardly know the difference!

**Borys**
Щиро дякую, Еріку. Як чудово, що завдяки футболу
ми стаємо друзями.
*Suggested translation: Thank Eric you so much.
Football makes us all friends.* ⚽ 🖤

**Eric**

You're right, son.
It does.
⚽ 💚

It's why I love it.
And you're very welcome.

**Borys**

ОДИН НУЛЬ НА КОРИСТЬ ФЛЕТФОРДУ!
*Suggested translation: FLATFORD TO THE ONE NIL!*

**Eric**

We're gonna get on just fine!
Donna – are you still there?

**Donna**

I'm here!

**Eric**

So while I've got you.
I had a thought.

**Donna**

Sounds dangerous!

**Eric**

I hope not!
You said you like pub quizzes?
Well they do one at The Crown on Thursdays!
My mum's happy to look after the kids.
And

*Dustin has joined the group 'Flatford FC'*

**Dustin**

Hi guys! 👋

**Donna**

Hello lovely!
Well isn't this quite the party?!

**Eric**
                                   It is.
                              Smashing.

**Dustin**
So glad we're all online at the same time!

                                 **Eric**
                                  Yeah.
                                 Me too.

**Dustin**
I just wanted to see if there was any chance that I
could tag along to the next Flatford game?

**Donna**
Of course!

                                 **Eric**
                                  Sure.
                       The more the merrier.

**Dustin**
Brilliant!
Simeon has a playdate with Adel and I thought it
would be fun.

**Donna**
I'm not sure about fun!
The last game shredded my nerves to ribbons!
But we'll be quite the party!
Flatford won't know what's hit it!

                                 **Eric**
                                   Yes.
                        So many of us now.
                              Smashing.

**Dustin**
Aw – you guys are the best!
Meet in The Crown for pre-match bevvies?

**Donna**
It's a date!

**Dustin**
I've got to dash – karate at six.
Byeeee!

**Donna**
Oh us too!

**Eric**
Oh Donna – before you go…

**Donna**
Yes?

**Eric**
So about the quiz night.
On Thursday.
At The Crown.

**Donna**
Yup?

**Eric**
I
(Sorry, sent too soon, my sausage fingers!)

**Donna**
Haha!
No worries!
I texted my accountant if he could 'hurry up and do
my wax' last week.

**Eric**

Well that should get your return done!
No, what I wanted to ask.
If you're up for it.
(But no pressure.)

**Borys**
Ну ж бо! Донна, він хоче піти з тобою на побачення!
(Деякі речі не потребують перекладу!)
*Suggested translation: Oh come! He want to go on the
big date with you Donna. (Some things are not needing
of the translating.)*

**Eric**

Ah.

Borys.

You're still there then.

**Dustin**

Me too, fyi.

**Borys**

Це краще, ніж Острів Кохання! Правда ж?
*Suggested translation: This is preferable than the Island of Love! Am I right?*

**Dustin**

You're not wrong!

Up high, friend! 🖐

**Eric**

Haha.

Er... lads?

**Dustin**

We're only playing!

Come on Borys, let's leave them to it.

**Borys**

Бажаю удачі, Еріку. Сподіваюся, ти забиваєш як гравець Арсеналу.
*Suggested translation: Good fortunes, Eric. I am hopeful you score like a Gunner.*

**Eric**

Bye, boys.

*Dustin has left the group 'Flatford FC'*

*Borys has left the group 'Flatford FC'*

**Eric**

Donna – I'm so sorry.

I didn't mean to embarrass you.

I'll leave you to it.

**Donna**
Yes.

**Eric**
Alright then.
See you on Saturday.

**Donna**
🥺

No, you girt nelly!
Yes!
I'd love to come to the quiz night with you...
Pick you up around 7?
(With Finley of course!)

**Eric**
Oh!
Right!
Of course!
Can't wait.

**Donna**
Me neither.

**Eric**
Super!
And if I might say.
This is... bloody smashing!
🥒

**Donna**
👀

**Eric**
Oh GOD!
Sorry!
My sausage fingers again.
I'm so nervous...
I really didn't mean that.
I'm so, so sorry.
I'm not like that at all.
I promise...

334

**Donna**

I know you're not!

**Eric**

I meant this one...

🖤

**Donna**

I know you did.

Me too.

See you Thursday.

🖤

# Hattie

There's no greater sight than watching kids be kids. And after all the nonsense at school, this trip is just what the little uns needed – me too as it turns out. Young Nora Thorpe is covering for me in the school kitchen ('93 – used to flash her knickers something shocking) and I'm enjoying the break.

The kiddies been up to all sorts today – climbing, kayaking, raft-building . . . They tried to get me up on the rope course, but I told 'em these feet ain't left the ground in near sixty years and they ain't starting today. They're having a blast at Radford House. Food ain't much cop, mind, but you can't have everything. Almond tart you could break a tooth on and some nasty stew what weren't fit for a dog. And I'm more than a touch suspicious that Fido might've been the main ingredient.

'You enjoying yourself, Hattie?' Ben asks after dinner.

''S all right,' I tell him. I ain't got nothing to say to that man and, besides, we gotta herd these munchkins into bed. They are high as little kites on fresh air and sugar – none of us is getting much sleep tonight – I'll tell you that for free.

But one kid ain't smiling.

Little Jacob Richardson. He's sitting at the dinner table, all alone. We still don't know what's happened to Jenna, his ma. The poor mite must be going through seventeen hells.

'Hello, my darling,' I say, pulling him into a big old cuddle. 'You ready for the midnight feast? Between you, me and the gatepost, I noticed that Matthew's got a bag o' sweeties the size of Santa's sack. You'll all be puking gummy bears for days . . .'

I got a tickle in me throat and try to clear it.

'I'm not hungry,' says Jacob, and I bet he ain't. He ain't touched his dinner, nor his lunch. I'll feed him up like foie gras when we're back at St Nonn's, you just watch me.

'Now listen here,' I tell him. 'I know you must be worrying yourself something rotten about your ma. No news is worse than bad news sometimes – your brain fills in all them gaps with 'what ifs'. But you remember what I told you?'

'You don't like "what if". You like "I know",' he chirps back at me.

'Smart lad,' I tell him. 'So at the moment we don't know nothing bad's happened to your ma. And if it ain't, think of all the fun you've missed worrying yourself daft for nothing?'

He screws up his little face and considers this. I don't wanna give the lad false hope. But it takes longer to find the living than the dead – they're still moving, after all. I'm praying bad news woulda travelled faster than this. And, if I'm wrong, why not let the lad have one good night before his little world goes the way of the tit?

'But it's not fair,' he says.

'What ain't?' I ask him.

'Me having fun,' he says, starting to sniff. 'I can't have fun if my mummy is hurting or she's broken something or she's—'

'Oh, now let's not go down that road,' I tell him. 'That's a one-way ticket to Bonkers Town, that. Cos I tell you what else I know. Wherever your ma is, she will be wanting you to have a good time. Am I wrong?'

He shakes his little head.

'And I promise you – from my lips to God's ears . . .' Urgh. Pesky cough. I give me lungs a right good clearing. '. . . second we hear anything, I'll come tell you meself.'

'You will?' He sniffs again.

'I don't care if it's four o'clock in the morning and you're bum-up, snoring in bed,' I say, making the Scouts' salute. 'I, Hatita Hughes, will drag you out in yer jammies and tell you what's what. I swear it on my ma's secret mince-pie recipe! And that ain't a vow I'm gonna break any time soon.'

He thinks about it for a minute.

'I do like gummy bears,' he says uncertainly.

'Then you'd better get yer little backside up to the dorm and get some down you before them lads beat you to it!' I tell him. 'Get to it! You know what Aleksander's like – that boy can gobble down my treacle tart sideways like one of them snakes! Give us another cuddle.'

He gives me a squeeze and I send little Jacob on his way with a pat on the bum. Come on Lord. You've had your fill of souls from Flatford lately. Appreciate you'd want some better company, mind. But not our Jenna, Heavenly Father. Not today . . .

'You're a treasure, you know that, Hattie Hughes,' comes a soft voice behind me.

'Oh, hush your noise,' I tell Al, swatting him as I walk past. 'Now, let's try to get these rugrats to . . .'

This bloody cough.

'You okay, Hats?' he asks, going all nurse-y on me. 'You've gone a bit of a funny colour.'

Oh Crivvens. That bloody dinner. Knew I shoulda checked that kitchen knew their arse from their . . .

'Hattie?' says Al as I cough up a lung. 'Hattie – what can I do?'

'Go get me handbag,' I gasp, handing him my room key. 'In my room. Number 226.'

'Someone should be with you . . .'

'Go!' I shout at him, leaving him in no mind where I need someone to be.

He sprints off, leaving me trying to calm the panic and find some breath. It'll all be okay, Hattie. We've been here before. Help is on the way.

Time don't half move slow when you're counting it in breaths. When they come and go easy, you don't notice the time they take. But as your ruddy throat starts trying to squeeze 'em outta you, you wish you'd valued each one, I don't mind telling you.

I hear Al sprinting back – ten years of running after them kids has kept the boy fit, I see. He shoves the handbag in my arms.

'Can I get you something?' he says, pulling the zip open. 'Do you need water for pills? An inhaler? A . . .'

He's been around the medical block too many times not to recognise what comes out of my bag.

'Hattie, I had no . . .'

I open the bloody EpiPen and jab it into me thigh. It hurts like all hell, always does. But, like sex and reverse parking, once you get it in, you're over the worst. And it bloody works. Almost instantly I feel my throat and chest open and the air returns to my lungs. I take some long, deep breaths. Al don't say nothing. But I know he's gonna.

'You're allergic,' he says finally. 'To what?'

'Seeds,' I say. 'Musta been some contamination in that ruddy kitchen.'

'Why didn't you tell them you have allergies?' he says, clearly looking me over for signs of wear. He's a good boy.

'Same reason I ain't told no one else,' I tell him. 'Because a) who's gonna keep on a dinner lady who could be allergic to the dinner? and b) because it's no one's business but mine.'

'People need to know, Hattie,' he says. 'You might need help . . .'

'I ain't had no one's help me whole life. I ain't gonna need it now,' I remind him. 'Only difference between now and five minutes ago is you know summit you shouldn't. I'm the same old warhorse as ever's been and I'll thank you to keep this to yourself.'

He looks daggers at me. But I know he'll do me right.

'Only if you promise to let me know if this happens again,' he finally says. 'And you promise you'll keep your EpiPen with you at all times . . .'

He trails off. Where's his head at?

'Hattie?' he says, serious as the grave. 'I need to ask you something. And you need to be entirely honest with me. It's really important.'

I nod, but I don't mean it. I don't like where this is going. I don't like it at all.

'The night Stitchwell died,' he says – and I think I know exactly where this is going. 'Neither Kiera nor Clive could find the onsite EpiPens. There is a theory that someone tampered with them, to stop Stitchwell getting her medication . . .'

'A theory by who?' I cry. Who's sniffing around Stitcher's death? And why?

'That's not important,' he continues, and I want to bloody differ. 'What is important is . . . did you have something to do with that?'

I go to fib. But he's no fool. The jig's up. Might as well fess up now. I sigh. And then feel bloody grateful I can breathe again.

'That night was all over the show,' I begin. 'Between Stitchwell calling everyone in and pissing 'em off and bloody Jesus statues in cakes and folk running around like headless chickens – I'm normally super careful about everything I eat and drink. But there am I, cutting the crusts off me egg sarnies and I nibble on one – never normally eat shop-bought bread, but I was peckish and there musta been some seeds on or in it, because moments later off I go – like what you just seen.'

He nods. The lad knows when to say nothing, which is more than most folk do.

'Now I always carry an EpiPen in my bag as you now know,' I tell him. 'But that night, like a daft old goose, I'd left me handbag in BuyRite. So I panicked . . .'

'And used the school one,' he fills in.

'I know I shouldn'ta,' I admit. 'But what was the alternative? And I knew there was another one – although why no bugger could find it is beyond me. Clive never were a details man . . .'

'So you used the one in the school office?' he asks.

'Well, I could hardly go into Stitcher's office and grab one outta her desk, could I?' I point out to the daft melon. 'Managed to keep this whole thing under wraps for forty year – I weren't gonna blow it! And I replaced it straight off when I was back in school at crack o' sparrow fart the next day with them poor looked-after kiddies . . .'

'So that's why it wasn't missing in the report,' he sighs, and looks more than a little relieved. 'Now it makes sense.'

I take another breath. I'm lucky I can. Stitchers had no such luck. Musta been a nasty way to go, that. Proper nasty.

'Look – don't get me wrong – I ain't no machine,' I say, taking his hand. 'Do I feel in part responsible? Yes I do. Will it haunt me to my dying day? Yes it will. I'll never know if that pen coulda saved her. And that's me punishment. Unless you decide to talk to the old bill . . .'

I watch him. I can't go to no prison. Not for her. Not for this.

He's wrestling. He's a good man.

Which is why I know he'll do the right thing.

'What good would it do?' he says. 'It won't bring her back. And, as you say, there was another pen . . . But in any case . . . I can't see any sense in ruining another life. Especially not yours. I won't talk to the police.'

His wording is a tad specific, which makes me worry who exactly he will talk to. But, for now, I just need to take the win.

'Now I'm sorry for giving you a fright,' I say, trying to stand, 'but there's thirty kids who are gonna be allergic to bed and I need to sort 'em all out, so . . .'

'You'll do no such thing – you need to be in bed yourself,' he instructs, being all nurse-y again.

'You cracking on to me, Nurse Bourne?' I tell him. 'Cos if you're just trying to get me into the sack, there's easier ways.'

'So I hear,' he says, planting a kiss on my head. Those who get kisses all the time dunno how good it feels to get one.

'Hattie . . . Maisie's Dad!' comes young Theo, running in like his bumbum's on fire. 'Aleksander just puked gummy bears all over the dorm and it's purple and it stinks!'

'On my way!' I say, pulling myself up.

'No. You're not,' says Al, pushing my key back in my hand and pointing me towards the dorms. 'I've cleaned up gallons of puke. And that's just at my house . . . Off to bed with you, Mrs Hughes. Call me if you need anything at all.'

I give up without no fight. He's right – I need to rest up.

And, in any case, I don't need him nor no one asking more questions tonight.

I think I got away with it.

Cos, after all, best place to hide a lie is in the truth.

# Kiera

Fucking residentials.

There's a reason we send them home at 3.20 at school.

It's 3am, I'm finally back in my own room and the score-sheet so far reads:

*3 x vomit (gummy bears, dodgy tummy, drinking shampoo for a dare)*

*4 x homesick (Verity, Matthew, Ollie and bloody Stella who has called three times to speak to William)*

*2 x fights (one play, one cat)*

*Room reallocations: countless (between the puking and the fighting, I have no idea where anyone is sleeping. Please God, don't let there be a fire alarm tonight. Or a fire).*

Al has been fantastic – I'm guessing not sleeping all night isn't new for him. Ben's being a trooper too – that man has the patience of a saint. But I'm done in. And I still haven't had five minutes to talk to Ben . . .

In truth, most of the reason I agreed to come when Rose dropped out is because Ben and I haven't really spoken since Clive. He's been putting out fires left and right with parents and I've been crazy with the house stuff – this buyer wants to move yesterday. And Taylor and Gracie are barely speaking to me. We went to look at new houses – flats really – over the weekend. Gracie cried the entire time. I can't expect her to understand now. But she will.

But it's more than that. Ben and I are avoiding each other. What happened with Clive could happen again. And if Clive had told anyone . . .

But that's one problem we don't have to deal with.

I'd hoped having some distance would calm me down, that the fright would knock some sense into me. I've got enough on my plate and he's incredibly distracting.

But it turns out I want to be distracted.

I think about going to his room. I haven't changed for bed yet and he's only across the hall – he gave me the room allocation sheet and I think it was his way of telling me . . . Or am I just reading what I want to into any and everything? Jesus Christ, Fisher, get a grip . . . And get some bloody sleep.

I've just got my T-shirt over my head when there is a knock at the door for the umpteenth time. There is a strict knocking policy here as there are no locks. I groan and cannot help myself.

'Khadija! If you and Beth are fighting over who likes Taylor Swift the most again, I'm going to come in there and shake you both off!'

The door opens gently.

'More of a Harry Styles man, myself,' comes the soft and gorgeous response. I smile. Then I realise my T-shirt is still over my head.

'All quiet on the Western Front,' he says. 'Theo and William are now in separate rooms, Riley and I have had a gentle chat about what we should and shouldn't put in our pyjamas and we even managed to fish Simeon's retainer out of the toilet with a coat hanger.'

'Nicely done,' I say, yanking my T-shirt back into position.

'Right back atcha,' he whispers with the sexiest wink and an unashamedly appreciative sweep of my body. He's hovering in the threshold, waiting for an invitation to come inside. I really shouldn't. It's late and . . .

'Come in,' I say, before my brain has time to get in the way.

He does and closes the door behind him, leaning against it once it's shut.

'How have you been?' he asks.

'Busy.' I smile, sitting on the bed to keep a safe distance. 'House stuff . . . it's been crazy.'

'Gracie told me you were moving,' he says with concern in his eyes. 'I hope it's for all the good reasons?'

'The right ones,' I confirm. 'It'll be fine – it's just a stress. And Taylor's being a total nightmare . . .'

'Not happy?'

'She's seventeen. She's never happy.'

He smiles.

'I bet. I was a nightmare at that age.'

'I was pregnant,' I say, and I realise it wasn't quite the joke I meant it to be.

'You were a child yourself,' he says softly. 'It's amazing how you've raised your family.'

'Wasn't given much choice,' I point out, sitting on the bed. 'Taylor's dad was never going to be involved . . .'

'Why not?' he interrupts. 'Jesus . . . sorry, it's none of mine, you don't have to—'

'Because he was one of my teachers,' I tell him, and I watch his eyes bulge. I learned a long time ago that it was that dirty bastard's shame, not mine.

'Fuck,' says Ben simply. 'I'm so sorry. I had no idea'

'Most don't,' I tell him with a weak smile. 'He was married, pervy and untouchable. I was seventeen, desperate for someone to love me and not old enough to know better.'

'Was he never . . . What happened?' he says, coming to sit on the bed next to me. 'Did you tell anyone?'

'Oh yeah.' I laugh bitterly. 'I told my form teacher. She told me I was a slut, entrapping a virtuous man with my sin, and I should give my baby to the church so it could be purged. Got me thrown out of school. A month before my A levels.'

'No,' he gasps. 'That's awful. Did you report her?'

'Ha! Not a chance,' I snort. 'The church owned the school. She was untouchable too.'

'Why?'

I turn and look at him.

'Because she was Claudia Stitchwell.'

I quite enjoy the shock on his face. I'll give my life this much. It makes a good story.

'Kiera, I—'

'Don't sweat it,' I tell him, patting his thigh. 'There aren't any right words. Trust me, I've tried to find them. It's dead and buried. As is Stitchwell. And I couldn't be happier about it.'

'I bet,' he says, this safe conversation drifting into a dangerous pause. We say nothing for a moment. I need him to be the first to speak.

'Kiera – I really need to talk to you,' he says, standing up again. 'What happened last week—'

Shit. I know where this is going and I need to get in first.

'Look – it's fine. I get it,' I say. 'It's just too risky, there's too much at stake, we've been stupid and we need to cool it. You don't need to spare my feelings.'

His face breaks into that sexy smile and he laughs gently.

'You know, for the brightest girl I've ever met, you can be really stupid,' he says with a cheeky grin. He's inviting me to play. But what's the game?

He kneels down in front of me and my innards turn gelatinous. What is it with this man? He's magnetic to me – the moment he's near, I just want to throw my body at his and see what sticks . . .

He takes my hands in his.

'What I was going to say,' he begins, smiling at me, 'is that what happened last week made it clear to me how I feel about you.'

My whole body is alive with static. These next words are everything. Or nothing. Or both.

'You're going to have to give me a clue,' I whisper. 'Maybe you could—'

Whatever silly shit was about to fall out of my face is stopped by a kiss. A long, slow, loving kiss. I don't want it to end. But I also want to hear what he has to say. He pulls away and our foreheads rest against each other.

'Kiera . . . when Clive . . . walked in on us last week, I don't mind telling you, I was terrified,' he begins. 'But a part of me – and not a small part of me – was also relieved. Darlin' – I don't want to be fooling around in dark corners behind locked doors. I want to be by your side. Holding your hand. Telling the world that—'

'Ben . . . don't say something you don't mean,' I whisper, closing my eyes. 'Please, please don't lie to me . . .'

'I'm not lying!' he insists, grabbing my face. 'Kiera Fisher. I am batshit, head-over-heels, cock-a-hoop, truly, madly, deeply in love with you! I think about you most of the day and all of the night. I want you. I want all of you. Your heart, mind, body – oh God how I want this gorgeous body – and your life.

I want to be part of your life. As your man. As your partner. As your love.'

I usually cry approximately three times a year – and one of those is when I watch *Home Alone* at Christmas. But hearing his beautiful, earnest, heartfelt words . . . the tears start running down my face.

'Do you mean that?' I ask him. 'Do you really, really mean that?'

'I do,' he says before I can finish it. 'I know this isn't ideal and I don't want anyone to get hurt. But love doesn't always grow where it's supposed to. And I'm in love with you. And I don't ever want it to stop.'

'Me neither,' I say, surrendering any last shred of restraint. 'I love you, Ben. I love you, I love you, I love you . . .'

He pulls me to him and we kiss again. But this isn't a kiss of lust. This is one of love. And it's perhaps the best one I've ever known.

We go into autopilot as he pulls me to my feet and tight into his body. All thought, all sense, all feeling is directed at him – I've heard the cliché about becoming one before, but tonight I get it. Urgent hands tear at anything between us, any barrier to our bodily affirmation, to our joyful surrender. He gently picks me up and places me on the bed, slowly leaning down until he's pressing down on top of me. Oh God – the weight of a lover's body is one of the greatest gifts sex ever affords – but still it's not enough. We won't be sated until we are locked together, indivisible, tangled, unified . . .

'I can't sleep,' comes the sleepy wail at the precise moment the door opens. 'I had a bad—'

Ben leaps off me like he's been stabbed. I pull some clothing around myself. But any child with the most basic involvement with Love Day will know what is going on.

Although this isn't just any child.

And I know she understands exactly what her sleepy little head has just witnessed.

'Mr Andrews?' Grace says incredulously. 'What are you doing with my mum?'

# Ben

I know I try to be a good man.

But, by Christ, I can be a stupid one.

It's 10am and I've not slept a wink. The look on Gracie's face . . . Kiera went after her, of course. But neither of them were at breakfast. We're now packing up to leave and I just want to know they're okay. I want to know that Kiera and I are okay.

My phone rings in my pocket. I ignore it.

'Mr Andrews?' little Sasha McCall asks, tugging at my sleeve. 'Do you have my travel-sick pills?'

'Er . . . go and see Maisie's dad. He's got all the medicines, sweetheart,' I tell her, looking around the carnage in the entrance hall of Radford House as we get ready to leave. 'And make sure you sit near the front this time, eh?'

She nods and scuttles off to find Al. I look around again. Where is Kiera . . . ?

The phone rings again. It's Finn. Urgh . . . I'm not in the mood for another round of emotional contrition . . .

Don't be stupid, Ben. He's your boy. Pick up the damn phone.

'Hi, darlin',' I coo, moving outside to a quiet patch of garden. 'I can't really talk – do you remember I said I was on the residential . . . ?'

'Daddy?' his little voice wails down the phone. 'Daddy – I want to come and live with you.'

My heart melts and ignites all at once.

'It's okay, fella,' I say more softly. 'It's okay. What's wrong?'

'Mummy and Don had a big fight and Mummy threw some marmalade at him,' he sniffs.

I hold the phone away from my mouth while I silently scream a swear.

'Mate, I'm so sorry,' he says. 'But you know that grownups fight sometimes. They'll make it up.'

'Don slept in the car last night,' he says. 'He's still outside.

He won't go and Mummy won't leave the house. I'm scared . . .'

'Mr Andrews,' comes a little voice at my elbow, 'Theo says that it's samesies on the coach on the way back, but that's not fair because he got the back seat on the way here and—'

'Okay, William – I'll be there in a minute,' I try to say as calmly as I can.

'Daddy!' Finn wails. 'Daddy – where are you going?'

'Nowhere – I'm not going anywhere, son. Just hang on in there . . .'

'Mr Andrews! Mr Andrews! Theo's getting on the bus and he's going to bags the back seat, look!'

'William!' I snap, making him jump. I never shout at the kids – they got enough of that from Claudia. He looks absolutely terrified, poor lamb. I try to soften my voice.

'William,' I say more gently. 'I've just got to finish this phone call and I'll be over there, okay?'

'Daddy – don't go!' Finn pleads. 'I'm scared, Daddy! I'm scared . . . I'm scared Don's going to hurt me.'

William walks chastely back towards the bus. I'll deal with him later.

'Finn, you need to listen to me,' I say. 'I'm going to hang up now . . .'

'No! Don't go, Daddy! I want to come and live with you!'

'I know, son, I know,' I say, trying not to cry myself. 'But we both know that's not possible right now. What is possible is that I can get you some help. I'm going to call Granny and Grandad and see if they can come and help you until I can get up there myself.'

Silence on the line.

'Finn? Finn, are you still there, pal?'

A small sniff tells me he is.

'Will they bring sweets?' he asks, and I feel a tsunami of relief.

'Aye – course they will,' I say, and hope he can hear the smile in my voice. 'So you just sit tight and I'll call Granny and I'll be up there tomorrow, okay?'

A stilted breath.

'You promise?'

'Cross my heart, hope to die . . .'

'Sstick a sausage in your eye!' Finn laughs. I love how easy it is to move the dial from tragedy to comedy at this age. Christ knows what I'll do when I can't.

'You just hang on in there, okay?' I reply, swallowing down my guilt. 'Daddy's coming soon.'

'Okay,' he sniffs. 'Love you most.'

'Like chocolate toast,' I tell him. 'Laters potaters.'

I hang up and try to calm myself. Fucking Don. Fucking Elena. And yet through the fog of my past life my future one shines through. Where is Kiera . . .?

'She went home,' a cold voice declares, answering my thoughts. I turn to find Hattie standing behind me, dead-eyed and hard-faced.

'I'm sorry?' I say, as if I don't know what she's talking about.

'Matt came and picked 'em up a couple hours ago,' she says. 'Little Gracie wasn't feeling so good.'

I try to scrutinise her, see what she knows. But Hattie is totally unreadable. My phone rings again. Oh, Finn . . . just give Daddy a second . . .

'I'm sorry to hear that,' I say. 'And I understand you were feeling bad last night? You okay now?'

'Nothing a good night's sleep couldn't cure,' she says. 'Most problems can be fixed by some time in your own bed, wouldn't you say?'

Shit.

She knows.

And, judging by the look on her face, the look on mine has just told her that I know she knows.

She leans in.

'Now I'm just gonna say this the one time,' she whispers malevolently. 'You wanna shit on your own lawn, that's none of mine. But the second you start making trouble for my Kiera, you make it so.'

She waits for me to say something. But I have no words I can trust.

'That girl's got her life together,' she continues. 'It's taken a while, but she's there. Matt's a good boy and he'll take care of her until the end of time. And that's what she needs. Someone stable. Someone reliable. Someone a bit daft, bless him – but that's what she needs. Not you. It's like what Beatrice says to Don Pedro in *Much Ado*: you're fancy enough to wear on the weekends. But Kiera needs someone she can wear in the week. You're a fantasy. A dream. A romantic lead in a cheap airport novel. Leave her to her real life. You ain't the hero of her story. You ain't no hero at all. I know that for a fact.'

'What do you mean?' I ask her. She stares me down.

'You know damn well what I mean,' she glowers. 'Stay. Away.'

She starts to walk off. I shouldn't say it. But it's out of my mouth before I can stop it.

'And you think he is, do you? You think Matt's the hero of Kiera's story?'

She turns back and stares me down.

'No, you dumbass,' she replies with a sneer. 'Kiera is.'

She walks off towards Sasha, who is already going a worrying shade of green.

I pull up my contacts and scroll down to some numbers I never thought I'd call again. I choose the landline – it's the only hope I have of getting an answer. I hit the number and feel my heart start to drumroll as the phone rings. I need them to pick up. But I really don't want to speak to them.

'Hello, 01463 934583?' comes the chirpy voice on the end of the phone.

'Caitlin?' I say as brightly as I can. 'It's Ben. I need your help. It's urgent.'

I'd not normally gabble all the information by way of greeting. But I know how short this call will be without it.

'You've a nerve phoning here,' Elena's mother replies. 'God help you if Arthur hears this—'

'Caitlin, I need you to go over to Elena's—'

'Sweet Jesus – is she okay?'

'Everyone's safe,' I assure her. 'But I've just had Finn on the phone. There's been some kind of fight with this . . . with this Don. Finn's scared and I just need you to go over and make sure everything's okay.'

Silence. She doesn't ask me who Don is. So she's met him, then. I try not to feel angry. Now's not the time. This is about Finn.

'Ben, I don't know what you think you're doing, but this doesn't concern—'

'*Ben?*' I hear an angry voice in the background. 'That man's got a . . . Give me that.'

The phone muffles and I have the uncomfortable sensation that I'm clenched in Caitlin's bosom. But after some angry grunts, the line clears and Arthur's unmistakably loud brogue takes over.

'Now you listen here, Andrews,' he bellows down the phone. 'I told you once and I'll not tell you again – you stay away from our girl!'

'Arthur . . . I know you're still angry with me, but—'

'You're damn right I'm still angry with you!' he roars. 'After what you did to Elena! To our grandson! You should be behind bars, you animal!'

Arthur always was one for hyperbole. But I'll let that one go.

'Arthur – I need you and Caitlin to go round to Elena's. Something is wrong and Finn is hiding in his bedroom—'

'I don't know what you're playing at,' he huffs. 'But whatever you think this is going to achieve, you are doing more harm than you could possibly know. Everything is fine.'

I'm so mad at this man. Does he not even care about his own grandson? But that doesn't matter right now. I just need someone to get to my boy.

'But Finn—'

'You keep your nose out of her life, or I'll keep it out for you,' Arthur threatens.

Enough.

'Finn is my son,' I remind him. 'I won't ever keep my nose out of his life. I'm his father.'

Arthur goes quiet and menacing.

'Well, we'll see about that,' he says. 'You'll be hearing from our lawyers.'

The line cuts dead.

What the hell did that mean? Surely Elena wouldn't . . .

She's not going to try to take him from me? Even she wouldn't stoop that low? Surely not . . .

I have to get up there. I start jabbing at the screen, trying to pull up flights. We should be back to school before lunch, we're under an hour away – I could be up to London late afternoon and on a plane by dinner time. I have to get home. I have to get back to my boy . . .

'Ben?' says Al, who I hadn't seen approach. 'You okay?'

'I have to find a flight – I need to get back to Scotland tonight. I have to . . .'

'Shit – is Finn okay?'

'Yes . . . no . . . I dunno – I just need to get home. I need to find a flight . . .'

I know I'm making no sense on no sleep. But I can't let them take my boy – he's all I have left . . .

'Hey,' says Al, putting a calming hand on my shoulder. 'Look. The kids are all on the bus, we've done the headcount and they're all waiting for us. We can't do anything standing here – let's get on the bus and I'll help you make all the arrangements you need, okay? Staying here is just going to hold you up. Why don't you take a beat to catch your breath, I'll teach them a mildly dirty song and we'll get on the road, okay?'

I look up into his reassuring eyes. Al has a lot of experience of dealing with people on the edge and it shows.

'Okay,' I say weakly. God, I wish Kiera were here. I need her, I need someone, I need—

My phone rings in my hand and I hesitate to turn it over. Is it Finn in pieces again? Is it Arthur or his lawyers? Is it Elena? Is it Kiera . . . ?

The final thought makes me turn it round.

But it's none of the above.

It's school.

Everyone knows I'm here and not to contact me unless it's urgent. I tap to accept.

'Ben?'

'Marcia?' I reply. She is normally the epitome of calm and cool, but even I can hear the tension in her voice. 'Everything okay?'

'We've had the call,' she replies.

I'm so tired and my brain's so fried I can't file her words in the right department.

'From who?' I ask, just as the obvious answer rears up in my mind.

'From Ofsted,' she groans. 'They're coming tomorrow.'

## Robocoppers
Priya, Al, Tanya

**Weds 30 Nov**
10.47

**Priya**

WHY IS NO ONE PICKING UP THEIR PHONE?!

**Al**
Because I'm on a bus with 30 children, half of whom
are sleeping, the other half puking.
It's chaos...

**Priya**

Oh shit of course – how was the trip?
Do you know where Tanya is?
I really need to speak to her?

**Tanya**
I'm here – I'm in the library doing some research.
Is everything okay?

**Al**
*Oh shit of course – how was the trip?*
I have a LOT to tell you.

**Priya**

And I'd love to hear it.
But Tan – the tests on the cake came back.

**Tanya**
Oh God.
Go on.

**Priya**

I asked my mate to check them twice.

**Tanya**
GO ON.

**Al**
FFS, Pri.
It's a food allergy test.
Not Santa's bloody naughty list.

**Priya**
The results are 100% conclusive.
There were no nuts in your cake.

**Al**
KNEW IT!
TAN!!!
This is amazing!
Shit – gtg – Riley just projectile vommed all over
Elijah's head 🙈

**Priya**
Tan?
Tanya – you there?!

**Tanya**
Sorry.
Sitting in the library.
Crying.

**Priya**
I'm on my way.

**Tanya**
You don't need to do that.

**Priya**
Yes, I do.
With you in ten.
But babe.
This was never on you.

# PARENTCHAT

Clearer Community Communication

## ST NONNATUS CE PRIMARY

*Ora et labora*

### Year 6 Tiger Class
click here for group info

### Weds 30 Nov
12.54

**Zofia**
Have you guys heard?!
Ofsted are coming tomorrow!

**Sharon**
Oh Christ.
That's the last thing Ben needs, poor bugger.

**Zofia**
Why?
He's fantastic – he'll be fine.

**Petra**
Has anyone got Archie's shirt and shorts?
At the moment, he's going in tomorrow in his pyjamas.

**Donna**
Hey everyone!
How was the trip?
Finley is knackered – he looks like I did when I was a club rep in Ibiza!

**Sharon**
*He's fantastic – he'll be fine.*
He is.
But if it's the same bloke as last time, he's screwed.

**Fatima**

*Finley is knackered – he looks like I did when I was a club rep in Ibiza!*
Khadija too!

**Stella**

William is still being sick from the coach journey.

**Dustin**

*But if it's the same bloke as last time, he's screwed.*
Why so?

**Sharon**

Because rumour has it that he went for the St Nonn's Headship the year Stitchwell got it.
Never forgiven the school for choosing her over him.
Accused the school of nepotism – and he was probably right.
Stitchwell was a relatively junior secondary school teacher when she got it.

**Jennie**

*William is still being sick from the coach journey.*
Riley's just thrown up again too.
Anyone know how to get vomit out of Nintendo Switch?

**Annie**

*Riley's just thrown up again too.*
Sasha too...
I'd assumed it was all the sweets she ate on the coach.

**Felicity**

Um...
Have any of you been asked to speak to the police again?

**Flo**

Ollie's honking too.
Oh God.
You know what this means...

**Sharon**

*Have any of you been asked to speak to the police again?*
About what, love?
I've been trying to take over Tash Tompkins's drug game.
But the hardest thing in my house is ibuprofen.
(And I include my Stan in that.)

**Zofia**

I heard the police were pulling people in left and right.
They must have some new information.

**Jane**

*You know what this means . . .*
No!
Not the dreaded Norovirus!
It wiped us all out last time!

**Petra**

*Has anyone got Archie's shirt and shorts?*
Okay, don't worry about it.
He's just vomited all over the rest of his uniform.
He's not going to school tomorrow.

**Sarah**

*They must have some new information.*
I heard they found Ben's fingerprints all over that nut oil bottle.
The one that fell out of Creepy Jesus at Parents' Evening.

**Sharon**

Noooooo!
And how do I keep missing you, Sarah love?
I want to invite Elijah to Matthew's party.

**Flo**

Flatford High folk...
Did you hear that a boy was excluded this week?
For upskirting in the girls' loos... 🙎

**Dustin**
Themis posted about this back along.
It's not the right way of going about it.
But at least it's giving these young women a voice.

**Stella**
*Not the dreaded Norovirus!*
Let's not leap to conclusions.
I'm sure they're all tired and have been eating far too many sweets.
There's no evidence there was any kind of bug on the trip.

**Sharon**
Oh come on Stella.
That's Archie, William, Riley, Sasha...

**Donna**
Oh – and Finley now.

**Sharon**
Hope chucked up last night at Radford House.
What more proof do you need?

**Al**
Hi guys.
Just been throwing up a lung 🙊
Must have been something I ate at Radford House.
What have I missed?

**Tanya**
OH MY GOD EVERYONE!
I've just got off the phone with Mike!
Jenna is alive!

**Sharon**
Oh thank God!

**Stella**
Praise the Lord!

**Dustin**
This is the best news!

**Flo**

Where is she?

How is she?

**Tanya**

So her convoy hit a landmine.

Her colleagues didn't make it – miraculously she did.

She's pretty beaten up – lots of broken bones.

But she was airlifted to a military hospital in Bahrain.

She's safe.

**Annie**

I'm just sitting here crying my eyes out 😢

(And Matthew's having a party?)

**Karen**

When's she coming home?

**Tanya**

There's the rub...

Mike is on his way to the airport. I have Jacob and Bea here.

But Jenna can't fly home on a commercial airline.

She needs a private air ambulance.

And they don't come cheap.

**Sarah**

How much?

**Tanya**

About £25K.

**Karl**

Jesus... could we fundraise?

It's the Xmas Fayre soon.

Put the funds towards that?

**Tanya**

Lovely thought.

But the last fayre raised just over £4K.

And with the best will in the world

people just don't have it to spare right now.

**Donna**
So when will she be able to fly?

**Tanya**
Weeks. Months maybe.
I've said we'll have the kids for as long as is
necessary.

**Sharon**
And we'll all help you love, you know that.
But poor little Jacob.
Don't get me wrong, thank Christ everyone's okay.
But no parents for Christmas.

**Tanya**
I know, it's so sad.
But let's do what we can to give him and Bea a good
time.
Let's get this wretched Ofsted out the way.
Then I know we can all pull together.
Good luck with the pukes everyone!
May the Dettol be with you...

# PARENTCHAT

Clearer Community Communication

## ST NONNATUS CE PRIMARY

### *Ora et labora*

**Weds 30 November**

Mrs Marcia Cox<<u>M.Cox@stnonnatus.flatford.sch.uk</u>>

To: <Whole School>

## Re: URGENT – OFSTED INSPECTION THURSDAY 1 DECEMBER

**Dear Self-Determining Care Providers,**

I hope that you'll forgive the extraordinary communication on a Wednesday, but, as you may already be aware, tomorrow we will be welcoming the inspectors from Ofsted to St Nonnatus Primary. This is an exciting time for our school to really demonstrate what a fantastic educational and pastoral community we are and we ask for everyone's help in ensuring that we really put our best foot forward. So in that spirit:

1) Can we please ensure that all children are dressed even more smartly than usual in the correct uniform and are neatly presented with no additions to the uniform policy. Our last report noted the proliferation of 'fluffy unicorn ears' in certain classes and we're very keen to show growth.

2) If anyone can spare some time this evening to help us with a last-minute spruce of the school, we would be incredibly grateful. With our caretaker position presently vacant, we are asking for all hands to the plough for a little spit and polish to ensure we really 'shine'!

3) Ofsted are keen to speak with children and their parents as part of their inspection of our school. We of course welcome your honesty as part of this process, but hope that you have made use of the feedback mechanisms in school should you have any significant concerns. Whilst Ofsted are thorough in their inspections, matters such as 'I don't like the colour of the walls' or 'we need reed diffusers' felt like an inefficient use of this opportunity during our last inspection.

4) It can be unsettling for the children to have new faces around school, so please assure your young people that these are welcome visitors to St Nonnatus and we're very happy to help them with their work. If perhaps it could also be impressed upon our children that these two days would be an excellent opportunity to show their very best Star Learning and only use their Good Choice Words, this would be appreciated as well.

5) Please do not park inconsiderately tomorrow. It sets such an unfortunate tone for the visit if the inspectors are unable to access the school in the first instance.

We are so excited for this opportunity to show off our wonderful school. We trust everyone will stay calm and act as normally as possible.

I leave you with the words of Lance Corporal Jones: 'Don't panic!'

Best wishes,

Mrs Marcia Cox

Office Manager
St Nonnatus Primary School

# Hattie

Hell's teeth!

It's like the bloody Shah o' Persia's coming to visit rather than a load of poxy inspectors!

We've only been back a couple of hours and everyone's losing their ruddy minds. They're cleaning and painting and decorating . . . as if bloomin' Ofsted give a monkey's uncle about the colour of the walls . . .

'Hattie,' pants Ben, running into my kitchen like a loon. 'Do you have the week's menus for me?'

'Since when did I ever run my menus past—'

'Hattie!' he says in a tone I don't care for. 'Menus. Now.'

It's a good job I'm in a good mood. Or he'd be in Thursday's cottage pie.

I amble over to the side and pick up the menus – deliberately drop them twice, mind, you don't speak to me like that – then wander back over.

'Okay, okay,' he says, scanning them. 'Make sure we have a vegan option tomorrow as one of the inspectors is a flexitarian. And drop the chocolate sponge for something with fruit.'

He ain't looking at me. But I'm giving him the look nonetheless.

'Ben?' says Karl, a big old pot of creosote in his hands. 'I've been around the playground – shall I start on the front fence?'

'Yes. Please,' says Ben gratefully, his phone going off in his pocket. I wonder if it's Kiera. I dunno what happened at Radford House, but it weren't good. He takes a look, eyes the heavens, then shoves the phone back in his trousers.

'You're gonna give yourself a heart attack carrying on like this,' I say hopefully. 'Calm yourself down, man – it's only a ruddy inspection.'

'Easy for you to say,' he says, before realising what an arsehat he's just made of himself. 'Hattie – I'm sorry, I didn't mean that. And when all this is over, I think we should take another look at the budget and see if we can't—'

'Oh, don't you try to butter my biscuits,' I huff, turning back to cleaning my surfaces.

'Okay,' he says distractedly as Marcia runs into the kitchen.

'Ben – I'm inundated with calls from Tiger parents – it seems several of them are suffering from a stomach bug. Looks like they picked something up at Radford House?'

'Fantastic,' he sighs. 'Should I . . . ?'

'I'm handling it,' she says. 'Just wanted to clue you in.'

'You're a superstar,' he says. And he's right. Place'd fall down without Marcia – she's a bloody goddess. Come a long way since being born into the circus.

Ben goes to leave, before pulling himself up short. He turns to me, all awkward like.

'Hattie . . . I know you don't want to talk to me about it,' he begins, 'but I just need to know . . . is Kiera all right? I haven't heard from her and I'm worried.'

I look at his face. I believe the daft sod. I just don't trust him.

'I don't know,' I tell him honestly. It's Gracie's interview at Shottsford House tomorrow – I'll drop in on them after, see what's what. I don't want him anywhere near them. 'But, if I know Kiera, no news is good news. So I'd worry about what's going on here if I were you.'

His phone rings and he goes to cancel it. But something stops him.

'Finn?' he asks – that's the name of his lad. 'I know, I know what I said, but this is a super big deal for Daddy and you're just going to have to—'

'Ben,' says Marcia, coming round the corner of the kitchen door again. 'Ben – you're needed at reception.'

Ben puts his hand over the mouthpiece of his phone.

'Marcia – I can't right now. I'm right in the middle of—'

'Ben,' she says firmly. 'You need to come. You too, Hattie.'

'Me?' I ask. 'What in the blue blazes do you want with me?'

'Finn – I have to go. But I'll call you tonight, love you,' says Ben, jabbing his finger on his phone.

'What now?' asks Ben. 'More sickness?'

'Yes,' Marcia sighs. 'Lots. But—'

'I'm sorry, but you're just going to have to field the calls,' snaps Ben. 'I've still got the accounts to prepare, the lesson plans to finish and I haven't even started on the safeguarding . . .'

'Mr Andrews!' she shouts over him in a tone that ain't going nowhere soon. 'You both have to come to the office now. PC Bob Alsorp is here. And he wants to talk to you both.'

'What the bloody hell's all this about, Bob?' I say with no small irritation as we sit down in the Tigers' classroom. 'Can't you see it's bloody chaos round here?'

'I know, Hats. Last thing I want to be doing too – I was on me way home, and Nora's made beef bourguignon. Saw that bloke off *The Apprentice* make it on *Saturday Kitchen*, reckon it's a blinder too—'

'Bob!' I snap at him. 'What's going on?'

'Oh, it's just one of them daft things I've got to fill out on a form,' he says. 'Won't take a minute, but I need to dot the t's and cross the i's. You know how it is . . .'

'Well, get on with it, then, man,' I huff. 'I've got a flexitarian to cook for.'

'Well, you should have a look at *Saturday Kitchen*. I tell you, they get up to all sorts on there – made a brownie outta beetroot the other week. I never seen anything like it . . .'

'BOB!'

'Sorry, Hats – me mouth don't know where me mind's at . . . So we've had a call – anonymous, probably some bloody loony what's seen it all on the news . . .'

'Seen what?'

'This bloody Clive Baxendale business,' he sighs, rubbing his forehead. 'A shooting brings out all the whackos, I tell you . . . But, as this mentioned you by name, I have to follow it up. Nothing personal, you understand. It's just—'

'My name?' I say, me old heart quickening. 'Why my name?'

'Well,' says Bob, taking the long route to the point. 'This nutjob says that they saw you.'

'Hardly need to bother *Crimewatch* with that bombshell, Bob . . .'

'Mind your lip, missy,' he laughs. 'Nah – this bloke – it were a bloke, took the call meself, Northern lad, sounded like one of them pop singers what used to wear their anoraks in all weathers – he says he saw you. Round Clive's. Around the time of the shooting.'

Bugger. Bloody Andy. Thought I'd taken care of him.

My mind races. All right. Thing is, truth be told, I was there. Thought I'd been careful. But Andy mightn't be the only one who saw – others could come forward and then I'll be right in the soup. Best place to hide a lie is in the truth. Think carefully, Hattie. Play safe.

'So all's I need to know is where you were around 11pm on the twenty-fifth of November.'

Yes.

I think that'll work.

'Well, I can tell you,' I start, slowly. 'I was at Clive Baxendale's house.'

'You were?' he says, startling.

'Yes I was,' I confirm, settling back in my chair. 'Before it all kicked off, mind – he'd left his wallet at school. Being the good Samaritan what I am, I went to drop it back round to him – he's on me way home. But there was no one there – he musta taken the scenic route. Place was locked up tighter than Fort Knox, so I popped it through the letterbox and went on me merry way.'

'Can anyone confirm this?' he asks, making a note on his pad.

'Yes, you bloody Herbert,' I point out. 'Your "anonymous" source. And I suppose you boys keep a record of what you found there – I'll bet you a pound to a penny, Clive's wallet weren't in his pocket.'

'I'll check it out tomorrow,' he says, folding his pad, 'but that all sounds good to me. Sorry to have bothered you, Hats. Knew it would amount to a whole heap of nothing.'

He rises to leave and I feel my fingers unfurl from the fist I never knew I was making.

'No bother, Bob,' I say cheerily. 'If anyone gets in touch linking me to Shergar and JFK, you know where to find me.'

'Will do,' he chortles. 'Oh – one more thing, save me some time. I need to talk to old slick out there.'

'Andrews?'

'The same,' he says. 'I've heard tell there was an altercation between Ben and Clive the night Clive died. Apparently punches were thrown? The body . . . er, Clive . . . was sporting a shiner, but we'd assumed that was from his attacker. Was there a bit of fisticuffs here that night?'

Oh, what the blazes to do now? Much as I'd love to chuck Ben Andrews right under the bus, the dirty bastard, the best thing for all concerned is to get the blue lights off St Nonn's for five bloody minutes. Priya and Tanya were there . . . But Priya were half-cut and – God forgive me – I can cast shade on Tanya's memory. Everyone knows she's been struggling. And Bob'll listen to me – we go way back . . .

'I wouldn't give too much weight to nothing anyone told you about that night. They were all rat-arsed on me punch,' I laugh. 'And Ben Andrews? He couldn't hit a bull's arse with a shovel! Might damage his manicure!'

I hold me breath. Bob's a smashing bloke. But he's a lousy copper. I just need to sow enough doubt in his mind.

'That's what I figured,' he laughs eventually. 'And your bloody punch would get the Archbishop o' Canterbury brawling! But, y'know . . .'

'Procedure,' I sigh. 'I wouldn't do your job for all the tea in China . . .'

'Oooh – speaking of tea, let's hurry this along, I can feel a storm coming . . . Send him in, would you, Hats – Nora says her sauce is perfectly thickened. And you know how I like a thick sauce . . .'

'No bother,' I tell him. 'See you tomorrow night down the Crown?'

'First one's on me,' he says. 'And thanks for the iced buns down the cop shop – always welcome.'

'Always happy to take care of you boys in blue,' I say. 'See you shortly.'

'See you, Hats,' he says, squinting at a picture of a snowman that don't half look like a todger. 'And don't pay this nutter no mind. It's all a nonsense. I know you no more did for Clive than you did for Claudia, God rest her soul. It's like I said back along, when we first spoke of it. You're the last person in the frame. After all, it's not like you're gonna kill off your own kin, is it . . . ?'

# Robocoppers
Priya, Al, Tanya

## Weds 30 Nov
17.38

**Tanya**
How you feeling, Al?

**Priya**
And what was it you wanted to tell us?
Oh yeah.
And what Tanya said.

**Al**
Urgh.
You'll be investigating my death next.

**Tanya**
Oh lovely.
I'm so sorry.

**Priya**
Me too.
Now really.
What were you going to tell us?
I'm guessing the police have the results of Tanya's
cake.
And the fingerprints on the oil bottle.
Bob's interviewing people left and right.

**Al**
Your concern is touching.
I have solved the mystery of the missing EpiPen.
Or one of them.
It was Hattie.
She had her own allergic reaction that night.
She used the EpiPen in the office.

**Tanya**

What?

Hattie's allergic? I never knew that?

Well at least that explains it.

Hattie wasn't up to no good.

**Priya**

Not necessarily.

**Al**

Right on cue.

**Tanya**

Oh dear.

What now?

**Priya**

So even if Hattie's telling the truth

A) bit convenient and

B) what about the other pen?

**Al**

She reckons Clive just missed it.

**Tanya**

Or, like you said, Pri – it could have been Clive.

His death doesn't prove his innocence.

**Priya**

No.

But it might prove someone else's guilt.

I think Clive knew something. Too much something.

There's also the cake.

If that wasn't what killed Stitchwell, it had to be one of
the drinks that Clive, Kiera or Ben delivered.

**Tanya**

Do you still think Ben could be the Stitchwell Love
Child?

Feels a bit elaborate for him to get to Stitchwell.

Get a job at the school etc etc.

**Priya**
Murderers often play the long game.
And it would give him a huge motive.

**Al**
He was in a right state on the trip, poor thing.

**Priya**
How?

**Al**
Dunno.
But before Ofsted, he was heading straight up to
Scotland.

**Priya**
Just as the police are closing in?

**Al**
I don't think he knew that, to be fair.
I think this was a domestic drama.

**Tanya**
Poor guy.
He's such a doting dad.
I can't believe Elena took Finn so far away.

**Priya**
Makes me wonder why...

**Al**
Of course it does.
Oh shit. Gtgs.gfdjslgsjklsl

**Priya**
Easy for you to say...

**Tanya**
Al?
You okay?

**Priya**
I think the only calls he's making are on the great white
telephone.
Has Verity escaped the lurgy?

                                                      **Tanya**
              Seems to have got it out the way the other week.
                                         👎 👎 👎

**Priya**
I'm poised with the bleach.
Anya is a champion puker.
She goes off like the Exorcist child...

                                                      **Tanya**
                                                  Good luck!
              And Al, if you read this – get well soon.

**Priya**
And if you do happen to think of anything else...

                                                      **Tanya**
                                                   PRIYA!

**Priya**
Just asking the question...

# Kiera

'Grace,' I say for the fifteenth time in the car. 'Gracie. You're going to have to talk to me at some point. You can't keep ignoring me.'

She keeps her little head turned to look out of the window. I have lived the past twenty-four hours on eggshells – she called Matt from the residential and told her to come and pick her up, so he of course came running. I thought she'd tell him there and then. But she didn't. Nor when we got home. Nor this morning. I haven't slept a wink – and not just because of the storm that came through last night. I should be at the school for Ofsted, but Grace's interview at Shottsford House has been in the diary for weeks. Ben and Hattie have been calling me relentlessly, but I can't deal with them right now. I just need to be with my little girl.

'Gracie, come on,' I say. 'We have to talk about this. I know what you saw was . . . upsetting.'

She huffs. Good. That's something.

'But I can explain . . .'

'Are you and Dad getting a divorce?' she suddenly blurts out. 'Is that why you're selling the house? Because you want to be with Mr Andrews? I'm not stupid, Mum.'

'No, baby, no you're not,' I tell her. 'It's . . . it's all really complicated. But you must understand that I love you and I never want to hurt you and—'

'But you're going to hurt Daddy,' she says. 'He loves you. He really, really loves you.'

I can hear the tears in her voice. God, I hope life is that simple for her. I hope she falls in love with the right person at the right time and never has to question herself and her choices. Not like her mum.

'I love your daddy, I really do,' I begin.

'It didn't look like that last night,' she says bitterly.

'Grown-up love . . . it's complicated,' I say again for want of anything better or more true.

'Do you love Mr Andrews?' she asks, and the simplicity of her question floors me.

'Yes,' I say, and even in this terrible time and awful place it brings me a flicker of joy. I love Ben Andrews. I'm going to share my life with Ben Andrews. Yes, this will be painful and messy and shite. But afterwards . . . afterwards we all get to be happy.

'You can't love two people at once,' she says, looking back out of the window. 'So you're lying.'

I grip the wheel harder. If only it were that straightforward.

'Look,' I say eventually, 'we have a lot to talk about – I realise that. And I need to talk to your dad and to Taylor. But for this morning – can we just focus on you? You've worked so hard for this, Gracie. This is your shot – I really want you to love your school and this taster day will give you a chance to meet your teachers, meet your friends . . . I don't want to take that from you. Please can we just put this down and let you have your morning?'

She says nothing. I'll take it as some kind of agreement, although I'm far from sure it is.

We drive through the grand gate of Shottsford House and wind our way up the mile-long drive that leads to the school. It is a complete mystery to me why one of the country's foremost public schools is here in Flatford amongst the farmers and the feckless, but life hasn't always dealt me the luckiest hand, so I'll take it. This is the life I want for my girl – this is the life she deserves. We drive past stables and hockey fields, we see the sculls rowing along the river. There's a theatre and a music school – and, for Gracie, a cutting-edge art studio. Yes, I know every kid should have this.

But mine's going to get it.

We pull up in front of Shottsford House itself, a sprawling redbrick neo-Georgian country house that could easily be from the set of *Bridgerton*. The very thought immediately catapults Ben back into my mind, but I stave him off. We have time. Lots of time. Today is about Grace.

We get out of our beaten-up Hyundai, which feels comedically out of place with the Jaguars and Teslas dotted around the car park. We stand before the main building and

I feel uncomfortably small. I glance at Grace, who looks totally swamped by the grandeur of it all. I put my arm round her.

'Geddoff,' she says, shaking me away and striding confidently towards the grand front door. That's my girl. Fake it till you make it, kid.

I follow behind and up the steps to the imposing entrance to this hallowed place. I look for a door knocker, or a secret handle or even a magic password – any would fit here. But fortunately, there is a security buzzer. This place doesn't let just anyone in.

I press the Reception button and announce our arrival. We're instructed to head towards the hallway as the door clunks open.

'You ready?' I say to Grace, whose mojo appears to have evaporated already.

'Mm-hm.' She nods nervously, looking at the door with big eyes. I can't wait for the day she takes all this in her stride. I want her to walk into this place like she owns it. Like she belongs here. Like she has every right.

Because she does.

We walk into a hallway that is only a couple of valets short of Downton Abbey. The ceiling sweeps up into a huge dome, which casts bright light onto the spiralling stairs below, ending on the wooden floor that runs the width of the building. There are huge sets of double doors running along it – only one is open and I glimpse a beautiful library inside with books from floor to high ceiling, students dotted around the room variously studying, whispering or giggling. I feel a wave of tears threatening to break. We made it, kid. We're here.

'Ms Fisher? Grace?' comes a cordial greeting from the smart, middle-aged woman striding down the hall in a red trouser suit. 'I'm Mrs Porter, headteacher. Welcome to Shottsford House.'

'Hi,' I say, shaking her hand a little too enthusiastically and wondering how much her suit cost. 'It's so good to meet you.'

'You too.' She smiles back as Grace stands silent and slack-jawed. I nudge her.

'Gracie?' I say with a strained smile. 'Remember your manners.'

'Oh,' she says, snapping to. 'Hi.'

She sticks out her hand and jabs Mrs Porter in the stomach. I hope my groan remained internal. But fortunately the head laughs it off.

'It's all a bit much, isn't it?' she whispers kindly, leaning down as my daughter turns puce. 'It's a bit like walking into Buckingham Palace at first. I still feel like I should curtsey every time I come in.'

Grace nods and blinks several times. She's terrified, bless her. Hang on in there, kid.

'Well now,' says Mrs P. 'Why don't we take a look around? It's a bit of a maze here, but you'll get the hang of it. Make sure you have comfortable shoes, though – it can be quite the hike from class to class . . .'

We walk down the hall and out of the building, which it turns out represents the tiniest proportion of the school. There are classroom blocks, science labs, a design and technology centre – even a bloody Greek amphitheatre. It's so much – too much for a small group of kids already born into privilege. But more than the facilities, I look at the kids. They have a . . . quality? Confidence? Arrogance? Entitlement? Maybe. But their shoulders are back and their smiles are broad. That's what I want for my girl. To walk through this world with her head held high.

'So what do you think?' Mrs Porter asks Grace.

'It's . . . really big,' Grace replies, her eyes the size of dinner plates. Where has her vocabulary gone today? But Mrs Porter smiles kindly again.

'It really is, isn't it?' she laughs. 'You see what I mean about the shoes . . . Let's go back to my office and get a cup of tea.'

We walk back through the grounds – how Gracie will find her way around here without an ordinance survey map is a mystery, but a champagne problem for now – and back into the building via a completely different route from the one we just took. We are now at the other end of the grand hallway, where Mrs Porter leads us through a glass panelled door into an area with two offices to the right and one to the left.

'This is where Mrs Thompson, our school administrator, and Mr Ryland, our business manager, live,' the head explains, gesturing to the two offices, which wouldn't look out of place in a boutique country hotel. 'The school would literally grind to a halt within the hour without them – not to mention that I'd never know where I was or what I was supposed to be doing . . .'

Her colleagues smile and wave politely from the grandeur of their offices. I think of Clive in his Dickensian alcove and mentally jive on his grave.

'Come on through,' she says, opening the door to the left. 'Fiona, do you think you could bring us some tea . . . and maybe some chocolate biscuits?'

She gestures to Grace with a smile. My daughter just stares at her, like she doesn't live for chocolate biscuits.

'Grace?' I prompt her. 'Mrs Porter asked you a question . . .'

'Er . . . yeah . . . okay,' Grace replies, scuttling into the office.

I tilt my head in a gesture of apology to the headteacher, who waves it away with a genuine *de nada*. What is wrong with Grace? I know she's mad at me, but this is a ridiculous self-sabotage. Mrs Thompson comes over and whispers in Mrs Porter's ear.

'Ah – great idea,' she says. 'Leave it with me. Mrs Fisher – would you excuse me a moment while I just attend to something? I'll be back in five.'

'Take your time,' I tell her. 'If we've got biscuits, you've got ages.'

She laughs and guides me through her door . . .

Jesus Christ!

This isn't an office.

It's a setting for an Agatha Christie denouement . . .

I nearly sink into the carpet as I walk in, which is approximately a foot deep. Mrs Porter's office is the size of the downstairs of my house, with a mahogany desk that I have an overwhelming urge to get valued on *Antiques Roadshow*. Previous incumbents stare down at me from the walls, interrupted only by the ten-foot-high windows that look out over the luscious grounds.

'Back in a minute,' she says with a wink, pulling the door

behind her. I wait until she's a respectable distance away before squealing and grabbing my girl.

'Gracie! Oh my God! How amazing is this place?'

She stands stiffly in my arms. I put her at arm's length.

'Oh, come on, baby girl,' I say to her. 'I thought we were putting that down this morning.'

'It's not that,' she says, taking a seat by the roaring fire that the scullery maid presumably put on at dawn. 'Well, it is. I'm still mad at you. But it's not just that. It's . . . this place.'

'The office?' I ask her. 'Oh, don't worry – you'll probably never see the inside of it again. You're a good girl . . .'

'Not the office,' she says in the smallest voice I've ever heard her use. 'This place. The school. I . . . I don't like it.'

I know I should sympathise. I should give her a hug and tell her it's okay to be overwhelmed and nervous. That it's all going to be fine.

But I'm so bloody angry with the ungrateful little bugger I can hardly see straight.

'*What?*' I say in the loudest whisper-shout I dare. 'What do you mean? It's got everything! All the facilities! All the opportunities! All the amphitheatres! Everything!'

'It hasn't got my friends!' she cries. 'Flatford High has facilities! Okay, not as fancy, but a test tube's still a test tube. And you always told me we make our own opportunities. And I don't even see the point of the amphitheatre – what do you do if it rains . . . ?'

'Stop it!' I hiss, getting right up in her thankless little face. 'Stop it right now! You have no idea how lucky you are! Most people would kill for this chance! This is what we've always wanted, what we've worked so hard for, what—'

'No!' she shouts, and I wince at what Mrs Thompson must be overhearing. 'It's what YOU wanted! And it's what YOU made me work for! I don't want it! I don't want any of it! I just want you and Daddy and Taylor and our house and . . .'

The tears spring up and stop her in her tracks. I feel like all kinds of arsehole. But I know I'm right. This will be tough – change always is. But change like this is for the best. She'll understand in time. I know she will . . .

'Gracie,' I say, more softly, trying to take her into a hug before I'm repelled. 'I understand. I really do . . .'

'No you don't!' she snarls. 'You only care about Mr Andrews. You don't care about us at all . . .'

I've taken a few backhanders in my time and I've never dealt one out to my kids. But in this moment . . .

'Oh no – no biscuits?' says Mrs Porter, walking cheerily into the room. 'I'm going to have to call Mrs T to the head's office for this . . .'

She takes in the scene in front of her and very quickly reads the room.

'There's been a lot to take in today, hasn't there?' she says gently. 'New place, new people. Maybe something more familiar will help. Come with me.'

Mrs P holds out her hand. Gracie looks at me and I nod. She wipes the tears from under her eyes and trots over to the headteacher, taking her hand like she did mine when she was tiny. I suddenly yearn for her to be that small again, to do a hard reset on life, to make different choices . . .

But I've made the ones I have. And, for the most part, I stand by them.

'I want to show you something,' says Mrs P, her eyes twinkling as we head off down yet another corridor. 'As you know, at Shottsford House, we are very proud of our artists.'

She signals to the pictures hanging on either side of the wall.

'I'm not going to lie – we take absolutely any opportunity to show off our art! We have exhibitions throughout the year, at school and beyond – we print images in the school newsletter every week and one of our art scholars gets to design the cover of our yearbook every year.'

I watch Grace's head bob from side to side as she takes in all the work. I start to feel uneasy. Please tell me that we're not . . .

'But all year round, we have this display, in the Turner Gallery,' Mrs Porter explains. 'Where we showcase the very best of the art that our students produce.'

Oh shit.

Oh no.

Oh no, no, no!

'Grace – we were blown away with your submission for the scholarship,' she says with a proud smile, stopping near the end of the corridor. 'Our artists in residence said they couldn't believe the talent and maturity from one so young. And so I'm incredibly happy to show you . . . this!'

Fuck.

She points to the last picture on the wall. It's a painting of a fruit bowl. I've seen it many times.

'You really are quiet today!' Mrs Porter laughs. 'First chocolate biscuits, now this!'

'I think she's just a bit overwhelmed,' I say, taking Gracie's shoulders and trying to lead her away. 'But I think we'd both like to give the choccie biccies another go . . .'

'You must be very proud of yourself,' Mrs Porter says to Grace.

My daughter looks at her blankly. I want to be sick.

'Why?' she asks plainly.

But this time Mrs Porter doesn't laugh. She looks at my ashen face, then back to Gracie.

'Because . . . this is your painting,' she says slowly. 'The one that won you the scholarship.'

Everything in my body clenches. Don't say it, Gracie. Please, just don't say it . . .

But she does.

'No it isn't,' she says, shaking her head innocently. 'I did a painting of our back garden. I've never seen this picture before.'

# Ben

Okay.

To try to keep perspective, the Ofsted inspection could be going worse. The school could be on fire. I could have forgotten to get dressed this morning. I could have puked on the lead inspector's shoes.

But aside from that.

It's fucking awful.

Everything that could be going wrong is. We are in the grip of a full-on plague – kids who clearly shouldn't have been brought into school are dropping like flies, often in a pool of their own vomit. The agency cleaners are refusing to come in because we have norovirus in the school and, having not yet replaced Andy, we're having to sort it as we go.

'Mind out the way, you great lug,' says Hattie, barging past, sleeves rolled up and carrying a mop and bucket. 'Little Lily Smith in Bumblebees has just exploded like a landmine.'

Hattie Hughes. There's an enigma wrapped in a riddle. Last night, when she came out of her talk with Bob, she walked past me and grabbed my wrist. Hard.

'Now you listen to me,' she whispered. 'You didn't lamp Clive, you hear? You keep your mouth shut about that or we're both in the cack.'

I didn't really know what to say. But she didn't look like she was up for a conversation.

'Okay,' I told her. 'Anything else?'

'If you're asked, Clive left his wallet at school and I took it to his house,' she whispered hurriedly. 'You stick to that, we're both in the clear, you hear me?'

Why would Hattie lie? And why does she need me to? And other people saw . . . Bob told me that it was my fingerprints they'd found on the groundnut oil bottle, but I pointed out that was hardly surprising given I bought it. He wanted to know why it was inside Creepy Jesus and I told him I could only guess it was a prank – the things we've found in CJ over the years . . . When I have five seconds to rub together, there's a lot to unpack.

But right now I don't.

It's like a war zone here. And, added to that, terrible weather last night has caused all kinds of storm damage – the leaky roof finally gave up the ghost, so I came in at 6am to discover the Early Years corridor looking like Noah's Ark. Thank Christ Marcia was here too – she got straight on the clean-up op – her time as a firefighter prepared her well for today – but the school, which was looking like a new pin last night, now looks like a humanitarian crisis.

And this guy . . .

'So,' says Mr Nutt, the Ofsted inspector, who is the bastard love child of Senator McCarthy and Satan. 'You have been in budget deficit for how long?'

We're in my office and it's been unrelenting. While the other inspectors have sat in classes, we've gone through everything – early years, phonics, maths, safeguarding, my last bowel movement – you name it. I understand him being thorough. Less clear on why he has to be a complete prick about it.

'As you know, I've not long been in post,' I explain for the fiftieth time. 'And, sadly, we are still untangling some of the financial misconduct of our late bursar. But I'm confident that with some gentle prudence and cutting of our cloth, we can be back in the black . . .'

'Confidence is not what I am seeking, Mr Andrews,' he says laconically. 'Action is what is required here.'

'And – as I hope I've laid out in my plans – should I be appointed to the role permanently, it will be my first priority,' I say as pleasantly as my clenched incisors will allow.

'Your first priority?' he leaps. 'So not, say, your dire reading attainment levels at Key Stage 1? Or the polarity in your maths SATs? Or your staff retainment issues?'

'I said "first priority",' I reply while digging my nails into my palms. 'Not "only", Mr Nutt. All of these things will need to be addressed. And I sincerely believe I am the man to address them.'

'Hmmm,' he replies. The prick.

I'm extremely grateful for the knock on the door. So should he be.

'Mr Andrews – I'm so sorry to interrupt – but I have an urgent call for you,' says Marcia. This is our code to interrupt a meeting and I'm glad for it.

'I'm so sorry – would you excuse me?' I say to Nutt. 'Perhaps Marcia could show you our lovely poetry displays in the hall . . . ?'

Before he can object, Marcia has ushered him out of the office. Always employ a former bodyguard as a school admin – that's my advice.

'With you in one moment,' she says to Nutt, closing the door behind him.

'Oh Jeez, thanks for that,' I say. 'I swear it would be less stressful juggling flaming machetes than dealing with this clown . . .'

'Sorry, Ben – not The Code this time,' she says. 'I've got Margaret Porter on the phone.'

'From Shottsford House?' I ask. 'What does she want?'

'Grace Fisher had her scholarship interview there today,' Marcia continues slowly.

'She did,' I say, warming at even this adjacency to Kiera. 'She's probably just calling me to formally confirm Gracie's place – can you put her off to later in the week?'

'I don't think that's it,' she says grimly. 'She sounds . . . It doesn't sound good.'

My guts churn. I don't know if it's the thought of something going wrong for Kiera or the stirrings of norovirus. But I try to quell it.

'Put her through,' I say as she returns to her office. This day, man . . . I sit down and try to breathe through the growing nausea. Don't panic, Andrews. You've seen off worse than this.

I pick up the phone and hear Marcia redirect the call.

'Ben?'

'Hi there, Margaret – sorry I've not been in touch. My feet have barely touched the ground since I took over.'

'I quite understand – it's a whirlwind and I'm happy to

catch up with you properly soon,' she begins. 'But I'm afraid a . . . situation has arisen today that we need to discuss.'

My guts rumble. I hope Margaret didn't hear it.

'Of course,' I say. 'Is this to do with Grace Fisher?'

'I'm afraid it is,' she replies. 'As you are probably aware, I interviewed Grace this morning to confirm her award of the Shottsford House Foundation Scholarship.'

'She's a lovely girl, isn't she?' I say quickly, trying to damp down whatever is coming next. 'A really bright star here at St Nonn's.'

'Absolutely,' she says, with words rather than feelings. 'But something came up during our time together that has left me deeply troubled.'

Oh Christ. Grace said something about me and Kiera. Shit, shit, shit . . .

'I have some serious concerns over the provenance of Grace's scholarship submission,' she says.

'I'm sorry?' I say, like I don't understand posh speak. I understand perfectly what she's saying. I just don't know what the bloody hell to say back.

'To put it plainly, Ben . . . I don't think Grace created the artwork for which she was awarded the funds. I think she cheated . . . or, more to the point, I think someone cheated on her behalf. I didn't get the impression Grace knew anything about the deception.'

I want to rush to defend Grace, to say that's impossible. But then I think of Kiera and the way she's spoken about that school . . . Kiera the devoted parent. Kiera the ambitious mother. Kiera the talented artist . . . Shit.

'I . . . I don't know what to say,' I finally splutter out incoherently. 'I know Grace to be very gifted and someone who would thrive at Shottsford House . . .'

'I'm sure both of those things are true,' she says gently. 'But you understand, Ben – my hands are tied here. Your school must have a record of what was supposed to be submitted . . . I don't want to conjecture what has happened, but if it doesn't match with what we based our decision on, I will have no choice but to revoke the scholarship.'

'Of course,' I say quickly, a chink of light opening up. 'I'm sure it's all a misunderstanding and we can clear it up – but can you bear with us? We've got Ofsted and norovirus in today and I'm not sure which one's worse . . .'

'Oh, you should have said – you must be up to your eyes in it,' she says.

'I'm up to my eyes in something, I tell you,' I try to laugh. 'But, I promise, the second we're over the worst of both, I'll be giving this my urgent attention.'

'I appreciate it,' she says. 'Good luck.'

'Thanks,' I say, replacing the phone.

Kiera, what have you done . . . ?

There is a knock at the door – it's Marcia again.

'Sorry, Ben – I've parked Nutt at the poetry. But we've had another two projectile vomits in Ladybirds and we've just had a call from the electricity board. They're doing some urgent storm repairs in the area, so we're going to be without power at some point between . . .'

The lights flicking off and the screams of children being plunged into darkness fill in the timeline.

'Well, that's just brilliant,' I mutter as the emergency lights power up. 'Okay, let's find torches, lamps, headlights, Victorian streetlights, anything that brightens the place up.'

'Already on it,' says Marcia, going back to her office as I head the other way back up the murky Early Years corridor towards the hall and Mr Nutt.

'You couldn't make it up!' I say brightly as I return to him. 'I know some schools try to keep you in the dark, but this is ridiculous!'

I laugh. He doesn't.

'Now – where were we?' I say, my voice far, far too high.

'You were telling me about attainment levels,' he says. 'We've noticed that they've dropped considerably since our last inspection.'

'Ah yes – the Covid ripple,' I say. 'Home learning was very inconsistent during the pandemic and we're still struggling to level up the kids who perhaps didn't have that support for whatever reason at home.'

'And what measures are you putting in place?' he says as we feel our way along the corridor towards Badger Class.

'Our main strategy relies on early identification and intervention,' I explain in the darkness. 'We're blessed at St Nonnatus with an enthusiastic team of parent volunteers who happily give of their time to—'

'Whoaahahahhahhhhhh!' I hear Nutt shriek, followed by a hefty thud.

'Mr Nutt? Mr Nutt? Are you okay?' I cry, feeling around for him. I get no response. I kneel down and the source of his accident immediately becomes clear when my trousers are soaked with vomit. And the upshot becomes even clearer as the inert form of Mr Nutt collides with my hand. He isn't moving. Oh shit – have we just killed the bloody Ofsted inspector?

Although . . .

I push the thought from my mind.

'Mr Nutt? Are you okay?' I shout at either his head, feet or arse – I cannot see a bloody thing.

A faint moan replies.

Thank Christ for that. I remember that my phone is still in my pocket – screw you, Stitchwell and your No Phone Zone policy – and go to switch on the torch. But, before I can, I see a message from twenty minutes ago.

**Kiera**
Don't send anything to Shottsford.
I'm coming in.
I can explain.

Desperate as I am to see her . . . one thing at a time.

I find Mr Nutt's arms and I pull him up to sitting. Just as I'm trying to reposition him, the phone rings. It's Elena. Fuck . . . I can't ignore it. I've been trying to get hold of her all night. I need to know what's happening with my son . . .

'Elena,' I say, dropping Mr Nutt to the floor with a thud. 'What the hell is going on up there?'

'Hello, Ben,' says a softly spoken voice. 'It's Don.'

I look up at the crucifix through the hall window.

You have got to be having a laugh.

'Don,' I say. 'I need to talk to you – if you are doing anything to my son . . .'

'That's why I'm phoning,' he says calmly. 'There's clearly been a misunderstanding.'

'Of course there has,' I say sarcastically. 'Because my son doesn't understand a grown man picking on him. Whatever you did to him yesterday . . .'

'That's why I'm calling you, Ben,' he says. 'I wasn't with Finn yesterday. Neither of us were. We went away overnight to celebrate Elena's birthday on Wednesday. Finn was with his grandparents.'

I want to shout at him, to tell him he's lying.

But then I think about my call with Arthur and Caitlin.

So that's why they weren't concerned.

Because Finn was with them.

He lied. He lied to me.

'It's clear that Finn is having some . . . difficulty . . . adjusting to my relationship with his mother,' says Don. 'I understand it entirely – I remember meeting my stepfather as a lad. I wanted to push him off a bridge . . .'

I quickly think of all the bridges in Inverness that would be fit for the task.

'I hope he will come to see me differently in time,' he continues, 'but I just want to reassure you that I want nothing more than Finn and Elena's happiness. So I thought this would be an opportunity for us to talk and sort this out. Calmly.'

I look at the vomit, the semi-conscious inspector and the massive hole in the ceiling.

'Now's not really the best time for me, Don,' I say.

'Oh, that's just typical,' says Elena, butting in. 'We try to be calm and reasonable and you are too bloody childish to even engage—'

'Elena, it's not that,' I say, as Mr Nutt starts to groan. 'I'm having a day – we've got Ofsted here and—'

'Oh, don't worry, I get it – I understand your precious career. It's why I let you keep it,' she spits. 'But you wonder why our son is making up stories? It's to get your bloody attention.'

The phone call cuts off. I hate her. I hate her so much.

Not least, because she's absolutely fucking right.

It will change. It will all change.

From tomorrow.

I call the school number.

'Hello, St Nonnatus Primary, Marcia speaking . . .'

'Marcia! It's me! I need the first aid kit in the EY corridor stat! And mind your step! It's like Pat Sharp's sodding *Fun House* around here.'

'On my way,' she says without question, which is one of the many reasons I love working with her. We were so lucky to wrestle her away from the Houses of Parliament.

Mr Nutt is coming to.

'What happened?' he says blearily.

'No drama,' I say calmly. 'You just took a wee tumble. Our first aider is on the way – we always have at least two on site at any given time. Our commitment to Health and Safety is unparalleled . . .'

He gives me a look. Pick your moment, Ben.

'Right,' I say to him before he can fully regain his wits. 'It's not long till home time – why don't we just pick this up tomorrow when you're feeling better, okay?'

Marcia comes running – carefully – down the hall, armed with a first-aid kit and a torch.

'You got this?' I ask her.

'I got,' she says. 'By the way – Kiera just got in. She's looking for you everywhere.'

Marcia's too smart not to know that it's connected to my call with Margaret, but she's too professional to comment.

'Thank you,' I say. 'I'll be back as soon as I can.'

With the pathetic light from my torch as my only guide, I start weaving my way around the school, looking for Kiera. After a fruitless five minutes, I return to my office, figuring that she'll find me there eventually. Turns out, she's there already.

'Ben,' she says, looking awful, 'I have to talk to you.' She's pale and shaking – she's clearly been crying her heart out. I just want to gather her up into my arms and make it all go away. But the place is still crawling with inspectors. And I'm awash with vomit.

'Come in,' I say, guiding her through the door. The second it closes, I go to give her a proper hug, but she pushes me away. She's manic. I've never seen her like this.

'Look – you have to understand,' she says, her eyes wild. 'All those other kids, the ones who already go there? They've got an advantage! They were born into money! They don't have to prove themselves! There's no test! No portfolio! No interview! Mummy and Daddy just write a big, fat cheque and they're in! *Their* parents get to do the work for *them*! It's not fair, Ben, it's not fair . . .'

'Shhhh,' I cajole, both trying to calm and quieten her down. 'I know – the system sucks. We all feel it . . .'

'And her artwork was good, it was so, so good!' she says, tears starting to fall down her face. 'It should have been enough! But I just . . . I just couldn't leave it to chance . . .'

Oh Christ. I try not to sigh. I'm Team Kiera all the way. But this is going to be a nightmare.

'As soon as we brought her portfolio into school, I swapped some of her pieces out with mine – not all of them. Just a few. I didn't think she'd ever see them again and she deserves it so much . . . You should have seen her the day we got the letter saying she'd got the scholarship. She was so proud . . . But then . . . then . . .'

I grab my trusty box of tissues and hand them to her. She blows her nose and tries to slow her breathing. She can't even look at me.

'And then Stitchwell found out.'

This time I do sigh. I know how that must have felt. Exactly how that must have felt.

'Oh, Kiera . . .'

'She told me,' she gasps. 'She told me the night she died. Showed me the letter she'd written to Mrs Porter. She was going to tell her everything. I couldn't let it happen, Ben, I couldn't . . .'

'So what did you do?' I ask cautiously.

She looks at me.

'What I had to do,' she says quietly. 'To protect my daughter.'

I don't ask. We've all done what we've had to do. Whatever our reasons.

She takes another moment to gather herself.

'At first, I just wanted to humiliate Bitchwell, make her feel as small as she'd just made me feel,' I say. 'I wanted her to die on that stage. So I put some of Matt's laxatives in her tea . . .'

'Classy,' I say with a smile. She doesn't return it.

'But Hattie caught me,' she says. 'Made me chuck it away, make her a new one. I kept trying to go to the office and get the letter, but someone was always in there – including you.'

'Sorry about that,' I say, trying the smile again. This time she half responds.

'You're forgiven,' she says. 'Then when it all kicked off, when she started choking like that, I did try to find the EpiPen, I really did – I swear on a stack of Bibles it wasn't there. But the letter was. So, while everyone was distracted, I took it. Stuffed it in my bag, took it home and burned it. I thought that would be the end of it.'

'Wasn't it?'

She raises her eyes to mine. Even red-rimmed and full of pain, she is still astonishingly beautiful.

'Clive,' she replies. 'Stitchwell made a copy. He found it. That's why . . .'

'Oh my love,' I say, finally gathering her into that hug. 'That bastard.'

'He got his,' she says. 'They both did. And they deserved it.'

I say nothing. I completely agree. And all our secrets are best off dead with them. So I just hold her. She's more like a teenager than a grown woman. She feels vulnerable, helpless, younger. I just want to kiss it all away. I want to take everything that has ever hurt her and make it stop. I can make her better – I just know I can.

'Ben,' she says from inside the hug, 'I need you to do something for me.'

'Of course,' I say. 'Anything. I love you.'

She looks up at me, tear-stained and pink.

'I need you to lie to Shottsford House.'

I close my eyes. I feared this was coming.

'Kiera. Darling,' I say to her. 'You know I can't do that. That's fraud – I could lose my job. I could go to prison . . .'

She looks up at me. Her eyes harden. And then she shoves me away.

'Oh, I see,' she declares far more loudly than I want her to. 'So you love me when it's easy? You love me when it's fun? When it's all hearts and flowers and sneaky shags? But when I actually need you to put your head on the block for me . . . ?'

'Kiera – sweetheart – please,' I say, hoping my quieter volume might encourage hers. 'We can talk about this later – I'm right up against it at the moment.'

'Don't bother,' she practically spits in my face. 'You keep your precious job. And you can stick mine while you're at it. Fuck you, Ben.'

She nearly yanks the door off its hinges and storms out. I want to call after her, but I need no more attention drawn to this. Thank God for the power cut. Hopefully no one saw her flounce out of here. I try to calm my anger – I love her, but how dare she risk my career to sort out her mess? I'm sorry for Gracie, truly I am. But what's for you won't go by you. She's a good kid. She'll do well anywhere.

The bell goes for the end of day and I could kiss it. I quickly try to wash the worst of the vomit from my trousers, narrowly avoiding puking myself, before pulling on my jacket to greet the parents. This has truly been a bin fire of a day. I don't normally drink in the week. But I can feel my special blend calling me from here.

I head out of the door and into the playground. It's always chaos at pick-up. But today it is eerily still, all the adults staring at their phones. And then at me.

'Hi, everyone,' I call. 'Glad to see so many of you still standing!'

Nothing. Not so much as a smile.

Stella McEnzie-Roberts comes and grabs her children from right in front of me.

'Disgusting,' she hisses at me, and gathers William and Henry in her arms.

'You should be ashamed,' says Rosie Thompson.

Jimmy Platt spits at my feet. In his pyjamas.

'I beg your . . . what on earth do you think you're doing?' I ask as people start hurrying their children out of the playground. I look to where Priya and Tanya are hovering on the far side of the playground, clutching their children and Al's. I shrug a gesture at them, but even they just turn away. Only Leanne Phillips stands there. Staring straight at me. Smiling.

'Mr Andrews,' comes a voice behind me. I turn round to see Mr Nutt, a dressing on his head and his suit flecked with vomit. He's holding his phone out in front of him.

'Would you care to explain THIS?' he says, thrusting it in my face.

Marcia is standing in the doorway, her usually unflappable face aghast.

I don't understand, what is . . . ?

But then I read the first line.

By the second, my eyes are starting to blur – this can't be happening . . .

I'm not sure I'm gonna make it to the third.

Because I'm already puking.

All over the lead inspector's shoes.

# * THEMIS SPECIAL EDITION *
# THE NONCE OF ST NONN'S!

The Goddess is back! And this time she's branching out to reveal that the latest perv to unnerve is none other than St Nonnatus Primary's very own Mr Ben Andrews! Yes, the man who put the head in headmaster is nothing more than a dirty old perv, preying on women young enough to be his daughter!

Last year he groomed a student from Flatford High on work experience. She was 16 years old. They had a sexual relationship until he decided he'd had enough. When our survivor reported him to the late Claudia Bitchwell, did she report him? Did she fire him? No! She paid our survivor off and made them sign an NDA! Don't believe us? Look at the screenshot of the contract and the cheque below!

Is this the man you want as your Headteacher?

Or will you make a stand and say No to the Nonce!

# Kiera

I race home like the devil himself is at my heels. I need to see her. I need to see my Taylor. How did I miss this? How have I been so stupid?

I get home and yank the front door open.

'Tay! Taylor!' I yell, taking the stairs three at a time. 'Taylor baby, where are you?'

I burst into her room, where she's sitting on the bed with Sebastian and Tilly.

'Mum, what the f—'

I grab her and I hold her to me. I claw at her, pulling her closer to me, wanting to absorb her inside me where I can keep her safe.

'I will kill him!' I shriek. 'I will fucking kill him! Did he hurt you? Why didn't you tell me, Tay, why?'

'Mum!' she shouts, pulling herself away from me. 'MUM! It wasn't me.'

I'm in such a state it takes me a moment to register what she just said.

'You . . . what?' I blather.

'Chill,' she says uncomfortably. 'It wasn't me that Andrews . . . that he . . . It wasn't me.'

I stare at her. What?

'I don't . . . I don't understand,' I say. 'Themis . . . the news-letter . . . that wasn't . . . ?'

'Oh, Themis was me,' she says, with no small hint of pride. 'Gracie came home in bits. She told me about the art scholarship. Then she told me about . . . him. About Andrews.'

This is information overload. One thing at a time.

'So if it wasn't you . . . how do you know?' I say, a small glimmer of hope starting to form. Perhaps Ben didn't do it. Perhaps Taylor has got it wrong. Perhaps . . .

'Because it was me,' says Sebastian, shuffling off the bed. 'He slept with me. Loads of times. Last year. When I did my placement at the school. When I was . . . my dead name. He told me . . . He told me he loved me . . .'

Oh God.

Sebastian.

Julia, as was last year.

A sixteen-year-old on work placement at St Nonn's.

How did I miss him? Another perv. Another school. Another innocent child.

Sebastian starts to cry.

'You must think I'm so stupid,' they sob.

I move us over to the bed and put my arm around them.

'Not at all,' I say. 'Men like him . . . they know exactly what buttons to press. This is totally on him. Not you.'

I hold Seb to me. I know exactly how they feel. Exactly.

'Mum . . . I'm so sorry,' says Taylor uncertainly. 'I didn't know what else to do. Seb was here when Gracie told me about you and Andrews. I didn't know what he'd done until then, I swear. Seb hadn't told anyone. And I didn't want you getting involved with—'

'Shhhh,' I say, pulling her to me. 'You have nothing to apologise for. I'm the one who's screwed everything up. What you did took courage. Stupid courage. But courage. And I'm proud of you.'

'Can I get in on that hug, please?' says a tearful Tilly.

We all sit there for a while, me holding these three lost and confused young people. I know how they feel. Exactly how they feel.

A few moments later, there is a little knock at the door.

'Gracie,' I say, wiping the tears off my face. 'How are you?'

'I . . . I . . . I'm sorry,' she stammers at me as the door opens wider. 'I had to tell him . . .'

And standing there, with a face like granite, is my Matt.

'Was he better than me?' is Matt's first question as we cradle cups of tea at the kitchen table ten minutes later. I know I've no right. But I pull a face.

'Really?' I ask. 'We're facing the imminent collapse of our marriage, life and family and you want to know if he was a better shag than you?'

Matt considers this for a moment.

'Yeah,' he replies. 'Yeah I bloody do.'

I sigh.

'I've been a complete and utter total dickhead of the highest order,' I say. 'I've been stupid and naive and reckless and I've made a horrible, terrible mistake.'

He considers this.

'Am I supposed to disagree or summit?' he whispers.

I snort despite myself and he smiles. I'd forgotten how cute his smile is.

'Matt . . . I am so, so sorry,' I tell him. 'You've never done anything but love me and the girls. I don't know what's wrong with me. I don't know why nothing is ever . . .'

'Enough?' he fills in, taking the word I didn't want to say from my mouth.

'Yeah,' I reply, slightly staggered. 'Yeah. Enough. It's not that I don't love you guys, it's just . . .'

I don't even know what it just is. I don't know what's wrong with me. I don't even have the words. I shake my head. I hear Matt take a deep breath.

'Now I'm not some poncy quack with a Harley Street office and a thing for me mum,' he says. 'But I have a theory if you're happy for me to have a crack?'

I shrug. Why not?

'Kier . . . it's not exactly a massive surprise, is it?' he begins. 'You had a kid when you were still a kid. You missed a bit. When I were eighteen, I were drinking and shagging and doing stupid shite every day. You were feeding and working and changing stinky shite every hour.'

I snort again. He's not wrong.

'Life don't like it when you miss a bit of the puzzle,' he says. 'You don't get the whole picture. So it ain't much of a shock that you wanna catch up.'

I have to laugh. That's it. He's nailed it. My husband. Buy-Rite manager and Freudian therapist. Who knew?

'And, more to the point,' he says, slugging his tea, 'you bloody well should. You're brilliant at what you do, but you're wasted. You're so talented, Kier. You should be teaching them classes, not cleaning up piss 'n' shit.'

He's saying everything I've been saying to myself for so long. But I have a question.

'How?' I ask. 'What gives?'

'We all do!' he says. 'For Christ's sake, I know you think we're all useless, but I can open a can o' beans like the next bloke. Taylor and Gracie are older now – they don't need you here all the time. Go back to school! Get your exams! Finish the bloody puzzle!'

'What about Shottsford House?' I sniff. 'We can't afford for me to—'

'Oh, you shat the bed on that one, kid!' he laughs. 'Gracie ain't going there now after what you did!'

I start to pant.

'Does she hate me?' I squeak. 'I was only trying to give her—'

'Aw, love – she don't hate ya.' He smiles, grabbing my hand. 'I won't lie, she was pretty pissed off about Noncy Andrews, but I set her straight. Told her we'd sort it out. But the painting? She gets you were only trying to help. Though you should have trusted her to do it herself – she thinks you don't rate her.'

'I know – it's so, so stupid. I've been so, so stupid!' I cry, hitting my head with my fists.

'That you have,' he says plainly, folding his arms. 'And that's your cross to bear, babe. But nothing's been done that can't be fixed. Bit of time. Bit of love. Bit of patience.'

I nod, ripping the drenched tissue in my hands.

'Now. Can I ask a question?' he says, leaning in.

'Sure.'

'Do you wanna leave me?' he says simply. 'Because I'm not gonna beg and cry and make a fuss like a big girlie ponce. If you want out, Kier, just say the word.'

I look at him. I look around our home. I think of our family. It's real. And it's here. Ben was a dream – a nightmare as it turns out. But he was something bright and shiny to distract me from the grey I've let my life become. He wasn't the answer. I'm the answer. And that just leaves Matt's question.

'No,' I say, yet another round of tears coming to my eyes. 'I don't want to leave you.'

'Oh thank fuck for that!' he says, breathing an enormous sigh of relief as he runs his hand across his shaved head. 'Cos I really didn't wanna have to beg and cry and make a fuss like a big girlie ponce . . .'

I snort again. Christ, I've been an idiot. He takes my hand across the table.

'Look,' he says. 'You know I'm nothing if not a practical lad. When you punch up like I have, you kinda expect this to happen. You're the hottest piece of ass in Flatford, Kiera Fisher, and I still can't believe I pulled ya.'

I smile.

'You're so romantic.'

'Get in.' He winks. 'But, Kier . . . you get one free pass, right? I love ya, but I'm not a mug. This don't mean you can go round the town copping off with all the fellas and I'll just sit home like a melon. You've had your freebie, okay?'

'Okay,' I agree.

'You mean it?' he says earnestly. 'One free pass? That's it?'

I nod. I do not deserve this man.

'Good,' he says, taking a sip of his tea. 'Cos while we're laying cards on table, Frieda nearly sucked me off at the Buy-Rite Christmas do last year.'

WHAT?

'You cheating—' I start to go off.

'Uh-uh-uh,' he says, waggling his finger at me. 'Free pass, right? And it never even happened – I ended up puking all over her top knot before she could get a latch on – it were a big night. But we're square. And Frieda weren't a nonce so I win on points.'

I am absolutely bloody furious.

And then I start laughing.

And he starts laughing.

And in this awful moment, both of us are helpless.

And then he bangs down his tea, comes round the table and grabs me in his great, big, sexy arms.

And then we start kissing. Like we haven't for years. Properly, passionately kissing. Like two people who know each other so well, but have more to find. Like two people in actual love. Not the carvings-on-the-tree love. The love that's the tree itself.

He sweeps me up off the floor and heads towards the stairs.

'Right, you,' he whispers in my ear. 'Girls have got twenty quid and me BuyRite discount card, so I reckon that gives me at least half hour to show you how a real lad shags.'

'Wow,' I tell him, running my hand down his face. 'It's like being married to William Blake.'

'Not much innocence here, kid,' he winks. 'But plenty of experience.'

I raise my eyebrows in admiration.

'You're learning a lot from those quiz shows, Mr Fisher.'

'Damn straight,' he says as we reach our bedroom. 'Speaking of which, let's crack on – it's *The Chase* at five . . .'

## Kiera Fisher

### Thursday 1 Dec
17.23

**Ben**
Kiera...
I'm so sorry.
Please let me explain.
It isn't how it sounds.
*Voice call*
*11 seconds*

**Ben**
Kiera?
Kiera please pick up...
*Voice call*
*5 seconds*

**Ben**
I can explain everything.
I was stupid...
I just need you to talk to me.
*Voice call*
*11 seconds*

**Ben**
KIERA!
PLEASE.

**Kiera**
Stay away from me you perv.

**Ben**
*Voice call*
*5 seconds*

*Calls to this number have been blocked*

401

# PARENTCHAT

Clearer Community Communication

## ST NONNATUS CE PRIMARY

*Ora et labora*

**Monday 12 December**

**Mrs Marcia Cox<<u>M.Cox@stnonnatus.flatford.sch.uk</u>>**

**To: <Whole School>**

**Re: Week commencing 12 December**

**Dear [insert new terminology here],**

It has been an extraordinary term here at St Nonnatus. We are aware that there has been a great deal of hurt and pain and that there remain a great number of unanswered questions. I shall attempt to summarise some of the most pressing here.

After an immediate suspension and internal investigation, Mr Ben Andrews's employment at St Nonnatus was terminated last week. We will continue to review the catastrophic safeguarding failings that led to the events surrounding his dismissal and are working with the affected parties to ensure they receive all the ongoing support they require. The actions of a single individual should not stain the reputation of an entire school, but we are mindful that there is a great deal of trust that must be rebuilt. And we will. Mrs Lucy Ellis, current headteacher of Flatford High, will be seconded to us as acting head until further notice.

As a result of the recent Ofsted inspection, the report has recommended that St Nonnatus is placed into 'Special Measures'. This means that they've deemed our school in need of additional support in order to ensure the necessary improvements. Schools that are placed into Special Measures are more closely monitored by Ofsted and we can anticipate regular visits from Her Majesty's inspectors across the coming school year.

Although the report was a big disappointment for us all, we are choosing to take a positive outlook and embrace the opportunity for growth. We are all fully committed to improvement and the extra support we will receive will help us to make rapid progress. As we constantly tell our students, we must learn to thrive in adversity and so it shall be. Ours is a community and together we can turn this ship around. We are excited to embark on the voyage with you.

You may be aware that the police have concluded their investigations into both Miss Stitchwell and Mr Baxendale's deaths. They have deemed Miss Stitchwell's passing to be a tragic accident as a result of her severe allergies. They continue to seek Mr Baxendale's assailant, although have exhausted all present lines of enquiry. We are mindful that both cases are a continued source of community and media speculation and we ask again that you use discretion about how and where your views are aired. Facebook polls are not an adequate substitution for due legal process.

After much discussion, we have decided to proceed with the Christmas Fayre **this Saturday 17 December**. This has long been a joyful focal point of the St Nonn's year and so much work has gone into it from the whole community. There is much for us to learn from the past few months, but much to celebrate too. And, ultimately, everything we all do is for the children, who perhaps need this happy occasion more than ever. As is our tradition, we invite them to bring along their letters to Father Christmas and they are encouraged to read them aloud as we have received word that he will be listening. I look forward to seeing you there.

I leave you with the words of our own school motto: 'Ora et labora: Pray and work.'

Best wishes,

Mrs Marcia Cox

Office Manager
St Nonnatus Primary School

# Tickly Tiger's Diary!

Date: Monday 12 December

This weekend I went home with: Adel

I was SO happy to get Tickly Tiger on Friday!

I cuddled Tickly in the taxi all the way back to Rainbow House and my key worker Tom was so proud of me that we all got pizza for tea! And it was a double celebration as we have a new member of the Rainbow Family called Mylo who is coming to stay for a while and he's 10 like me! We all watched Star Wars in the Games Room. Except Mylo because he wanted to stay in his bedroom.

On Saturday I had THE BEST playdate with Simeon. We went to watch Flatford FC play! Simeon's Dads let me have burger and chips AND a coke and I wore a Flatford scarf – and they even let me keep it at the end! I tried to give them two pounds to pay for it, but Barney said it was a present and I told him it wasn't my birthday until April and he said it didn't matter and then Dustin cried a bit. I put my scarf on Tickly, but it was a bit big for him and he doesn't like the dark, so I took it off. Flatford lost, which isn't surprising with a 3 4 3 formation that doesn't suit their attacking style of play. But it was still brilliant. Tickly and I have written Simeon and his Dads a letter to say thank you.

When I went back to Rainbow House, I went to see Mylo in his bedroom as I thought he might like to hear all about it. But he was very sad. I was very sad when I came to Rainbow House. But then I found some happy and I told Mylo that. And then I told him about Flatford FC and he said that they rely too much on their midfield, which I didn't agree with, but I didn't say anything because he was a bit less sad and I didn't want to make him more sad again. He really liked Tickly Tiger, though, and as Mylo didn't have time to bring any teddies, Tickly decided to stay with Mylo in his bed. I know that if anyone can help Mylo to find some happy, it's Tickly Tiger.

On Sunday, we all played table football in the Games Room and I beat Tom, even though he said I cheated because I spun the handles, but we never play that rule, so it doesn't count and I still won. Then we played real football outside and then we watched The Lego Movie on Sunday night. Tickly really enjoyed the film. And it looked like Mylo did too.

# PARENTCHAT

Clearer Community Communication

## ST NONNATUS CE PRIMARY

*Ora et labora*

### Year 6 Tiger Class
click here for group info

### Tuesday 13 December
10.32

**Felicity**
OMG!!!
Where do we start?!

**Zofia**
I always had a funny feeling about Andrews.
Never really liked him.

**Sharon**
I still can't believe it.
Just goes to show – never trust a pretty face.
And I still reckon Bitchwell was murdered.
I'm desperate to find out whodunnit.
Not least so I can buy them a pint...

**Tanya**
Has everyone signed up for their bar shifts on the
Doodle poll?
We're still a few hands short on Saturday...
And I'm sure we could all use a drink!

**Felicity**
*I always had a funny feeling about Andrews.*
Does anyone know where he is?

**Flo**

*I'm desperate to find out whodunnit.*
I reckon it was Ben.
Stitchwell knew about his fling with the student.
Told Baxendale.
Boom.

**Petra**

Hi – has anyone seen Archie's shoes?

**Karen**

Tanya – I've got Beth's story for Hattie's book.
Shall I drop it round?

**Zofia**

*Does anyone know where he is?*
I heard he went back to Scotland.
There's a For Sale sign on his house.

**Karl**

*Has everyone signed up for their bar shifts on the
Doodle poll?*
Could anyone swap with my 11–12 shift?
I've double booked with the Dolphins' Chocolate
Tombola.

**Fatima**

*I reckon it was Ben.*
I think Clive killed Stitchwell.
She knew about his dodgy finances.
The burglary was karma.

**Felicity**

Has anyone heard from Leanne?
I just hope her Seb is okay.

*Sarah has joined the group 'Year 6 Tigers'*

**Sarah**

Hi everyone!
I'm BACK!

**Flo**
*I've double booked with the Dolphins' Chocolate Tombola.*
Can you ever commit to one thing at once?

**Tanya**
*Shall I drop it round?*
Thanks love – that would be fab.
It's going to be amazing.
I've got so many beautiful stories and pictures.
She's going to love it.

**Jane**
*Has anyone heard from Leanne?*
Spoke to her last week.
They've taken an early family Christmas holiday.
Get away for a bit.

**Sharon**
*I'm BACK!*
Hello love!
Where you been?
Weekend away?

**Dustin**
Is there any more news on Mike and Jenna?

**Zofia**
Did you hear about Kiera's Grace?
They took her scholarship to Shottsford House away.
Cheating apparently…

**Stella**
*I think Clive killed Stitchwell.*
Might I remind you about Marcia's request not to idly speculate?

**Sharon**
Absolutely.
Knock yourself out.
I still reckon it was Ben.

**Sarah**

*Where you been?!*

Ha! ☺

Nice to know I can be away for nearly TWO MONTHS and no one notices!

**Priya**

*Cheating apparently . . .*

Not cool, Zofia.

We can dish out on adults here.

Not kids.

**Dustin**

*Could anyone swap with my 11–12 shift?*

Yes please!

I'm 1–2, but I'm supposed to be on the BBQ, so suits me perfectly!

**Sharon**

*They've taken an early family Christmas holiday.*

Good.

Best thing for them, poor loves.

**Tanya**

*Is there any more news on Mike and Jenna?*

They're together in the hospital.

Jenna's recovering.

But they still can't get her home.

So Mike is probably going to have to come back on his own.

**Karen**

*Nice to know I can be away for nearly TWO MONTHS and no one notices!*

Huh?

Confused.com!

Where have you been?

**Karl**

*I'm 1–2, but I'm supposed to be on the BBQ, so suits me perfectly!*
You're a legend, mate.
Beers after?

**Zofia**

*We can dish out on adults here.*
*Not kids.*
You're right.
My bad.
Sorry.

**Felicity**

*So Mike is probably going to have to come back on his own.*
Oh no... and leave Jenna there?
Alone?

**Sarah**

*Where have you been?*
My dad hasn't been well in France.
He's better now – but sod all signal in the mountains!
Can't believe I missed all the drama!
Even if no one's missed me!

**Dustin**

*Beers after?*
How about during?

**Tanya**

*Oh no . . . and leave Jenna there?*
It's looking that way.
Poor Jacob.
Everyone's been great at looking after him.
But the poor boy must be totally bewildered.
And missing his mum.

**Felicity**
*My dad hasn't been well in France.*
I'm so sorry to hear that.
I saw your sister at drop-off.
Just assumed you were busy at work.

**Karl**
*How about during?*
Done 👍

**Sharon**
*Even if no one's missed me!*
Hang on the bell...
Help an old lady out...
Sarah love, are you saying you haven't been on this group for two months?

**Jennie**
Does anyone know a good private investigator?

**Sarah**
*Sarah love, are you saying you haven't been on this group for two months?*
Yes! Not since before half-term!
Like I say, bugger all signal at my Dad's.
And I dropped my old phone at Elijah's Splashworld party in half-term.
Then Dad kicked off.
Never had a chance to log back on here.

**Laura**
I think it belongs to No 73 – they have the same spade.

**Laura**
Sorry! Wrong group!

**Zofia**
*Never had a chance to log back on here.*
Um...
Scroll back up the chats.
We've been talking to you for weeks!

**Jane**

*And I dropped my old phone at Elijah's Splashworld
party in half-term.*
You should've gone for the Platinum package.
They take the pictures for you.

**Petra**

*I've got so many beautiful stories and pictures.*
Sorry Tanya.
Archie did a lovely collage.
But... you know...

**Annie**

*And I dropped my old phone at Elijah's Splashworld
party in half-term.*
Elijah had a party?

**Sarah**

*We've been talking to you for weeks!*
Okay guys...
This is really weird.
Whatever 'Sarah' you've been talking to.
It's not been me.

**Sharon**

WHAT?

**Jane**

No?!

**Karl**

You sure?

**Felicity**

That is super creepy.
Why would anyone do that?

**Tanya**

Oh Sarah...

**Flo**

*You sure?*
Yeah, Karl.
I think she probably is.

**Priya**

*It's not been me.*
Then who was it?

**Zofia**

Oh my God!
Must be some kind of scammer...
Have you checked your bank etc.
Could be ID fraud.

**Fatima**

Similar thing happened to my cousin.
Someone stole her identity online.
Used it to buy an annual pass to Monkey World.

**Priya**

That's a weird scam.
I mean, it's not like 'Sarah' asked us for anything.
No money, no personal details.
That's how these things usually work.

**Sarah**

*Have you checked your bank etc.*
Thanks Zofia – yes I have.
All is well.
But I don't understand.
Why would anyone pretend to be me 👻?

**Sharon**

Because you're fabulous, love!

**Zofia**

True.
But that is freaky.

**Jane**

It really is.

**Karen**

You okay, Sarah?

**Sarah**
Yeah.
Just a bit weirded out.
Oh – and by the way?
Has anyone got this week's spellings?

# Robocoppers

Priya, Al, Tanya

## Saturday 17 December
10.13

**Priya**

Bloody hell.

That was a frantic week.

**Al**

Jesus, tell me about it.

I've been in school every single day.

Millie's Christmas concert on Tuesday.

Leo's prize assembly on Wednesday.

The Tigers' Christmas disco on Thursday.

And I was helping Hattie bake for the cake stall all yesterday!

I have got ZERO enthusiasm for the Fayre today.

**Priya**

Me neither.

I just want to bury myself in a onesie
and a tub of Quality Street.

**Tanya**

Don't you bloody dare say that!

I've been here since 7am!

Counting on you guys!

**Al**

Don't sweat, babe.

We'll be there.

I think everyone could do with letting their hair down.

Is Kiera there?

She hasn't been in school all week.

**Tanya**

She is, bless her.

Sticking pretty close to Hattie.

Tongues are wagging about Shottsford House.

But you know Kiera, she'll front it out.

**Priya**

*Tongues are wagging about Shottsford House.*

Oh let them.

She was only doing what she thought was best for her kid.

**Al**

WOW!

Priya Mistry In Defending Kiera Fisher Shocker!

**Priya**

Sod off.

I just get it.

She hasn't had a fair shot.

She wants her daughter to have one.

**Al**

Well Grace seems relieved, tbh.

It'll be good for them – for all of us – to have a break.

It's been a helluva term.

**Tanya**

Amen.

And I'm glad the police have called it on Clive and Stitchwell.

We all need to move on.

**Priya**

Hmmmmm...

**Al**

Priya!

You promised!

**Priya**

I know, I know.

There's just so much that doesn't make sense.

If Stitchwell didn't die from the cake, how the hell did she ingest the nuts in a drink?

Why would a burglar shoot Clive, an overweight middle-aged man that my Anya could overpower?

And there's still the question of the money.

Who has the Stitchwell fortune?

**Tanya**
I guess we'll never know.
And I'm happy to leave it that way.

**Al**
I agree.
Some things are better off buried.
And Claudia Stitchwell and Clive Baxendale are two of
them.

                                                        **Priya**
                                    Some coppers you'd both make...
                                        So what's the deal today?
                        I missed last year – we both had Covid.

**Tanya**
Oh it's such a lovely day!
Each class runs their stall.
There's music and games.
The kids read their letters to Santa.
There's loads of food and drink...
Oh Al – tell me Hattie made Joanie's secret mince
pies?
They will keep me going today!

**Al**
Oh yes.
We made dozens.
They should be in rehab they have so much brandy
inside them.

**Tanya**
Perfect! 😋

                                                        **Priya**
                                                        Joanie?

**Al**
Hattie's mum.
Used to run the local bakery.
Best baker in creation.
(Present company excepted, Tan.)

**Tan**

You're too kind.

Although I admit, most of my recipes are Joanie's.

I've prised them out of Hattie down the years.

What time are you guys getting here?

**Al**

I'm going to leave shortly.

We're just having to negotiate an elf costume situation.

Shall I pick you up on the way Pri?

**Tanya**

Brilliant.

I could really use your help.

The Christmas tree in the hall is wonky.

And we've got a slight situation with a missing lizard from the reptile man...

**Al**

Ha – brilliant!

I'm well trained.

I've pulled Hammy the Hamster out of every crevice in this house.

**Tanya**

HAMMY'S STILL ALIVE?

HOW???

**Al**

Er, technically he's Hammy the Fifth.

The kids didn't even notice.

Even when he changed colour.

Pri? You there?

Wanna lift?

I've got the S-max, so we can get you, Anya and your chair in.

(If you don't mind sharing with a grumpy elf.)

**Tanya**

And I've noticed that you haven't signed up for one of the spare bar shifts.
You WILL be roped in!
Pri?
Have we lost you to the Quality Street?

**Priya**

I've just been reading back over the group chats.
Al, I'll take that lift.
We need to get to the fayre.
And you owe me a tenner.

**Al**

Sure.
And... why?

---

**Tanya**

You can't seriously think one of them would actually kill Stitchwell?

**Priya**

Can't I?
Twenty years on the force and a tenner says I can.

**Al**

I'll take your money.

---

**Priya**

So have your cash ready, Bourne.
Because I think I've just figured out
who killed Claudia Stitchwell.

# Kiera

I'm not going to hide away. Shoulders back. Smile wide.

It's been a week. I cried off sick to get my head straight. Taylor and I had a big heart-to-heart. She's right – I have been putting Gracie's needs over hers. I apologised and I will do better. In return, she's going to try to settle down at school – Themis has given her a taste for justice, so she now wants to go to uni and study law! God help anyone she cross-examines. I know I barely survive it . . .

Gracie is starting to forgive me, which I must say is largely down to Matt. He's been incredible. In oh so many ways . . . Grace is actually really relieved about the scholarship and, on some level, so am I. She's sitting the tests for Flatford High's grammar stream in the New Year. I'll be keeping a close eye. But she's got her head screwed on right.

The equilibrium nearly took a knock when we exchanged on the house yesterday. The girls are still furious they are losing their home, but we'd be crazy to turn down this buyer – they don't seem to care about anything. It's been the easiest sale – and now at least we can put in an offer on somewhere else.

So next year is going to be a lot – new home, new schools, new life. But today it's the Christmas Fayre and I'm going to enjoy it.

And manning the bar is really bloody helping.

'Bloody hell, Hats – how much mulled wine did you make?' I ask as she pours another vat of it into the cauldron.

''Tis the season,' she says. 'You all right?'

'I will be,' I tell her, and it's the truth. 'The girls are getting there. And Matt's been . . . amazing.'

'Told you. You got a keeper there. So you keep him,' she says.

She puts down her pot and looks weirdly at me. And then she pulls me into a massive hug. It takes me a bit by surprise –

Hattie's not a big one for big emotion. But it feels good. Really good.

'It's all gonna be all right,' she tells me. 'You just see if it ain't. Because there's loads that care about you, Kiera Fisher. So let 'em. And I'm top o' the list. I love you, gal.'

'Love you too, Hats,' I tell her. Because I really, really do.

Is that . . . ? Is that a tear in her eye? Bloody hell. I don't think I've ever seen Hattie cry.

She must have really gone at the mulled wine.

'Right,' she says, pulling herself together. 'I'm gonna go make some more o' this – back in a bit.'

'Hattie, we really don't need any . . .'

But it's too late. She's on her way to the kitchen. It's where she's happiest. It's where she belongs.

I turn to the stage, where Sasha McCall is reading out her Santa letter.

'Dear Santa,' she reads with a big grin. 'For Christmas I would like the Pony Palace stable, the Pony Palace horse box, seven Pony Palace ponies, the Pony Palace grooming set and a Smiggle voucher. I've been really good. Love Sasha.'

A gentle ripple of applause goes around the hall. These letters are so cute. In a totally grasping way.

'Oh my God,' says Tanya, hurtling over and throwing a mulled wine down her neck. 'You haven't happened to see yellow grass snake, have you? It's chaos at the Reptile stand. It's like a miniature Jurassic Park . . .'

My mind flits back to Ben. We've had enough slimy creatures roaming this hall, thank you very much.

'I'll keep an eye out,' I tell her as she necks her second glass. 'How's Hattie's book turned out? I'm really sorry I couldn't do the artwork. I . . .'

We both know why I haven't done it, so I don't feel the need to say it out loud. But I feel really crap about it. I look at the floor, unable to look Tanya in the eye. I feel a warm hand on my wrist.

'Your family needed you,' she says kindly. 'And that must always come first.'

I look up into her smiling face. There's not an ounce of

judgement in her eyes. Just support. Hattie's right. There are people who care.

'Oh look,' I tell her, happy to distract from the intensity of the moment. 'Verity's up with her Santa letter.'

'Ah – this could be helpful,' says Tanya. 'She's keeping dead quiet to prove Father Christmas doesn't exist.'

'Dear Father Christmas,' grins Verity from behind the mic. 'For Christmas I would like all the children of the world to be safe and happy.'

A delighted moan echoes around the parents. Verity grins even more broadly.

'And a puppy. Love you, Santa!'

She does a little curtsey and heads off stage.

'Oh Christ,' says Tanya, chugging back some more mulled wine. She's gonna be laced by lunchtime. And why not? She's worked so hard to pull all this together. She works hard to pull this whole community together. I should be more help than I am.

It's barely gone 11am, but the bar's already getting busy, so I get to serving everyone. I get a few funny looks. Stella McEnzie-Roberts can stick her orange juice up her sanctimonious arse. And after how much I've seen of Theo Thompson's, Rosie can keep her side eyes to herself. But, broadly, everyone is pleasant enough. That's the great thing about a school community. You're only the headline gossip for so long – someone else will be in Dispatches before long.

'Bloody hell,' comes a horny whisper in my ear as I feel a pair of strong arms encircle my waist. 'Your poncy bottled lager might be a bag o' shite, but I'll have whatever the barmaid's serving . . .'

He pulls me round and gives me a massive great snog, much to the delight of the line and the disgust of our kids.

'Gross!' Gracie moans, while looking slightly pleased.

'Get a room,' Taylor scoffs. 'Can I have a fiver for the chocolate tombola?'

'Absolutely not,' I protest as Matt hands over a tenner.

''S all right, love.' He winks. 'I'm cleaning up on the general knowledge bingo! Chips are on me tonight . . .'

He smacks me on the bum with another wink as Gracie drags him away to relieve him of more of our disposable income. I bet Shottsford House doesn't have glitter tattoos.

The hall suddenly goes weirdly quiet. Little Jacob Richardson is at the microphone, looking nervous as all hell. I don't know if he can feel the hearts going out to him. But there are about three hundred pointing his way right now.

'Dear Father Christmas,' he says, his little hands shaking. 'I'm not writing to ask for a present. Christmas is when miracles happen, like the baby Jesus and the *Doctor Who* special. And this year I'd like a miracle, please. I want my mummy back. That's all. I don't care if she's a bit broken and messy like Mike says she is, because my swingball has only gone one way since the summer and I still love that. I just want her home. In our house. With Mike and Bea. Even if Bea is doing her menstrual cycle like we learned on Love Day and it makes her a bit of a psycho. I've asked God too, so I don't know if you're friends, but perhaps you and God could do it as a joint present? My two aunts do that, even though they live in different houses and it's only ever a five-pound book token, which doesn't even buy one book and . . .'

He is drowned out by a collective gasp from the entire St Nonn's community. And then the clapping starts. And then the cheers follow. And then the tears.

Because wheeling up behind him – as broken and messy as a dodgy swingball – is Jenna Richardson.

Jacob is a little confused for a moment. I don't think he expected his letter to get quite that response. But then a tearful Tanya turns him round. And he can't believe his little eyes. He quickly turns back to the mic.

'Although, Santa, if you want to give me a present too, I'd really like the Mario Kart upgrade package, thanks, bye . . .'

He pauses for a moment.

And then he runs to his mummy.

Mike's crying. Jenna's crying. Bea's rolling her eyes.

And we're all in pieces.

Thank God for Hattie's mulled wine.

The hall erupts in cheers and everyone's hugging and raising glasses to a beloved family. There's a lot that's wrong with a community like this.

But, fuck me, there's a lot that's right.

'Wow,' I say, turning back to my next punter. 'That was . . .'

Oh great. It's Priya.

'Hey,' she says.

I nod in response.

'How are you?' she asks.

'Fine,' I say stiffly. 'You?'

'Fine,' she replies. 'Look . . . Kiera. I know we're not exactly the best of mates—'

'You must have been a great detective—'

'But I really need to talk to you. You got a minute? It's important.'

Al comes up behind me and puts a reassuring hand on my shoulder. I take the money belt off from round my waist and hand it over. I don't think I like this . . .

We seek out a quieter corner of the hall and she gestures for me to sit down.

'Can I ask you one thing?' she asks, with both of us knowing she's going to ask it anyway. 'And it's really important. Are you the Stitchwell Love Child? By which I mean, were either of the Stitchwells your parent?'

I spit a mouthful of mulled wine across the floor.

'WHAT?' I laugh. 'You think Bitchwell was my mum? Or the Randy Rev my dad?'

'I'm sorry to intrude,' she says, 'but it's incredibly important that I know.'

Something in her face tells me I need to be straight with her. So I am.

'No,' I say, shaking my head. 'I'm not related to the Stitchwells. My dad was a squaddie who passed through the camp. Knocked up my mum who was a troubled kid – she had me, gave me to the church, then buggered off.'

'And Taylor?'

Okay, this time I nearly choke.

'Jesus! Now you think my Taylor is one of the Randy Rev's bible bastards? And that I shagged him? Jesus – he was a pensioner when I was a teenager! I mean Handy Pandy was bad enough – he was in his forties, the filthy perv . . .'

'Thank you for your candour,' she says. 'And I just want you to know that I'm sorry for what you've been through.'

'Thanks, but don't sweat it,' I say, replenishing my wine. 'My shame died with Handy's heart attack. And he gave me Taylor . . .'

'That's an incredibly courageous perspective,' she says admiringly – that's unusual. 'But I was talking about Ben.'

I freeze. What does she know?

'The disabled loo is right next to his office,' she whispers. 'You guys were either really into Quiz Night, or . . .'

I loll my head back. Great. That's me back in Dispatches.

'I haven't told a soul and I won't,' she promises. And I find myself believing her. 'Anya's dad was my boss in the Met. We had a torrid, passionate affair. Told me he loved me. Told me he was leaving his wife for me. Told me we'd start our own family. And yet when I told him I was pregnant with Anya . . .'

She doesn't supply more details and I don't need them. Jesus. Is there a woman alive who hasn't been screwed over by a man?

'So I know how it feels to be everyone's bit of scandal,' she says. 'They won't be hearing anything from me. But, for what it's worth, I'm sorry.'

She reaches over for my hand. And I give it to her.

'It is what it is,' I tell her. 'I could break my heart over it, or I could get on with my life.'

'And you're making the right choice,' she says. 'Your life isn't his to take. So don't let him.'

We smile at each other. Survivors both. We get it.

We head back to the bar, where Tanya is handing Al a piece of cake.

'Bloody hell, Tan – this is your best one ever, I swear it,' says Al with a mouthful of chocolate sponge.

'It's Hattie's mayonnaise – it's a game-changer,' Tanya laughs, looking at me and Priya. 'How we all doing?'

'We're good,' says Priya, smiling at me. 'But I really need to talk to Hattie . . .'

'Shoot – I've got to go and do the speech for her birthday present,' says Tanya, a slight slur already in her words. 'I'm going to sob my heart out, I just know it. What if she decides to retire?'

'Oh, relax – she won't go anywhere. I guarantee it,' I tell them. 'Flatford's in her blood. Twenty quid says she'll still be here for her ninetieth . . .'

'I hope you're right,' says Tanya. 'Right, wish me luck . . .'

She heads off to the stage with some encouraging words from her friends. It would be nice to be part of a group like that. Perhaps I should try harder to be in one.

'This cake . . .' Al says, stuffing his face. 'Don't tell Tan, but I don't know if it's hers or another "Hattie surprise"!'

'What do you mean?' Priya asks.

'Er . . . hi, everyone!' comes Tanya's voice through the microphone on stage. 'Can you hear me?'

An enthusiastic roar goes up from the crowd.

'He's talking about Hattie's magic food swaps,' I explain. 'Where she fake bakes someone else's cake. She's always doing it – that woman is to baking what Bootleg Barry is to bent bank notes . . .'

'So, as you might know,' Tanya continues, 'today is a special day for a special member of our St Nonnatus family.'

'Hold on . . . you're telling me that Hattie can . . . fake food?' Priya says.

'I swear to God, even its creator wouldn't know the difference,' I tell her. 'It's a gift. A twisted gift. But a gift.'

'So that's how . . .' says Priya, pulling out her phone and frantically searching.

'For over forty years, Hattie Hughes has served up love and lunch at our school canteen,' says Tanya, starting to tear up. 'She is the hero of so many St Nonnatus stories and, today, we get to give her one all about her.'

'What's got your goat?' asks Al through his cake crumbs.

'The cake,' Priya mutters. 'It *was* the bloody cake . . .'

'Have you been at the mulled wine?' I ask her. 'Cos you know you could fuel a space mission to Mars on this stuff . . .'

She keeps frantically scrolling through the phone.

'Don't you see?' she says. 'It *was* the cake that killed Stitch-well.'

'No, it wasn't,' Al scoffs. 'You're losing your mind. The tests cleared it – there were no nuts in Tanya's cake. Stitchwell wasn't killed by cake.'

She stops and looks up at us both.

'Yes, she was,' she says with a tremble in her voice. 'It just wasn't Tanya's.'

'So I know that so many of you wanted to thank Hattie for everything she does for our community,' Tanya continues. 'As anyone who knows Hattie will tell you, the only thing she loves more than a sweet sherry is a good book.'

The hall lets out a ripple of laughter. But Priya and Al aren't smiling.

'Oh God,' says Al, finally putting his cake down. 'There were two of them . . .'

'Of course there were,' Priya groans. 'It makes perfect sense. Spiking Tanya's cake with nut oil was too risky – anyone could have eaten it. The trick was to get Stitchwell to eat *her* one, already filled with oil – and make sure everyone saw it – then change it out for Tanya's safe one . . .'

'Creepy Jesus!' Al exclaims, making several parents turn around.

Priya nods. 'The perfect distraction.'

'What you pair on about?' I ask. I look down the corridor for Hattie. She'll pretend to hate all this. But she'll love it really.

'And so we've spent the last few weeks,' says Tanya, 'asking everyone who wanted to do something for Hattie to write down something about her – a story, a picture, a poem. And wow – does St Nonnatus have talent!'

More laughter. But still Al and Priya look like they're at a funeral.

'Hattie was at BuyRite the same time as Ben, right?' says Priya, finally finding what she's looking for on her phone. He said she was behind him in the queue. Look at what she bought:

```
43857    Champagne                              28.99
33858    Luxury chocolate ice cream              2.99
76400    BuyRite Special Selection Brie          2.69
49594    Red wine                                8.49
2435     Durex Intense                          11.00
10349    BuyRite Basics Bleach                   0.79
6893     Masking tape                            1.69

         Thank you for Buying Rite!
```

## BUYRITE

### Buy more, pay less, buy rite!

```
Mon 24 Oct                                     16.11

58432    Rice Wine Vinegar                       2.90
59382    Soy Sauce                               2.75
50293    Groundnut oil                           2.00
981233   Pork ribs                               5.62
00293    Cornflour                               2.45
8762     Garlic                                  0.24
59203    Chinese 5 Spice                         1.10
8350     Spring onions                           0.55
5023     BuyRite Basics Chicken stock cubes      1.00
19845    BuyRite Basics 50 Paper plates          2.50
19473    BuyRite Basics 50 Paper cups            7.50
19029    BuyRite Basics 1ply Napkins             1.00

         Thank you for Buying Rite!
```

'No – the nut oil was Ben,' says Al. 'We established that ages ago.'

'Not his receipt – the one after it!' she urges. 'Look . . .'

## BUYRITE

### Buy more, pay less, buy rite!

```
Mon 24 Oct                                     16.14

00854    BuyRite Ex Power Dishwasher Tablets    3.10
006987   Cocoa powder                           4.00
005485   Mayonnaise                             1.20
00854    BuyRite Basics Cleaning Wipes          1.30
```

'Shit,' says Al. 'The cocoa powder Stitchwell banned . . . extra strength dishwasher tablets to boil the evidence, wipes to clean up after herself . . . even her secret mayonnaise . . .'

'Wow, you guys,' I say, slow hand-clapping them. 'School cook buys stuff for a kitchen. Sherlock must be shitting in his grave.'

'We've taken all of your contributions and we've made them into this . . .' says Tanya, unveiling a beautiful coffee-table book with THE BOOK OF HATTIE HUGHES painted across the front.

'She was making sandwiches and savouries that night,' Priya muses. 'The pong of all that egg and tuna would be an excellent way to mask the baking smells . . .'

'And Ben wasn't lying about the cookery class. It was her who told Ben it was Chinese ribs,' says Al keenly. 'So she didn't even need to incriminate herself – she just got him to buy the nut oil. All she had to do was take it from him.'

'And she's got notoriously sticky fingers,' Priya adds, going back to her phone.

'Wait . . . you think Hattie killed Stitchwell?' I say, finally cottoning on. 'Oh, come off it! She's going to find this hysterical . . .'

'But what was her motive?' Al asks. 'Not the job, surely . . .'

'Erm – have you two completely lost the plot?!' I laugh.

'I think that might have been part of it,' Priya grimaces as she triumphantly finds the next thing on her phone. 'But mainly it was because of this.'

---

**Sharon**
Oh sure!
He loved half the bloody town!
Talk about tending your . . . flock.
He had a massive affair with my Aunty Pat.
And she was just one.
He was at it with Mary Smith who used to run The
Crown, Joanie Hughes in the bakery, Connie Rogers
when BuyRite was the haberdashers – and he cleaned
up at the camp when the boys were on deployment.

---

'Joanie Hughes was having an affair with the reverend,' Priya continues. 'Hattie's mum.'

'So was half the town,' I confirm. 'So what?'

'So Hattie . . . Hattie is the Stitchwell Love Child?' Al gasps. Priya nods.

'It wasn't Stitchwell that had the illegitimate child,' she says. 'It was her dad. Hattie inherited his allergies. But she wanted to inherit his money.'

'And so, without further ado, can I please invite up to the stage,' says Tanya, sniffing back tears. 'Our beloved, beautiful, bookish dinner lady . . . HATTIE HUGHES!'

A huge cheer goes up around the hall. I can't wait for Hattie to hear all this. She's gonna laugh her arse off.

Priya is scrolling through her phone again.

'No cake,' she mutters. 'In all the reports of what was in the bins, there was no cake . . . How did she get rid of the second cake? Where the hell do you hide a whole chocolate cake in a primary school . . . ?'

Verity and my Grace try to push past us.

'Oh God,' says Al, standing in their way and putting a hand on each of their heads.

'Girls, I want you to tell me something – you're not in any trouble,' he starts. 'The night Miss Stitchwell died – you both had a bad tummy ache. Do you remember? You were sick?'

The girls look shiftily at one another and nod.

'Had Hattie been giving you some treats?' he asks with a smile.

The girls giggle conspiratorially.

'Hattie? Don't be shy!' Tanya shouts from the stage when she doesn't appear from the crowd. 'Hats?'

'What did she give you to eat?' Al asks with a cheeky smile. I stare at Grace. She vommed for England that night. She just had that stomach bug . . .

'She told us not to tell,' says Verity.

'That's fine,' says Priya. 'No one's in any trouble, I promise. We just want to . . . thank Hattie.'

Grace looks at me with a naughty smile.

'We ate a cake,' she giggles. 'A whole chocolate cake . . .'

My mind glitches. Typical Hattie. I can see Priya putting two and two together and making seventeen.

'Hattie?' Tanya calls awkwardly from the stage over the dying applause. 'Where are you, lovely?'

'Of course,' sighs Priya. 'She's not here. She's done a bunk.'

'Don't be daft,' I say, putting down my glass as Al hands Priya a tenner. 'I saw her less than an hour ago. She'll be in the kitchen stirring her brew. I'll go fetch her. If I'm not back in ten minutes, call the police . . .'

I laugh. But Priya doesn't.

The hall is chanting now.

'Ha-ttie! Ha-ttie! Ha-ttie!'

I head out into the corridor and bump straight into Mike Richardson.

'Hey!' I say, giving him a massive hug. 'That was a moment! You guys okay?'

'We will be,' he says, his tired eyes red from crying. 'Are you heading to the kitchen? I really need to thank Hattie.'

'For all the cakes for Jacob while you were away?' I say. 'Oh, she loves it – even if his pancreas won't . . .'

'No,' he says, looking surprised. 'I assumed you of all people would know . . . It was Hattie that got Jenna home.'

I feel a cold chill start to flurry in my chest.

'What?' I say.

'Hattie paid for the air ambulance,' he says, tears coming to his eyes again. 'The pilot told me. I have no idea how we begin to repay her, but I have to tell her how much—'

'This can't be right,' I tell him, my words shaking. 'Hattie's as poor as a church mouse. There's no way she could afford that.'

'Well, she did,' says Mike with a massive grin. 'And I want to tell the world – so long as it's okay with her. I just want to check . . .'

'Give me a minute,' I say, approaching the closed kitchen door. 'She really can't stand a fuss. Let me sound her out. I'll bring her back to the hall.'

'Right you are,' he says. 'But she's an angel, Kiera. An earthbound angel . . .'

That's school life for you. One minute you're a murderer. The next a saint. Let's clear all this up . . .

I push the door open with a cheery shout.

'Hats!' I cry. 'Get your wrinkly arse out here. They're all calling for you! And wait until I tell you what's being said. You're gonna laugh . . .'

But two things hit me in quick succession.

One – the kitchen is absolutely freezing – the fire door is wide open.

And two?

Hattie isn't here.

The kitchen is totally empty.

Except for an envelope.

An envelope with my name on it.

*My darling girl,*

*Now I never was one for goodbyes, Kiera my love, and you don't need me snivelling all over you. So I thought I'd do it this way and I know I'm right, so let that be an end to it.*

*You're not daft. And if you haven't figured it out by now someone soon will. Except maybe Constable Bob, God love him, never was the sharpest knife in the drawer, thank the Lord.*

*It was me.*

*I bumped old Stitchers off.*

*And I'd do it again tomorrow.*

*I've always admired the long game. Count of Monte Cristo. Hamlet. They all had the right idea.*

*Revenge is a dish best served cold, they say.*

*Well, it also works in a bloody great chocolate cake.*

*I know all the rumours about the Stitchwell Love Child – and well I should, I started most of 'em (and being 'Sarah' was a big help – I tell you, I can't bloody believe the things they get up to on them chat groups, could get a person hung . . .)*

*But it's me.*

*The Randy Rev knocked my ma up then tossed her away like an old hanky. She were in love with him for her sins – tried everything to get his attention, even giving me a daft bible name. Hatita. A biblical servant, apparently – the die was always cast. My name means "bending of sin". Which, if rumours are to be believed about what the rev did to my ma over the iced ring doughnuts, sounds about right.*

*But he let her live and die with nothing while he and his family sat on their piles of gold. It weren't right. But Stitchers had a couple o' years on me – I nicked her DNA off a tea cup years ago to prove we're kin and all's I had to do was wait until he croaked to claim what was rightfully mine. I knew the rev never made no will, young Ricky Williams ('85 – nice lad, always took the goldfish home for the holidays) was* the Stitchwell family lawyer like his pa before him and he despaired of it. Don't get me wrong – I hated Claudia, but I didn't always mean to kill 'er. I hated the way she treated everyone. I hated what she did to you and it had always been the plan to set it right once the rev was pushing up daisies.

But then the silly old goat found out I was her sister.

That night, she called me in to tell me that her pa confessed on his death bed that I was his, and that I was the product of sin. She told me that I'd never see a penny of his money – she'd made him write a will on his deathbed to prevent any of his bastards from claiming on his estate. She showed me the will – taunted me with it. And then told me she didn't want me working in her school, that my original sin would infect the kids! Infect the kids! Those were her words. She was gonna make up some cock-a-hoop nonsense about catering budgets to get it past the governors, but we both knew the truth.

She was punishing me. So I decided to give her a taste of her own medicine.

I left that office in a fury, I don't mind telling you. I didn't know how I was gonna do it – but I was gonna do it that night. I scoured the school for anything – bleach, rat poison, I woulda choked her to death with a bloody glue stick if it'd got the job done.

And then I saw Tanya's cake.

That greedy harridan never could resist a slice of Tanya's choccie cake and so I knew what I had to do. I wouldn't have touched Tanya's cake – what if some poor other bastard with a nut allergy had a slice? I'm not a killer. I'm an avenger. So I went down BuyRite to get another one. And I'll tell you something for free:

Do you have any sodding idea how hard it is to buy something full o' nuts these days?!

Everything was bloody nut-free or too obvious for her to eat it. So I had to make another one from scratch. Tanya got that recipe from my ma – I can do

434

*it in my sleep in five minutes flat. The secret is to use
a fat other than butter – keeps it moist. Mayonnaise is
great. And a great slug of nut oil helps too.*

*Now I ain't daft – I know that your Matt's place
would keep records and it would be dodgy as a nine-
bob note if I left a record of me buying it meself. But
salvation arrived when that dozy bugger Ben turned
up – I always suspected he was a wrong un – and so
I got him to buy it instead. Soon as we got back to
school, I nicked it out his office – no one never notices
me shuffling around the place – and I was away.*

*'Course, everyone can smell a lovely choccie cake
cooking, so I found every stinky thing I could – egg,
tuna, onion – to drown out the smell. And not half
hour after I got back, it was done. It were full of
oil – even put it in the icing just for good measure.
Cooled it in me freezer, iced it, then put it in Tanya's
cake box. I let her put it out for Stitchers to grab a
piece, then I created all that fuss and bother with
Creepy Jesus (all's it took were a bit of veggie oil on
the floor) and I were away. Pretended to 'fix' Tanya's
cake (matching the slice that Stitchers took outta
mine – I even suggested that lovely Fliss Jameson
popped a bit in her freezer cos I didn't want anyone to
get in no trouble) and took Tanya's real cake out for
everyone to have at it. All's I needed to do was pop the
nut oil bottle back in Ben's shopping and no one would
be any the wiser. He musta found it and hidden it from
the coppers in the Creepy Jesus – covered in his
fingerprints, the idiot. I wore gloves.*

*But then you put a spanner in the works, my love.
Remember you slathering me face in that icing when
we cleaned up? It was full of nut oil – and, like my
beloved sister and father before me, I'm allergic as all
hell. Not to seeds like I fibbed to young Al. To nuts.*

*So I'm scrabbling around for me bag with me
EpiPen in – and it's only then I realise I left it at the
ruddy shop cos me nerves were all in jitters. But the
Lord works in mysterious ways. Just I was injecting*

myself with the one from the office, I thought of the one in Stitchwell's desk. That would have to go too. So I 'helped' her to look for her bible and swiped her EpiPen while I was at it. (Got mine back when your Matt gave me my purse – used it to replace the one what I took from the office and put Stitcher's back when I was looking after the kiddies in care, before the coppers knew it was missing – didn't want no one getting into trouble on my account and I needed to get rid o' that bloody will in her filing cabinet.) Then all that was left to do was to run everything through a bloody hot dishwasher to hide the evidence – and pop the rest of the cake down two little girlies I knew were safe to eat it.

Why am I telling you this? Well, honestly, I gotta tell someone. I'm really quite bloody proud of myself. I thought I'd done a bang-up job. But then bloody Clive told me he'd found a copy of the rev's will – bloody Stitchwell and her bloody duplicates – so he had to go too. And after what he did to you, that one were a pleasure, I don't mind telling you. I'd helped him get that gun off Bootleg Barry – in return for extra budget for the good custard, mind, I ain't no pushover – and he kept it in a bloody petty cash tin under his sink! I picked that lock inside two breaths. Now don't get me wrong, I ain't a monster, I did feel badly for what I done to Andy – at least till he grassed me up to Bob for being round Clive's that night. It weren't him nicking all the bits from the kiddies. It were me. I needed a patsy and he strikes me as a survivor. If he looked through his bag again later, he'd a found ten grand in cash. He can disappear. Just like I can.

There's not much to commend being Stitchwell's bastard, but it has worked out all right in the end. I've put in a claim for probate as his rightful heir – finding me birth certificate round Clive's was a big help – we'll have to see what comes of it. I've got Katie Blevins ('76 – breath like a badger's bum, poor love, I used to crush polo mints into her water bottle) working on the

*probate claim and she reckons I've got a decent poke.*
*But there's inheritance and there's inheritance. I knew*
*that neither of them trusted banks, so the night*
*Stitchwell died I went round there and had a poke*
*about. And guess what I found under her bloody bed?*
*One. Million. Pounds, Kiera! Those tight buggers had*
*saved up over a million quid in cash! I had it out of*
*there before she was cold.*

*Now it's no easy thing to bank a million in notes –*
*everything leaves a bloody paper trail these days.*
*But remember young Jimmy Collins ('84 – dribbled*
*something biblical), used to manage the local bank*
*back when it was a Midland? Well, he's taken all his*
*banking know-how and now runs the dodgy casino up*
*in Easthampton. I once gave some bullies of his a dose*
*of the pukes with some raw eggs in their milk – course*
*you could do that back in the eighties, Thatcherism an'*
*all – and he was more than happy to help me launder*
*the lot (for a very reasonable kickback too if you have*
*the need).*

*So I'm all set. Whatever comes of the will, it's*
*more than I'll ever need in my short lifetime, that's for*
*sure. So you'll be getting a call from the solicitors on*
*Monday. It's me what bought your house, gal. For*
*you. Don't you go moving them girls from their home.*
*Consider it reparation. For what Stitchwell did to you.*
*For what that bastard Pandy did to you. For what you*
*bloody deserve. You'll also find a hundred grand in*
*cash in your handbag. Now don't you go spunking it*
*on some private school – Gracie will do just fine at*
*Flatford High. She's a bright girl, as is your Taylor. But*
*that money is for education – for college, university,*
*whatever they want to do. For you too, my love. You*
*have so much in you. Go find it and God speed.*

*Well now I have a plane to catch. I'm hitching a*
*lift back on Jenna's ride here. Turns out little Mattie*
*Watkins ('89 – terrible squint, had to wear a Fireman*
*Sam plaster over his left eye) is now a pilot! He used*
*to sit in my kitchen while I patched him up after a*

*walloping from his pa, so he was happy to help the Richardsons out – even did me mates' rates, which was good o' him. He's gonna drop me in Germany and I'll make my way from there. Bootleg Barry ('92, wanted to be an elephant when he grew up, strange lad) has done me a smashing new passport – even says I'm 57 like nature intended!*

*Vanuatu is calling. Tropical climate and palm trees. Also happens to be a non-extradition tax haven – needs must. I dunno when you'll read this and what you'll do with it when you do. But I know you'll love me enough to sit on it until I've got where I need to go. I know what I done was wrong and I'll have some explaining to do when the Almighty calls me home. But this world won't suffer without Stitchwell and Baxendale in it. I'm no serial killer. My work here is done. Although that Ben Andrews had better watch his back in a dark alley. My sources tell me he's living in his ma's spare room in Inverness, can't get arrested, though he should be. I'm sorry I never told you what he done – that was wrong. I hadn't long known meself – the night I done Clive in, I nicked Stitchers' black book and had a good read. I've posted it to your Taylor if you fancy a gander. The things folk get up to in this town . . .*

*And so, my darling girl, I take me leave. Like the old count says: 'How did I escape? With difficulty. How did I plan this moment? With pleasure . . .'*

*Enjoy your life, my lovely. Your story ain't half told.*

*Think of me fondly, Kiera. I love the very bones of you.*
*Your friend,*
*Hattie*
*xxx*

# PARENTCHAT

Clearer Community Communication

## ST NONNATUS CE PRIMARY

*Ora et labora*

**Monday 19 December**

**Mrs Marcia Cox<M.Cox@stnonnatus.flatford.sch.uk>**

**To: <Whole School>**

**Re: week commencing 19 December
END OF TERM NEWSLETTER**

Dear Whatever the Bloody Hell You Want to Call
Yourselves This Week,

It]s Marcia herre. Have done some drinking.

Cant be rased.

Happy xmas. Lve you all.

I leve you with teh wrds of me:
{Learn how to park a fcking car.

Mrs Marcia Cox

Office Manager
St Nonnatus Primary School

# Tickly Tiger's Diary!

Date: Monday 19 December

This weekend I went home with: Anya

This weekend, Tickly Tiger cuddled under a blanket with us, watched Christmas movies and did sod all.

It was brilliant.

Priya & Anya

# The Flatford Gazette

Wednesday 21 December

## Local Dinner Lady Cooks Up A Murder?

Authorities have put out an all-ports alert for long-serving St Nonnatus dinner lady, Hatita Hughes (57), who is wanted in connection with the murders of headteacher Claudia Stitchwell and school business manager Clive Baxendale.

The arrest warrant was issued yesterday after Priya Mistry, a former Metropolitan police officer, submitted a dossier of new evidence linking the catering manager to the crime.

'No one is above the law,' Ms Mistry told the *Gazette*. 'Whatever Hattie's motives and motivations, the fact remains that a crime has been committed and the perpetrator should face justice.'

Miss Hughes's current whereabouts remain a mystery. It is believed she is still in the country after her passport was discovered in a police search of her home, where ballistic evidence linked her to the gun that killed Mr Baxendale.

The news has been met with stunned disbelief in the community, where Miss Hughes was a beloved local character. Anyone with information regarding her movements is urged to contact Robert Alsorp of the Flatford Police, who also appealed for anyone to come forward with Miss Hughes's fabled fruit-scone recipe.

## Council Apologises For 'Offensive' Christmas Lights

'We thought they were candy canes,' it says of the adult illuminations.

## Local Man Gets OBE In New Year's Honours

Barry 'Bootleg' O'Connor nominated by local MP Jerry Jenkins for 'services to finance'.

# PARENTCHAT

Clearer Community Communication

## ST NONNATUS CE PRIMARY

*Ora et labora*

### Year 6 Tiger Class
click here for group info

**Weds 21 Dec**
13.41

**Tanya**
Happy End of Term everyone!
We made it!

**Al**
Thank God!
I'm absolutely knackered!
Now we just have to buy, wrap, shop, cook...

**Stella**
I just wanted to publicly congratulate Priya.
I'm a firm believer in law and order.
What you did was entirely the right thing to do.

**Jane**
I just can't believe it...
Hattie?

**Zofia**
I always thought she was dodgy...
And did anyone else hear?
Apparently Andy is coming back as caretaker next
term!

**Priya**

*What you did was entirely the right thing to do.*
That's kind of you Stella.
It wasn't just me.
Tanya and Al have been a huge support.

**Al**

Too kind.
But you were right.
And I'm so glad that the force has recognised it.

**Tanya**

Yes!
Huge congrats on the new job, Priya.
Flatford will be so much safer for
having you back on the force.
On another note...
I just wanted to thank you all for
making the fair such a success.
We raised over £6,000!

**Sharon**

That's amazing sweetheart!
Well done everyone for all your hard work.

**Karl**

*Apparently Andy is coming back as caretaker next term!*
I'm glad.
The kids loved him.
And I owe that man a drink.
(Although I might ask him to make it – those
cocktails...)

*Kiera Fisher has joined the group 'Year 6 Tigers'*

**Kiera**

Hey everyone.
Just wanted to wish you all a Happy Christmas.

**Sharon**

Aw – same to you, love 🎄

And good to see you here!

Now you can talk balls with the rest of us!

**Stella**

Sharon…

**Sharon**

I meant Christmas balls 😇

**Priya**

*Just wanted to wish you all a Happy Christmas.*

Great to see you, Kiera.

Looking forward to lunch next week.

**Kiera**

Me too – I'll see you at Amelia's party.

**Jenna**

Hey everyone!

I just wanted to thank you all for everything you've done for us.

The care you took of my Jacob 🖤

**Flo**

It was all our pleasure.

It's so good to have you home.

**Mike**

It really is…

**Annie**

*Me too – I'll see you at Amelia's party.*

Amelia's having a party?

**Sarah**

[It's me! The original and still the best!]

I think we're all ready for Christmas!

Here's to a quieter Spring term!

**Donna**

It's been quite the baptism of fire!
Most exciting thing to happen at my last school was conjunctivitis season!
Have a great Christmas everyone.
(Oh – and Eric and I are hosting Xmas drinks round mine on Friday if anyone fancies it...)

**Felicity**

*Amelia's having a party?*
Oh love – didn't Sasha give you the invite?
She's on the list!

**Annie**

Oh!
Great!
When is it?

**Felicity**

Friday.

**Annie**

BOLLOCKS – WE'RE AT CENTRE PARCS!!!

**Zofia**

*(Oh – and Eric and I are hosting Xmas drinks round mine on Friday if anyone fancies it . . .)*
You are, are you?
You and Eric... ?

**Donna**

*You and Eric . . . ?*

**Eric**

*You and Eric . . . ?*
Smashing! ✎

**Eric**

No!
I mean 💜

**Donna**
You sure, love? 🙂

**Sharon**
Behave you young lovebirds!
I'll be round!
You know me, never miss a party.

**Priya**
Me too!

**Kiera**
I'd love that.

**Tanya**
Count me in!

**Dustin**
*(Oh – and Eric and I are hosting Xmas drinks round mine on Friday if anyone fancies it . . .)*
Sorry, we'd love to.
But we'll be settling Adel in.
He's coming to stay with us.
Indefinitely.

**Tanya**
OH MY DAYS!
This is the best news!

**Al**
Nice one you guys!
(I'd recommend a sitter, but...)

**Stella**
It's a wonderful thing you are doing.
Happy Christmas Dustin and Barney.
Sending your whole family joy.

**Dustin**
Thank you Stella, that means the world.
Same to you and yours.

**Felicity**
Well what a fantastic way to end the year 🙂
Have a great Christmas everyone (sod the diet).

**Karl**
Season's greetings!

**Dustin**
Happy Christmas everyone!

**Zofia**
Wesołych Świąt!
*Suggested translation: Happy Easter.*

**Karen**
Happy Hanukkah!

**Borys**
Щасливого Різдва!
*Suggested translation: Halloween is Joyful.*

**Flo**
Happy Appropriated Pagan Festival!

**Stella**
Merry Christmas one and all.

**Petra**
Has anyone seen Archie?
I think he's lost himself 🙂
(Although we are genuinely missing his jumper, PE shorts and left shoe if anyone has seen them.)

**Mariam**
عيد ميلاد سعيد
*Suggested translation: Get well soon.*

**Sharon**
*Has anyone seen Archie?*
Is he clearly named? 🙂

**Mike**
See you all next term!

**Jennie**
Does anyone know where to buy a live reindeer?

**Priya**
Love you, you crazy biatches!

**Tanya**
Tigers are the best!

**Al**
Someone's been at the egg nog early!
Happy Christmas.
God (or your personal equivalent) bless us. Every one.

**Priya**
AND FUCK THE SPELLINGS!

**Laura**
Oh yeah, big Daddies.
Come to Mama.
I want you both to drill me hard like a dirty Black and
Decker...

*Laura has left the group*

# Acknowledgements

It occurs to me as I come into land on this, the seventeenth novel I have written, that I still have absolutely no idea how these books come into existence. I sit, I type, I swear, I cry, I gain at least five pounds, nothing gets washed . . . but how so many words end up in roughly the right order remains a mystery to me. I do know, however, that I do not achieve this alone – and this book in particular owes its life to the great many people who have kindly given of their time and expertise to illuminate my ignorance.

In the order that I spoke to you, then – my enormous thanks go to Gary Lacey for his insider supermarket knowledge, Andrew Bradley for his invaluable experience of coroner proceedings, Michael Braycotton from the Disabled Police Association for helping me to develop Priya's story, Nadine Matheson for her legal advice (again – you must check out her books), Nazima Pathan for her medical knowledge (again – you must also check out her books), Catherine O'Shea and Simon Pollard for their extensive insight into the extraordinary mechanics of running a school, Emma Short for her pathology expertise and CSI Suzi for letting me ruin her Moroccan holiday with my endless questions. There were several more of you who didn't wish to be named – but if you helped me with anything from cooking the books to the inside track on rural black markets, my thanks go quietly your way.

In this, as in all things, I must thank my wonderful agent, Veronique Baxter, along with all her colleagues at David Higham Associates who support this career and its author. I first suggested this idea to Veronique over lunch and it made her drop her fork. This is now the benchmark for all my pitches. V – you work tirelessly on my behalf and I can never thank you enough. Thank you for all that you so brilliantly do.

A book is only as good as its editor, so what to say about Toby Jones . . . ? Jones, you are pedantic, exacting, blunt as a spoon and give me no quarter whatsoever. In short, you are precisely what I need. This second tome – indeed year – of ours has been lacerated with laughter and, as I'm sure you realise from the respectful and deferential manner of my communications, working with you is ceaselessly joyful. For me, anyway. I don't wanna bore you with it . . . but you're all right. To you and all your fantastic colleagues at Headline, thank you for your brilliance and your bants. Who knew publishing could be this much fun?

This, as I suspect most of mine are, is a story of friendship and I'm very lucky to be surrounded by so many beautiful ones. Lisa T, Lucy M, Tim S, Emma S, Katya B, Piers T, Ross M, Maya L, Steve C and Louie S, thank you so much for keeping me afloat in the swirling waters of the literary world. This book is dedicated to two women who kept me sane during my primary-school years and one who we tragically lost while I've been writing about them. They were all part of a community at the best school my family ever had the privilege to be a part of. I shan't name it to protect the innocent – but it was a very special chapter of my life that I've loved revisiting in these pages. Team Tigers – this one's for you.

For my home team . . . I am a woman overly blessed with love – albeit also laundry. To my family, you are beautiful and brave and brilliant and I adore you. Everything I do, I do for you. And to fuel my own pitiful narcissism – I am an author after all.

And finally, to all the readers, bloggers, reviewers, judging panels and booksellers who have supported this latest iteration in my daft career, I thank you, humbly, for all that you have done to get my adult books off the ground. *Over My Dead Body* was a step into the unknown for me and you greeted us both like friends. My deepest gratitude to every last one of you.

As I write, the world is riven with pain and conflict and, like so many, I struggle to make sense of what humans are capable of inflicting upon one another. But, as I often say to my young readers, I do believe that darkness can make the light more luminous. What we can't control without, we can strive to improve within. And if enough of us commit to treating each other more gently I can't help but feel the world will be brighter for it.

Sending you peace, love and the safest of chocolate cakes,
Maz xxx